The Murders of Conky Whallop

This is a work of fiction. Names, characters, places, and incidents either are the product of the author's imagination or are used fictitiously, and any resemblance to any persons, living or dead, business establishments, events, or locales is entirely coincidental.

First published in Great Britain by

Watledge Books

Copyright © 2022 David Wake

All rights reserved

This paperback edition 2023

1

ISBN: 979-8864956267

The moral right of David Wake to be identified as the author of this work has been asserted by him in accordance with the Copyright, Designs and Patents Act, 1988.

Cover by Dave Slaney.

Also by David Wake

NOVELS

The Derring-Do Club Adventures

The Empire of the Dead
The Year of the Chrononauts
The Invasion of the Grey
Death on the Suez
The Sisterhood of the Death Goddess

The Thinkersphere Series

Hashtag
Atcode
Plus Sign

Stand Alone Novels

I, Phone
Crossing the Bridge
Roninko
The Murders of Conky Whallop

NOVELLAS

The Other Christmas Carol

ONE-ACT PLAYS

Hen and Fox
Down the Hole
Flowers
Stockholm
Groom

NON-FICTION

Punk Publishing (with Andy Conway)

For

The Cambridge Lunch Club

THE MURDERS OF CONKY WHALLOP

David Wake

WATLEDGE BOOKS

Foreword

By Chief Inspector, Sir Reginald Kilroy, CBE, QPM

On the eve of his retirement

It is with some reluctance that I tender my resignation after, dare I say it, a distinguished career. Retirement is a time for reflection, certainly. I remember those many enquiries that I had a hand in solving and the numerous criminals I have brought to book. Sadly, though, my early career was blighted by one of the most infamous cases in the history of criminal investigation.

It is important to remember that the backdrop for these shocking circumstances was the most pleasant and peaceful English village, perhaps just the kind of place to which one dreams of retiring.

Even its name, without the connotations of the horrors that occurred there, can be considered quaint and olde-worlde, harking back to a better, more pleasant age of cricket on the green, homemade jam sold for charitable causes at jumble sales and good old-fashioned pints by a roaring log fire in the Red Lion with a ploughman's lunch.

But this was no *Madingley, Six Mile Bottom, Stow cum Quy, Trumpington, Wendy* or *Wimpole* for it will forever be a name to raise the hairs upon the back of the neck and chill the blood. I refer to none other than that halcyon collection of cottages by the River Huh.

Conky Whallop.

I hear you gasp. Yes. Of course.

For, as we all know, beneath that veneer of English respectability, there festered those dark forces of malice, resentment, jealousy, envy, gossip, revenge and... murder!

So, it is perhaps time to explain the small part I played in this affair, my very first case as a detective, and state for the record my part in uncovering the shocking truth of those dark days. It was an investigation full of twists and turns, blind alleys, wrong moves and cunning misdirection that would have tried the most experienced of inspectors, let alone a new detective constable. But luckily, I had help from the unlikeliest of deputies – my posse.

You see, it all started with three old ladies and a body on page one.[1]

_____

[1] Editor's note: Books always start on page 3, so it's impossible to have a body on page 1. The body in this book does not appear until page 7.

1. A Body on Page One

It was a dark and stormy night.

"It's just terrible," Annabelle said, wringing her hands again as if there was any more anguish to squeeze out. "Diane's going to be so cross."

"Yes, dear," Pat said as she folded away her half-moon reading glasses.

Such had been the news that the two old friends had already started on the muffins.

"Pat, how can he do this to Di?"

"It's the modern age."

"But the parish magazine has been printed – *printed* – for nearly 75 years, come rain..." – the lightning flashed outside – "...flood, storm, war and even the Great Hornet Invasion."

Pat looked away from her friend and twitched the net curtains aside to stare into the void. The lampposts around the Green tried their best against the dismal weather.

Through one cone of light, a lone figure battled the elements.

"Mrs Entwistle's out late[2]," Pat said.

"Visiting her son?" Annabelle asked.

"She's going that way."

Mrs Entwistle disappeared into the darkness between the street lamps. A sudden flash of lightning illuminated her for a final time before the night swallowed her.

"Isn't her son in the Caribbean?" Pat said.

"She's probably checking his house for any post," Annabelle said. "Although, people should stay indoors in this weather."

Thunder pealed and the doorbell rang.

"That'll be Diane," Pat said.

She went to open the door, seeing Diane's silhouette in the stained-glass window. Outside, the begonias of Pat's lovely, prize-winning garden thrashed about in the storm.

---

[2] Editor's note: This is a clue.

Diane stood in the rain, her sheepskin coat flapped about in the wind, and thunder raged in her eyes.

"Di, come in, come in," Pat said, "before you catch your death."

Diane wiped her wellingtons on the welcome mat, then slipped them off to come into Pat's drawing-room in just her stockings. She wore sensible everything except for a couple of loops of pearls.

Since they'd first met at Infant School, they'd been friends through three marriages, four children, six grandchildren and two hundred years between them.

Pat with her half-moon glasses that she wore to magnify the twinkle in her eye and the Times crossword. Her cardigan's armour consisted of leather patches for elbowing. She didn't use her stick indoors, so her knee clicked as she sat on her upholstery.

Diane had a reputation as a battle-axe as a lawyer used to treading the boards of amateur theatre, the boardrooms of local government and the boards put out over muddy fields at protests. She forever appeared at odds wherever she went, but she always earned a begrudging respect.

Annabelle, the youngest barely into her free bus pass, dressed stylishly in a dark outfit so popular in over-50s dating app profiles. However, her long hair was already streaked with own-brand age-defy auburn. Her twinset was green with red, showing that she'd been distracted when getting ready for their meeting, but then the cancellation of the parish magazine was likely to put anyone under strain.

"I'm so sorry, Di," Annabelle said.

"It isn't your fault, Belle," Pat pointed out.

"The vicar–" Diane said.

"Now, now, Di, we must be understanding," Pat said.

"The vicar–"

"Yes, but he may have a point," Pat said, "after all, everything is being connected to the internet, five gee-ups and all that."

"The vicar–"

"And we don't need to worry..." Pat said, mouthing 'Annabelle' and pointing to her friend. "And I'm sure you explained our feelings without... Oh! You lost your temper again?"

"The vicar's dead!" Diane said.

"Well, that's a little strong," Pat said, "it's only a parish magazine."

"I'm sure you can settle your differences," Annabelle said. "I mean, he's the vicar and we have to talk to him on Sundays at the very least."

"He's dead," Diane insisted. "Knifed in the back."

"It is a kind of betrayal to turn the parish magazine into a blog... is it? Blog?" Pat said and she looked to Anabelle.

"Unless it's filmed," Annabelle explained, "then it's a vlog."

"I'm sure that can't be a word," Pat said. "Perhaps in a cryptic, but not in Scrabble."

"No, Pat, Belle, listen," Diane said.

"Yes, Di," Pat said.

"The vicar is lying on the floor in the church with a knife in his back."

A dreadful silence filled the room, except for the hammering of the rain outside, the rolling thunder and the whirring of Pat's old fridge.

"Whatever is he doing that for?" Annabelle asked.

"I think he's dead," Diane said.

"Think or..." Pat asked.

"I wondered if you'd give me a second opinion."

Pat glanced at the paisley curtains, so thick and capable of keeping out the cold and uproar. "On a night like this?" she asked.

Diane nodded.

"Do you want to come too?" Pat asked Annabelle.

"Oh, well..." Annabelle said.

"That's settled," Diane said. "We're all going. Come on."

They tended to do what Diane said as she could always marshal her arguments. She was also their chief editor and a church keyholder. So, the three old ladies donned their wellingtons, coats and rain hats.

Pat unfolded her walking stick, Diane turned on her torch, Annabelle shivered and they were off.

They crossed the lane, gripping on to each other and went along the row of shops by the Village Green. At the end of the High Street, they turned and struggled up the hill to the church. Diane's torch shone ahead picking out the looming horse chestnut tree and the ominous, gothic stone of the church. A path led from the lychgate through the small graveyard to the porch.

Diane handed her torch to Pat and reached into her pocket for the church key.

"It's b-b-bitter," Annabelle said.

Diane fumbled with the big, mediaeval object that matched the heavy, oak door. The sky flashed as Diane unlocked it, but, when she pushed the heavy oak, they didn't hear it creak as the thunder choose that moment to roar.

Inside, the torch faltered and dimmed.

"Oh bother," Diane said.

"Where are the lights?" Pat asked.

Diane pointed.

The large switchboard was full of brass twiddly bits and a 'pat-tested' sticker. It wasn't Pat that tested it (or that it had even needed testing as it wasn't a portable appliance), but another of the vicar's new-fangled ideas.

Nothing happened.

"Fuses," Diane explained.

Pat nodded.

They found the packet of remembrance candles and a box of matches. Diane struck a spark and lit a candle, lighting two more, one each for Pat and Annabelle.

The flames cast vast shadows onto the walls and the darkness sulked about as they crept down the aisle. Under the reproachful gaze of stone angels and stained-glass saints, they kept their peace and the quiet hung heavy. The medieval stone kept away all the insignificant sound and fury of the outside world.

"I was giving him a piece of my mind," Diane started explaining, "about... well, everything. You know, the parish magazine, guitars instead of the organ and the nonsense with Mrs Entwistle's flower arranging. It's all change, change, change!"

"Well, quite, yes."

"When..." Diane trailed off until even the echoes went quiet.

"When?" Pat prompted.

"When I realised he wasn't listening."

"Typical man," Annabelle said.

"He was just sitting there on the front row with his back to me and he didn't look round once."

"What was he doing?" Annabelle asked.

"Ignoring me," Diane said.

"Oh, how rude."

"So I... tapped him on his shoulder and he fell there."

They rounded the front pew and there was no more need for explanation.

Beneath the eagle gaze of the lectern, the vicar lay sprawled on the tiled floor, his hands clawed and his prematurely bald head reflecting the warm glow of their remembrance candlelight.

An ornate knife stuck out of his back.

"Well?" Diane said.

"Well, what?" Pat said, standing back.

"Pat, you were a nurse."

"Of sick people, not... this."

Diane gave Pat a look.

"Reverend Pendle-Took?" Pat tried, her voice wavering.

There was no answer.

So, Pat leant her walking stick against a pew, bent down and reluctantly felt at the fallen man's neck.

"Well?" Diane asked.

"There's no pulse."

"Oh God," Annabelle said. "Oh, sorry Lord."

"But my hands are too cold to feel anything," Pat explained.

"Oh, thank God," Annabelle said.

"Let's turn him over," Pat said. She reached for his shoulder, but one-handed, she wasn't strong enough to turn him over. Annabelle took Pat's candle from her and then, two-handed, they still weren't able to manage it. So, Diane helped, and, three-handed, the vicar rose gently and rolled onto his side.

Reverend Pendle-Took's eyes stared out of his gaunt features, wide, blank and full of disapproval.

"He's dead," Pat decided.

"Oh…" said Annabelle.

Diane began to let go.

"Wait," Pat said. "I think there's something caught underneath."

"What?" Diane asked.

"Let me... hold him."

The two others did and Pat reached.

"A bit more," Pat said. She tugged gently, teasing it free.

"What is it?" Diane asked.

"A piece of paper."

"This is a terrible accident," Annabelle said. "If only he'd let Mrs Rawlings polish the silver. She's slow, but careful. The Reverend Pendle-Took didn't know how to do it properly, so the knife probably slipped."

"I doubt he slipped, Belle," Diane said.

"What do you mean?"

"It's not an accident."

"Suicide!" Annabelle said. "Oh, how terrible. Is that his suicide note?"

"It's not suicide, Belle," Diane said.

14

"Oh, what could it be then?"

"A bit more," Pat said.

They all rolled him further, but the sheet of A4 just wouldn't quite slide out.

The oversized, fancy handle sticking out of his back caught the tiled floor and he turned no more. His frame held the last corner of the paper and so it tore when it came free.

They let go.

The vicar rolled back into the recovery position from which he was never going to recover.

"Well?" Diane asked.

"Yes," Annabelle said. "What is it?"

Pat dug out her half-moon glasses and held the sheet of paper up to the feeble candlelight. It was blank on one side and steeped in blood, but the other had the familiar line drawing of the church over the title banner.

"It's from the parish magazine," Pat said. "He was lying on page one."

2. A Process of Elimination

A sinister, black SUV sped from the right, turned onto the A-road and narrowly missed Pat, Diane and Annabelle as they hurried into Miss Fairfax's driveway. For a fleeting moment, they caught sight of the occupant, underlit by his dashboard, his black hair swept back from his widow's peak and his dark saturnine beard streaked with the grey of forbidden knowledge.

"Sir Victor!" Pat exclaimed.

"Never mind him," Diane replied as she raised her fist to the door.

Bang-bang-bang-bang-bang!

"There's a bell," Annabelle said.

"Oh!"

Ding-ding-ding-ding-ding!

Miss Frances Fairfax lived just over the road, which was very convenient as she was the churchwarden. She appeared at the door looking flustered. Her hair, full and black,

16

also had a widow's peak. Tousled would be a kinder description of its state.

"Yes?"

"May we use your phone?" Pat asked. "Much obliged, thank you."

Pat swapped her walking stick for the churchwarden's slab of black glass and then Frances had to show Pat how to use it. Frances was one of these modern people who didn't have a landline.

Pat pressed '999'.

"The police, please," she said. "Mrs Patricia Thomas. Number two, Gladstone Road, Conky Whallop, CB... look, there's been a murder."

"Murder?" Frances asked.

"Yes," Pat said, "the vicar."

"Not George!"

And then, there followed a long, interminable wait.

"Tea or something stronger?" Frances suggested.

"Perhaps Horlicks or cocoa?" Pat suggested.

"Scotch," Diane said.

"Oh, well, it is quite late, so is there decaf or mineral water?" Annabelle asked.

And then everything seemed to happen at once with a sudden whirl of sirens, screeching tyres, running police and flashing lights.

A nice woman police officer took Pat's address and an unpleasant male sergeant told them to go and wait there at once.

"Well, really," Diane said. "I happen to know your Chief Constable."

"You know Demon Clough!" the sergeant replied. "I mean, the Chief Constable?"

"Benjamin, yes."

"Could you wait there, Ma'am, *please.*"

They made their way downhill and around the Green. Behind them, the police cars blinked, their multi-coloured lights streaking the church tower not with the friendly colours of Christmas lights, but with garish

18

blues and reds. They'd parked on the grass verge and by Mrs Entwistle's cottage despite the signs.

"What was Sir Victor Pendle-Took doing at Frances's at this late hour?" Annabelle asked.

"What indeed?" Pat replied. "I thought they looked like peas in a pod."

"And on the same night that his brother was killed," Diane added.

"Aren't there rules about it?" Annabelle said. "After all, she's the warden and he's a lay preacher."

"People will talk," Diane said.

"I suspect they already are," Pat said.

They tutted about this on their way back to Pat's cottage. By this time, the storm had abated, the Divine having arranged respectful weather for the deceased.

Midnight approached before the police got around to interviewing them.

"It's murder," said a drenched police officer.

He stood in the middle of Pat's drawing-room in his angry stab vest with a belt of pepper spray, taser and handcuffs. He brandished his warrant card in one hand and his other fist rested on his Monadnock PR-24 side-handle baton. To complete his uniform, he wore black combat trousers and Disney Jungle Book socks.

"Who'd want to kill the vicar?" Annabelle said.

Pat glanced at Diane.

"Sherry?" Pat said.

"I'm on duty," said the constable. He put away his warrant card and took out a notebook and pen. "So..."

"Mrs Patricia Thomas."

"This is your house?"

"Yes."

"And Mr Thomas?"

"Passed on. Illness, eleven years ago."

"My condolences. And you found the body?"

20

"No, he was in hospital and... Oh, I see. Diane did."

The officer looked to Annabelle.

"Annabelle," Annabelle said. "Mrs Harrison. Belle."

"And Mr Harrison?"

"Which one?"

"Erm..."

"Well, my first husband–"

"We've no time for that now, Belle," Pat said quickly. "She lives alone, officer."

"Hmm... and Diane?" the officer said.

"By a process of elimination," Diane said, "that would be me – Diane Richards."

"And Mr Richards?"

"Miss."

"Ah... hmmm." His pen wouldn't write as the paper was wet. "So, you found the body?"

"Yes."

"And it was in the locked church?"

"Shouldn't we wait for an inspector?" Diane said.

"Inspector?"

"Or chief inspector?" Annabelle added. "Like Chief Inspector Japp or Chief Inspector Morse."

"Morse was only ever an inspector, Belle dear," Di said.

"Oh... I'm sure he was... that's a shame. He was nice."

"You are unlikely to get a chief inspector or an inspector," the police officer explained. "Or a detective sergeant. Or even a detective constable."

"Oh... but the vicar?" Annabelle said.

"I am on first name terms with the Chief Constable," Diane said. "I'm sure if I had a word with Benjamin, he'd send an inspector."

The police officer flinched.

"I'm sure that's not necessary," he said. "You're not going to be one of these

22

witnesses who demands a lawyer present, are you?"

"Of course not," Diane said.

"Good."

"I am a lawyer."

"Well, we in uniform are perfectly capable of carrying out a simple murder enquiry."

"If you insist."

"I insist," he insisted. "You'll find that the good old trusted methods of rank-and-file policing will suffice here. We don't need any of your new-fangled psychological profiling, computer modelling or infrared remote-control fingerprinting. A crook is a crook as my dad used to say – he were in the force too – and that's all there is to it."

"If you say so."

"I'm an old-fashioned copper. I might not look it, but it were the way I were brought up."

Pat glanced down and, sure enough, Mowgli peeping out from his combat trousers was the original animated version.

"Now Miss Harris... son, you found the body?"

"Yes."

"We can vouch for that," Annabelle said. "Pat and I saw Di unlock the church."

"It was locked?"

"Yes."

"Who else has a key?"

"The vicar, obviously," Diane explained, "the curate, Mrs Entwistle as head of the Flower Arranging Committee[3], Mrs Jones as treasurer of the tea–"

"Does she?" Annabelle asked. "I thought she only had keys to the Parochial Hall."

"She has a key to the church too," Diane said. "It's a symbol of office."

_____

[3] Editor's note: This is another clue.

"And you have it for what reason?" the policeman asked.

Diane stopped fiddling with her pearls and straightened up on the Habitat sofa. "I am the chief editor of the parish magazine."

"I see." He tried writing this and succeeded in making a hole in the damp paper.

"The curate's wife has a key," Annabelle said.

"No, she doesn't," said Diane.

"She does, I've seen it."

"Not as the curate's wife, but as the supervisor of the cleaning ladies."

"Same thing."

"It is not! If someone else took over the supervision then the key would pass to them and the curate's wife would not have one."

"But she has one now?" said the officer.

"Yes."

"Anyone else?"

"Just Mr Boseman the choirmaster, Frances the warden and Betty the organist."

"That's nine keys?"

"Yes," Diane said, "and there's a spare in the vestry. It would normally be issued to the other churchwarden, but Major Naseby refused to take office."

"So the key would be…"

"Locked in the church."

"Ten keys… hmmm."

"So, who could it be?" Annabelle asked.

Pat put her right index finger on her left little finger.

"Well," she said, "not the vicar, obviously, and Mrs Entwistle wouldn't hurt a fly–"

"She did put those daffs around the font when they were well out of season," Annabelle pointed out.

"Yes, shocking," Diane agreed. "Daffodils are for spring."

"AND," Pat said, "the curate's wife wouldn't kill someone in the church as she'd have to supervise the cleaning up and the curate wouldn't dare inconvenience his wife, Mrs–"

"I didn't," Diane said.

"Diane didn't," Pat said, reaching her left thumb. She switched to her other hand. "Mrs Jones rarely goes into the church, Mr Boseman is a very upstanding member of the community, so he's above suspicion, and Betty the organist has bad eyesight."

"Bad eyesight," the constable said.

"It was dark in the church," Pat explained.

"The fuses had tripped," Diane added.

"Yes, so Betty the organist wouldn't have been able to see anything."

"I see," the constable said.

"That's nine... who have I forgotten?"

"Frances," Annabelle said.

"Miss Fairfax is the new warden," Pat continued, "and I can hardly imagine that she would leave the vicar like that."

"You mean dead?"

"No," Pat said, "on the front row. He's the vicar, so Frances would have insisted that he die in his proper seat in the chancel. She's very particular."

"I see."

"Did any of these nine have a motive?" the policeman asked.

"Oh no," Annabelle said.

"Hardly," Pat added, "Conky Whallop is a respectable village. We just don't go in for that sort of thing."

"I did," Diane said.

"Di?" Pat said.

"He was going to cancel the parish magazine," Diane explained. "He said it wasn't exciting enough and he felt it could be done just as easily with an email list. I mean, an email list, I ask you!"

"But that's not a motive for murder," Pat said.

"No... I suppose not," Diane admitted.

28

"Right... any idea about his next-of-kin?"

"His brother, Sir Victor, that's Sir Victor Pendle-Took, lives on Orthodox Crescent," Pat said. "He's an Architect."

"Well, he calls himself an Architect," Diane said, "but that house of his–"

But before she could finish, the police officer's radio crackled a garble that eventually sounded like a voice.

"...repeat Delta One Nine, this is <crackle> and <crackle><crackle> please, over."

"Repeat, please," the police officer said, thumb on the button. "Over."

"Repeating <crackle><crackle><crackle>."

"Repeat. Over."

"Repeat... what? <crackle> say again."

"I said... repeat... REPEAT. Over."

"<crackle><crackle><crackle> please <crackle>."

"Oh for..." Delta One Nine said, but then he realised that he was in a room full of gentle old ladies. He clicked the radio off and fished out his phone. "Excuse me."

The man stepped into the hall, although he had to raise his voice to be heard over the mobile network, so Pat, Annabelle and Diane were able to wait for him to finish without having to lean closer to the door. Clearly, the village's campaign against a new mast had other advantages besides avoiding an obvious eyesore.

"Yes? Yes. The vicar... another death? Who? Surely that's not connected? Right."

Pat, Diane and Annabelle turned towards one another with open mouths, but they straightened up quickly when the officer came back into the drawing-room to face their attentive and innocent expressions.

"So, ladies, thank you for your assistance and if we've any further questions, we'll be in touch."

"Thank you, officer," Pat replied.

And with that, the police officer disappeared into the night, coming back briefly to wipe Mowgli and Balloo on the welcome mat before collecting his combat boots. He left

Pat, Diane and Annabelle standing in the hall with their matching puzzled expressions.

"Someone else has been murdered," Annabelle said.

"You are jumping to conclusions," Pat said.

"What other conclusion is there?" Diane agreed. "But who?"

"And by whom?" Pat said.

By now it was very late, but none of them wanted to go to bed. It was also dark and the leafy lanes, crescents and avenues of Conky Whallop were stalked by a murderer... a double murderer!

"Who would murder the vicar?" Annabelle asked.

"Someone with a key," Pat replied.

"And who would murder whoever else has been murdered?" Annabelle said.

"Well, I was with you," Diane pointed out.

"Not when the vicar was killed," Pat said.

"No, but I was with you two when you found the vicar, and I was with you whenever it was that whomever was killed by whoever is the murderer."

"That's true," Pat said, "though maybe the first murderer isn't the second murderer."

"That's unlikely, isn't it?" Diane said. "There being two murderers, I mean."

"Maybe they are like buses?" Annabelle said.

"Buses come in threes," Diane pointed out.

"Oh, sorry."

"So," Pat said, "maybe the question is who's next?"

"Oh, that's a horrible thought," Anabelle said. "Pat, how could you think that?"

"Perhaps this isn't over and someone's going to eliminate everyone in the village."

"Oh, that's... Pat, you're teasing us."

"Perhaps."

"Honestly, who would commit murder?"

"I could murder a sherry," Pat said.

"Scotch," Diane said.

"Me too," Annabelle said.

"I've got a blend, I think," Pat said. She fetched the drinks, poured generous measures and then they sipped silently, unsure what to say. The clock ticked towards its one o'clock dinging.

"We have to investigate," Diane said suddenly.

"Whatever for?" Pat asked.

"Like Monsieur Poirot and Miss Marple," Annabelle said.

"Exactly," Diane said.

"I love Poirot, David Suchet is adorable, and you can sing the theme tune... *trust a trader dot com.*"

"That's the advertising jingle of the sponsor," Pat pointed out.

"Oh... is it?"

"Yes."

"How disappointing."

"Di, why do we have to investigate?" Pat asked.

"Because we're the editors of the parish magazine!" Diane said.

"What's that got to do with the price of tea?"

"It's our chance to be proper investigative journalists."

"Do we have to?" Annabelle asked.

"Yes," Diane said.

Pat raised her sherry. "Then the game's... what is it?"

"Afoot."

3. The Evidence Box

The next day, Pat rose late due to the disturbed night. They'd arranged to meet on the High Street at 11:15. She put on her nice blue hat, unfolded her walking stick and set off on the short walk to the shops. The air seemed fresh after the thunderstorm and fluffy clouds scudded overhead in the Cambridge blue sky. Gulls yawked above despite the lack of nearby seaside.

Strangely in Conky Whallop-on-the-Huh, everything carried on as normal – and why shouldn't it? Except for the police presence, the foreboding air of menace and the gathering of staring on-lookers, all was as it should be. After all, the villagers were *British*. For the locals, it was still the Golden Age before extended phone numbers, bifocals and the EU referendum of 1975.

When she reached the shops, Pat popped her half-moon glasses on to peer at her Accurist: 11:14 and some seconds.

Good, she thought.

The village itself had a picture postcard look with a wide pavement in front of the shops, each a delightful discovery of independent retail, their doors beneath hanging baskets of flowers and all the street furniture painted black and traditionally made. The paving was flagstones, not common tarmac, and cars had a hard time with the speed bumps, road narrowing and the pedestrian crossing. It was a zebra as the Parish Council hadn't liked the concept of buttons and beeping.

First, there was Pheasant's Café with teas, coffees, health drinks, freshly pressed fruit juices and cinnamon cakes. Pat often enjoyed a hot chocolate there, but today she hadn't the time.

Next came the Oxfam shop where Annabelle volunteered. It sold donated gifts such as knick-knacks, letter openers, collectable ornaments, garden gnomes and homemade candles. Along from there, was Baxter's the Butchers, Conkies Bakery and then Celia's, which sold new gifts such as knick-knacks, letter openers, collectable ornaments, garden gnomes, home-made candles and picture postcards of the village.

On the far corner stood the Red Lion, now Chiang's Oriental Emporium, which specialised in Peking cuisine and pizzas.

The police cars were still swarming around the church and Mrs Entwistle's cottage, and there appeared to be another collection on the other side of the Green in Tinsel Lane.

Villagers were abroad too: Mrs Entwistle included. Mr Henderson and Mrs Pilkington trundled about on their mobility scooters.

Pat saw Diane and waved her walking stick aloft to call her over. Diane's powerful stride meant she reached Pat just as Mrs Entwistle did.

"Have you heard?" said Mrs Entwistle. She wore her blue rinse under a plain headscarf.

"The vicar," Diane said.

"I know."

"Diane and I," Pat said, "found–"

"Shhh, shhh," Diane said. "Terrible news. It was last night, sometime between five and seven."

"Really?" said Mrs Entwistle. "The police won't let me inside the church and I need to sort out the dead."

"The dead!" Pat said.

"The dead flowers... they'll be looking very sad."

"Of course," Diane said. "Very good of you to keep up standards."

"Thank you," Mrs Entwistle replied. "Flowers will be such a comfort to everyone during these trying times."

"It is appreciated," Pat said, and then she added for no very good reason, "Where were you yesterday evening?"

"Me? I was at home. I didn't go out. At all. Dreadful storm. Nicer weather today."

"Do you know who else died?" Pat asked.

Mrs Entwistle glanced left and right, and then down at her sensible shoes. "No. Someone else? No."

"Terrible business," Pat added.

"Yes, terrible, anyway," Mrs Entwistle said, "twenty-five past already, I must be getting along."

"Of course."

"Well, good day."

"Good day, Mrs Entwistle."

"Good day, Mrs Thomas."

"Good day, Mrs Entwistle."

"Di."

"Angela."

Mrs Entwistle left them on the corner and hurried to the butcher's.

"So," Diane said, "she has no alibi."

"She has," Pat said, "because she lied."

"Oh?"

"Before you arrived last night, I saw her going along the Green towards her son's."

"Did you now?"

"Tinsel Avenue way."

"Hmm."

By way of checking Mrs Entwistle, they had a butchers in the butcher's window at the smoked bacon and famous sausages: Mrs Entwistle was having something sliced. Baxter, proud in his white and blue apron, weighed the meat and popped on a label.

He asked something.

Mrs Entwistle pointed into the display.

"So," Diane said, "she murdered the vicar and then went to her son's."

"Her son is in the Caribbean."

"What? Again? How does he afford it?"

"I've no idea, but she's forever having to water his plants."

"It was raining," Diane said. "All the gardens will be soaked and the water butts will be full."

"House plants, Di."

"Oh."

40

"Why didn't she just murder him and go home for a nice mug of Horlicks?" Pat mused. "She could have watered the house plants a day late, surely?"

"If I'd murdered someone, I'd want something stronger than a Horlicks."

Pat nodded.

"So not Angela," Diane said.

"I saw Mrs Entwistle," Pat said, "and she could have gone to the church before going to her son's house."

A woman with a bright red-and-white dress, designer hat and matching clutch bag struggled towards them across the Green. She held a distasteful bin bag out at arm's length.

"Curate's wife is about," Diane observed.

Realising the danger, Pat and Diane popped into the Oxfam shop to see if Annabelle was there.

The bell above the door rang – *ting-a-ling* – but no-one greeted them as they went in. Above the counter, the clocks on the shelf read 11:42 am, 9:40, 00:00 flashing and ten to two. Their friend was in the back room sorting out all the bric-a-brac people had brought in into various piles: tat, broken, recycling and landfill.

"Belle! Belle!" Pat called.

Annabelle came into the shop holding a tea towel. She was wearing red with green today, the opposite mismatching of last night.

"How can I... oh, Di, Pat, have you heard?"

"Yes, Belle," said Pat. "We were there."

"No, not the vicar, though that is terrible, so terrible. But Sergio has been killed."

"Sergio?"

"Not Sergio?"

"Yes," Annabelle said. She leant forward and lowered her voice. "It was a car... I mean, a moped accident."

"He was foolish to be out on that moped in the middle of a storm."

"Oh, the storm had passed before he went out," Annabelle said. "It had stopped by eleven, I think."

"I suspect the roads were still wet," Diane said. "And who would want pizza at midnight?"

"Lots of people do," Annabelle said. "Night workers, students and people with insomnia, those with nothing in for breakfast."

"And those being questioned by the police at all hours," Diane said.

"Were we really up until two last night!?" Pat said.

"Yes, and what's worse..." – Annabelle leant forward again – "...it was a hit-and-run."

She stood back upright and nodded, knowingly.

"Hit-and-run?" Pat said. The vicar on one side of the Green and then Sergio on the other.

The bell above the door tinkled as Mr Boseman came in, its *ting-a-ling* tuneful for the choirmaster's entrance. He was a genial gentleman with a pencil moustache and a trilby. He removed his hat to show off his receding hairline and public-school education to the ladies.

"Mrs Harrison, Annabelle... and Mrs Thomas, Miss Richards, excellent, even better."

"We were just discussing poor Sergio," Annabelle said.

"Really, what's he done now?" Mr Boseman asked. "Annabelle, do you have the time?"

"Yes, it's... oh dear, ten to two."

"It's ten to twelve," Di said.

Pat squinted at her watch too: it was more like 11:47 and then, in two ticks, 11:48.

"You were saying about Sergio?" Mr Boseman said.

"Killed in a hit-and-run?" Annabelle said.

"No! Poor Mrs Chiang."

"Mrs Chiang?" Di said.

"Sergio delivers for them," Mr Boseman explained. "I've often... well, I've seen him collecting deliveries."

"And the vicar too," Pat said.

"Vicar?"

"Murdered."

"Mrs Thomas! Surely not?"

"In his own church, I'm afraid."

"That is shocking."

"Where were you yesterday evening at about seven?" Pat asked, nonchalantly checking the scarfs-and-hats rail.

"I'll tell the police I was at home," Mr Boseman said, "with my wife."

"Of course," Pat said.

"You will have to tell the police," Diane added.

"Will I? I will. Of course. Why?"

"As choirmaster, you have a key to the church."

"But there's no choir," he pointed out, "so they won't be interested."

"You still have a key," Diane countered.

"That's merely ceremonial."

"It still opens the door."

"The vicar was locked inside," Pat explained.

"Oh. Right. I see."

They stood for a while, taking all this in during the long awkward silence.

One of the clocks ticked on the shelf.

Mr Boseman took his watch off and checked it. "Well, five to twelve... I must be going. Ladies."

Ting-a-ling and in breezed the curate's wife.

"Darlings," she said.

"Ah, it's twelve o'clock, noon," Mr Boseman said as he passed her. He replaced his trilby, then lifted it again to the curate's wife as he left, pulling the door to with another bright *ting-a-ling*.

Pat checked her watch: 11:53.

The curate's wife came up to the counter.

"I have these... well, I don't need them anymore and what with my Gary being your curate, I thought, charity would be best."

She deposited the bin sack by the till and then looked around for something to wipe her red glove on as it must have been contaminated by the fresh plastic black bag.

Annabelle gazed into the sack.

"They're rustic," the curate's wife explained. "Tweed. I won't be needing them when I move back to London."

"You're going back to London?" Pat asked.

"Well... it's still... but, you know, a new posting. Exciting, isn't it?"

"You'll have to hand your church key back," Diane said.

"Yes, obviously Diane, no need to harp."

"Where were you last night?" Pat asked.

"That's rather personal, but if you must pry, I was at a soiree down in the Smoke, you know. Cocktails and divine hors d'oeuvres, and such lovely people from, like, the theatre and finance worlds, you know."

"I'm afraid we don't," Pat said.

"I got back so late and I had a lie-in. Beauty sleep is so important. Anyway, I thought–"

"You've not heard," Diane said.

"Heard what, Diane?"

"The vicar's dead."

"Dead? What do you mean, dead?"

"He was murdered," Pat explained.

The curate's wife gave Pat such a stare, her finely carved eyebrows lowered and her long, mascaraed lashes almost entwining before her sparkling blue contacts.

"Really?" she said.

"Yes," Pat said. "In the church."

"Oh. That explains all the boys in blue."

48

"Once the police have finished with the crime scene," Diane said, "it'll need cleaning."

"Oh?"

"And you are in charge of the cleaning."

"Ah."

The curate's wife curled her lips down at the edges, revolted at the thought.

"How did he... you know?"

"Stabbed in the back," Diane explained.

"Oh dear," Annabelle said.

"Was there... much... mess?" the curate's wife asked.

"I imagine," Diane said.

"It's just that Mrs Partridge is, like, on holiday and I offered to step in. A little light dusting, I thought, not... anything... messy?"

"You'll have to get down on your knees," Diane said.

The curate's wife glanced down at her knees and her foundation paled as if it had been bleached.

"And scrub," Diane finished.

"The police will want a word too, I imagine," Pat said.

"Me? Why me?"

"You have a key."

"Of course, the curate's wife should have a key."

"No," Diane said, "you have a key because you are in charge of cleaning, not because you are the curate's wife."

"Same thing, Diane, obviously."

"No," Diane said, "it's not the–"

"I must talk to my husband," the curate's wife said. She left like a hurricane of matching red-and-white and the bell still rang after she'd slammed the door behind her.

"She has an alibi," Pat said, "as does Mr Boseman."

"Two down, six to go," Diane said.

"Though it depends on when she did get back from London."

"She seemed genuinely surprised," Annabelle said.

"She said she was meeting theatrical types," Pat pointed out, "which includes actors and actresses."

All three of them gazed out of the window and watched the curate's wife hurry across the Green, clutching her clutch bag and holding down her designer millinery – *step-step, step-step, step-stepping* – on her red high heels.

One of the clocks on the shelf chimed the hour: they read 12:02 pm, 12:00, 00:00 flashing and ten to two.

The bell rang yet again, discordantly – *ting! ting!* – and Mr Boseman returned. He saw them, coughed, and lowered the brim of his hat over his dark glasses.

"It's twelve o'clock," he said in a gruff voice. He smoothed his pencil moustache and kept his finger on his stiff upper lip as he left again.

"What was that about?" Di said, when the bell, unaccustomed to such regular treatment, had finally finished *linging*.

!!!

On her way home, Pat took a detour towards the flashing police blue and ghastly red of the patrol cars on Tinsel Lane. She stood for a time by the fence to the Village Green, leaning on her walking stick and watching.

About 300 yards away, men in white overalls bent down by the road checking a tyre track. Further down others in blue overalls struggled with the mangled remains of a moped. The accident must have occurred at the top end of Tinsel Lane, and the impact had driven the moped downwards.

She checked her watch: 12:25... no, 12:26 exactly.

Nearby, a policeman was pulling a cool box out of the hedge. It advertised pizza delivery. The officer looked up and down, trying to connect it with all the other crash debris. How had the cool box come off the moped and travelled uphill?

And in the gutter by Pat's feet lay a pizza box.

Littering always irritated, but this pizza box was fresh. It should have been soaked by last night's storm.

Without quite knowing why, she bent down and tugged it out. It came away easily – her knees cracked as she stood up: "Ah" – and she pushed it into her big bag.

When she looked back, a police officer glanced back at her: she was sure he could see her face burning bright red.

Back in her cottage, she folded away her walking stick, put the kettle on and checked the time: 12:42. Good, she thought, over an hour before *The Archers*. After she'd spooned a little Oolong into her tea infuser, she took out the pizza box and unfolded her half-moon glasses.

On the top was a ticket with the address of a flat in nearby Upper Whallop, probably in the student district. It was dated today, which confused Pat for a moment until she realised that it referred to last night's early hours.

The contents were well squashed; the cheese, pineapple and anchovies resembling soup.

The Chiang's were on the far side of the village. Upper Whallop was west, so why had Sergio driven along the High Street and up Tinsel Lane when the A-road was in the opposite direction?

Sergio must have had a delivery to do on the east side of the village.

She turned the box over and a dirty mark cut across it. The big, solid impression suggested the thick tyre track of a big, solid, thick car.

The hall clock dinged one o'clock.

Her watch was ten seconds fast.

"Poor Sergio," Pat said as she scraped the pizza remains into the bin. She kept the box.

4. On the Case

Detective Constable Kilroy jumped from the plain clothed car, straightened his plain clothes, plain tie and plain light jumper. He'd ironed his brand-new coat, a fresh expensive Mackintosh, until it was as sharp as a pin ready for his first day.

"Killjoy!"

Kilroy sighed and went over to the uniformed sergeant.

"It's Detective Constable Kil*roy.*"

"You wanna see the crime scenes?"

"Obviously."

"Church," the sergeant said, pointing to the obvious building, "Tinsel Lane or–"

"In order, sergeant... what's your name?"

"Drax, Constable."

"Detective Constable," Kilroy corrected. "I'll see them in chronological order, Drax."

"Right you are."

Sergeant Drax led the DC up the hill to the church.

As he went, Kilroy saw the villagers gathering like frozen automatons, staring back as he approached the lychgate.

A constable was on duty keeping the curious at bay.

The sergeant went ahead between the graves and then through the quiet, peaceful interior of the church, heavy with its history and settling dust, to the chalk outline.

"Stabbed," Drax said, helpfully.

"I have read the report."

"In the back."

"I have read the report."

"Sitting there in the front row."

"I have... never mind."

Kilroy stepped back and then turned around doing a little dance to view the scene from various angles. He mimed stabbing, and then danced a two-step to bring himself into what he thought was the proper spot.

"Must have known his killer," Kilroy said.

"Everyone knows everyone in places like this."

"Hmm."

The second crime scene required them to cross the Village Green. The villagers were still there, frozen to the spot, but they'd moved from their initial positions as if they were all playing musical statues and the tune only played when no-one was looking.

Tinsel Lane had tyres tracks and a forlorn evidence marker kicked into the gutter. The yellow stand had '2' stencilled on it.

Sergeant Drax conducted with his hands as if operating a car coming down the hill, hitting a moped and scattering debris down towards Brighter Avenue. It seemed straightforward.

"And the third?" Kilroy asked.

"Didn't you read the report?" Drax replied.

"It hasn't been written yet."

So, Sergeant Drax led DC Kilroy down Tinsel Lane, along Brighter Avenue and into Orthodox Crescent. Number 3 was called *Brahms Cottage*. The sign had musical notes surrounding the number and name.

Another uniformed constable stood on guard.

"Evening Frank."

"Evening Sarge."

"This is DC Kill... roy."

Frank nodded to Kilroy. "Path's still here."

"I see... and the husband?" Kilroy asked.

"Down the station giving a statement."

"I see."

"This way," Drax said and he led the way inside.

They found the pathologist at the back of the house in a downstairs room. It had been converted into a bedroom.

"Doctor Lake," Sergeant Drax said, "this is Detective Constable Kilroy."

Doctor Lake wore corduroy, but somehow on her, it seemed dashing and provocative. Kilroy felt his mouth go dry and–

"I'm up here," Doctor Lake said.

"Sorry, Miss... Ma'am."

"Doctor."

"I was just admiring your stethoscope."

Behind him, the sergeant coughed and managed a "'scuse me." His footsteps pummelled away before laughter echoed back along the hall.

"I see," Doctor Lake said. She took her stethoscope from around her neck and shoved it into her Gladstone bag, away from any admiring eyes.

"Well?" Kilroy asked.

"She's dead."

Kilroy looked at the bed, the body, then quickly at the quaint bedroom full of nick-nacks and then back to the buxom–

"Are you all right, Detective?"

–utterly professional pathologist.

"Yes... er, Doctor Lake, I'm going to ask for a time of death and you're going to say there's no way you can give me an accurate time of death, but approximately?"

"Eleven fifty-five and seven seconds."

"How can you be so precise?"

"She was bed-bound and had a monitor for her heart connected to a computer and then the internet. When it shows fluctuations, it sends a text. The heart stopping counts as a fluctuation. She can't have died much before then, two, maybe even three seconds earlier. Of course, brain death would be anything up to two minutes after that."

"I see."

A carriage clock lay on the floor by the bed, the glass smashed and the time frozen at five past twelve. It must have been knocked from the bedside table when the death occurred, the clock being fast... or broken ten minutes later for some reason.

"Who found the body?"

"The husband, Zephron Boseman, at one o'clock."

"Hmmm."

"There's a note," Doctor Lake explained. She handed him a transparent evidence pouch.

Kilroy read it through the plastic.

Dear Zephron,

I am so sorry to be a burden. I love you too much to hold you back.
You can still make beautiful music with someone.

Love,

Belinda.
XXX

"And then she killed herself?" Kilroy said.

"Yes," Doctor Lake said, and she pointed to the bedside cabinet. A glass stood there full of white residue.

"I see."

"It was an overdose of barbiturates," Doctor Lake explained, "and a bullet to the head before multiple stab wounds to the chest."

Kilroy looked at the body, its eyes staring upwards disconcertingly with a neat hole in her forehead.

"Poisoned, shot and stabbed?"

"Not necessarily in that order," Doctor Lake added. "She could have been poisoned, stabbed and then shot."

"Yes... right."

"I doubt she could have drunk an overdose of barbiturates after she'd been stabbed and shot."

"No."

"Well, I'll leave it in your capable hands, I'm sure."

When DC Kilroy was alone, he went and stood at the foot of the bed. He mimed shooting her, then mimed the stabbing and finally mimed drinking a glass of barbiturates.

He checked his watch: 6:37, 15°C, 103 bpm.

Back at the porch, he met Sergeant Drax again.

"Is there anywhere to get something to eat?" Kilroy asked.

"There's a Chinese down on the High Street. Does pizza."

"Thank you."

Kilroy noticing his Mackintosh had the slightest of creases down the seam. He smoothed it down.

"Three deaths, eh?" said the sergeant. "A proper serial killer."

"Technically, he's not a serial killer until he's killed four."

"Whatever you say, Killjoy."

"Kil*roy*."

Chiang's was at the end of the row of shops on the High Street and did both Chinese and pizza. It had clearly once been the village pub. Kilroy went in and smiled: the new décor harked back to a luxuriant age, decadent with its reds and gold.

A woman in a tight cheongsam of dark blue and gold embroidery approached. She greeted him with a bow and said, "May I help you?"

"Do you have a table for one?"

The woman adopted an expression of sadness. No-one should be alone, her pale face and bright red lips seemed to say.

"Of course, this way," she said, indicating the empty restaurant.

Kilroy chose the table furthest from the window and sat with his back to the wall. After checking the menu, he ordered calamari for starters, whole fish in a sweet and sour sauce with noodles, Hong Kong style, for his main, and jasmine tea.

"Excuse me," he said, "do you know the vicar?"

"Takeaways. Always Chinese. Always Peking duck with other choices, never the same."

"Oh... and Sergio?"

"Pizza with anchovies."

"I meant about his death."

"Shame. Awful business. How we going to cope?"

"He delivered for you?"

"Good worker."

"And the night he died?"

The woman looked upwards. "Buffalo with olives, Margherita, pepperoni, pepperoni. Regular order, good customers, ghastly hall."

"Sorry?"

"Ghastly hall. Students."

"Oh."

"You ask many questions."

Kilroy fished out his warrant card. "I'm a detective constable," he said proudly.

"Detective constable, not inspector?"

"No, you see, most crimes are investigated by detective constables. It's not like the television."

"No?"

"Do you know the Bosemans?"

"Eat in, every Wednesday. Peking duck, egg fried rice, prawn crackers, sometimes lemon chicken."

"Ah... anything else?"

"White wine."

"And?"

"They sit where you sit."

As he sat where they sat, Kilroy went over the case making notes: vicar, murdered; delivery driver hit-and-run, accident or deliberate? Finally, as the calamari arrived, Belinda Boseman, suicide plus extras.

He dunked a squid ring in the sauce.

66

This was his first case, he remembered, so he ought to celebrate. A bottle of wine, maybe, but he was driving and on duty.

Or was it, like buses, his first three cases?

5. The Plot Thickens

Diane invited Pat and Annabelle over to her house. She'd been working on a new edition of the parish magazine.

"But we've done one already," Annabelle said. "Our special, commemorative last edition."

"Yes," Diane said, "but now we've news, actual news."

"The death of the poor vicar, and poor Sergio and now poor Mrs Boseman."

"I went with the vicar."

She held up a sheet of A4 paper upon which her rinky-dinky printer had emblazoned: *Minister Mercilessly Murdered* along with *'News Editor Diane Richards discovered the body'* and *'Exclusive'*.

Pat took it off Diane to have a look. She hadn't put on her half-moon glasses, so she held it at arm's length.

"Don't you think it's a little tasteless?" she said. "'Butchered by a bloody bayonet in the back' – is that really necessary?"

"Artistic license for the alliteration."

"Oh, really, Di."

"It's standard journalism," Diane said, taking back the page and holding it near her heart, except that her pearl necklace got in the way.

"And it wasn't a bayonet," Pat said. "I'm sure it was that ornate paperknife. The one that's too big to use properly."

"The vicar complained that the parish magazine wasn't exciting enough, so it's a way of honouring him, really."

"Hmmm," Pat hummed.

"Full colour, I think."

"That will be expensive."

"Nonsense... and we don't have a big print run."

Annabelle had the list: 27 people in the village and 3 mailouts.

"This is a sort of suspect list," Pat said.

"Yes!" Diane said seizing upon the thought. "And we must investigate."

"Three deaths... and three of us."

"Yes, split up and cover more ground. Good idea."

"Three deaths?" Annabelle asked.

"Mrs Boseman," Pat said.

"Oh no! How?"

"There seems to be some confusion over that point," Pat said. "Mrs Entwistle said stabbed, Mrs Jones said poisoned, Mrs Kovalyov said shot, Mrs Pilkington said bludgeoned and Mrs Perceval swears blind that she was electrocuted by foreign agents."

"That eliminates strangled," Annabelle said. "Sorry."

"Right," Diane said. "We investigate all three deaths."

"How do we divide them up?" Annabelle asked.

70

"Well," Pat said, "Diane found the vicar, so that makes sense."

"Pat, you were in Mr Boseman's choir," Annabelle said.

"Yes, I was," Pat agreed. "Which leaves Sergio for you, Belle."

"Oh, but I didn't really know him."

"Well, he must have been at the Chiang's to collect the pizzas for delivery, so perhaps that's the place to start," Pat said. "I found a pizza box on Tinsel Lane near the accident."

"Did you?" Diane said.

"Yes. And it was being delivered to Upper Whallop–"

"That's not towards Tinsel Lane."

"No, so one of the other deliveries must have been on the lane. If we knew where...."

Both Pat and Diane looked to Annabelle.

"Oh," Annabelle said, "I could go and ask."

!!!

Pat bought a bunch of flowers at Celia's, a simple display as she thought Mr Boseman would not want too much trouble.

She rang his bell: it played a lovely little tune.

That, and the musical notes on the house nameplate, reminded her of the choir practice all those years ago. It was a shame that the choir had withered to a chorus, an ensemble and finally a trio before they'd called it a day. Shame, as it had given Mr Boseman something to take his mind off the withering of his wife. She had gone from a strong, forthright woman to requiring a Zimmer frame, a wheelchair and finally a downstairs bed.

While Pat waited, she folded up her walking stick.

The door opened.

"Pat!"

"Zephron." She handed over the flowers. "I'm so sorry."

"Thank you."

They stood for a moment, one on each side of the threshold. He was a handsome man with his pencil moustache and his genial nature. If Pat had been forty years younger? Today, however, he seemed as if he had less notes to the bar and more tipples from the bar. His voice had a quaver to it.

"Pat... come in."

"If it's no trouble."

Pat went in and along the hall. As she passed the downstairs bedroom, she glanced at the medical bed with all its supports, machines and equipment like a private hospital ward deposited in a mock Tudor house. It was taped off as a crime scene.

"I'm not allowed in the room," Mr Boseman said as they reached the kitchen. "Not that I need to go... Tea?"

"If it's no trouble."

He fussed with the crockery and kettle, unsure what to do. He'd looked after his wife, so he did know what to do, of course, but somehow the tempo had been removed from his song.

"Zephron, what happened?"

"Oh Pat... she was... the police... it makes no sense."

"I'm so sorry."

"They say she was murdered," Mr Boseman said.

"Murdered! How awful."

"And the vicar... and Sergio... what are we to do?"

"How was... I mean... was it... the same?"

The kettle boiled. Mr Boseman filled the pot. The tea stewed awhile.

"She was shot, stabbed and poisoned," he said, finally. "It makes no sense."

"Shot, stabbed and poisoned?"

"Yes." He seemed bewildered. "Can you believe it?"

"No, it's... but when?"

"Yesterday," he said, "around twelve. You and I, Pat, and Mrs Richards and Miss Harrison and the curate's wife. We were talking at the exact time that my poor Belinda was murdered."

"Oh, dear."

"She'd suffered enough."

"That's a comfort, I suppose, that she's not suffering any longer," Pat agreed. "And at the time you came into the Oxfam shop twice?"

"Twice?"

"Don't you remember?" Pat said. "You came in for the time... twice."

"Once... I don't remember. It's all so confusing."

"Oh, dear."

Pat took over and made the tea. They drank, standing by the counter, letting the tea work its magic.

The doorbell played its tune.

"You have visitors," Pat said. "I'll go."

"Yes. Thank you for coming over, Pat."

"My pleasure," Pat said and then she bit her lip.

Mr Boseman took her back down the hall and Pat saw the downstairs bedroom again, a place bereft of life.

Outside stood a man in a smart Mackintosh.

"Hello," he said, "I'm Detective Constable Kilroy. Mr Boseman, if I could ask you some questions."

"Certainly officer," Mr Boseman said. "I've just made a pot of tea."

"Thank you."

"Does your inspector take tea?" Mr Boseman asked, looking around.

"It's just me, sir."

"I see."

"Well, I'll be going," Pat said. She brattled her walking stick and the three sections jumped into one like a magician's wand. "Take care, Zephron, and if there's anything you want."

76

"Yes, thank you, Pat."

Pat and this Detective Constable Kilroy locked eyes as they passed.

"Who was that?" she heard him say.

"Oh, that's just Pat... Patricia Thomas, she's–"

But the door closed and Pat heard no more.

!!!

"Mrs Chiang," Annabelle said, "I wonder if I might... er, peruse your takeaway menu."

Mrs Chiang bowed, her hands pale against the rich blue of her ornate oriental dress. Her dark hair artfully arranged in a bun through which chopsticks had been stabbed. She looked so elegant, sophisticated and organised. Annabelle knew she'd got her twinsets confused again: beige with peach, neither of which went with her hairdo's auburn splendour with no ammonia or parabens.

"Very good," Mrs Chiang said, "we have good pizza and much prized Cantonese food."

"Lovely."

Annabelle checked the glossy print, unfolding it from its thirds, and examined the lushly illustrated Chinese fare and then the sparsely decorated pizza menu with its bewildering choice. It seemed that anything could be dropped, drizzled or deposited upon a deep-dish, double-dough or Detroit-style crust.

"And I wonder if... this is the same as your restaurant menu?"

"It is."

"And I wonder if... you have a wine thingummy."

"Of course," Mrs Chiang bowed again and fetched a cardboard list slipped into a leather cover.

Annabelle considered the French, New World and Australian options. There were four different types of saké – imagine – and Japanese whiskies.

"And, er, that is... that's a lovely bracelet."

"Glastonbury festival wristband."

"Lovely."

"Five days."

"Oh. That's erm, yes."

"Anything else?"

"Well, I wonder… er… that is… er…"

The phone rang, shrill and demanding.

"Please to excuse me," Mrs Chiang said. She bowed, took tiny steps to the angry, black faux Bakelite contraption. "Chiang's Chinese and Pizza! May I help you?"

Annabelle smiled at her and stepped away as if to give Mrs Chiang some privacy as she took down an order of 35, 46, 72, extra 120 and so forth.

A delivery book lay upon the counter.

Annabelle flipped it into the wine menu and then went through it as if flicking through the world's vineyards. Today, yesterday, Wednesday evening, later, over the page and a final order delivered by 'Serg'. It listed four pizzas to the same address, Gastrench Hall, a student residence in the next town.

"...forty minutes to an hour," Mrs Chiang stressed. She'd added up all the numbers to reach £35.50, which was nearly a pound-a-minute waiting time.

The phone tinged once with the slam.

Annabelle flustered everything onto the floor.

Mrs Chiang scurried over to help and raised a quizzical eyebrow once the wine list, leather cover and the delivery book had been recovered.

"Thank you, Mrs Chiang, most helpful."

Mrs Chiang's raised eyebrow did not even quiver.

"Have a lovely festival," Annabelle added.

"It was last week."

"Oh, lovely."

Annabelle made her escape.

As she left, she collided with a man wearing a Mackintosh.

"Sorry," they both said at the same time.

"Detective Constable Kilroy," the man said.

"Oh... yes... sorry. Annabelle Harrison."

"Do you work here?"

"Oh, no sorry," she said and then she hurried away.

"I am Mrs Chiang," Mrs Chiang said.

"Mrs Chiang," Annabelle heard the man say, "I have a few questions, I'd like-"

But Annabelle had stepped out onto the High Street and heard no more.

!!!

Meanwhile, Diane checked Frances the warden's big blue BMW SUV, pleased to see that the rear hatchback door had a dent.

She imagined the trendy SUV reversing, smashing into poor Sergio's moped, squashing the pizzas and... except that there was only a single point of damage. A moped was a long object and would surely have scratched all over the paintwork as the powerful SUV's sophisticated styling mangled the 50cc bike to the point of insurance write-off.

And Frances would have had to drive backwards, which seemed unlikely. The churchwarden was a very forward lady.

Diane didn't like Frances, who was new to the village and didn't understand the country ways and their traditions. But, unlike the curate's wife, she had fitted in, even bludgeoning her way to gaining a church key!

Although a warden was important, of course, it wasn't a long-term post like, say, parish magazine's chief editor.

Diane stood up and ooh... her back.

"Diane?" It was Frances.

"I was just... dropped my... keys," Diane said holding up her keys and thankful that she kept them in her coat pocket rather than any handbag. It was a heavy, obvious bunch: her house, back door and the big church key.

"That explains why you were on your knees."

"Yes."

"I thought you might be praying."

"Me? Oh no."

"It doesn't explain why you dropped the keys there."

"No?"

"No."

"Well... you have a bump on the back of your car."

"I got it a couple of days ago."

"Really?"

"Yes."

"Yes?"

"I hit a stupid bollard," Frances said. "You'd think an architect would be able to design a straight driveway."

"The vicar's brother, Sir Victor?"

"That's the one."

"Wasn't he here the other night?"

"No."

"I thought I saw him driving out."

"You must be mistaken."

"I'm sure–"

"No."

Frances stood impassively, smart casual to perfection, her hair tidy, and her feet bare even though she was standing on the gravel path.

"We need to talk," Diane said.

"Then you'd better come in."

Usually churches had two wardens, but Conky Whallop's last election had been rife with controversy[4]. Major Naseby, the other warden elected, had objected on the grounds that Frances was a woman.

"I'm not sexist, *but*," he'd said, "either she goes or I do," and then he had gone.

---

[4] Editor's note: Highlighted in the July edition of the parish magazine, *Woman Wins Warden War*.

So, Frances, a lovely ex-headmistress recently moved up from Brighton, was now the only warden and, in her early forties, young to bear such a burden.

"Tea or something stronger?" Frances suggested.

"Best keep a clear head."

"Plenty of tonic then?"

"Yes."

Frances paused in her main room and indicated the options. The lovely Regency building had a Grade II listing: it had a beautiful exterior with its ashlar stonework complementing the yellow brickwork and an interior boasting a modern, open plan living space complete with a building enforcement notice that the council hadn't been able to fight in court due to lack of funds.

Diane pondered whether it would be best to talk on the black leather sofa, around the dining table or seated at the breakfast bar. The floor throughout the ground floor had been done in marble to link all the zones together, so it wasn't clear where she should go. A proper cottage had a drawing room for guests. While she thought about it, Frances mixed two Bombays and Schweppes.

Frances made the decision and sat on the leather sofa pulling her legs up under her. She was still barefoot.

Diane felt over-dressed in her sensible blouse, sensible skirt, sensible coat, sensible patent leather shoes and frivolous pearls.

She took a swig of gin.

"Frances, I know that we haven't seen eye-to-eye."

"Go on, Di."

"Well, the church needs... this is a terrible time, you understand, and we should all stand together."

"Agreed."

"So, well, basically, the police will suspect those of us with keys to the church."

"Why's that?"

"Because the vicar was locked inside the church."

86

"So, whoever killed George must have locked the door after they left."

"That's it."

"Or they were still inside when you found the body."

"I hardly think... oh!"

Diane slurped some gin and tonic, seeing the dark church interior in the brightness of the ice cubes and the sunshine colour of the lemon. Could someone have been hiding behind a pillar, lying between the pews or skulking in the vestry? Anyone could have been inside from flower arrangers to cleaning ladies and... murderers. They'd have seen her.

"But you are right," Frances said, "we form a suitable shortlist... the curate, his wife, Mrs Entwistle, Mrs Jones, Betty, Zephron Boseman, you and I – I rang Mrs Jones and Mrs Entwistle as soon as I knew... oh, and there's the other warden's key in the vestry."

"That was still there."

"Maybe they replaced it."

"After they'd locked the church."

"Ah... perhaps not."

"So," Diane said, "eight suspects."

"Eight?"

"Yes, eight."

"How so?"

"Well, I didn't do it."

"No, Di, and neither did I."

"Nobody did... except one."

"Who would?" Frances said. "He was like a father."

"Father is rather a catholic phrase for a Church of England warden to use."

"I meant he was like ministering father to his flock."

"Yes, he was a kind and dutiful man."

"To his flock."

Diane took another sip of the fiery gin.

"He wasn't the saint you all think he was," Frances added.

"Do you have an alibi?" Diane said.

"Yes, I was... here all evening."

"What were you doing?"

Frances jiggled her chunky tumbler in reply.

"Any witnesses?" Diane asked.

"My, you are inquisitive, aren't you?"

"Parish magazine."

"Oh. Ha-ha!"

"So any witnesses?"

"Alas, I was alone. I watched some Xena Warrior Princess on Amazon Prime."

Diane startled and dropped her glass. It shattered, leaving shards of glass, ice and a sharp lemon slice on the marble flooring.

"Sorry," Diane said, "just slipped."

"Don't worry," Frances said, easily. "Mrs Entwistle will sort it. It's her day."

"I'm sorry?"

"She's my cleaner. Saturday afternoon. Although she will insist on bringing flowers for all the vases."

Diane saw the tulips for the first time: tulips weren't in season. Nor had the daffodils around the font back in the church.

"Will that be everything, Di?"

"Yes, Frances."

Frances uncurled from the sofa to indicate that the interview was over and followed Diane through the hall.

When Diane opened the door, she revealed a very surprised man in a Mackintosh. His hand raised, caught in the act of knocking.

"Ah," he said, "Mrs Fairfax, I'm Detective Constable Kilroy. I'd like to ask you some questions."

"I'm Harrison," Diane said.

"Sorry... er... Mrs Harrison."

"Miss."

"Oh. Sorry."

"You want Frances," Diane said. She smiled coldly and stepped aside to reveal Frances.

"Ah, Mrs Fairfax."

"It's *Miss* Fairfax," Frances said.

"Sorry, Miss Fairfax."

"Well," Diane said, "I must be going. Good day, Frances, good day, Inspector."

"Detective Constable."

"Really?" – she looked about – "Where's the inspector?"

"This is my case."

"I expect he'll be along shortly," Diane said.

"No," he said, "you see, inspectors–"

"Good bye, Frances."

"Diane."

Diane scrunched down the gravel path. There was another SUV parked next to it, silver, and it too had a dent.

"Detective, would you like a cup of tea or something stronger," Frances said.

"I'm on duty, though–"

But Diane overheard no more.

6. The Usual Suspects

It was Annabelle's turn.

She made a cold collation with items from Marks and Spencer's and laid it out on her dining room table. Coffees and teas were ready, richest hot chocolate and a plate of all-butter shortbread squares.

And then disaster – utter disaster.

"Oh!"

She'd put them on the table before she'd realised.

"Those will never do," she said to herself.

But the kitchen drawer didn't have any others.

How could she have been so muddle-headed?

She'd thought she'd been doing so well as she'd managed to find a twinset that matched, marigold with marigold.

The Church Committee was a peripatetic organisation and each of them was responsible for hosting the monthly meeting in strict rotation. Just as the planets aligned in the heavens, and so Capricorn had to be careful about money and Taurus would meet a tall, dark stranger, it was predictable. Only more so! Planets were wandering stars that might retrograde back into any constellation, but whoever hosted the Church Committee was a fixed-point set in stone. Rules had been laid down in the 17th century to cover Lent, early Easters, Parliamentarianism, witchcraft, illnesses and even sudden death.

The vicar was dead, the curate indisposed due to an emergency meeting at the Bishop's, the choirmaster had a bereavement, Miss Fairfax still had a pass because she'd done that emergency meeting due to the Pentecost fiasco and it was still British Summer Time, so, naturally, and obviously, the duty fell to the Junior Parish Magazine Editor.

Everyone knew that.

Annabelle knew that.

So, why, why, why had she been so remiss?

She blamed herself; after all, there was no-one else to blame and she was to blame.

The doorbell rang: *ring!*

Annabelle stood in her dining room caught by indecision. What was she to do? She had let the side down: the church, the magazine and herself.

The church always forgave and Annabelle knew that by next week, she would have forgotten, but the magazine! Diane was not one to forgive or forget.

The doorbell rang again – *riingggg!!!* – loud and insistent.

Annabelle put the offending items back on the table as there was nothing to be done about it.

Pat stood in the porch in her thick coat and hat caught in the act of folding up her walking stick.

"Belle."

"Pat," Annabelle said, "I'm so sorry about the Christmas napkins. I didn't have anything else."

"I'm sure no-one will mind."

"Terrible news."

"Terrible."

Such was Annabelle's discombobulation that she made Pat a cup of tea without even asking if she wanted one.

Ring!

"Belle."

"Frances, do come in."

Frances the warden wore a white blouse, black trousers and a man's waistcoat. She didn't have a coat as she'd come in her SUV, which had heated seats – imagine that.

"I'm so sorry about the Christmas napkins. I didn't have anything else."

"What Christmas napkins?"

"Tea?"

"Coffee."

"Of course."

Frances took her coffee strong with a small dash of cream that made such a delicate spiral until Frances put a teaspoon in and churned it all together. She left the saucer on the kitchen table.

Ring! Ring!

"Belle."

"Mrs Entwistle, do come in," Annabelle said. "So sorry about the Christmas napkins."

"Is it Christmas?" Mrs Entwistle said as she removed her headscarf from her blue rinse.

"No, Angela, that's not for ages yet."

"It comes earlier every year."

"It's not Christmas, I just didn't have any others."

"Are there mince pies?"

Mrs Entwistle had coffee with too much milk and a biscuit even though she knew there was a buffet to come.

R-ring-r-ring-ring, ring... ring.

"Belle."

"Betty."

"I'm not late, am I?"

"No, no, and I'm so sorry about the Christmas napkins."

"Well, hark the herald."

"Sorry?"

Betty the organist had hot chocolate.

R-r-r...

"Belle."

"Mrs Jones, do come in and I'm so sorry about the Christmas napkins."

Mrs Jones had tea, although she wrinkled her nose up at it.

"Milk?" Annabelle asked.

"Isn't the milk already in the cup?" Mrs Jones said.

"No. Sorry."

Mrs Jones sniffed at the tea with her sharp nose.

Ring. Ring. Ring.

"Belle!"

"Yes?"

"Curate's wife!"

"I know, I know, come in, come in," Annabelle said. "And I'm so sorry about the Christmas napkins."

"I've brought dessert."

"Oh, you shouldn't have."

"I must keep my hand in," the curate's wife replied. "It's nothing really, just some sugar fancies on a filo pastry base and glazed strawberries with a soil and spun caramel arches."

"Soil!"

"Chocolate soil."

"You're so clever. Tea?"

"Tea?"

"Or coffee or hot chocolate."

"Any gin?"

"Rather early for gin... sherry?"

The curate's wife poured her sherry into a black coffee.

Ring-ring.

"Belle."

"Di. Napkins, sorry, Christmas."

"Eh?" Diane was late and smelt of gin.

"Tea or coffee?"

"What are you implying?"

"Nothing. Sorry. They were all I had."

Once everyone had a drink and they were settling in the front room, Annabelle helped herself to a sherry. After all, everything was going pear-shaped and so she felt she needed some Dutch courage. She checked the label – M&S Spanish courage.

100

"Belle?"

"Pat?"

"Agenda?"

"Oh sorry." First Christmas napkins and now this.

"No-one sent anything through," Diane pointed out.

"Oh, yes, no-one sent any items," Annabelle said, relieved that it was only the whole evening that she'd ruined because of the Christmas napkins.

"Who's chair?" Frances asked.

"It's my chair," Annabelle said, half-rising to show it to everyone.

"I meant, who is chairing the meeting?"

"Oh. Of course. Sorry."

"You do it, Frances," Diane suggested.

"Very well," Frances said. "Apologies?"

"I'm so sorry about the Christmas napkins," Annabelle said. "They were all I had and what with the vicar being... they were all I had. I am so sorry."

"I meant has anyone sent their apologies for absence," Frances said.

"Oh, yes, of course," Annabelle said. "But I am sorry."

"Frances," Diane said, "we're all here."

"Ah, good point," the churchwarden admitted. "What's the first item?"

"No-one sent any," Annabelle said. "Diane said."

"Then I guess it's the vicar," Frances said.

"Oh dear."

They sat in silence for a while.

"We should organise a memorial service," Frances said.

"Well, yes," Pat said, "but perhaps not in the church."

"The parochial hall then."

"We'll have to have a new vicar," Diane said.

"Perhaps we should wait until after the memorial and Reverend Pendle-Took's funeral," Pat said. "And for the police to finish their investigation."

"That would be tactful," Frances said.

"Who will they appoint?" the curate's wife asked.

"It's for the diocese to make recommendations," Frances explained. "There's usually three candidates and we see who we think is most suitable."

"I see."

"Unless, on account of the... well, what happened," Frances said, "they decide to promote your husband."

"Gary!"

"Yes, the parish knows him, he knows us, ideal really."

"Oh, that would be lovely," Annabelle said.

"Oh yes, that would be marvellous," Betty said, "you'd be a proper country vicar's wife."

"Yes," the curate's wife said. "Lovely."

"Let's vote on it," Annabelle said, raising her hand.

Betty followed suit.

"If the diocese suggests him, that's when we vote," Frances said.

"Oh." Annabelle lowered her hand.

"What about the other murders?" Pat asked.

They all eyed one another.

"What are you suggesting?" Frances asked.

"I thought a card for condolences."

"Oh yes," Annabelle said, "one of those big ones that everyone can sign."

"One for Mr Boseman," Diane said.

"Poor man," Betty said.

"And Sergio," Diane continued. "Do we know where his family are?"

Mrs Entwistle took out her handkerchief and blew loudly, sniffing and crying.

"And the vicar was unmarried," Diane said.

"You'd think," Frances added.

"Doesn't he have an uncle in Torquay?" Mrs Entwistle said. "Lord something-or-other."

"Lord Bishop Barnaby," Diane said.

"Death's door," Frances added. "Apparently."

"Oh, poor man," Betty said.

"So, just a card for his brother, Sir Victor," Pat said, "and perhaps for the Chiangs. Sergio worked for them, after all."

"Good idea," Frances agreed.

"This can't come out of the tea money," Mrs Jones said. "The tea money is only to be used for tea, milk and biscuits."

"Don't the contributions cover that?"

"Of course," Mrs Jones said, "but the tea money is for the tea."

"We could all chip in," Annabelle suggested.

"What? From the tea money?" Mrs Jones said, appalled.

"It'll come out of the church petty fund," Frances said.

"Well, so long as that's understood," Mrs Jones said.

"Anything else?" Frances asked.

Everyone shook their heads.

"Belle?"

Annabelle racked her brains, trying to remember if there was any other business.

"Ah," – she remembered – "there's the buffet?"

"Does the buffet have turkey slices and pigs in blankets?" Diane asked.

Annabelle could have murdered her with a look.

"I think that's it," Pat said.

"So, no apologies" Frances said, summing up and glancing at Annabelle, "and we buy cards for the vicarage, Mr Boseman–"

"Poor man," Betty said.

"Victor and Sergio's employers."

Everyone nodded.

"The buffet is in the dining room," Annabelle said. "Please, help yourself."

Everyone queued up, took a plate and then a napkin, but they returned both when they saw the cold meats. To celebrate, when one of God's servants had been taken up so early and so violently, with the birth of Our Lord himself held in their hands in all His glory of holly, robins, snowmen and three-layered absorption, felt wrong, even blasphemous.

"I do have gin in the cupboard for Christmas," Annabelle remembered. "And whisky and port."

"Now you're talking," the curate's wife said.

So, they all sat back with plates of dessert and a glass of gin (Frances and the curate's wife), whisky (Diane), port (Pat and Mrs Jones) or sherry (Betty and Annabelle).

"It's only half-past," Annabelle said. "Meetings usually take longer."

"There's normally a lot of talk about the flowers and tea money," Frances said.

"Lilies, I thought," Mrs Entwistle said.

"Not from the tea money," Mrs Jones said.

"We could play Bridge," Annabelle said.

"Or Cribbage," Pat said.

"Cribbage is too prone to cheating," Diane said.

"Or Happy Families?" Annabelle said.

"With bets?" Diane said.

"Not from the tea money!" Mrs Jones insisted.

"For matches," Pat said.

"Rummy?" Diane said.

"I've a gin," the curate's wife said.

"Now you're talking," Frances said.

108

"My husband never let me play card games," Annabelle said. "Is Rummy the one where you lay out sets of three cards?"

"That's it."

"I don't know..."

"It's time you learned," Diane insisted.

And they made Annabelle fetch the cards.

7. Forensics

It was late.

Kilroy rubbed his eyes and nursed his coffee.

His new Mackintosh drooped on the hook in the hall. It had crinkled along one side and the folds were being reinforced as it dangled there. He wondered about using a clothes hanger.

He sat at the table in his kitchen and in front of him he'd laid down a run of manila envelopes. It was a set of three forensics reports.

There was also an email, printed out and bulldog-clipped to the collection. It explained that the pathology lab was busy – very busy – and they did not take kindly to so many demands on their time. Detective Constable Kilroy was new and so allowances had been made, but it would be wise, in their opinion, if he refrained in future from gathering so many murders all at once. Just advice, you understand, it said, but advice he should take to heart.

He slid his side plate to one side to generate some space before he opened the envelopes and shuffled the reports into chronological order.

Number 1: vicar, knife in the back, lung punctured... couldn't have been killed that long before he was discovered.

Kilroy sipped his coffee. He'd waited until he'd finished his late-night jam on toast before looking at the reports. Imagine, he thought, what pathology would say if he got strawberry conserve smeared all over their blood splatter pattern analysis.

Number 2: Sergio McNally, multiple trauma consistent with a car accident... run over, simple as that, but was it an accident or deliberate?

"Damn."

His coffee dribbled down the analysis of the tyre pattern. He tried flicking it off only to create a brown mud-like stain over the photographs of the sprawling carnage.

"Damn, damn."

Number 3: Mrs Belinda Boseman, bed-ridden due to... Kilroy scrunched up his eyes and tried to pronounce the mixture of Latin syllables, but it was all Greek to him. Probably best to avoid trying to say that out loud to anyone.

She died of a barbiturate overdose and then, post-mortem, she'd been stabbed and shot. Or shot and stabbed. Someone had really wanted to kill her. What could an old lady have done to warrant such a reaction?

His notebook had lists of suspects, keyholders for the first, no-one for the second and Mr Zephron Boseman for the third.

The second involved finding a car, probably a small van or large SUV according to the report.

The third... well, Mr Boseman was the obvious suspect being tied to a bed-bound wife and in possession of a – Kilroy whistled – large life insurance policy. Except Mr Boseman had, in addition to a large collection of choral music on vinyl, an alibi. It sounded water-tight.

He checked his notes again: Mr Boseman had met Mrs Harrison, Annabelle; Mrs Thomas, Patricia; and Miss Richards, Diane, in the Oxfam Shop, as well as Celia in Celia's, Baxter the Butcher in the Butcher's and Trent in Conkie's Bakery and the curate's wife, and most likely Uncle Tom Cobley and all.

Everyone along the High Street, in fact.

The whole village.

Thick as thieves these country types.

But if it checked out, then he could cross off an awful lot of suspects. They all gave Boseman an alibi and he gave them all the same. Kilroy counted: seven, not including Uncle Tom Cobley and all, to cross off the suspect list.

Kilroy had talked to Mr Boseman at his house, Mrs Chiang at Chiang's Chinese and Pizza and the lovely Miss Fairfax the warden in her impressive house. Each time he'd met some old lady leaving. They were everywhere. Everyone in these places knew everyone else's business. Perhaps, he should just question random old ladies.

Because answers were not being forthcoming.

Patience was what was needed.

He found a pack of cards, shuffled and laid out the columns. A two went on a three straight away and then he was stuck.

The first card he selected was a joker.

"Oh great," he said to himself.

He flicked through the pack to find the other joker, but it wasn't there. It was on the table already hidden in plain sight, much like a murderer in a village where everyone knew everyone else.

Kilroy dug into the arrangement to find it and replace it with a random card from the pack.

Was this somehow suggesting, like Tarot, that there were two killers in Conky Whallop?

The next card he picked explained the rules of bridge.

What he needed, he thought as he placed the next card, a five, on a six, was a card for each of the suspects. The trouble was these cards fell into three suits: vicar, rider and wife. But each card might belong to more than one suit and the suits themselves may turn out to be the same.

He found himself standing by the drinks' cabinet with his hand on a bottle of whisky. It wasn't a weekday, but even so, it wasn't a day to be weak.

Back at the kitchen table, a two wouldn't go anywhere.

Was there a link?

He couldn't see how the murder of a vicar could connect with the murder of a pizza delivery boy. Or to a housebound wife of a choirmaster. Or the vicar to the wife, except that the husband was the choirmaster.

He checked the reports, but found nothing about any choir.

Had Sergio been in it?

It seemed from reports that the teenager had been in trouble, minor stuff – possession of cannabis, graffiti art and bald tyres on his moped. Kilroy checked the scene of crime report and the moped had brand new, regulation depth tyres. The road had been wet, but it still seemed likely that he'd been hit rather than losing control. Also, according to the report, he hadn't been a regular at the church since his baptism.

Kilroy would have to go to church.

That filled him with a certain dread.

This Sunday, he thought, to get it over with. It would be a good opportunity to see the congregation all together like in a police line-up.

Sunday was tomorrow, he realised.

For some reason, he was back at the drinks cabinet. This time, as it was a Saturday, he poured himself a little snifter and then topped that up with another generous measure.

Back at the kitchen table, a seven went on the eight, but the five... wait a moment!

He dug out the police report.

A uniformed constable had interviewed Miss Richards.

116

Ah-ha!

She'd found the vicar and the PC had interviewed her in Mrs Thomas's cottage. He'd also questioned Mrs Thomas herself and a Mrs Harrison. Those three had all been together in the Oxfam shop to give Mr Boseman an alibi.

That seemed oh-so-very convenient.

An image of the whole village gathering to commit murder sprang to mind.

He took another slug of whisky and cheated out a six of hearts.

Thomas, Richards and Harrison... thick as thieves.

They were all editors of some parish magazine.

This was where to start.

8. The Murder Game

"Right, Rummy," Diane said, "Aces low or high, runs can wrap around, you can draw one card from the stock or discard pile, or the whole discard pile, aces and picture cards are ten points, face value for the others, rummy when you are all out, no discard, doubles points, jokers wild."

She shuffled and dealt each player six cards in rapid succession.

"What are the stakes?" Frances asked.

"Penny a point."

Frances nodded.

"Oh dear," Annabelle said as she tore a robin away from its holly perch and made a small snow-like drift with plucked scraps of three-ply. She throttled the napkin as if she was twisting the life out of the redbreast.

"Bye then," Mrs Entwistle said as she put her headscarf over her blue rinse ready to brave the elements.

"I best be off too," Betty said. "I thought I'd look in on Mr Boseman. See how he's doing."

"Very thoughtful, Betty," Pat said.

"Oh," said Annabelle, her destroyed napkin discarded, "sorry."

"I'll see them out," Pat said. "You enjoy your game."

Diane shuffled the extra hands back into the deck.

Pat closed the door behind the two ladies and then peered through the window to see Betty turn towards Orthodox Crescent and Mr Boseman's. However, instead of turning towards the church and her cottage, Mrs Entwistle turned in the opposite direction.

"Water the flowers, ridiculous," Pat said to herself.

"You in, Pat?" Diane asked.

"No, I'll tidy up," Pat said. "It's all right, Belle."

Pat cleared the dishes and washed them up in the sink rather than risk the technology of the dishwasher. There were only teacups, saucers, side plates with crumbs, dishes with chocolate dessert stains and quite a few glasses.

From the other room, she heard the sounds of rules explained again, cards played and another round of drinks suggested. All phrases wafted through the serving hatch as if they had been shuffled.

While Annabelle, Diane, Frances, Mrs Jones and the curate's wife played a few hands, Pat sneakily helped herself to another sherry, and settled in an armchair to listen to the conversation. She wasn't eavesdropping, exactly, but rather nodding off in the comfortable upholstery with her ears open. It made a change from soaps about country life.

"Shame about the vicar," Mrs Jones said. "I never really saw him as I'm on teas."

"A surprisingly nice man," Frances admitted. "Not what I was expecting."

"He didn't interfere with the running of the church?" Diane asked.

"Not at all," Frances said. "I run a tight ship."

"He interfered with the parish magazine."

"And he tried interfering with the teas," Mrs Jones said. "Could the money do this? Could it go to charity? Could it buy things for the food bank? No, it could not! It's the tea money. Tea. Money. Couldn't be more obvious. But the poor this and the disadvantaged that and the needy the other. Well, I told him. Ducky, I said, the poor, the disadvantaged and the needy can come into the hall like everyone else for a cup of tea. That's why we have tea money."

"Didn't the money people paid for – I'll deal – their tea cover the costs?" Frances said, taking the cards. She'd unbuttoned her man's waistcoat and looked quite the poker player.

"People paid a subscription for the parish magazine," Diane said. "That mostly covered costs."

"Always asking for money, our vicar," Mrs Jones added.

"Bets?" Frances said.

"They call it good works," the curate's wife said. "Glass is empty, Belle."

"Oh, sorry," Annabelle said. "Here."

"Cover the bottom of the glass."

"Sorry."

"When."

"Your turn, Belle," Francis said.

"Oh, yes, sorry. Do I say 'gin' or 'rummy'?"

"Oh for... beginner's luck again, Belle?" Diane said.

"You deal, Di," Frances said. "Our luck has to change sometime."

"I'd better make tracks," Mrs Jones said. "I've another Skype with my financial advisor."

"If you are short before pension day," Diane said, "you could dip into the tea money."

"Miss Richards! The very idea!"

Mrs Jones let herself out leaving behind a trumped harumph and a flush of startled looks.

"Oh dear, she's upset," Annabelle said.

"Serves her right, stuck up–" Diane stopped herself.

Frances snorted and the curate's wife guffawed.

"What? What?" Annabelle asked. "What is it?"

"Maybe she killed the vicar," Diane said.

"Why?" Frances asked.

"Caught him with his hand in the tea money?"

They laughed again, except for Annabelle.

"But Reverend Pendle-Took wouldn't do that," Annabelle insisted.

"Wouldn't have dared," Diane said.

Pat thought that Annabelle was like a minnow amongst sharks in an ocean of gin.

"Did you kill him, Frances?" Diane asked.

"Not saying," Frances said.

"Or you?"

"Why would I kill the vicar?" the curate's wife replied. "So Gary can do more pastoral work?"

"He likes pastoral work, doesn't he?" Frances said.

"Yes," the curate's wife replied, "but this! All this! It's so country. Village life is, like, so dull. Nothing happens."

"We've had three murders."

"That's my point. Where was I? Yes. Like dull. Even these cosy murders, they're so dignified."

"Hardly."

The curate's wife leaned back in her chair, dangerously tipping backwards. "In London, I was somebody. Not a curate's wife. I mean, what is that? Junior vicar for... whatever's sake. I made cakes, not your country bake-off cakes, but artistic creations. None of your Victoria sponge and fruit stodge, but delicately spun caramelised sugar filagree, you know... things! Creations! Art!"

"Your toffee apples at the fête were particularly nice," Annabelle said.

"I'm reduced to making toffee apples," the curate's wife wailed.

"Oh yes," Annabelle said. "Zara Pheasant's apples are always the best. She wins the fruit award every year."

The curate's wife tilted forward, the front chair legs connecting with the ground such that she jerked to a halt. She reached for her glass of gin as if to sob uncontrollably into it.

"I think the Church Committee meeting has come to an end," Diane said.

"Shall I minute that?" Frances replied.

"Poker?" Diane suggested.

"Pound stakes?" Frances said.

"I'm in," the curate's wife said.

"Done."

"Oh," Annabelle complained, "but my second husband never let me play poker,"

"He's not here, Belle," Diane said.

"No, but..."

"In or out?"

"Oh... in."

Diane shuffled, cut the pack one-handed and dealt.

Pat popped the empty sherry glass on the coffee table and settled herself again. She was just going to rest her eyes, just for a minute, you understand.

"Right," Diane said, "standard Texas hold 'em, gin bottle is the dealer's button, they have to take a shot, one pound ante, pot limit, two cards each, five cards on the street, no bugs, but eights wild... any questions?"

"What are trumps?" Annabelle asked.

"There aren't any trumps, Belle."

126

"Oh, sorry."

Pat yawned.

There must be, she thought, a line leading from the church to Tinsel Lane and then to Orthodox Crescent, something linking the vicar, Sergio and then Mrs Boseman, but her thoughts floundered as she couldn't think of any reason why anyone would want to murder any of them.

Distantly, a similar conversation mirrored Pat's mental wandering.

"The King of Spades is like the vicar," Annabelle said.

"'Cos he buried people," Diane said.

"And the Queen of Hearts is like Mrs Boseman," Annabelle continued. "She was so sweet, despite everything, and the Jack of Diamonds is like Sergio."

"Rough diamond," the curate's wife said.

"Have you noticed that there are Jacks, but no Jills?" Frances added.

"It's not a winning poker hand, Belle," Diane said.

"I know, sorry, but I've two other kings, so that makes three of a kind."

"That's... beginner's luck," Frances said.

"Oh, sorry, I don't know."

"Shall we up the stakes?" Frances suggested. "Two pounds ante?"

The King of Spades made the sign of the cross and the Joker leapt out from behind a stone pillar. He struck at the King with an Ace of Spades. All jolly strange, Pat thought. "Thou shalt not bet more than the pot," the King pronounced.

Pat sat bolt upright, suddenly awake, and fished out her notebook from her handbag.

As the others raised, folded and called, she jotted down some notes.

Vicar – victim.

Curate – jealous of vicar, promotion?

Warden (Frances) – trad v modern.

Flowers (Mrs Entwistle) – argued about daffs.

Teas (Mrs Jones) – money.

Choir (Mr Boseman) – angry about choir.

Organist (Betty) - ?

Curate's wife - ?

Editor (Diane) – loss of magazine.

Must keep this secret from Di, Pat thought. She glanced at the others to check that they were still engrossed in the game.

"I'm going to have to throw my pearls into the pot," Diane said. "Belle, have you been taking poker lessons?"

"Oh no, my school was all the normal subjects," Annabelle replied.

"My boarding school was practically directed," Frances said.

"Needlework, sewing, baking, that sort of thing?" Annabelle asked.

"Brick laying, metal work, gutting fish."

"Oh."

Pat went back to her thoughts.

If the old vicar was out of the way, Pat speculated, then it might be possible to gently guide a new vicar to get rid of all these new-fangled modern ideas about guitar music – *oh, Betty did have a motive* – reform the choir, have daffodils throughout the year, keep the tea money sacred and save the magazine.

"Well done, Belle, you've a natural knack at this," Diane said.

"That's right," Frances agreed.

"Let's play for folding money, otherwise we won't have a chance to win anything back," the curate's wife said.

"It's only fair," Diane added.

"Oh... do we have to?"

"Yes, Belle."

"Oh... all right."

Was that enough of a motive, Pat wondered, and were there other, more unknown motives?

An Uncle, a Lord no less, in Torquay on death's door?

His brother, Sir Victor?

Did any of these suspects have a motive to murder Sergio or Mrs Boseman?

Pat went down the list.

The vicar was dead.

Did the curate's pastoral care extend to mercy killing for the poor suffering Mrs Boseman?

Did Frances murder the vicar to run the ship tighter?

Did Mrs Entwistle need funerals to use up her lilies?

Did Sergio borrow from the tea money?

Did Mr Boseman miss the choir that much and had he, who had stood by his wife for so long, reached the end of his tether?

Did Betty want the choir back that much?

Did the curate's wife, currently bidding ten pounds, need her husband to get on in the world? Pat added that to her list.

Did Diane lose her temper?

Did anyone on the list order pizza?

"I've got another of the all-the-same suit, but this time with the picture people," Annabelle said, showing her cards to reveal a royal flush.

There were moans all round.

"Sorry," Annabelle added.

"Your husband should have let you play poker," Diane said. "You'd have made a fortune."

"Oh no," Annabelle said, "he wouldn't allow me as I always won."

Diane threw her cards down on the table. "I give up."

Pat, looking at her list, knew the feeling.

9. Identity Parade

Kilroy spilt marmalade on his dressing gown, but it rinsed out. He went upstairs to change into his interview suit. It looked professional in the mirror, but he felt uncomfortable wearing it.

He slipped the reports into his briefcase and collected his Mackintosh from the peg in the hall. It was showing signs of overuse for the past week. He'd asked a lot of questions wearing it, after all. Yes, he thought, he would use a coat hanger, so he fetched one from his wardrobe and hung it up ready for his return.

Always best to be prepared.

He was halfway along the A-road in his silver SUV on the part that was the ring road around Upper Whallop, when he realised that he'd left his packed lunch still in its Tupperware on the kitchen table.

It was too late to go back.

He came upon Conky Whallop suddenly, the patchwork of country fields giving way to stone cottages, yellow brick houses and timber-framed buildings. At the top of the hill, the church stood proudly, its tower resembling one from a fairy story. Bells rang from its belfry.

He slowed, glanced to his right at the Green. Figures merrily in their Sunday best, hats bright, took the short cut across the grass. The perfect English village harked back to a Golden Age, jubilee picnics on trestle tables and bunting connecting the branches of the old oaks and horse chestnut trees. It promised peace, a sanctuary one could retire to if you wanted a serene and quiet life.

Kilroy shook his head: he was just starting his career as a detective, so it was far too early to think about retirement.

He drew up into the church car park. He'd made sure he was early, but even so, there were already cars lined up between the faded white lines. One bay was reserved for the warden and contained a big, blue BMW that had been reversed into position.

He parked his SUV and checked the regulations: two hours, no return in four. He took out his 'Police Business' card and plonked it on the dash. If he found the right people to talk to, he might be here longer than two hours.

"Are you allowed to do that?"

Kilroy recognized the speaker as one of the old ladies he'd seen the day before, but he wasn't sure which. They all looked alike.

"Police," Kilroy said, "Detective Constable Kilroy."

"Just a detective constable?"

"That's right."

"Not an inspector?"

"No."

"Or a chief inspector?"

"No, it's a falsity put about by television dramas that inspectors actually investigate crimes. Mrs..."

"Miss Richards. I'm the *chief* editor of the parish magazine."

"Really?" Kilroy said taking in her no-nonsense tweed and pearls. She was a formidable looking woman. "That sounds important."

"It is," Diane said. "And I'd have expected a chief inspector. We have had three murders."

"They may not all be murders."

She snorted. "I'm on first name terms with the Chief Constable," she said.

"Chief Constable Clough?"

"That's him."

"Richards..." Kilroy said. "Didn't you find the first victim?"

"I did."

"I'll need to talk to you, Miss."

"I've answered the police officer."

"I'm the detective," Kilroy said. "What would you have me do, Miss Richards?"

"Di!"

"Die?"

"Di... call me Di, it's short for Diane."

"Oh."

"I notice the front of your car has been damaged," Diane said.

"I keep meaning to get it fixed," Kilroy said. "I don't seem to find the time."

"No peace for the wicked."

"Exactly."

"I'll be in the hall, if you need me," Diane said and she walked away, speaking briefly to a woman who was opening up the Parochial Hall. Diane pointed back at Kilroy.

"Cooeee," the other woman shouted, waving.

Kilroy waved back. He felt foolish with his hand raised, so he lowered it before wandering over.

"Excuse me," he said. "I'm looking for Mrs Jones and Mrs Kovalyov."

"Well, you've found her, Ducky."

"Good, er..."

"Cup of tea?"

"That would be lovely and you are?"

"Teas."

"No," Kilroy said, "I'm not teasing you. If anything, I'm the one being teased. Who are you?"

"Teas... I make the cups of tea."

"Oh! Teas."

"I did say."

She turned and led the way into the hall. It had squares of lino and Mrs Jones moved like a queen across and then straight into the kitchen.

Kilroy moved like a detective, cautiously, a methodical step at a time.

"Round there," the woman said, pointing.

Through some double doors, he entered the large hall with noticeboards between every window. Hard plastic chairs surrounded square Formica tables. At one, three old ladies sat over cups and saucers, clearly plotting and conniving like witches. Kilroy recognized them as the three witches who had dogged his footsteps. No, not witches, he must be professional.

He turned to the large hatch into the kitchen.

The woman was there.

"Tea," she said pouring brown liquid into an array of cups standing upon saucers. They already had too much milk filling the green, canteen china.

"Thank you."

The tea was weak.

"I'm Detective Constable Kilroy," he said.

"I know, word gets around."

"And you are?"

"Isn't it obvious?"

She wasn't playing the organ, so, "Mrs Jones?"

"Got it in one."

"Can I ask you where you were on the evening the vicar died?"

"I don't know, Ducky, can you?"

"Where were you Wednesday night?"

"Dreadful business, don't you think?"

"Yes.... where were you on Wednesday night?"

"Let me see," she said and she pondered looking up to her left. She put her finger to her sharp nose. "Wednesday night, Wednesday... Saturday Church Committee, Friday *The Crown*, only a repeat, Thursday bingo, so Wednesday would be... that would be the day the vicar died."

"Yes."

"Dreadful business."

"Yes."

Give me strength, Kilroy thought, and he took a sip of tea. It tasted so lukewarm and weak that it seemed to suck energy from his bones rather than imbue any reviving properties.

140

"I was at home," Mrs Jones said. "I was doing the accounts. Skyping with my financial advisor."

"Accounts?"

"That's twenty-five pee."

"Sorry?"

Mrs Jones pointed at a saucer without a cup.

"Yes?" Kilroy asked.

"Twenty-five pee for the tea."

A cappuccino cost £3.45 in London, so the price of tea here dated back to the 1930s. How was it that people born during flower power, or later as punks or dyed-in-the-wool New Romantics, always ended up in the same nylon, pinnies and the pointless hats that old people had been wearing since the Dark Ages? They probably thought of 25p as five shillings. However, considering the strength of the tea, it was still daylight robbery.

Kilroy fished out a 50p piece, part of the coins he kept in case a pay-and-display wouldn't accept a card or an App. It clattered in the saucer.

"No change, I'm afraid, Ducky."

"Was anyone with you when you did the accounts?"

"Percy."

"Is Percy your husband?"

"Good heavens, no, he's a Maine Coon."

"A what?"

"Grey tabby."

"Oh."

"Must get on," Mrs Jones said. "Tea needs to stew a little."

"Yes," Kilroy agreed.

He glanced into the hall, where the three old ladies were suddenly looking at nothing in particular.

As he approached, he enjoyed watching them squirm and avoid eye contact, a jiggling and neck stretching that lasted until it was obvious he was coming over to talk to them. He put his briefcase on an empty seat, his Mackintosh over the hard, creasing plastic back of it and then he stood over them.

"Ladies," he said, "I'm Detective Constable Kilroy and you three have been following me around."

"Oh no," Pat said.

"Never," Annabelle said.

"We were simply going about our business in the village," Diane said.

"It is more that you are following us," Pat added, "as we arrived wherever first."

"Oh yes, Pat, that's good," Annabelle said.

"Mere coincidence," Diane said.

"Once maybe," Kilroy said. "Twice is coincidence. Three times is something else."

"Circumstantial evidence at best," Diane said.

"There have been deaths in the village," Pat said, "and we have been doing our civic duty."

"As members of the church," Diane added.

"Indeed," Pat continued, "and so we are all likely to visit the same people to offer comfort, solace and support."

"I have a question," Kilroy said. "You don't need a lawyer present."

"That's for us to decide," Diane said. "And we do have a lawyer present."

"Oh yes?"

"I'm a lawyer... was a lawyer. I still have an office on the High Street."

"It's all right, Di," Pat said. "Detective, please, ask your question."

"What have you found out?" Kilroy asked.

"Plenty– Oh... ah."

"Hmmm."

Pat continued, "The vicar must have been murdered by someone with a church key and that's nine–"

"Eight," Diane said.

"Eight suspects."

"I know this," Kilroy said.

"And poor Sergio was run over by a large car that will have dents on its bumper."

"I know this too."

"And Mrs Boseman... well, we were hoping you could help us?" Pat asked.

"She was... it is none of your business."

"We are only trying to help, Detective Constable."

"That seems unlikely."

They seemed to him as if butter wouldn't melt in their mouths but their homemade treacle toffee would bind the teeth together.

"Would you mind?" Diane said, holding up her cup and saucer.

"Not at all."

He took the cup from the old lady and returned it to the hatch. Mrs Jones pointed to where to leave the used cups.

"Another?" she asked.

Rows of green cups with milk already poured lined the counter.

"No," he said, "thank you."

By the time he got back to the table, Mrs Harrison was holding out her cup and saucer.

"So sorry," Annabelle said. "Would you be so kind?"

Kilroy took her cup back. He had thought that his promotion to detective constable would mean that he would no longer be making the tea, but he'd soon learnt he had to make the tea for detective sergeants and detective inspectors and detective chief inspectors and now, apparently, old ladies.

"Another?" Mrs Jones asked.

"No, thank you," he said placing the cup down next to the other one.

"Oh... you've had two."

"I haven't really, they're not mine."

"That'll be fifty pee."

"I've paid fifty pence."

"For yours, that's two more."

Kilroy took a deep breath ready to argue the point, but instead, it calmed him enough to fish inside his pocket. He found a pound, dropped that into the dish, but retrieved his original 50 pence piece.

"Change," he said. He felt very pleased with himself as if he had won some kind of victory.

When he got back to the table, Pat placed her cup into her saucer with a clink of cheap china.

"And you?" the detective constable said to Mrs Thomas.

"Oh, I'm quite finished," Pat replied. "Thank you."

"Your cup?"

"Oh! That too."

Instead of handing him her cup, she removed her half-moon glasses. Her eyes became smaller, more cunning in appearance as if she was up to something, but Kilroy couldn't imagine what.

"You ladies are not to involve yourselves in this," DC Kilroy commanded. "Stay safe indoors, do the crossword, knit, bake a cake."

His piece said, he smoothed down his Mackintosh, picked up his briefcase – now she handed him her cup and saucer! – and left them to ponder his advice.

"Well really?" Miss Diane Richards said, rather too clearly.

"Yes," Pat said, "and I finished today's crossword."

"I'm not knitting," Diane said.

"I've got a recipe for lemon drizzle," Annabelle said.

Their humour made him smile and–

"Excuse me."

It was Mrs Jones pointing at the saucer of money. He had 50p for Pat's 25p cup of tea and the dish only had a £1 coin in change. He'd lost this round of the game too.

On his way out, Kilroy relieved himself in the gents of as much of the two sips of tea as he could. He could still taste sour milk on his walk across the car park to the church.

He paused to check the larger cars and used his phone to photograph the bumpers and radiators grills, making sure to include the number plate in at least one image.

And then – nothing else for it – he walked into the shadow of the gothic architecture. Beneath the gaze of gargoyles and nosy old ladies, he entered the sanctuary of the church.

10. Thou Shalt Not Bear False Witness

Inside the church, he met two ladies he knew: Miss Fairfax and Mrs Thomas. Mrs Thomas must have nipped across ahead of him, spritely despite her walking aid, while he was in the Gents'.

"Ladies."

"Detective Constable."

"Detective Constable."

"Good morning."

"Good morning."

"Good morning."

"Mrs Thomas, are you still following me?"

"I was here first, Detective Constable."

"I'm surprised you're having a service."

"The curate felt that Reverend Pendle-Took's flock would need spiritual guidance," Pat informed him.

"And the show must go on," Frances Fairfax, the warden, added.

"I was hoping to talk to… er, Betty the organist."

Frances waved him into the church and pointed towards the altar. "On the right," she said.

Kilroy walked up the aisle, taking in the old pews of dark wood, the stained-glass windows, the white stone, the wooden pulpit, the eagle lectern and the organ. The church was steeped in religion and history: everything seemed to be marked with a dedication to someone taken too early, resting in peace or not forgotten.

Some of the stones at his feet appeared to be indoor graves to rich, late believers, their tombs disturbed by footsteps until their names had been rubbed out.

He reached the smaller, higher section of the church, the chancel. On one side the empty choir stalls waited. One the other, a big stocky woman was fussing with pages of music under an impressive array of pipes.

Kilroy coughed.

The woman looked around and the pages of requiem fluttered to the floor.

"Are you Mrs Betty Kovalyov?"

"Who else would I be?"

"I'm Detective Constable Kilroy. I'd like to ask you some questions."

"Now? Before the service?"

"You've been a hard woman to meet."

"That's me, a hard woman," she said, "I need to be to work the bellows."

"You have a key to the church?" he asked.

"Oh yes," Betty said. "I need to get the old girl going in the morning."

A brass plaque told the story of how the original organ had been donated to the Spitfire Appeal by mistake. The resulting brass and mahogany fighter plane had not saved three nearby places of worship and so their damaged organs had been recovered and amalgamated to create the current, rather eclectic, musical marvel.

"Where were you on the night that the vicar died?"

"Me?" Betty looked at the detective constable with utter surprise. "Why are you asking me?"

"Because you have a key to the church and so you are a suspect."

"Why would I want to kill the vicar?"

"I don't know, but I do need to eliminate you from my enquiries."

"Really?"

"Yes. So, where were you when the vicar was killed?"

Betty turned to check the stops, pulled out the Bombarde and the Fagotto, then pushed them back in again.

"I was at home," she said.

"And your husband will vouch for that?"

"Vlad?" She selected the Vox Angelica and twiddled a few playful, soft notes that sounded slightly flat. "Yes, of course, I'll make sure he does."

At the back of the church, Kilroy found Mrs Thomas setting out copies of the parish magazine. She was finding it tricky to put them on display while also hiding the lurid headline.

"Mrs Thomas."

"Pat, please, Detective Constable."

"I suppose you heard that."

"Well, quite, the church echoes so."

"And you needed to put the magazines out just now."

"In time for Sunday Communion, yes."

"Can I ask you a few questions?"

Pat glanced towards the organ, now suspiciously quiet despite the powerful presence of Betty the organist and so many pipes and bellows.

"Perhaps in the vestry," Pat suggested.

154

She led the policeman along the aisle and then through an archway beside the pulpit. This led to a small room with cupboards and a large central table.

"The vicar puts on his vestments here," she explained, "and when we had a choir, they put on their surpluses and wotnots."

"What happened to the choir?"

"Mr Largo went to live with his daughter in Eastbourne, Ethel had a falling out with the choirmaster, Mr Boseman, and Desmond's voice broke."

"Just three?"

"Numbers had been dwindling since 1847, I believe."

"Ah."

"You had questions?"

"Do you know of anyone who has a large SUV-style vehicle in Conky Whallop?" Kilroy asked.

"The vicar."

"Not a likely suspect."

"And Frances the warden, that's Miss Fairfax, you've met her. The curate's wife has one with heated seats. The vicar's brother, Sir Victor Pendle-Took, has one, sometimes two – he's an architect – and then there's yours."

"Hmmm."

"And Major Naseby has a Land Rover."

"That's quite exhaustive."

"I do my research."

"Did they all get on with each other?"

"Well, I'm not one to gossip," Pat told him, "but Miss Fairfax had a falling out with Major Naseby."

"What about?"

"Something to do with Major Naseby having the attitudes of a dinosaur. Miss Fairfax had some progressive ideas when she moved here from living with her sister, Mrs Eunice Fairfax, in Brighton."

"So, she's quite a newcomer?"

"Frances? I suppose, but she fitted right in and she's now the warden."

"I thought it took years to be accepted in a place like this."

"Oh no, we are welcoming," Pat replied. "Oh, well, quite, perhaps three generations to be really accepted."

"As short as that?"

"On average."

"It must have been with her sister-in-law," Kilroy said. "As she was a Mrs and the warden is a Miss."

"Not every bride changes her name when she gets married, Detective Constable."

"I suppose not."

"I took Eric's name, of course."

"Of course," Kilroy said. "As for the cases, do you have any theories?"

"I have a lot of theories... mere speculations, perhaps. We are so short of any actual facts."

"Don't I know it."

"Of course," Pat said, "you could check the records to see who has a handgun."

"Handgun?"

"The one that shot Mrs Boseman."

"It didn't kill her."

"But it did shoot her."

"How did you know that?"

"Oh... merely an idle... I thought... well, quite."

"She was also stabbed and poisoned."

"There's no police register of knives or poisons."

Kilroy considered this mild, old lady and decided that she was razor-sharp on the inside. Nothing got past her, he realised.

!!!

Pat considered the detective constable. He was trying his best, she realised, but underneath his crumpled Mackintosh, he was like a little boy playing at police work.

Someone who needed looking after, she realised.

"What's through here?" Kilroy said, pointing to another door.

"That's the office," Pat said. She went and tried the door and it opened. It led to a small room with a modern desk and computer at odds with the octagonal layout. Opposite, by an arched window that let in a sliver of daylight, there was yet another door.

"Would this be where the knife came from?" Kilroy asked.

Pat pointed to a neat pile of unopened correspondence. "Paperknife."

"It was rather large and ornate for a paperknife."

"Everything is large and ornate in a church."

Pat picked up a piece of paper from the desk. It was a brochure and receipt for new vestments: £380 seemed a lot to Pat, but then the vicar's usual robes had been old, and a lack of funds meant that he'd had to make do and mend, a tricky task for an unmarried clergyman. It was a shame that he hadn't lived to wear these fine gothic chasubles with their front and back panels decorated in orphrey of the highest quality, according to the description. They boasted every liturgical colour.

"Strange," she said.

"What?"

"The vicar spending money."

"What's this?" Kilroy said. A notepad had the words '*Reverend then Lord*' written on it.

"Vicar's handwriting," Pat said leaning over.

"Hmm," Kilroy said. "And, I suppose, anyone can get into this office?"

"I'm afraid so."

"Is the door to the outside always bolted?"

"Yes," Pat said. "We had a break-in back in 1974, so it's always locked and bolted now."

"The key?"

"All of them are here in this locked key safe, along with the spare front door key."

Kilroy checked the steel box bolted to the wall. "The combination?"

Pat shrugged.

"Who would know it?" Kilroy asked.

"The vicar... perhaps the curate and the warden."

"Hmmm."

"And they all have keys so they are unlikely to have stolen the spare in order to kill the vicar."

"No, I suppose not."

"And the back door hasn't been opened," Pat pointed out.

Kilroy raised an eyebrow.

"The ivy has grown over it," Pat explained. "I checked."

"You've been busy."

"Have I?" Pat checked her watch. "We ought to join the congregation. The service will be starting soon."

"Yes... oh." Kilroy shuffled about. "I won't have to sing, will I?"

"You can mime."

Kilroy breathed a sigh of relief.

"Everyone does," Pat said, "that's why we desperately need a choir."

11. Thou Shalt Not Kill

The singing was truly dreadful, full of flat baritones and sharp sopranos. Pat had become used to it, but her conversation with the detective constable had prompted her to hear it afresh.

Diane belted it out.

Annabelle's singing had a beautiful, if mumbled, purity.

Pat herself mimed, her mind full of dissonant thoughts.

They all sat near the back in the same row as the curate's wife and the warden.

The church had a full house, even if the house of the Lord was not full. The village never filled the pews to capacity, even at Christmas when visiting relatives swelled the numbers and carols replaced the dirges. However, on this second Sunday of the month, a lot of villagers, who usually had perfectly reasonable excuses for every holy day, had come to witness.

Even so, it was easy from the back to see everyone, the sidesmen and woman, the warden, all of the flock: twenty-nine, Pat counted.

Some of the congregation had overdone it the night before – Pat on sherry, Annabelle and Frances on gin, Diane on whisky and others on who knew what. They said a silent prayer to themselves: never again, and please let the sacramental wine be served soon.

"Let us remember those we have lost," the curate said, "the dearly departed so tragically taken from us. We remember the Right Reverend George Pendle-Took... Sergio McNally... and Belinda Boseman..."

The main door banged open.

"Let us remember them in our prayers," the curate continued, "and let us observe a three-minute silence."

Frances the warden intercepted the sudden arrival, Mr Boseman, who wore a black tie instead of his usual red musical number. She thrust a copy of the Book of Common Prayer and a Hymn Book into his hands, and directed him to the rear pew reserved for latecomers.

Members of the congregation turned to find out who was tardy and then they nodded sympathetically.

Mr Bosman took his seat, alone in the pew that was only ever used when the hour sprang forward.

"Let us pray," the curate announced.

Everyone struggled down onto the kneeling cushions.

"Ah."

"Ooh."

"Oh."

It gave Pat a chance to ferret in her handbag for her notebook and pencil. She used her hymn book as a writing surface.

Key – 8.

She crossed out 8, picking up the embossed letters beneath as if she was brass rubbing, and then wrote a few more words.

Key ⁓✎ 9.
Pizza.
SUV.
Poisoned, shot and stabbed.

Was the knife used to kill the vicar the same one that didn't kill Mrs Boseman because she had already been poisoned? No, that had been left in the vicar, and was now presumably in an evidence box, but was it from the same cutlery drawer?

No, the vicar had only had one paperknife.

Fiddlesticks, she thought, if only she'd had more time to read those forensics reports, but that nice detective constable had been so quick returning their used cups.

It seemed unlikely that anyone would poison someone, and then stab and shoot them? People who were acting in a frenzy of mad rage rarely stopped to change weapons unless they ran out of ammunition.

She stared at the great oak beams spanning the space, trying to recall such an incident in all her years as an amateur sleuth watching *Poirot, Marple, Morse, Lewis, Barnaby, Poole, Goodman, Mooney* and *Parker.*

166

Nine detectives and nine suspects![5]

"Please be seated," the curate announced.

Everyone struggled back up onto their pews with a few audible "ooh"s.

Pat's knees clicked.

Diane put her hand to her back.

The organ blurted out a sudden fanfare – *ta DAA!!!*

The curate seemed irritated by this. He was doing a good job, perhaps too good a job. Did he kill the vicar for more of the limelight?

Pat scanned around for the other suspects: the curate sitting in the vicar's seat, Mrs Entwistle sat in the middle near the display of lilies; Mr Boseman over there watching the organ; Betty was sitting at the organ; Sir Victor looking so like his brother, the late vicar; Mrs Jones was in the Parochial Hall

———————————————

[5] Editor's note: Agatha Christie's plots traditionally had nine suspects, but never nine detectives. Once there was nine victims.

turning weak tea into over-stewed tea; Frances sat on the aisle end of the back pew that was reserved for the warden; the curate's wife sat at the other end and Diane fidgeted beside her.

Pat felt guilty adding her friend to the nine, but she was a suspect. She had a key and, now she thought about it, she'd argued with the vicar over the future of the parish magazine. Was that a big enough motive? But surely, Diane's weapon of choice was not a dagger but a sharp tongue.

The service moved on a few pages in the Book of Common Prayer.

"Thou shalt not commit murder," the curate said.

"Amen," the congregation replied, "Lord, have mercy."

This was the sixth commandment, the ones that followed seemed like a list of motives: adultery, stealing, false witness, coveting.

Frances the warden stepped out and directed the sidesmen and woman to start the collection. The brass plates went along the rows while everyone sang to Betty's thunderous playing.

Pat put her usual fiver onto the motley collection of silver and brass. There were a few other notes, twenties, and a fifty she knew Sir Victor added.

It was the architect, Sir Victor Pendle-Took, who stood to go forth and give the reading. He had a dark saturnine beard flecked with grey, his dark hair swept back. His physique boasted of pitting sirloin steaks and fine, red wine against his personal trainer's tough regime. He stood proudly at the lectern, right over the spot where the tiles were now scrupulously clean and the surrounding carpet was dusted white from the chalk outline. He seemed more like an evangelical preacher than a layperson as he stared over the beak of the eagle. He suggested a judge directing the jury or the Lord towering over a fallen Lucifer.

He'd be a suspect if he had a key.

Pat shook her head.

Had Reverend Pendle-Took done anything to call down righteous, or unrighteous, retribution?

She needed to find out what he had been up to, apart from buying expensive vestments. Perhaps with his uncle on death's door, he was expecting to come into money. She'd have to check that.

"The lesson is taken from Genesis, Chapter 4, beginning at verse eight", Sir Victor announced. "And Cain talked with Abel his brother: and it came to pass, when they were in the field, that Cain rose up against Abel his brother, and slew him. And the Lord said unto Cain, 'Where is Abel thy brother?' And he said, 'I know not...'"

There was a lot Pat didn't know.

For example, perhaps her list of nine weren't the same suspects for the murders of Sergio and Mrs Boseman?

Glancing around she saw others: Major Naseby sitting diagonally away from Zara Pheasant, Baxter the Butcher, Celia, Trent the Baker, even Detective Constable Kilroy, who was stuck in the middle of a row like a round peg in a square hole.

When she had been growing up, Zara Pheasant had been a wild child in the village, scrumping for apples, ringing doorbells at all hours and running, swearing and smoking. Although she was no longer a teenager, she was still a tearaway. She'd know Sergio too.

"...and the Lord said unto him," Sir Victor read in his deep voice. "Therefore whosoever slayeth Cain, vengeance shall be taken on him sevenfold. And the Lord set a mark upon Cain, lest any finding him should kill him. And Cain went out from the presence of the Lord, and dwelt in the land of Nod, on the east of Eden."

Major Naseby startled: he'd been in the land of Nod.

Why couldn't all murderers have marks on their foreheads? It would make detection so much easier.

"This is the word of the Lord," Sir Victor said.

And the congregation answered, "Amen."

Sir Victor Pendle-Took closed the bible and returned to his place at the far end of his pew.

The Gospel was Matthew 5:21: Those who kill are in danger of judgement.

"That's a little heavy, considering," Diane whispered.

"Well, yes, quite," Pat agreed.

"What was that?" Annabelle asked.

"Shhh," Frances replied.

The curate climbed the steps to the pulpit as if he was a mountaineer on the final ascent of Everest and he'd forgotten his oxygen. He stood erect and faced the congregation. Everyone's eyes stared up at him, even Betty gazed into the mirror above the organ keyboards.

He did well, Pat thought, except for a last-second flicker of his eyes to the side.

"Dear friends, thank you all for gathering at this most difficult time. How this unspeakable evil – yes, evil, could be committed beggars belief. We are all a family brought together in our worship of the Lord... how can... the Lord Jesus Christ teaches us forgiveness. We must forgive, but how can we forgive? We must be strong."

172

The congregation nodded and for once they were not nodding off.

"We must remember the Reverend George Pendle-Took as..." – the curate paused – "It is incredible to me that one of us here must be the Judas responsible for this unspeakable crime."

He scanned the pews left-to-right, front-to-back and then took in the sidesmen and woman, the warden; he even glanced backwards at the organist.

"We should all search our hearts and confess our sins. Only then can you be truly saved," the curate announced with his finger raised ready to point and accuse. "Let us pray."

The congregation struggled down onto their embroidered kneelers, put their hands together and bowed their heads.

Pat found herself on autopilot for the rest of the service. The curate had seemed so angry and upset, so unlike a reverend. It made her inclined to cross him off her list. A man in the service of the Lord wouldn't harm another man in the service of the Lord, surely?

"...and lead us not into temptation, but deliver us from evil..." she was saying. They'd reached that bit.

Finally, the curate went to the altar and began preparing the plate and chalice for the communion wafers and the red wine.

Frances got out of her seat to begin directing the worshippers from their pews to the chancel. The sidesmen and woman stood attentively, ready to help those with dodgy knees. Mrs Perceval needed two helpers as her legs were well past their best. Mr Henderson had remembered his stick for once.

"One of these," Diane whispered.

"Hush," Pat said.

"What was that?" Annabelle asked.

Pat noticed that Frances had stopped Sir Victor as he went to walk up for communion. The warden leaned forward to whisper. Pendle-Took's eyebrows raised and his high forehead creased. He nodded before he joined the line moving towards the altar with its promise of body and blood. Frances

174

glanced left and right, and Pat had to look away quickly.

She saw, fuzzy without her half-moon spectacles, her list. Should she cross off the curate, underline the warden?

And then Frances reached them, and Pat shoved her notebook back into her handbag as it was their pew's turn.

"Ooh."

"Ah."

"Oh."

They'd been sitting for too long on the hard, wooden benches.

They processed slowly. Pat didn't need her stick, but she was grateful for the banister at the steps from the nave to the chancel. As they moved forward, Betty's strange interpretation of Bach became louder, the organ pipes lofting the notes into the arched roof above the empty choir stalls to reverberate and echo.

Sir Victor took a moment to finish. He stood, bowed and made his way back to his pew.

In the empty place at the end of the altar rail, Pat knelt on the plush cushion. To her right, the vacant spaces began to fill up. Diane, Annabelle, the curate's wife and then – heralded by a whistle from the organ and the usual sigh from the congregation – Betty the organist struggled from her seat.

It was quiet then, focussing the mind on what was happening with all its myriad, tiny details.

"The body of Christ," the lay preacher said.

The wafer stuck to the top of Pat's mouth.

Finally, bringing up the rear, Frances the warden knelt beside the curate's wife.

"The blood of Christ," the curate said, handing Pat the chalice.

Pat took a sip, glad to use the opportunity to free the wafer from her palate.

She said a silent prayer for Eric Thomas, a proud man who fought to the end and was now gone to a better place, and then she struggled to her feet.

"Ooh."

"Ah."

"Oh."

The curate's wife helped Pat to the steps with a smile until they'd reached the banister.

Again, as Pat descended, she saw the rows of villagers, the regulars topped up by rubbernecking occasionals in their uncomfortable Sunday best and posh hats. They'd risen early on the Holy Day for the juicy gossip – *murder, imagine?* – in person rather than simply reading about it in the broadsheets and colour supplements. Most likely they'd soon regretted coming to a service bereft of carols.

They were all there, Pat thought, except for the Chiangs, who were not C-of-E, and Mrs Boseman on account of her being bedridden... oh, and dead.

The list of suspects, Pat realised, was twenty-nine.

Unless a madman with a lockpick, two knives and a gun had escaped from a lunatic asylum in an SUV.

By the time they were back in their pew, an organ whistle announced that Betty was back in position for the final hymn – Number 384, *Oft in Danger, Oft in Woe*.

When the final twiddle of organ music faded in the rafters, the curate gave the blessing, "Go in peace and serve the Lord."

Everyone stood and began filing out. The rush to leave was always embarrassing. Pat hesitated and finally caught Diane and Annabelle's eye.

They nodded back.

Up by the altar, the curate tidied away all the paraphernalia of sacred worship. He was in his own territory behind the defensive barrier of the altar rail and it was his onerous task to finish the sacramental wine, knocking back the holy, cheap Aldi house red. The wafers would be kept for the next week in a specially prepared Tupperware container: the keen front row must wonder why the Body of Christ was always stale.

The three ladies made their way against the exodus.

"Curate," Pat said, "could we have a brief word?"

"I..." he replied, "...find I..."

He was choking and tried to unfasten his dog collar.

"Curate?"

The man looked towards heaven and keeled over the altar rail. The chalice fell from his grip, bounced down the chancel, and rolled to come to rest at Pat's feet. The tiniest dribble of red stained the carpet like a drop of blood.

When she looked back, the curate was quite dead with his hand pointing at the wall opposite the organ, but the claw could have indicated the stained-glass last supper, the flower arrangement or the magnolia paint.

Like a supernatural herald, the church organ whistled, a fanfare of trumpets that sounded as if the host of heaven had been caught off guard.

Finally, an angelic voice screamed.

12. Motive, Opportunity and Method

Pat watched.

Frances clambered into her car and drove away, stopping briefly at the entrance to indicate and check for oncoming traffic. The rear bumper had a dent

Pat hadn't seen it before as Frances had backed into her space until she was practically touching the wall. "I wonder if that nice detective noticed that?" Pat muttered.

"Noticed what?" Diane asked.

"Nothing."

The oncoming traffic turned out to be three police cars. They came into the church and parked diagonally across the white lines. Pat thought it was lucky for them that Frances the warden had left: she'd have had words.

A uniformed police officer went over to the nice detective constable.

"Another one?" Sergeant Drax asked.

The DC nodded.

"Where were you?"

"Out here," Kilroy admitted.

"Four deaths, so you've got your serial killer," the sergeant said. "Happy, Killjoy?"

"It's Detective Constable Kil*roy*."

"Where's the stiff?"

"In the church and I'd appreciate it if you'd show some respect," Kilroy said, nodding towards the many old ladies watching the show.

"Right you are."

The police officers all went inside, donning blue latex gloves and blue socks over their shoes. What was the collective for police, Pat wondered: an investigation of police, a hello-hello-hello, a thin blue line?

"I feel really shocked," Annabelle said.

"Quite, we all are," Pat admitted. "It's hard to believe what's just happened."

"Stiff upper lip, eh," Diane added. "Let's go and have a coffee."

"Good idea, we can compare notes," Pat suggested. "Come on, Belle."

They were parched: Mrs Jones's teas in the Parochial Hall had long gone cold as the police hadn't let anyone inside. Names and addresses had been taken in the car park.

Pat checked her Accurist watch and then waved her walking stick to show the way down to her cottage. En route, they overtook Mrs Perceval on her mobility scooter.

"It can go faster," Diane said to her.

"More haste, less speed," Mrs Perceval cried, waving her umbrella at the bright blue sky.

Once back inside her cottage, Pat checked her watch again before changing into her slippers.

"I'll put the kettle on," Pat said.

"Shall I get the biscuits?" Annabelle asked.

"Please."

182

They each had one of the nested tables. Pat, sitting in the centre, had the largest and the plate of ginger snaps. After the terrible shock, they needed fortifying. Perhaps even a sherry; after all, one sip of red wine didn't go far.

"Right... vicar?" Pat said.

"One of the nine... not the vicar, so seven keyholders," Diane said.

"Eight."

"You are counting me?"

"We have to be thorough," Pat said. "We need to establish your alibi for the police."

"Yes, of course. That's very thoughtful."

"What is your alibi?"

"I went to the church to talk to the vicar... oh! I don't have an alibi."

Pat fished out her list of suspects.

Vicar – victim.

Curate – jealous of vicar, promotion?

Warden (Frances) – trad v modern.

Flowers (Mrs Entwistle) – argued about daffs.

Teas (Mrs Jones) – money.

Choir (Mr Boseman) – angry about choir.

Organist (Betty) – reform the choir.

Curate's wife – promotion for husband.

Magazine (Diane) – loss of magazine.

"The curate... oh dear, poor man, Frances the warden, Mrs Entwistle, Mrs Jones, Mr Boseman, Betty, the curate's wife and... Diane, sorry."

"It can't be the curate," Annabelle said, "he's... dead."

"Can we cross him off?" Diane said.

"Technically, no," Pat said. "He could have killed the vicar and then someone else killed him."

"Surely not," Annabelle said. "Two killers? In Conky Whallop? It's bad enough having one."

"Or four."

"Oh my, what will people think?"

184

"Any of them could have done it," Pat said.

"You saw Mrs Entwistle," Annabelle said.

"True, but only for a moment, and there's time to walk from the church."

"I wondered what you were doing checking your watch," Diane said.

"But wouldn't Di have passed her coming from the church to fetch us?" Annabelle said.

"Yes, quite," Pat said. "I wonder if we can eliminate anyone else?"

"What about Sergio?" Diane said.

"It could be a hit-and-run," Pat said.

"The pizzas he was delivering all went to Gastrench Hall," Annabelle said, "over in Upper Whallop."

"That can't be right," Pat said. "Sergio drove to Tinsel Lane. That's entirely the wrong direction. There must have been another delivery."

"There wasn't."

"It's the wrong–"

"I can't help that, but he was booked for four pizzas to Gastrench Hall and nothing else. I saw the book in Chiang's."

"You must have got it wrong."

"Pat! I know what I saw."

"You must have seen something else."

"I had plenty of time to read it."

"Belle–"

"Two pepperonis, one Margherita, and one buffalo with olives," Annabelle insisted. "All to Gastrench Hall and nothing else."

Pat considered this. "All right, but why?"

"I don't know, but it's a clue."

Pat swirled the pot, thinking, and topped up everyone's cups. "He went to Tinsel Lane," she said.

"Four pizzas to Gas–"

"For some other reason."

"And was killed for it," Diane said.

186

"Yes, quite, I think," Pat said, "that he must have delivered something else and someone searched his delivery box for it."

"For pizza?" Diane said.

"Well, no, whoever it was, they threw the pizzas away."

"Something else?"

"Yes."

"Perhaps they didn't like the topping," Annabelle said.

"No, Belle, something else."

"Chicken wings?"

"No."

"Garlic bread?"

"You don't kill people for garlic bread."

"A dessert?"

"No."

"Cheesecake... oh, they threw the cheese pizzas away."

"It's not food, Belle."

"Ice cream?"

"No, Belle."

"Perhaps he wasn't delivering," Diane said, "perhaps he was collecting."

"Ah yes," Pat agreed. "A delivery on the side."

"Waffles?" Annabelle said.

"To Gastrench?" Diane asked.

"Or on the way," Pat added.

"We could work it out," Annabelle said. "The size of the box minus the four pizzas he was delivering."

"Belle," Pat said, "it's not food!"

"She's right though," Diane said.

Pat held up her hands signifying the size of the delivery box. Diane held her thumb and finger to show the depth of a pizza box.

"Four," said Annabelle.

Pat shuffled her hands down four inches or so.

"Plenty of room for something," she said.

"A cake," Annabelle said.

"It's not food, Belle," Pat insisted. "There's no other food outlet open at that time and certainly not in Tinsel Lane."

"A hat."

"I beg your pardon?"

"It's the size of a hatbox."

Pat glanced at the space between her hands: it could be a hatbox.

"Whoever did it must have damaged their car," Diane said.

"Frances had a bump on her car," Pat said.

"I didn't see one," Annabelle said.

"On the back."

"I saw it too when I went to her house," Diane said. "She could have killed the vicar, run Sergio over and then killed Mrs Boseman and now the curate."

"A lot of other cars to check," Pat said. "So we've not narrowed it down at all."

"What about Mrs Boseman?" Diane said.

"Poor Belinda," Annabelle said, "bedridden and now dead."

"Poisoned, shot and stabbed," Pat said.

"Really? How awful."

"Or poisoned, stabbed and shot."

"Does it make a difference?" Diane asked.

"It might," Pat said.

"One person making sure?"

"Or three people?"

"You wouldn't kill someone if they were already dead," Annabelle said.

"Mr Boseman must be the chief suspect," Diane said.

"He was with us when she died," Pat pointed out.

"Was he?"

"According to a computer, she died at five to twelve," Pat said, "but there was also a carriage clock broken at five past twelve."

"That could have been changed," Diane said.

"And her computer thingummy?"

"That could have been changed too."

"It was backed up to the cloud."

"Eh?"

"I don't know what that is either, but it means that she was killed at exactly eleven fifty-five and seven seconds."

"So the carriage clock was ten minutes fast?" Annabelle asked. "Mrs Boseman would never have allowed that."

"It doesn't make any difference," Pat said. "At both times, Mr Boseman was in your charity shop. We all saw him."

"We did," Annabelle said. "He came in twice. That's once for the cloud and again for the clock."

"He could still have poisoned her," Diane said. "You know, left it in her cocoa."

"Not in the morning," Annabelle said.

"Why not?"

"Cocoa... in the morning."

"In her tea then." Pat tapped her notepaper with her pencil, breaking the point.

"And the curate?" Diane asked.

"Heart attack?" Pat said.

"It looked like poison."

"The same poison as Mrs Boseman?"

"The same killer?"

"Perhaps."

Pat went into the kitchen to fetch her sharpening knife. She knapped at her pencil to create a new point, catching the flakes on a sheet of newspaper. The little shavings fell on all that was dreadful in the world: economic downturns, politicians lying, more politicians lying, youth fashions, yet more politicians lying, local drug problems – honestly, she didn't know why she had the paper delivered.

The doorbell rang.

Pat answered it, knife in one hand and sharpened pencil in the other.

The man at the door startled.

"Sorry," Pat said.

"Mrs Thomas."

"Detective Constable Kilroy."

"May I come in?"

"Please."

He came in.

"Shoes."

"Oh. Yes."

He struggled to take off his shoes, crumpling his Mackintosh as he tried to bend down.

"Let me take your coat," Pat offered and then she realised she was still armed with a Stanley knife and a pointed pencil.

"The pencil is mightier than the sword," Kilroy said.

"Sorry... oh, please go in, I'll just put this away," Pat said and she scurried to the kitchen to put the knife back in the drawer and tuck her pencil behind her ear. She also found another cup and saucer.

Kilroy padded into the drawing-room and met the others.

"You're all here," he said. "You ladies are following me."

"We were here first," Pat said.

"Pure coincidence, I assure you," Diane said. "We were investigating."

"Investigating?"

"We are the editors of the parish magazine."

"I read your latest. Quite the headline."

"Thank you."

194

He sat where Pat indicated and she handed him a cup of tea. He eyed it suspiciously and then he drank gratefully from the darkly brewed liquid. All the nested tables had been taken so he was forced to hold his cup and saucer, and the ginger snaps were just out of reach.

"What's the collective noun for a group of old ladies?" Kilroy pondered aloud. "An interference of old ladies?"

"A helping of ladies," Pat suggested.

"Poison is a woman's weapon," Kilroy said.

"You're not suggesting one of us?"

"Mrs Boseman was poisoned and it looks like the curate was poisoned too."

"Was the curate poisoned?" Diane asked.

"It looks like it, but I'll have to wait for the forensics report," Kilroy said. "Doctor Lake wouldn't be pushed into saying. Not even time of death and I was a witness to when."

"Yes, well, quite," Pat said. "In the meantime, we could discuss one of the other murders."

"The trick is to solve motive, opportunity and method," Kilroy said.

"No-one would want to kill anyone in Conky Whallop," Annabelle said.

"Well, that's motive out of the way," Diane said.

"Opportunity is tricky," Pat said, "because it's such a small village. You can walk from one end to the other in twenty minutes, so anyone can get anywhere."

"And there's no CCTV," Kilroy added.

"So much for opportunity," Diane said.

"How about method?" Pat suggested.

"Who owns a big car in the village?" Kilroy asked.

"Sergio's hit and run?" Pat said.

"Was it a big car?" Annabelle asked.

"The forensics report suggested... sorry," Pat said. "Detective Constable, you first."

Kilroy's eyes narrowed. "The forensics report suggested a large car or van."

196

"Frances the warden has a large car," Diane said, "and it has a dent."

"It doesn't," Kilroy said. He took out his phone and checked the images.

"At the back," Diane said, triumphantly.

"Back?"

"And cars have a reverse gear."

"And hers has heated seats," Annabelle added.

"I hadn't thought of that," Kilroy said, "but why?"

"Sergio's behind her, so she pops it into reverse," Diane said, miming with her hands up as if holding a steering wheel and glancing over her shoulder. "Crunch, crunch."

She bounced up and down on the comfy armchair.

"Oh please don't," Annabelle said.

"But why?" Kilroy repeated. "Why would she kill a delivery boy?"

"Oh... plenty of reasons," Diane said. "He forgot her order or he... I'm sure there might be something."

"Motive," Kilroy said, "and we can check her paintwork to see if the damage is consistent. You often find paint from the other vehicle, even a moped."

"Sergio's moped was red," Pat said, "and Frances Fairfax's car is blue, so it ought to show up, but the tyres are wrong."

"Tyres?"

"Oh dear, I meant to, but with one thing and another."

Pat got up, sloped into the kitchen like a naughty girl spotted passing notes in class, and fetched the pizza box.

"I found it under a hedge," she explained when she got back.

Kilroy's frown deepened as he examined the tyre tracks.

"We got tyre tracks from the scene," he said, "so I suppose no harm done."

"But tyre tracks on the pizza box means that the delivery was searched and then the car drove off."

"Ah!"

"And the search wasn't for pizzas."

"So what were they searching for?"

"Exactly."

"It's a potential motive."

"Robbery of a pizza?" Diane said.

"No, robbery of something else," Pat replied. "You see, Detective Constable, he was supposed to be carrying four pizzas and there were three other pizza boxes in addition to this one at the scene. What's more, there would be about this much space left in his delivery box."

Kilroy examined the gap between Pat's hands. He raised his hands as well almost as if he was going to take the empty space off her as another piece of evidence.

"Who else has a big car?" he asked.

"The vicar," Annabelle said.

"He has an alibi," Kilroy said.

"What's that?"

"He was being murdered."

"Oh!"

"Anyone else?"

"Sir Victor Pendle-Took," Annabelle said. "He's an architect and he can afford lots of cars. He usually has two or three, a big one, a sporty one, a red one and so on. Maybe he killed his brother, family argument, and then–"

"Without a key?" Pat said.

"He knocked," Annabelle continued. "The vicar let him in and then, when he was making his getaway, he hit Sergio by accident."

"And then searched the delivery box?"

"Yes, and locked the church and somehow put the key back in the vicar's pocket."

"And Sergio drove the wrong way for what reason?"

"Er... he was lost," Annabelle finished, and then she looked at the others' expressions. "Sorry."

"Does this Sir Victor have an SUV?"

"Oh yes," Annabelle said, "and a sports car."

Kilroy showed her his phone and Annabelle nodded.

"No marks on it," he said.

"So that leaves... someone from outside the village," Pat said.

"Oh, thank goodness," Annabelle said. "Imagine having a murderer here in Conky Whallop."

"You could check the speed camera on the A-road," Pat said. "If they rushed off quickly and went to Upper Whallop, then maybe it caught them."

"Hmmm."

"So, Detective Constable," Pat said, "what do you think the collective noun for a group of old ladies might be now?"

"I think the correct term is a bevvy of ladies."

"In that case maybe a sherry, Pat?" Diane said. "Officer?"

"Not for me, I'm on duty."

"It's a murder of crows," Pat mused, "so what's the collective for a group of murderers?"

"Hopefully, a catch of murderers," Kilroy said.

"They might not be working together," Pat said. "What's the collective for police?"

"It's a posse of police."

"Shall we join your posse then?"

"We could," Diane added.

"Oh let's," Annabelle said.

They looked at the detective constable and he said, "Do I have a choice?"

13. Whodunnit?

Pat rang Diane first thing after her cup of tea, Monday morning.

"Conky Whallop, 153."

"Di, it's Pat."

"Hello, Pat."

"You have a key to the church."

"Look, Pat, I'm not a suspect–"

"On you?"

"Yes. It's a sign of office."

"Then let's meet on the High Street and see if we can do a little snooping."

"Will the police let us?"

"Oh, yes," Pat said, "that nice detective constable practically asked us."

They met at the shops soon after. Several cars had been parked in the various bays with a couple of mobility scooters plonked on the pavement.

"SUVs," Diane said, pointing.

Sure enough, two monstrosities bookmarked either end of the eight spaces.

"That's the detective constable's car," Diane said.

"Is it?" Pat said. "And the other?"

"I'd guess it's Pendle-Took's."

They had a quick shufty through the windows and saw a copy of *Architecture Today* and *Private Eye* on the passenger seat.

"Pendle-Took," Diane confirmed. "I don't know how he can show his face in the village, what with that monstrosity of a house and–"

"Now, now, Di."

"And that building he designed falling down."

They checked the front and rear, but the car's green metallic paint was unharmed.

204

"Not him then," Diane said.

"We need to check the church," Pat said.

"And Mrs Entwistle."

"Well, yes, church first and then perhaps you and Belle might ask Mrs Entwistle a few questions."

"Sounds good," Diane agreed. "Church it is then."

They made their way up the hill, feeling guilty. The church's lychgate was still taped off with a blue-and-white barrier, which Pat raised with the end of her walking stick, so they could nip underneath.

Pat gave the surroundings a few furtive glances as Diane put the huge key in the lock. Despite the sunshine, they both shivered. This is what they had done during the storm less than a week ago to find the vicar dead.

In they went and the door slammed behind them.

The main window beamed coloured light over the altar and choir stalls as if angels were singing 'look here'.

Pat folded up her walking stick and took a deep breath.

The spot below the eagle lectern gleamed.

"The police will have searched," Diane said.

"Yes."

"What are we looking for?"

"Something... anything..."

The next port of call was the organ. Pat shuffled over, but to seat herself properly, she had to put her foot down. The organ *whistled*.

"Quiet!" Diane said.

Pat put out her hands over the keys. "Shall I?"

"No, shhh!"

"I know chopsticks."

"Shhh, Pat don't."

Above the three keyboards, a music rest awaited a few sheets of notes and over that a chrome rearview mirror caught Pat's eye. In the reflection, she could see where the choirmaster, Mr Boseman, would have stood if there was still a choir. She could also see the pulpit and the first row of the pews and – craning around – the altar. She could also see the eagle lectern and the back of the church simply by looking to her right.

"Betty has a good view," Pat said.

"So she'd have seen something."

"Or been the one... there's no way she could get out without everyone seeing."

"Or hearing."

Pat looked at the altar again.

"Betty does that," Diane said.

"Does what?"

"Shifts about like she wants to powder her nose."

"She's looking at the altar for her cue to play the voluntary."

"That makes sense."

"Could the curate have gone into the vestry and then Betty could have nipped out and poisoned the wine?"

Diane considered this, "No, he was cleaning up when and we were watching. We saw him drink the dregs."

"This is impossible," Pat said. She shuffled back – *whistle* – out of the organ seat.

They both went to the altar feeling sacrilegious as they opened the altar rail. Pat walked around the altar in silence. It was a simple table covered in an ornate cloth. There were no hidden doors or anything.

"He was here, behind the altar," Pat said.

"Behind the altar rail too," Diane added.

"Drank the same cup as everyone else." Pat mimed his actions.

"Could it have been in a wafer?"

"How would you be able to predict which one he'd eat?"

208

"Maybe it was targeted for someone else."

"It can't be targeted."

"Someone at random?"

"That's a nasty thought."

They came out to stand between the choir stalls.

Pat looked down. Between her sensible shoes was a dark stain, the Blood of Christ spilt upon the meadow green Berber. She bent down to the carpet to examine it. Someone should have sprinkled salt to absorb the red wine – it was too late now. The mark would be there for all time or until the Parish Council agreed to replace the carpet and that would be expensive. At least, the vicar had the good sense to die on the tiles.

She put her hand out, half expecting the patch to be wet. It wasn't, but there was something hard in the centre. She felt around it and picked it up. It was black and like a peppercorn.

It must have rolled out when the cup spilt the wine.

Pepper in the sacramental wine?

A poison made of pepper?

She ought to hand it to that nice detective constable.

"What is it?" Diane asked.

"I don't know."

Pat had a little envelope in her bag, she was sure, and she fished inside to dig it out, but it was awkward. She didn't want to put the evidence down just anywhere, so she looked round and saw one of the collection plates. She plonked the tiny ball in that... and it rang like a bell.

It wasn't a peppercorn, it was metal!

Arsenic was a metal, Pat thought, so perhaps this was how the poison had been put in the wine.

"How odd," she said aloud.

She rolled it around and it clinked like an evil, little ball-bearing and realised what it was.

"What is it?" Diane repeated, staring at it too.

"It's a clue."

It went into the envelope.

Although they checked further, there was nothing else to find, except a copy of the parish magazine stuffed behind a flower display.

"Well, really," Diane said. "Some people just don't appreciate how much work I... we put into the magazine."

Diane locked the big church door with her key while Pat kept watch. Once that was done, they scurried to the pavement before adopting that pleasant strolling gait that said they had all the time in the world and weren't up to no good.

"It's moved," Pat said.

"What's moved?"

Pat pointed her stick at the parked cars: Pendle-Took's big, green metallic SUV was now parked next to the detective constable's.

"He was with Frances on the night of the murder," Pat said.

"And Frances denied it," Diane said.

"Did she now? And when everyone needs an alibi too."

They both went into Pheasant's Café to discuss matters over a glass of her freshly pressed apple juice.

"What would you like?" Zara asked.

"The apple juice, please," Diane said.

"Coming up... and you, Mrs Thomas?"

"Well, no, I'll have a tisane, thank you," Pat said.

Pheasant's Café was pleasantly hippy with a rough, distressed charm that came from charity shop furniture, hand-me-downs and permanent borrows. A lick of paint, though, was not something it needed. What it needed was a proper colour scheme. Instead, the paint came from all the various leftover tins that Zara Pheasant had scrounged over the years. Matt and gloss alternated with beige, magnolia, livid orange, lime green and burnt umber like a Piet Mondrian on a day when he'd drunk too much coffee. But Zara was young and so allowances had to be made if the village was to hold onto any of her generation.

"Right," said Pat, moving the salt shaker to the centre of the table. "The curate was here, Betty here..."

Diane handed her the pepper.

"And... let's see."

Soon, and with condiments from the nearby table, there was a collection of salts, peppers, ketchups and mustards arranged like a crazy chess game.

"And?" Diane asked finally.

"Oh, I don't know," Pat admitted.

"Perhaps we should examine Mrs Boseman."

Pat shifted the arrangement until she had three peppers surrounding a salt.

"Stabbed, shot and poisoned," Pat explained.

"With a suicide note?"

"Yes, quite, but it's tricky to commit suicide three times in one morning."

They examined the arrangement again.

"What about Sergio?" Diane asked.

Pat shifted the objects around and then ran over a ketchup sachet with the condiment box. The rustic wood split the sauce and it bled onto the table.

"Oh dear," Pat said.

They mopped up with paper napkins.

"Big car?" Diane said.

"Yes, that's all we know."

"Well, that's that then," Diane said, wiping the last of the red off her hands.

"There's the vicar," Pat said. She shuffled the positions again until she had a line of eight items, one for each suspect. There were peppers and salts galore, and it confused her as to which was which, but it didn't matter. Staring at them wasn't helping.

"What game are you playing?" Detective Constable Kilroy said, suddenly looming over them in his creased Mackintosh.

"Detective Constable," Pat said, "I have a present for you."

"Really, I don't need any jam or crochet work," Kilroy replied, "and it could be construed as receiving gifts. Thank you all the same."

"Quite. Do sit down, Detective."

Kilroy sighed and slid a chair over to join them.

"It's a clue," she said, handing over the envelope.

He felt the envelope suspiciously, feeling the hard pip in the corner.

"What is it?"

"I don't know," Pat admitted, "but it was in the carpet where the wine has left an awful stain."

"The curate's death…" – Kilroy opened it and checked the contents – "…and you got this from the church?"

"Yes."

"You are not supposed to go in the church."

"You're welcome."

"What is it?" he asked.

"It's lead shot."

"Do you always find clues?"

"I try," Pat admitted.

"This is not a game," Kilroy said.

"Oh, but it is."

"Murder in the dark," Diane suggested.

"And we are in the dark," Pat said. She looked out of the window at the bright sunshine and, between the writing advertising speciality teas and fruit smoothies, Pat saw Sir Victor clamber up into his green metallic SUV. He glanced to his right, his eyes looking directly into the café before he zoomed away with only the briefest of savage braking for the speed bump.

They had seen him leave Frances's house; she was sure.

"I can't help feeling that we've been very, very stupid," Pat said.

"Your curate was killed with poison," the detective constable said. "There were traces left in the wine. He wasn't shot."

"Mrs Boseman was shot," Diane said.

Both Pat and Kilroy answered: "Wrong sort–"

"Sorry, you first," Pat said.

"Wrong sort of gun," Kilroy said. "I'm afraid no-one has been killed with a shotgun."

"Of course," Pat said, "but it is a clue and relates to the method."

"How can lead shot relate to the method?"

"Well, it most certainly doesn't relate to motive or opportunity, does it?"

"No, but–"

"Whoever did whatever it was they did, they must have had access to a shotgun thing."

"A cartridge."

"Exactly."

"So, you want me to check who has a gun licence?"

"Yes, indeed."

"Again?"

"Yes, but not for a... low calibre handgun, wasn't it? For a shotgun."

"For a poisoning?"

"Exactly."

"I'm going to be a laughing stock."

14. Police Records

Of course, Detective Constable Kilroy knew exactly how to access the police station's computer system and pull together a plethora of useful information, sort and filter that data, and narrow his field of enquiry down to a list of suspects. Conveniently, all the residents of Conky Whallop came within the same postcode sector.

The Foal Lane Police Station had a canteen and interview rooms, cells and offices, and a big open-plan area full of computers.

Kilroy hung his Mackintosh on the peg, nodded to a few colleagues and got himself a coffee. He logged on, which took a while as the system wanted him to change his password.

It didn't agree with his first few attempts: they were too weak, too long, too short, too obvious, didn't have a special character, didn't have a numeric, were too like his National Insurance number, too... so it became a random splurge of keyboard nonsense that he had to painstakingly write down on a piece of paper and hide in his drawer.[6]

So, *click-click-clickety-click–*

Backspace-backspace.

Click.

Backspace.

Click-clickety-clickety.

Return.

Who had a criminal record?

_____

[6] Editor's note: This has long ago been proved to have no security value, but continues to be promoted. The truth is that people can't remember these esoteric codes. Any system that allows brute-force login attempts deserves to be hacked, but it's the systems admin people blaming the users as usual.

1. Kovalyov, Vladimir (Doctor)

2. Pheasant, Zara (Ms)

3. Richards, Diane (Miss)

4. York, Benita (Mrs)

All bound over to keep the peace for killing squirrels, trespass, protesting and tax evasion, respectively.

Who owned a gun licence?

1. Kovalyov, Vladimir (Doctor)

2. Naseby, Archibald (Major)

Issued and up to date: a .38 for defence contracting and a shotgun for hunting, respectively.

"Oi, Killjoy, what you doing?"

"Checking gun licences," Kilroy replied, keeping his head down.

"Which case, your stabbing or your poisoning?"

"The poisonings."

"Ha, only Killjoy – here listen, only Killjoy would check gun licences for poisoning."

DC Wragg moved away to spread more malicious nonsense, his bald head leaning back as he roared with laughter, but at least he left Kilroy in peace

Who owned an SUV or similar?

1. Fairfax, Frances (Miss)

2. Kovalyov, Vladimir (Doctor)

3. Naseby, Archibald (Major)

4. Pendle-Took, Victor Edward (Sir)

Vladimir Kovalyov was the only one on all three lists, but he hadn't appeared in the investigation yet. Kilroy had heard the name, though.

He checked – Betty the organist was Mrs Kovalyov. He'd have to wait for ballistics to confirm the bullet size. Kovalyov, Vladimir (Doctor) had a .38 and a *machine gun!* What sort of defence contracting was he doing in a sleepy village like Conky Whallop?

He grabbed the phone and dialled forensics.

"DC Kilroy here."

He found a pen.

"Kil*roy*," he had to repeat.

But no paper.

"Has ballistics found out what the bullet was that killed Mrs Boseman in Conky Whallop?"

He opened the drawer and...

"I know she was poisoned, but she was also shot."

...rummaged through all the dead pens, scissors, an old apple – *yuk!* – that went in the bin.

"Yes, the bullet size, please."

He found a piece of paper with 'hXFk9854kj]$}' written on it for some reason.

"Thanks, thirty-eight, got it."

He made a note, although it was something he'd remember, and then hung up.

And Vladimir Kovalyov had a .38 – interesting.

Kilroy printed out a collection of pages on the network's printer: the lists, addresses, a summary of criminal records. The circle whirled and he was third in the printer queue, except that it had gone through to the second-floor printer.

As he went to get his pages, he ignored the pointing and laughter while he queued.

"Those your poison bullets?"

"Very funny."

"Just a bit of fun, Killjoy."

His pages finally appeared, smeared with lines of ink, but for once, readable. Kilroy fumed as he took the stairs and stomped round and round in circles.

"Killjoy?"

"Oh, for– Sir. Yes, sir."

Kilroy stood still, not to attention, but his feet were together and his head tilted down, not bowing, but respectful. He noticed that his shoes were polished to perfection.

"So, how's the investigation going?" Inspector Rex Raymond asked. The senior officer was tall, square-jawed, his hair shorn to a number one and his regal nose broken twice, once in rugby and once arresting a litterer. His piercing blue eyes looked down on the detective constable as he waited for the answer he wanted.

"Fine, sir, early days."

"Early days... no progress then."

"I wouldn't say that, sir."

"What would you say?"

Kilroy glanced around the open-plan office at the Foal Lane police station only to see his colleagues with their heads down, studiously writing reports. He'd have no help from that direction, but he knew that already. As a new boy, it was sink or swim.

"I'm waiting for forensics on the curate poisoning," Kilroy pointed out. "They have a backlog."

"On account of all the murders in Conk... that village."

"Yes, sir."

"It's early days for you too, isn't it?"

"Sir?"

"Not long a detective," the inspector said. "Better get your finger out, Killjoy."

"Sir, with respect, it's Kil–"

But the inspector had breezed out of the open plan area as abruptly as he'd blown in.

Kilroy found he'd crumpled his sheaf of printout. There were people he'd like to poison, shoot and stab... or poison, stab and shoot.

Back at his desk, he picked up his phone, then slammed it down and marched to Forensics on the third floor to pick up the reports directly. This felt like getting his finger out.

He might even get to talk to Doctor Lake.

"Doctor Lake's at lunch," her assistant told him, "and it's in the internal post,"

So, Kilroy marched to the basement and made the civilian specialist down there find the big, fat envelope.

It was a long walk back up, so he took the lift.

"What's that, Killjoy?" another detective asked.

"My forensics reports."

"The one with the silver bullets?"

"Yes."

The others in the lift sniggered and Kilroy concentrated on the floor number.

Back at his desk again, his computer had got bored and had logged him out. He couldn't get back to the login screen, so he turned the machine off-and-on again.

"Come on, come on," he said at the thing as it attempted to hypnotise him with its circling dots. He typed in his user name, Kilroy_768, and then fished in his desk for the piece of paper. Very carefully, he typed in the stupid password: 'hXFk9854kj]$}38'.

It didn't work.

"For... *arrghh*."

He tried again, super carefully, 'hXFk9854kj]$}38' and it didn't work again. Hang on, was that a square bracket or a '1', so 'hXFk9854kj1$}38' and then he was locked out of the system.

As it turned off-and-laboriously-on again, he saw that the 'X' could be a capital or a large, small letter.

'hxFk9854kj]$}38'.

'hxFk9854kj1$}38'.

'hXfk – *backspace* – K9...

He rang IT support.

"DC Kilroy... fourth floor. I can't get into... yes, I've turned it off-and... yes, twice. I can't get into the system, my password isn't working."

He grabbed the piece of paper, knocking his printouts to the floor.

"Yes, yes, I'm trying to," he said and then, consulting the scrap of paper and taking great care, he read out, "hotel capital x-ray capital foxtrot niner eight five four kilo Juliette right square bracket dollar right curly bracket three eight."

As the computer support technician tapped away in his ear, Kilroy glanced at the printout on the floor, but it was too far away to read.

"I know it's complicated."

Give me strength, he thought, I bet those old ladies don't have these issues.

"Yes," he said, "I wanted to choose something simple too, but your system wouldn't let me."

The cord was long enough for him to get down on his hands and knees to recover the printouts.

"I know it doesn't work."

Vladimir Kovalyov lived at 4 Gladstone Road, Conky Whallop–

"No, I can't open a support ticket," Kilroy said. "I'm locked out of the system."

He got his personal mobile phone out of his pocket and tried the address on Google Street View.

"No, I can't send you an email with a screenshot as I'm locked out of the system."

The houses around Number 4 were large with double garages and no numbers on their doors.

"Kilroy seven, six– Yes, Kilroy underscore, seven, six, eight."

There was an SUV with a blurred numberplate parked outside one of them.

"No, *roy*... Romeo Oscar Yankee."

Why did people not have house numbers?

"Not Juliette, Romeo – *Romeo!* Romeo Oscar Mike Echo Oscar."

Why did people never park their cars in their garages?

"No, that's the bit that's not working."

Gun and SUV... two of the murder weapons.

"No, please, listen, don't email it to me and close the support ticket, I still can't get into– Hello? Hello?"

He gave up.

He'd visit these suspects, but there was someone else he wished to talk to first. He didn't mention this to any of his colleagues, of course. If they made fun of him requesting firearms licences for a poisoning, he would never hear the last of the humour if they find out who he was consulting.

His Mackintosh lay beneath the peg, trampled.

!!!

Kilroy didn't stand to attention or even still, his toes twitched as if their freedom meant they wanted to run and skip, but his feet were together and his head was bowed, though tilted to one side to hear the old lady's voice better. He noticed that his socks were mismatched.

"These crimes may not be connected," Pat said, "but they are connected."

"I see," Kilroy said, although he did not.

"Everything in a village is connected."

"You all know each other's business and yet, no-one knows who murdered who."

"Murdered *whom*. But yes, quite. Although we all know each other's business, everyone has secrets."

"Even you?"

"Oh, most especially me."

Mrs Thomas's drawing-room appeared quaint and cluttered to Kilroy's minimalist tastes. None of this came from IKEA with efficient storage and easy to clean surfaces. Instead, nick-nacks and curios lined the mantlepiece and wasted space on the shelves, each one delicately fragile and a nightmare to dust. Like their owner, they collected things that didn't match.

Like his socks.

Conky Whallop was having its effect on him.

Kilroy handed over a set of reports.

Pat took out her half-moon reading glasses and flicked through the notes on bleeding, injury, poison, shooting, stabbing and death with obvious relish.

"Ah," she said and then she added, "Ah. Ah-*ha*... ah."

"Well?"

"Sir Pendle-Took, Kovalyov, Frances and Major Naseby... two of those have large cars."

"Who are they?"

"Sir Pendle-Took is an architect and lives in that monstrosity up Orthodox Drive. He's the late vicar's brother," Pat explained. "Kovalyov calls himself an inventor and he's married to Betty the organist."

"Yes."

"And Major Naseby lives out in the Manor."

"Hmmm."

"Major Naseby has a Land Rover."

"That could still be the car that hit Sergio."

"Kovalyov's licence was revoked," Pat said, now on another page. "That'll be because he was shooting squirrels, but I see that he's been granted a new one."

"Something to do with a defence contract, all top secret and above my clearance."

"It's robotic soldiers, a preliminary trial to see if British research can compete with Boston Dynamics and their Big Dog, Little Dog, Spot and so on," Pat said. She looked up and saw Kilroy's incredulous expression.

"I see your clearance is higher than mine," Kilroy said.

"As I said, everyone knows everyone's business in an English village."

"So, what do you think?"

"It's difficult to untangle it all, isn't it? It's like trying to unknot and sort differently coloured wool into separate balls in the dark while wearing gardening gloves."

"Perhaps we should concentrate on one case at a time."

"Well, if you think that would help?"

"Yes, I think so."

"Well, how about the freshest?"

"The curate was killed with arsenic, not lead poisoning. That amount of lead wouldn't kill someone and certainly not quickly."

"Yes, I know that," Pat said. "I'm quite capable of asking my nephew in Australia to look it up on Wikipedia. It's obvious that the lead ball in the chalice was arsenic, isn't it?"

"It's not arsenic," Kilroy said. "It's black, not silver."

"I see. Some other poisonous metal? Polonium perhaps?"

"Hardly and that's radioactive. It's simply lead shot as you suspected."

"So... he did die of lead poisoning?"

"Lead poisoning is slow and drawn out," Kilroy said, exasperated that they'd gone in a full circle so quickly, "and a single ball of lead wouldn't kill him."

"He was shot!" Pat said. "No, he was poisoned... was the poison somehow fired into him?"

"He'd have bled to death... it makes no sense."

"Perhaps he was shot at, but they missed?"

"Where's the rest of the shot pellets?"

"And we'd have heard it, wouldn't we?" Pat said, looking up at him over her glasses. "Perhaps whoever used a silencer?"

"Silencers are still quite loud," Kilroy said. "Films give people the wrong idea. The preferred term nowadays is 'suppressor'."

"But the organ was playing quite fortissimo, wasn't it?"

"You don't get suppressors for shotguns."

"Well, quite. Anything else? Let's see..."

Kilroy shrugged and sat down on the sofa.

Pat adjusted her glasses to look closer at the paperwork.

"Nothing unexpected or helpful," Kilroy said.

"Calcium carbonate, tannins..."

"Just what you'd expect in wine."

"There's a lot of sugar."

"Cheap wine."

"Wasn't it anti-freeze they used to make wine sweet that caused a lot of problems?"

"Not present here."

"There's potassium sorbate, potassium metabisulfite, sulphur dioxide..."

"That's wine."

"And arsenic... perhaps the curate drank more than anyone else," Pat suggested. "Maybe it needed a certain dose."

"There was enough to kill an elephant," Kilroy said, leaning over to indicate a table of figures. "It would have made everyone ill at least, even in a small dose. Or more likely killed them. The curate was only in his late thirties and most of the congregation are elderly... no offence."

"None taken, I'm sure."

"So that's that."

"Arsenic, sweetener and lead... does that make anything chemically?"

"I'm sure it would," Kilroy said. "Just as I'm sure the forensics woman would have pointed that out in her report and her scathing summary."

"Oh dear, I'm sorry."

"And it's not lead shot."

Pat perked up. "Then what is it?"

"I mean, it is lead shot, but it's not lead. Modern pellets are made of steel, bismuth or a tungsten composite. Those metals are less reactive, so it's safer."

"Of course," Pat said, "Lead is dangerous and you wouldn't want guns to be dangerous."

"It's a dead end."

"The chalice must have been poisoned between when Frances the warden took communion and when the curate drank what was left over."

"That would make sense, except it would have been seen... I'd have seen it."

"There was me," Pat said, "Di and Belle, the curate's wife... and Betty and the warden is always the last. They bring up the rear, check for stragglers and it lets the vicar... sorry, the clergyman know that everyone has had communion."

"Right."

"So someone must have poisoned the cup or bottle between then and when he drank the leftovers."

"There was only poison in the cup, not the bottle."

"Obviously, otherwise the whole congregation would have keeled over with arsenic poisoning," Pat said. "We all drank from the cup, all of us, you, me, the whole village. Apart from the Chiangs."

It was Kilroy's turn to perked up. "Chiangs?"

"They run the Chinese restaurant on the High Street and they aren't C of E. They're probably some Chinese religion or, heaven forbid, Methodists."

"Do they have a motive?"

"They weren't in the church."

"Ah. No."

"The cup was left in full view of everyone on the altar and no-one went up there except the curate," Pat said. "So it can't have been the cup."

"But it was."

They sat for a while in silence, each bereft of any inspiration. The moment stretched. A clocked ticked. Kilroy managed to glance at his watch without appearing rude, but all he saw was 21°C, 98 bpm. Why did old ladies always have their homes at greenhouse levels of heating? It was that or they had hypothermia.

"More tea?"

"I'm fine," Kilroy said.

But Mrs Thomas reached for the pot anyway and poured tea into his cup.

"Seriously, I don't need any more tea."

"The Blood of Christ," Pat said.

"Pardon?"

240

"And you drink," Pat said. "Mime it."

"Right." Kilroy picked up the cup out of its saucer and mimed drinking.

"Then I say 'Peace be with you' take it back and hand it to the next person."

Pat took the cup off him and then handed it back to him.

Kilroy mimed drinking again.

"Peace be with you," Pat said, taking it back again. "Finally, Betty and Frances, and then the curate put it back on the altar."

Pat put the cup down on its saucer on the tray.

"There's still wine in the cup and wine in the pot," she said, touching the teapot. "Everyone goes back to their pew... the curate stays... Betty off to his left... he says the Peace..."

"He said his piece in his sermon," Kilroy said.

"Peace, not piece... everyone starts to leave... he drinks the leftovers..."

Pat mimed drinking the cup and then she made an appalling choking noise before falling back into her armchair – dead!

There was an awful silence, brooding and tense.

Despite the central heating setting, Kilroy felt suddenly frozen. He was sure his own heart had stopped: zero bpm.

"Mrs Thomas?"

She didn't move!

"Mrs Thomas."

She was dead, victim number five and he was the only possible suspect!

"Mrs Thomas!"

Kilroy reached out to touch her neck. Perhaps, he thought, he should hold his watch against her wrist.

"Oh, Mrs Thomas…"

"So, you see–"

"Ah!!!"

"Are you alright, Detective Constable?"

"Yes, fine."

His watch registered a million bpm, the little heart symbol flashing like a strobe light. He fought to control his rapid breathing.

"So," Pat carried on, "no-one approached the chalice. You and I were witness to that as was everyone else."

Kilroy picked up his cup and stared at the cold tea. It was brown and looked like a thick porridge version of a single malt. He took a gulp, even cold it was exactly what he needed after such a shock.

"More tea?"

"Hmmm."

Kilroy resolved to visit this Major Naseby and Vladimir Kovalyov – shotgun cartridge and a .38, there must be something in that. And he mentally added Sir Victor to his list of people to question.

Pat poured a little tea from the pot.

Kilroy placed his card on one of her nested tables.

"If you think of anything else," he said

"Milk?"

"Hmmm."

What he desperately needed was a clue.

"Sugar?" Pat suggested.

15. A Locked Door Mystery

"Anyone at home?" Diane called out. She bent over to stare through the letterbox – thank goodness it was set at waist height – but she couldn't see anything.

"She's not in," Annabelle said. "We should go."

Squinting, Diane could see through the frosted glass a fat bunch of keys dangling from the lock on the other side.

"We could reach in and get the keys."

"Oh... is that wise?" Annabelle said. She looked into the bay window, her hand above her eyes to see inside rather than admire her own reflection.

"Perhaps we should try around the back," Diane suggested.

"Really?"

Diane was already ambling around to the back door. They should have gone there first. Mrs Entwistle came from a long line of

Entwistles, who had lived in Conky Whallop for several centuries. They had been mentioned in the Domesday Book when the village had been known as Lower Whallop and the large horse chestnut that gave the place its new name had been a mere sapling. She was one of those country folk who left their doors unlocked and complained about how the cities had become cesspools of crime.

But the back door was locked, bolted and the key turned so that the deadbolt stuck out. It had also been splintered open.

"Oh... dear," Annabelle whispered.

"Something's happened?" Diane said.

"Should we?"

"No," Diane said as she put her hand to the fractured handle and pushed the door. It ought to have creaked as it opened, but it didn't.

"We ought to call the police," Annabelle said.

"Let's find out what to tell them first," Diane said.

A red light winked on the dishwasher to inform anyone who looked that the cycle had finished. The dishes would sparkle and the glasses would have a ghostly hue, all ready to go into the shabby chic kitchen cupboards. The homely decoration was at odds with the new appliances. On the window ledge, some pots grew flowers and herbs within rings of spilt soil.

"Hello," Diane whispered to try to attract attention and remain undetected.

"It's only us," Annabelle added.

They crept to the hall despite having shouted for attention. The front door had its curtain pulled open letting any draught that might steal through the double-glazing waft coldly towards them. From inside, the keys dangling in the lock suggested some terrible interruption. It was a big bunch containing modern door keys and one large, old-fashioned monster – the church key.

"Locked door," Diane said.

"New carpet," Annabelle said.

They heard voices – men talking about cutting, killing and deadheading.

They tiptoed to the front room, which was a lounge containing a new, three-piece sofa and armchairs. It smelt of leather and polish. Knick-knacks crowded the mantlepiece and some even perched upon the ultra-thin, HD television set. Bunches of lilies had been laid out in readiness on the coffee table next to the radio.

"Oh dear," Diane said.

"What... oh!"

In the armchair furthest away, sat Mrs Entwistle, her head lolled to one side, mouth open, eyes wide and staring vacantly. Her hair formed a blue halo over her crown and her hands lay beside her, one clutching an empty teacup, the dregs still slipping towards the lip as if to cast a prophecy away.

"Di, is she... oh no."

"Belle, there's no need for you to see."

"Oh, poor, poor Mrs Entwistle."

Diane went to the coffee table and turned the radio off, silencing *Gardener's Question*

Time – "...which will kill the weed to the root and..." – with a click.

Mrs Entwistle blinked, startled, jumped to her feet, shouted, "What!" and swung the cup. It flew towards Diane, who ducked, and then it connected with Annabelle, who screamed.

Mrs Entwistle screamed too.

Diane yelled.

Annabelle switched to shrieking.

Then they all clutched at their chests and collapsed onto a sofa or armchair. They squeaked as they regained their breath and squeaked as they wriggled on the new leather upholstery.

"You nearly gave me a heart attack!" Mrs Entwistle yelled.

"Sorry," Annabelle said.

"We nearly gave you a heart attack," Diane shouted. "What were you doing pretending to be dead?"

"Has the Archers finished?" Mrs Entwistle asked.

"What?" Diane said.

"I must have nodded off."

"Nodded off... you were dead!"

"Clearly not, Miss Richards!"

"Mrs Entwistle, you were quite dead to the world."

"Is Nigel Pargetter all right?"

"He's dead!"

"Dead? When? How?"

"He fell off a roof," Diane said.

"Oh dear."

"He's not been in the Archers for years."

"Really?" Mrs Entwistle said. "I must have been nodding off every afternoon."

"Sorry," Annabelle said again. She touched her head and winced.

"What are you doing sneaking around my house?" Mrs Entwistle demanded.

"Oh... sorry, but I'm bleeding," Annabelle said, taking her hand off her head and feeling the cold, thick liquid between her fingers.

"It's tea, Belle," Diane said.

"Tea?"

"From the cup."

"Oh, sorry."

"Your back door has been forced," Diane said.

"What did you do that for?" Mrs Entwistle said.

"We didn't," Diane said. "We found it like that."

"Let me see," Mrs Entwistle said, trying to ease herself out of her armchair. She plodded to the kitchen with Diane and Annabelle in her wake.

"See," Diane said.

"Someone's broken in," Mrs Entwistle said.

"Or broken out," Annabelle pointed out.

"Belle, they'd just turn the latch," Diane said.

"Oh, sorry."

Mrs Entwistle looked up at the ceiling. "Maybe they're still here."

Both Diane and Annabelle stared up at the Artex stipple pattern.

Quietly, and with purpose, the three women armed themselves with frying pan, rolling pin and meat tenderiser. They stalked together into the hall.

"Should we split up to cover more ground?" Annabelle suggested.

"Would you like to go into the dining room on your own?" Diane said.

"Oh, no, sorry."

Mrs Entwistle popped her head around the dining room door.

"Clear," she said.

They turned as one and examined the stairs that led upwards and around, and then tilted their heads as if pointing an ear at the upstairs would help them hear an intruder better.

Diane went first.

When she reached the foot of the stairs, she raised her fist as she'd seen special forces do in films and the other two crashed into her.

"Shhh..." she said.

"Sorry," Annabelle said.

There was still no sound at all.

Taking a firm grip of her weapon, Diane started up the stairs.

"Careful of the... never mind," Mrs Entwistle said.

Diane winced as the loud creak of the second step scraped across the blackboard of her soul. When she took her foot off, it creaked again. Diane put her foot down on the third step and Mrs Entwistle pushed her so she could clamber up.

Then the three of them passed their weapons up and down to each other when it became their turn to avoid the second step.

"And the ninth," Mrs Entwistle said.

They repeated the process, shuffling their deadly kitchen implements, until, hand-over-hand on the banister like mountaineers, they had climbed the north face of the stairs to the landing.

Three doors gave them a choice: bathroom, bedroom and bijou boxroom.

Mrs Entwistle tried the bathroom, tapping the door open to reveal the eye-wateringly bright salmon décor. She stepped in, swished the shower curtain and then she shrugged to the others.

Diane tried the bijou boxroom, but the door stuck on something. She tugged and pushed and finally got it open. The room was so packed with large compost bags, boxes of weedkiller and 5L bottles of pesticide that there was no hiding place. She too shrugged to the others.

Annabelle stepped towards the bedroom door. If there was an intruder, then this was the last hiding place possible. She hesitated, swapped weapons with Diane and then with Mrs Entwistle. Finally, she pushed the door open, raised the meat tenderiser and stepped inside.

After a while, Diane said, "Well?"

Annabelle opened her eyes.

The bedroom was devoid of intruders.

The three of them stood by the bed ready to pan, pin and tenderize.

"I feel somewhat foolish," Mrs Entwistle said.

"Nonsense," Diane said, "your lock has been forced."

"I know."

"You need to call the police," Annabelle said.

"Oh no," Mrs Entwistle replied, "they'll be far too busy with the murders. I wouldn't want to be a bother."

"It's breaking and entering," Diane said.

"Breaking," Mrs Entwistle said, "but not necessarily entering."

"Mrs Entwistle, Angela! For goodness' sake!"

"Brrrr," Annabelle said, suddenly.

"What?" Diane demanded.

"It's cold like someone has stepped over my grave."

"It shouldn't be, the heating's on," Mrs Entwistle said. "Wait, it's the window."

She went over and rattled it closed.

"Perhaps we frightened him away," Annabelle said.

Tiles from the bay window roof clattered and tumbled, shattering on the path outside. A deep voice swore and footsteps sounded on the paving.

"We have now," Diane said.

By the time they reached the window, the intruder had long taken to his heels.

"We should call the police," Diane said.

"No, no, no," Mrs Entwistle said. "I wouldn't want to be any trouble."

256

"But it was breaking *and entering.*"

"And exiting and breaking," Annabelle said. "Your bay window will need repairing."

"No, no," Mrs Entwistle insisted. "It's fine. Let's have a cup of tea."

And with that, Mrs Entwistle strode off down the stairs, creaking on the ninth and second steps leaving Diane and Annabelle to stare at each other in exasperation.

When they'd both creaked downstairs after her, they found Mrs Entwistle fussing in the kitchen with her phone.

"I'm glad you've seen sense," Diane said.

"Hello," Mrs Entwistle said into the handset, "I need a back door repaired, please..."

"Angela?"

"Ah, thank you, Conky Whallop, the cottage by the church, you can't miss it."

"Well, Angela," Diane said, "We must be off."

"Oh... yes, sorry," Annabelle said.

Mrs Entwistle let them out of the front door, opening it with the bulky set of keys.

"Do call again," Mrs Entwistle said, shutting the door. They heard the key turn and the bunch rattle.

"She's hiding something," Diane said.

"What was in the spare room?" Annabelle asked.

"Gardening supplies."

"Perhaps the man was trying to steal them."

"Hardly, it would have taken him several trips up and down those stairs," Diane said. "Mrs Entwistle can't have carried those bags upstairs."

"Couldn't she?"

"And she wouldn't," Diane added. "She'd have put them in her shed, surely?"

"They must be for her son."

"Why would he need to hide compost bags?"

"I don't know."

"Perhaps he's making explosives?"

"That's fertiliser, Di, not multi-purpose fast grow."

To return to the village, Diane and Annabelle had to go past the church. A forlorn notice flapped in the breeze held on by a single, rusty drawing pin. It announced a collection in memory of the late vicar, which seemed such a long time ago.

"I must go back to the shop," Annabelle said.

"And I've an idea to find a motive."

"A motive to kill someone!"

"No, a motive for someone else."

"Other than Mrs Entwistle, because she wouldn't murder the vicar."

"She had lilies ready."

"Oh, Di, honestly."

16. Legal Proceedings

So, Diane laid in wait, watching, observing, planning and ordering another flapjack. Her patience over two pots of tea was rewarded when Mr Tome made his way over the road to his old Mercedes.

Diane thanked Zara Pheasant, left the café and sauntered to the gap between Baxter's and Conkies. No-one noticed the black door unless they were in trouble.

The brass plaque announced 'Richards, Somerset and Tome – Solicitors'.

She buzzed.

"Yes?"

"Emrys, it's me."

"Who?"

"Diane."

"Who?"

"Miss Richards."

"Oh, yes."

The door buzzed angrily and Diane pushed it open, but it stayed locked.

"Emrys!"

"Yes."

It buzzed again and Diane gained access.

One of the reasons Diane retired was the steep staircase leading up to the reception. It was murder on the dodgy back. The solicitors had rooms above both Baxter's and Conkies. When she'd originally chosen her office, Diane had avoided the meat smells and gone for the gentle aromas of baking.

Emrys never left his desk, Diane thought. He had his hand out ready.

"I haven't brought any protest leaflets," Diane said.

"Oh. I see," Emrys said, taking his hand back. "Well, Miss Richards, Mr Tome isn't here."

"Isn't he? Oh dear. What a shame."

"He won't be back all day."

"Oh... that is a pity. Oh well. I've just a few things to check for one of my special clients."

"Just your special clients?"

"Of course."

These special clients consisted of Pat and Annabelle, nowadays, and their Last Wills and Testaments were pretty much fixed. Annabelle's was the only tricky one due to all the pensions from her various late husbands.

"That's fine," Emrys said. He looked as if he was about to rise, but no, he sank back into his leather office chair.

Diane went past him and into the office area. She checked her own room: the dust settling created a strangely reverent appearance. Solicitors should always reside in old rooms.

So, to business.

Someone... the curate, warden, flowers, teas, choir, organist or cleaning had to have a motive. Something legal that would stand up in court was what was needed.

She got the computer working and checked the names of the key holders systematically.

The curate was new to Conky Whallop and there was no mention of him in their records.

Frances Fairfax was also new, six months, and had asked about women's rights regarding inheritance. Tome had noted that he'd explained all about feminism to her, but she'd disagreed with his opinion. Oh, to have been a fly on the wall during that exchange.

Mrs Entwistle had enquired about avoiding death duties. Tome had advised giving money to her son in various amounts, but, apparently, Matthew Entwistle had been giving her money, so that had put the kybosh on that.

Mrs Jones had not consulted Richards, Somerset and Tome since they'd done a property search on her house. Was she still planning to move?

Mr Boseman had been in to arrange a power of attorney concerning his wife. Tome had done the paperwork, but that had been a few years ago.

Doctor Kovalyov had had several legal cases, but these all involved the squirrels, hornets and other run-ins with the Parish Council. His wife, Betty the organist, was not mentioned except as his next-of-kin.

Finally, the curate's wife was as absent in their records as the curate himself.

It was a dead end.

She checked Pendle-Took: there was the Reverend and Sir Victor. The vicar had made a new will very recently. Tome had drafted that. Sir Victor had consulted them briefly and then moved his business elsewhere. This was because the 'Richards' component of Richards, Somerset and Tome had led the campaign against his building work. Sir Victor had cited a conflict of interest, threatened them with the Bar Council and now he consulted Hickson, McEwan and McKenzie in Cambridge. They had proved remarkably adept and Conky Whallop was now graced with Sir Victor's design of an award-winning eyesore.

Diane drummed her fingers on her desk where she'd worn out the red leather.

There was nothing she could weave into a motive to kill the vicar. Unless the Reverend Pendle-Took had bullied the curate into avoiding lawyers, been misogynistic near Frances, given Mrs Entwistle money to increase her death duties, stopped Mrs Jones from moving, visited Mrs Boseman to turn her against her husband, claimed he was going to persuade the Parish Council to ban Kovalyov's experiment or had had a go at the curate's wife about her fashion sense.

It was hopeless.

Her investigations thwarted, Diane turned off her computer and went back to the reception area.

Emrys was not alone.

"Sir Victor!" Diane said, surprised.

Sir Victor Pendle-Took gazed at Diane with his penetrating eyes. His dark, saturnine features were the sort that made ladies weak at the knees. Diane's knees were made of sterner stuff, it was her back that always played up.

"Sir Victor is here to see Mr Tome," Emrys said.

"Are you?" Diane asked.

"Yes," Sir Victor said.

"Of course," Diane said. "Come in, come in."

"I thought you'd retired."

Emrys started to rise. "Miss Richards, I–"

"Yes, thank you, Emrys, that will be all," Diane said, waving him back before turning to Sir Victor. "Oh, I keep my hand in, particularly for our most important clients."

"I'm not your client," Sir Victor said. "Indeed, I–"

"Figure of speech. Tea?"

"No, thank you."

"Good, good."

In fact, very good. Emrys wouldn't leave his post to make something as trivial as a pot of tea, so there was no-one to make the tea. She led him into Tome's office, indicated the green leather of an expensive chair and sat herself behind the desk.

"Now," she said, "what can I do for you?"

"I'd like to see my brother's will."

"Your brother's will," Diane repeated, wondering where that might be kept.

"The Reverend George Philip Pendle-Took," Sir Victor said. "I'm his executor and you are his solicitor."

"Of course, of course."

She stood up and ambled to the filing cabinet. Under 'P' there was 'Pheasant versus Naseby' and a 'Naseby versus Pheasant', the latter there because 'N' could no longer accommodate any more 'Naseby versus Pheasant's.

"It's in the file box," Pendle-Took replied.

"Of course, of course," Diane replied, "I was checking for any codicils."

She found the box file on the shelf and Pendle-Took bravely reached up for it.

There were only a few sheets held by the nasty lock spring.

"Now," Diane said, "are you allowed to see this before the funeral?"

"Yes."

"Do you have a death certificate?"

Pendle-Took produced a sheet and Diane checked the facts.

"And proof of who you are, Sir Victor?"

"You know who I am," Pendle-Took replied. "We've known each other for years."

"Ah yes, but there's a matter of form."

Pendle-Took frowned and fished into his pockets. "Bank card?"

Diane shook her head.

"Golf club membership?"

Again, a shake.

"Membership of my professional association."

Diane took that... it had lapsed.

"This has lapsed."

"Oh for heaven's sake, Richards," Pendle-Took said. "With Hickson, McEwan and McKenzie, it's just a handshake."

"If your lodge would have women members."

"You're in the golf club now!"

"I rarely play given the eyesore that–"

"For God's sake, you can only see my house–"

"You call that a house."

"From the seventeenth and eighteenth and not from the street because of those damned hedges you and your protest committee insisted upon."

"You can–"

"Let's be professional," Pendle-Took said. He rose to his feet and shoved his hand out towards her.

Diane shook it, unaware of any strange grips or finger movements.

"There," Pendle-Took said, sitting back. "That wasn't so difficult."

"All right, I'll give you the highlights," Diane said. She glanced at the Will. "Let me see... this is a very recent will."

"Yes, I knew he'd changed it."

"Well, let's see... you are the executor, the bulk of his estate goes to the church fund and a – good heavens – large bequest to–"

"Yes, yes," Pendle-Took said. "I'm not interested in the money unless he's trying to fob me off with debt."

"Yes... no, I don't think that will be a worry."

"It's titles."

"Oh."

Diane went back to the top, took in the fancy curly font of *'Last Will and Testament'* – why, oh why, didn't they just use a typewriter? – and then scanned down more carefully.

"There's nothing about titles here."

"No bequests for siblings or offspring?"

"Off-spring! The Reverend?"

"Are there?"

Diane checked again. "No."

"Excellent, thank you," Sir Victor said. "As executor, I will need a copy of the will."

"Of course," Diane said. "Will that be–"

"Yes, thank you. Just bring it round to my house."

Pendle-Took stood, held out his hand, thought better of it and swept out.

Bring it round to his house!

The cheek.

She wasn't his errand boy.

She was a solicitor with her own office and her name on the brass plaque.

And what was all that really about?

Diane went over the will again, going over each word, but there was nothing about titles, siblings or offspring. The title of 'Reverend' wasn't something one could bequeath anyway.

Diane mulled this over as she returned the document to its rightful place via the photocopier. She needed to show Pat... although there was the issue of confidentiality. But Diane was retired, so perhaps she wasn't covered by that and she wasn't a practising solicitor anymore... as such.

However, there was the matter of the large bequest to Miss Frances Fairfax. That was a motive and the warden had a key.

She made two copies.

And Pendle-Took asking about off-spring – what was that about?

Perhaps he knew something about his brother that the rest of the village with all its interrogators, inquisitors, investigators and women's institute members had not discovered.

Something in the vicar's past before he came to Conky Whallop perhaps?

The Reverend George Philip Pendle-Took had been happier with his dusty books, afternoon naps and long interminable sermons than he had with the pleasures of the flesh.

But he had been young once.

Diane had been young once and had previously been able to skip down the blasted stairs without holding on to the banister like grim death.

17. The Game's Afoot

"Please, call me Vlad," the man said. "Vlad the Inventor."

He didn't look like an inventor. He looked more like a businessman, someone in finance, as he stood in the hall dressed in an expensive-looking three-piece double-breasted bespoke tailored suit with matching tie, the pinstripe as sharp as the seams.

Vlad led the way, marching stiffly to the front room and Kilroy followed.

"Please, sit down, Inspector."

"I'm a detective constable."

"Not an inspector?"

"No. Sorry."

Kilroy glanced around the piles of apparatus, boxes overflowing with equipment and wood stacked in the corner. A couch and one chair were the only furniture devoid of paraphernalia. When

Kilroy sat on the shabby sofa, he felt the creases transferring to his Mackintosh.

Vlad stood to attention by the comfortable armchair.

"Would you like to sit?" Kilroy said. Despite being in his own home, the man seemed ill at ease.

"I'd love to sit," Vlad said. He remained standing.

Kilroy took out his notebook and pen, and put them down on the coffee table amongst the collection of remote controls. Engineering blueprints hung on the wall, framed and at odds with pastel wallpaper: blue and white precision versus red and pink impressionism.

"I am hated by the village, you know," Vlad said.

"I didn't."

"Because of a minor infestation problem."

"Oh yes?"

"We had a few pigeons in the garden and it's... As an inventor, it's my calling to identify a need and create a solution."

"That sounds... wise."

"So, I created a device to turn these flying vermin into pigeon and mixed nut pie."

"Pigeon and mixed nut?"

"The oils in hazelnuts, walnuts and almonds produce a lubricant that solved a sticking problem with the mechanism. Pure pigeon pie came out more like a flan."

"I see."

"But the pigeons needed to position themselves above the vertical scoop. I engineered a ledge. But they wouldn't," Vlad said, raising one hand and making a fist with the other. Then he realised that he didn't have a screen or a remote for any PowerPoint, so he lowered his hands again. "I devised a way of enticing them into position. However, the bait became a readily available food source, which unfortunately increased the pigeon infestation."

"That would be a problem."

"And the machine worked so well – it was a success – that the pigeon and nut pies overflowed the hopper, and that attracted a lot of rats."

"Ah."

"And squirrels."

"Squirrels are nice."

"Not in the numbers that appeared."

"Ah."

"And those philistines in the Parish Council won't allow the machine to be perfected. It's typical of the religious to hold back progress. You've seen the backward types I have to deal with," Vlad said, waving a stiff arm in the general direction of the village.

"There are other things you could invent."

"I have," Vlad said. "For example, this is my crease-free suit."

"I could do with one of those for my coat."

"Hmmm, yes, a Mackintosh. It would no longer be waterproof, but it would be easier to get on and off."

"It's already easy to get on and off."

"I meant in comparison to this suit."

"Ah."

Kilroy eyed the militarily erect inventor in a new light.

"How did you get it on then?" Kilroy asked.

"I invented an auto valet."

"Can't it take it off again?"

"Of course!" – Vlad relented – "It's simply that the suit prevents me from bending over to reach the controls."

"I could help."

"No need, I've nearly finished building a robot butler that will be quite capable of operating the auto valet."

Kilroy's expression seemed unconvinced.

"These are just bugs to be ironed out," Vlad said.

"Or not ironed out, if it never creases."

"No, they will be ironed... oh, humour. Yes. I see. *Ahem*. Very droll."

"You have a gun licence."

"Yes."

"Can you tell me about your firearms?"

"No."

"But you do have a thirty-eight and a machine gun."

"I'm not at liberty, you understand."

"Because it's a defence contract?"

"I can't say, but it would be if the fools at the Ministry of Defence would green-light the funding."

"Where are the guns now?"

"Locked in the garage safe."

"Can you show me?"

"I'm afraid not."

"I'm a police officer, so you can rely on my discretion regarding any defence contract."

"I still can't because I installed an anti-theft device of my own design and, when testing it, I sealed the safe in a polymer resin."

"I see."

"The smell was terrible."

"Ah."

"No, it's a selling point. The stench will drive away potential thieves."

"Yes, I can see that," Kilroy said. "I will still have to take the guns in for checking. Ballistics and the cartridges."

"Oh, very well, I'll start the dissolving process."

"When will that be complete?"

"Seventy-two hours."

"Right... then let me know when I can send someone round to collect them."

"Very well."

Kilroy handed him a card, which Vlad attempted to put into his top pocket but the suit jacket's elbow wouldn't bend enough. Kilroy took his card back and left it on the coffee table.

"Is that all?" Vlad asked.

"I wanted to ask you about your wife."

"Betty? What about her?"

"Well–"

"Very understanding woman."

"I simply want to confirm where she was on Wednesday evening?" Kilroy said. "It's perfectly routine."

"Checking everyone's alibi, eh? No problem with Betty. She was at choir practice. Every Monday and Wednesday."

"She sings?"

"No, screeches like an owl, but she plays the piano," Vlad explained. "She's the church organist too. I don't go myself, it's a lot of superstitious nonsense, but she seems to like it."

"The church choir?"

"That's it."

"I thought the church choir had been disbanded."

"No."

"Well, there we are then," Kilroy said. He checked his notebook: SUV undamaged, he'd checked it before ringing the doorbell, and firearms unavailable until Friday. "In that case, I won't take up any more of your time. Mondays and Wednesdays from?"

"Seven," Vlad said. "I use the opportunity to work on my fried-egg-on-toast maker, mark three."

"Does that work?"

"Not exactly."

"Ah. Well. Er," Kilroy said. They'd reached the front door and Vlad stood stiffly to one side. "If you'd let me know about the guns."

!!!

The gun's blast ricocheted off Kilroy's car. He ducked.

"And stay away!"

"Major Naseby!" Kilroy shouted as he crouched down further.

"I'll call the police!"

"I am the police."

"What?"

"I'm the police."

"Speak up, man."

"I'm investigating the recent deaths in Conky Whallop," Kilroy shouted, louder now. "I'm Detective Constable Kilroy."

"Rubbish."

"I assure you, I am."

"They'd send an inspector, surely?"

"No, sir, it's a common fallacy that inspectors investigate all murders."

"Are you sure?"

"Yes."

"Well, what do you want?"

"I want to ask you about your shotgun."

"I've got a licence."

"Yes, I know."

"Then what's the problem?"

"Can I stand up, please?"

"I don't know, can you?"

"Without being shot!"

Major Naseby shouldered his shotgun, so Kilroy risked standing and moved around his car, although he kept his hands raised until he was sure it was safe.

His SUV had scrapes and pockmarks on it, bright silver gashes that stood out despite the silver paintwork.

"You've put dents in my car!"

The major glanced at the shining, but peppered car. "A bit of hammering'll get that out."

284

"No, it won't."

"Get a Land Rover then."

"What are you doing with your shotgun out anyway?"

"Pheasant."

"It's not the shooting season."

"No, Pheasant," the major insisted, "bloody woman's been stealing my apples again."

"Sorry. Pheasants carrying off apples?"

"Zara Pheasant. Lives in the village."

"Oh."

"Well, come in, detective, if you are coming in."

The major led the way into his manor house, a quaint timber-framed two-storey building with a wing that leaned alarmingly. Kilroy followed, wiping his shoes on the welcome mat.

"What are you doing that for?" the major asked. "You a cissy?"

"No... I... I wanted to ask you if any shotgun cartridges had gone missing."

"What for?"

"Routine procedure."

"Pah!"

The major stopped by a cupboard in the kitchen. On top of the big pine table, pine worksurfaces and pine chairs were dirty plates stacked like a crockery version of Jenga.

"Box here," said the major. "Should be forty. Just bought 'em."

The major lent his shotgun against the wall in the corner and started removing his scarf and gloves. The man had a ruddy complexion that testified to clean outdoor living and neat indoor drinking.

Kilroy examined the drawer to find two boxes of shotgun shells, each with twenty cartridges. One was still wrapped in cellophane and the other was open. There was space for a four-by-five grid of shells.

There were obvious gaps.

286

"There are three missing," Kilroy said.

"What?"

"I said–"

"Don't stand there," the major said, "I'm deaf on my right side for some reason."

"Could that be because you're always firing your gun?"

"What?"

"Could that... there are THREE MISSING."

"Fired one over your car as a warning shot."

"Warning shot? It hit–"

"And there's another in the second barrel."

The major popped his shotgun open, removed the spent cartridge and dropped it in a bin. It hesitated on the peak of the rubbish and then fell on the floor amongst the other detritus.

"That's two. What about the third?"

"There can't be an odd number," Naseby said, "obviously... two barrels. Stands to reason."

"Look for yourself."

The major harrumphed over and glanced down: "There! See! Ah!"

"One's missing," Kilroy said.

"Yes. Blasted nuisance. Wait a moment."

The major took the unspent cartridge from his shotgun and slotted it into the box.

"There! Even number. Much better."

"I'll take one as evidence," Kilroy said. He slipped one out and placed it in his Mackintosh pocket.

"Suit yourself... oh, blast, it's gone back to being an odd number."

"Sorry."

One in the bin, one in his pocket and that was an odd number, so, one missing. Could this explain the infamous shotgun pellet that somehow poisoned the curate?

"Do you have many visitors?"

"Not many."

"Why does that not surprise me," Kilroy said quietly.

"What?"

"Any visitors in the past few weeks?"

"People from the church down in Conky Whallop."

"Who exactly?"

"Curate, late Wednesday night," Major Naseby said. "Some stuff and nonsense about thou shalt not kill, but he admitted that thou shalt not steal is also a commandment."

"Thou shalt not kill?"

"The Pheasant woman."

"Anyone else?"

"I only want to kill the Pheasant woman."

"No, I mean, any other visitors?"

"Other women."

"Other women?"

"I don't know, they all look alike," the major said. "That Entwistle woman, that curate's wife, Betty... married a Russian, you know, and Richards."

"Diane Richards?"

"How would I know?"

Kilroy glanced at the shotgun leaning against the wall.

"You should lock that up?"

"Why?"

"It's a legal requirement and someone might steal it."

"No-one'll steal that," the major said, "I've got a shotgun. I'd shoot 'em."

"You can't shoot people."

"Why not? Free country."

"No, you can't, it's against the law."

"Someone nicks your property," the major said, "bang-bang. They don't do it again. Reasonable force is quite legal, I assure you."

"Not if... no."

"A man's got a right to protect his apples."

"You can't shoot Zara Pheasant."

"Why not?"

"She's not in season."

Kilroy checked the major's Land Rover, which showed dents, bumps, dings, hammering and scrapes galore, but none with red moped paint.

!!!

Sir Victor Pendle-Took was not in, despite extensive bell ringing.

Kilroy had a look round the modern, architecturally interesting building. It was (he had looked it up) a fine example of country brutalism, a new movement intent on overturning the idea of fitting in with the surroundings and instead, dominating the setting. This design movement was typified

291

by sweeping driveways, poured concrete, steel cantilevered balconies and protest campaigns.

At the back – and he didn't need a warrant as he was simply checking to see if Pendle-Took was sitting on a veranda – was a building site. Concrete mixers and hardcore stood ready to fill a large excavation to create a huge patio that would resemble the South Bank building, the old Birmingham Library or a Second World War bunker.

No-one was around.

No fancy SUV was parked on the sweeping driveway.

He peered inside at the vast auditorium of open plan living and shivered. Pendle-Took was obviously loaded. For a start, his heating bill alone would be more than a detective constable's salary.

When Kilroy walked back to the front, someone else came towards him up the drive, a tall man, blond with piercing blue eyes.

"Are you Sir Victor Pendle-Took?" Kilroy asked.

"Nej, are you?"

"No, I'm Kilroy, Detective Constable." Kilroy held up his ID.

"Ja."

The man had been in the act of reaching into his jacket for his own ID, but he changed his mind.

"And you are?" Kilroy asked.

"Ande, er... I am... Jack Ketch."

"Oh?"

"I am a mördare... er, mechanic for executing the building work."

"I see... he's not in."

"Ja." The man paused as if he didn't know what to do and then added, "Tack."

They both left together, but turned in different directions to go to their cars. As Kilroy drove away, he saw the other man shaking his head to a colleague in a silver Saab. They both looked similar, tall and blond... they could be brothers, Kilroy thought, even twins.

The Saab was still parked, when Kilroy
turned the corner and made for the A-road.

On the way home, Kilroy stopped at an off-
licence, but thought better of it and decided
to have an early night.

18. Murder in the Dark

In her head, Diane rehearsed exactly the right pithy phrase for the piece of her mind that she would most certainly give him. Bring it round – honestly?

And at this time of night as well.

Although to be fair, she had delayed bringing the Will round until it was that time of the night. Late enough to cause real annoyance when she rang the doorbell, but not too late that she couldn't get home to be in bed with a hot toddy, a hot water bottle and a hot detective in another episode of a dark Scandi crime drama. She hadn't been sleeping well recently, binge-watching until the English dawn disturbed the Nordic noir.

The clouds parted and the moonlight was surprisingly bright when she reached the monstrosity of failing words that was the award-winning architect's abomination of a house.

Won a Design Award – madness!

She took a breather against his hedge when she arrived. She still had to storm across the vastness of his brick driveway with enough vim left to drive her sharp words home.

She knew that the vicar had included Frances Fairfax, the warden, in his will. Something she was sure the vicar's brother, Sir Victor, would have an opinion about, surely? She'd ask in a roundabout way.

A pair of stone gargoyles guarded the gate and, as soon as she crossed the threshold, a security light caught her in its sudden glare.

Diane threw her hand in front of her face and had to look away, down at her feet. Two immense shadows boxed across her sensible shoes, struggling with each other.

With a premonition trickling down her spine like icy water, Diane stepped to one side and hid behind the pristine and undamaged metallic green SUV.

Something metal clattered to the floor.

A swear word, but in a foreign language.

She heard the oomph and kerfuffle of a struggle.

For all her righteous anger, she suddenly wanted to be home with an Ovaltine and an episode of a safe, cosy mystery – a *Father Brown* perhaps – that was well lit and had the politeness to stay behind the flat panel of her television.

Diane risked a glance.

The security light went dark.

She could see absolutely nothing in the pitch black.

Flash!

The flame leapt horizontally, briefly illuminating two men frozen in the moment of killing and death.

Diane felt, more than heard, the thud of the explosion.

Flash-BANG.

Flash-BANG.

Gunshots, unmistakeably.

She half-expected a theme tune, but these were real. At the side of the house, out of range of the motion detectors, a man had shot and killed another man.

Diane ducked back behind the comforting bulk of the SUV, but her movement caused the security light to activate again.

A patch of daytime appeared in the driveway.

"Is anyone there?"

Diane stayed still even though she was bent over and her back would give her jip come tomorrow.

A footstep sounded upon the brick herringbone weave.

Another.

"Who's there?"

Any moment, he'd round the vehicle and she'd be discovered.

Diane mustered all her courage to cry out: "*Meeooow.*"

The pause lengthened.

Perhaps she should have tried a fox?

She was struck by how quiet it was in the village, how silent and still without the hubbub of traffic and people. Those damned hedges she'd campaigned for blocked out any chance of calling for help. Three ear-splitting gunshots and no-one came running to see, no triangle of twinkling nosiness beamed out from a curtain-twitch and no flashing blue lights materialised.

The man snorted.

His footsteps became rapid and, thankfully, receded.

The security light went out, throwing a comforting blanket of darkness over everything.

Diane dared not move.

She heard, distantly, the ghastly noises of a man struggling to drag a body. A wooden gate banged, open... closed, and then the sounds became muffled.

Thinking it safe, but with a plaintive *meow*, Diane scooted through the dazzle of the security light, around the stone gargoyle and down Orthodox Crescent so quickly that she was down by Brighter Avenue before her thoughts had a chance to catch up with her.

She had recognised the voice: Sir Victor Pendle-Took.

But who had he just shot?

!!!

"Yes, yes," Pat said, tying her dressing gown cord and opening her front door.

Diane was standing flustered in the porch.

"Pa..." she managed.

"Come in."

Such was Diane's agitation and Pat's concern, that she kept her shoes on all the way to the drawing-room.

"Sit down, Diane."

"Yes, no and yes."

"Yes?"

"Sorry... habit... sit down, not sherry, but a whisky."

"Oh."

Pat fetched a whisky.

Diane gulped it down.

"Pen–" but Diane started coughing as some of the blend went down the wrong way.

"Deep breath, Di."

Diane breathed and then swallowed.

"I've just seen Pendle-Took–"

"Sir Victor?"

"Yes... how many Pendle-Tooks do you know?"

"There's the vicar... oh! Go on."

"I saw him kill someone."

Pat was taken aback. "Really?"

Diane mimed with her finger: "Bang-bang."

"Really?"

"Actually, bang-bang-bang... he fired three times."

"With a gun?"

"Yes, Pat, with an actual gun, and not with a cap gun, a staple gun or a water pistol, but a real one."

"A thirty-eight?"

"What? No idea. It was big, it went bang, I didn't stay around."

"It's just that it might be the gun that didn't kill Mrs Boseman."

"What? I don't know."

"Di, whom did he kill?"

"I've no idea."

"Why not?"

"It was dark."

"Perhaps you were confused and didn't really see anything because it was dark."

"Pat," Diane said, warningly. "I know what I saw and heard. He shot someone, the fire from the gun lit up everything..."

"And?"

302

"I saw... yes, I saw a man, I knew it was a man, and he was... tall."

"A tall man?" Pat mulled this over. "Mr Boseman?"

"Tall and thin."

"That would be... hmm, country life doesn't produce many thin people."

"The curate's wife is thin."

"She hasn't been in the country long enough and she's a woman."

"Oh yes."

"What were you doing there anyway, Di?"

"I was delivering the vicar's Will," Diane said, handing over the crumpled photocopy.

A thought struck Pat. "You don't have an alibi for this murder either."

"Don't start," Diane said. "I don't have a gun and I'm not a tall, thin man."

"That's the victim," Pat said. "You said Sir Victor killed a tall, thin man."

"Yes, that's it," Diane said.

"I wonder if it's connected to any of the other murders?"

"When we started investigating, I thought it would be like the television. Rosemary and Thyme, Tommy and Tuppence, Hetty Wainthropp – I endeavour to watch a broadchurch – but that's just pie in the sky. I'd give it up in a heartbeat," Diane said, waving her glass to request another measure. "Killing isn't cosy murder."

"And the vicar being stabbed in the back is cosy murder, is it?"

"That's not what I meant."

"It's what you said."

"Sorry. I feel guilty about that."

"We have to tell the police."

"Do we have to?"

"You saw a murder and... Di, this is important," Pat leaned forward to gain Diane's full attention. She put her hand on Diane's and stopped her glass from trembling. "This time, we know the identity of the murderer."

!!!

To say Detective Constable Kilroy was unhappy was an understatement, but he was also too tired and bleary-eyed to care.

He sat upon Mrs Thomas's sofa in his mismatched socks, one inside-out.

"...and so, we rang you," Miss Richards finished explaining.

"You did give me your card," Mrs Thomas added.

Kilroy nodded, understanding: there was no way, what with five murders, that he'd stay on the case. A detective sergeant would be assigned and Kilroy would be making mugs of tea in the portable incident room.

Or they'd send a full inspector, which would be far worse. Someone like Inspector Raymond and Kilroy would be running errands and collecting dry cleaning.

All those people who had doubted that a mere detective constable could solve the case, all those fans of Inspector Morse, Inspector Frost, Inspector Dalglish, Inspector Rebus, Inspector Etcetera... inspector, inspector, inspector... they'd be right. He'd have failed on his first case and it would forever be a black stain on his record. How many successes would he need before this would cease to count when new cases were assigned? He'd never achieve a 100% record now.

"So?" Miss Richards said.

But there was a way, Kilroy realised – all he had to do was solve the case. The Chief of the Precinct in his mind slammed his fist down upon the table and gave the maverick cop 24 hours, otherwise, it was back to traffic.

"I'll go to Pendle-Took's and have a look," he said.

"Do be careful," Mrs Thomas said.

"You don't want us to come with you," Miss Richards said. It was a statement, not a question.

"There's no need," Kilroy replied. "You stay here and I'll be fine."

He sat on the stairs to put on his left shoe and he realised that 24 hours was probably generous: the imaginary chief would only give him 12 hours.

And as he put on his right shoe, he realised that 12 hours was also optimistic. He checked his watch: 23:15. The night shift had logged the case as the old ladies had rung the Foal Lane number on the card and the next shift started at 07:00, but an eager inspector might be in at 06:00.

He had six hours, maybe seven, to sort out nearly half-a-dozen murders.

Resolved, he double-knotted his shoelaces.

Despite the short distance, he drove.

In the warmth of his car, he had a chance to think and it all began to fit together. He'd been so stupid not to figure it out earlier. Pendle-Took with a gun fitted the murder of Mrs Boseman, so Pendle-Took must have shot her, poisoned the curate, run over the moped delivery rider without scratching his paintwork and stabbed his brother, the vicar.

Although there were a couple of details that would need clarifying.

There was the question of the church key, *that damned key*, but wait! The vicar had a key and Pendle-Took could have copied it.

Kilroy slowed down as he reached the architect's modern building, a brooding dark shadow lit by the full moon and the feeble street lights. He parked down the road and popped open his boot. Inside, he had a stab vest and utility belt. He put these on, careful to make sure they fitted correctly and conscious that the Velcro ripping made an alarmingly loud sound.

He took three steps towards the foreboding scene and common sense made a fleeting appearance.

"This is DC Kilroy," he said to his phone once he'd connected to the police station. "I'm at Dundraftin, Orthodox Road, Conky Whallop— Yes, that village and I suspect a shooting. Send backup... yes... no, I can manage... sorry, you're breaking up, signal f– f–ailing."

He hung up, readied his torch and moved forward to confront a man armed with what the witness had described as a 'bloody big gun'.

308

Suddenly, something savage loomed over him caught briefly in the torchlight. Kilroy came face-to-face with a monster.

It was a stone creature, some sort of contorted ape holding its head as if in pain. Another statue crouched on the other gatepost with its hands over its eyes as if embarrassed by the owner's lack of taste.

The driveway beyond was huge, a vast desert of interlocked brickwork.

He shone his beam over the dark shape of the SUV and green metallic paint glinted.

The space was empty otherwise.

He stepped–

"Arrghhh."

The security light was stupidly bright.

He stumbled forward and came to the side of the house. This had to be where Miss Richards said she had seen the struggle and gunshots.

He checked the ground and–

"For... hell."

The light had gone off and Kilroy couldn't see a thing.

Maybe he should wait for backup.

No, he would solve this on his own.

He got his torch working again and scanned the ground. There was nothing, except a tinge of oily dampness from a recent shower.

The triple garage stood apart from the house and in between the buildings, a gate stood closed.

He tried it – the latch clicked up.

On the other side, a garden disappeared into the gloom and a vast concrete patio spread out in front of him. There was evidence of building work. Stacks of bricks and pallets of hardcore make the ominous scene more like the battlefields of the Somme or Ypres than a landscaped garden. Mind you, thought Kilroy, given the country brutalism of the main house, perhaps this was deliberate.

He stepped in something damp and he sank into it.

The patio was wet cement.

He slurped his ruined shoe out of it, shook his foot and spread a damp Pollock of mess.

"Oh, for... hell."

He shone his torch about the garden, perhaps seeing eyes reflecting the light. Foxes or cats maybe? He tried the French windows, but they were locked, so he shone his torch inside, scanning back and forth. His beam touched a shape on the floor, pink and bloated with wide eyes stared back at him.

A woman cried out!

Kilroy reacted, his training coming to the fore. He grabbed the handle, slipped due to the cement on his shoe and fell to the floor. His head connected with the glass and the A++ triple-glazed Krypton proved unforgiving.

The woman screamed again and again.

Kilroy saw red dots waving about and finally resting on his chest.

"Tango One... target acquired... permission to engage!"

"What! No, no, please, I'm police," Kilroy shouted, dropping his torch and showing the palms of his hands.

"Get on the floor!"

"I am on the floor. I'm police, I'm–"

"Get on the floor!"

"DC Kilroy."

"Get on the floor!"

"The woman... help her."

"Get on the floor."

Kilroy kept his hands up and struggled to his knees. The firearms officer jumped forward, pushed him down into the squelch of wet cement.

"Stay down!"

"Tango Two to Tango One," a voice crackled over the radio. "In the house now. Dead body. Room one, clear. Hall now."

"Kilroy, Detective Constable."

"Where's your warrant card!"

"In my inside pocket."

"Roll over!"

Kilroy did so, realising that his Mackintosh was now taking the brunt of the grey, sticky filth.

"See, I'm–"

The firearms officer, Tango One, grabbed it off him.

"Ground floor, clear," the radio announced. "Heading upstairs."

"DC Kilroy!" Tango One said.

"Yes, I tried to explain and–"

"What are you doing here?"

"Waiting for backup."

"We're backup."

"I know!"

What was going on in the house, Kilroy wondered: dead body, firearms officers ignoring the screaming woman – she screamed and screamed!

"Upstairs, clear! Bright pink bathroom!"

Kilroy struggled to his feet aware that Tango One was just standing there, his Heckler and Koch MP5 dangling carelessly from his shoulder, its red laser sight flickering across the floor as if a demented pet owner was tormenting kittens.

Someone was laughing, a kind of evil cackling that haunted Kilroy with its knowing mockery, a sound louder than the gasps of the woman.

"It's Killjoy, all right," said an all too familiar voice, DC Wragg. "Checks firearms for a poisoning and calls in the armed police for an accident."

"The man was shot," Kilroy insisted.

"No gunshot wound," DC Wragg said, stepping through the French windows and back into the garden. "He fell over backwards, mate."

314

Kilroy snatched his warrant card back from Tango One and traipsed cement footprints across the cream carpet of the crime scene.

Sir Victor Pendle-Took lay on his back, naked and with a peculiar expression on his face to go with the plastic bag over his head.

"Impaled on the fireplace spike," the policeman said.

"I can see that," Kilroy snapped.

The fireplace fender had a matching spike at each end, a fleur-de-lys carving: the left one had a body stuck on it.

"He was watching porn," the officer said. "Must have got excited and fallen over backwards."

"Yes, I can see that."

Two lesbians continued to gasp and cry out on the huge, widescreen opposite the fireplace.

"Can you turn that off?" Kilroy asked.

"We're just getting to the good bit."

"Turn it off!"

"Killjoy."

316

19. Black Bag

Bags had been left in the shop doorway –
again.

Why did people do that?

People might steal them.

Not in Conky Whallop, obviously.

Annabelle sighed as she often did. The other
shopkeepers were opening up: Baxter the
Butcher rattled his shutters open, Celia put
out displays and Conkies started their ovens.
Chiang's were quiet as their business didn't
open until lunchtime. Breakfast was served
at Pheasant's café.

The black obstacles meant that Annabelle
had to reach to put her key in the lock and
then step over them to put her foot on the
welcome mat.

She switched the lights on and fussed at the
counter before going to the backroom to
turn on the kettle. The cups were
mismatched, lonely orphaned survivors from
broken sets donated over the years. One

good cup amongst others rejected for the chips on their shoulders.

Once the red light was on, Annabelle resolved to get the black bags in as soon as possible. She heaved them over the welcome mat, two at a time as they had big knots – easy to grip, but tricky to untie.

The bric-a-brac went on a shelf. She found a home for unloved teapots, old plastic toys, DVDs and even a vintage VHS tape. The latter went into a bin along with a thought that they'd eventually appear on *Antiques Roadshow.* Perhaps she had already thrown away something that would be worth millions.

Clothes went on the table: a man's jacket, a shirt, trousers, Calvin Kleins, socks and shoes... a full set.

The kettle clicked off.

She added milk and sugar. She'd had to buy a new bottle of milk on the way in today.

Revived, she checked the clothes and found a tear in the jacket. In the olden days, this would have been repairable and repaired. Perhaps, she thought, she could darn it and no-one would notice, but then she saw the stain around the rip. It would need cleaning too and a sale never covered the cost of dry cleaning.

The shirt was ruined as well, torn at the back in the same place as the jacket, although its stain was far more noticeable. A dark red smear had spread out as if someone had made a hole using a ketchup bottle and the lid had come off.

She took her cup and saucer through to the shop itself and happened to walk past the bookshelf. Romance and crime thrillers vied for space – hearts broken and mended, hearts stabbed and murdered.

"Oh!"

The cup and saucer tumbled from her hands, tea spiralling down to splash on the floor. The crockery bounced, rising intact, but fracturing when it hit the ground again. Sharp shards lay on the steaming carpet.

One more crockery pair for the dustpan and brush, and burial in the bin.

She tiptoed back to the storeroom.

The stains on the shirt were obvious.

She'd seen blood before.

And a dead body – the vicar recently, her father, mother, two husbands, friends and many others during that incident in the Far East all those years ago.

The shirt had an ordinary collar: the vicar had nothing but shirts with dog collars, Sergio had worn bright t-shirts or his delivery polo-shirt uniform, Mrs Boseman had worn a blouse and, finally, the curate had worn dog collars like the vicar.

She went to the phone on the counter, dialled Pat's number and waited for an answer, all the time entwining the curly cord around her fingers.

"Pat?"

"Yes."

"Sorry, but there's been another murder!"

"Indeed, Diane witnessed–"

"Here in the shop."

"Oh."

320

Pat came round straight away.

Thank goodness for retirement, Annabelle thought, glad that her friend lived so close and only needed to grab a cashmere scarf and folding stick to be out of the door.

Annabelle took Pat to the back room and even flipped the sign to say they were closed.

"Diane saw Sir Victor shoot someone," Pat explained, "and now I hear–"

"Hear?"

"Not gossip."

"Of course, Pat, go on."

"Yes, well, I hear... was informed by Detective Constable Kilroy that Sir Victor is dead."

"Oh," Annabelle said, "but no, this is another one."

"Another one, Belle?"

"Yes."

"Who is it?"

"I don't know."

"Where's the body?"

"Here."

"These are clothes."

"Look at the rip and the blood on the shirt."

"Oh yes," Pat said, "just like the vicar."

"You mean... in the back?"

"Yes."

"Oh dear."

"The jacket is expensive," Pat said, examining the evidence, "well-made, double-breasted, not designer, tasteful... no tie."

"Does that matter?"

"A tie might reveal their regiment–"

"Major Nasby."

"Or golf club."

"Sir Victor Pendle-Took."

"Or university."

"Doctor Kovalyov."

"Or seminary."

"The vicar!"

"Wrong sort of collar."

"Oh yes. Sorry."

Pat switched her attention to the jacket's pockets, but they had nothing but lint. Next, she tried the trouser pockets, again nothing.

"There's grey dust on the shins and knees," Pat noted.

"Pat, what about the shirt pocket?"

"No-one leaves anything in a shirt pocket," Pat said, checking the breast pocket and sure enough there was nothing... wait!

Her fingers touched a scrumpled wad of paper.

"What is it?" Annabelle asked.

"Looks like a piece of a letter," Pat said. She showed it to Annabelle. "It's smudged."

"Oh dear."

"I can't make it out even with my glasses," Pat said peering through her half-moon spectacles.

"Wait! We've that detective game."

Annabelle rushed into the shop and came back with a large, board game. With practised expertise, she sliced the Sellotape with her nail and took out the contents: cards, dice, board and finally, a magnifying glass.

"Ah-ha! Perfect, Belle."

"Elementary, my dear Holmes."

Annabelle set about reading the paper using her sharp eyes, a pair of reading glasses at 50p and the magnifying glass.

"It says..." Annabelle said, squinting, "...Na report... match... bother!"

"Shall I try?"

"No, it actually says 'bother'."

"Oh."

"Bother assist… there's a letter I can't make out."

"What are they?"

"Pat, if I knew the letter, I'd just say it."

"I meant, do it like a crossword. You know, 'A' something, 'B' something."

"Oh, right… 'B' something 'other'… 'A' something something, then 'S', 'I', 'S', 'T', something, something."

"Brother and sister."

"Oh, yes, 'na report match brother and sister."

"Are the letters 'N' and 'A' in capitals."

"Yes."

"DNA match."

"Oh, you are clever, Pat. Yes, that's it."

"These clothes belonged to someone who had a sister and they had a DNA test to prove the relationship."

"Which one, the brother or the sister?"

"It's a man's jacket."

"Oh yes."

"Someone's dead," Pat said, summing up, "and we've no idea who."

"And we still haven't solved any of the other murders."

"Well, yes, quite."

"Perhaps a list might help organise your thoughts, Pat."

"I've made lists," Pat snapped, "and even a list of the lists."

"Cup of tea, Pat?"

"How's that going to help! Oh... I'm sorry, Belle."

"It's all right."

"We'll have to tell that nice detective about these clues," Pat said. "He didn't come back the other night."

"No... I have hot chocolate."

"That would be lovely."

326

Annabelle went back to the back room with its kitchen and began fiddling with the kettle, cups and so forth. She had to go back to the shop to find a new cup. Pat watched her friend and it made her wonder about poisoning.

Pat kept her eye on the new cup as it travelled about, hot chocolate added, kettle bubbling and wondered... but the curate was in charge of the chalice the entire time.

"Someone poisoned the cup after the Body and Blood of Christ," she said aloud.

"Is that blasphemy?" Annabelle asked.

"How?"

"How it's blasphemy or how was it done?"

"It's a mortal sin to kill and murder is one of the ten commandments."

"Thou shalt not kill," Annabelle said as she added the water.

"But how was it done?" Pat said, taking the offered hot chocolate and letting its cup warm her hands.

"When we prayed at the altar rail," Annabelle said, "everyone was kneeling and everyone had their eyes closed. Perhaps someone snuck over the rail, slipped something into the cup and then crept back."

"The curate would have seen them," Pat replied. "Betty the organist would have seen them. She would have been watching in her mirror for her cue to change music. And the entire congregation was watching that nice detective constable included."

"Oh, yes... Betty herself?"

"She waits until everyone has left."

"Oh, Pat, maybe she didn't."

"She did, because she didn't make a noise like a kettle boiling."

"Gurgle-gurgle click?"

"No, a whistle," Pat said. "To get out of her seat, she has to use the last pedal as a step."

They went back into the shop area and tested one of the coffee tables that were for

328

sale. Annabelle found a set of six coasters with seascapes on them. Outside it was sunny and peaceful looking, and the Cadbury Fairtrade Bournville hot chocolate was particularly strong and almost took their minds off the five murders.

Tap-tap-tap!

"Huh?"

20. Red Handed

"It's Mrs Entwistle," Diane said through the letterbox.

She tapped on the window again, disturbing their hot chocolate, with woodpecker rapidity before Annabelle had opened the door.

Once they were together in the back of the shop, Diane repeated her accusation. "It's Mrs Entwistle."

"What has she done now?" Pat asked.

"She murdered the vicar and the curate."

"The vicar and the curate?" Pat asked. "Why?"

"She hates clergymen."

"Are you sure you're not suffering from shock?"

"No, of course not."

"And she's not likely to have killed Mrs Boseman."

"The wife of a choirmaster."

"Or Sergio."

"Perhaps he was considering becoming a monk."

"Sergio!"

"I don't know, I don't know," Diane admitted, "but she's up to something. She's acting very suspiciously. Belle and I went to her house and she wouldn't report her broken door."

"Well, quite."

"Look, Sir Victor shot someone–"

"Which the police–"

"And Frances Fairfax inherits from the vicar."

"Does she? Why?"

"I don't know."

"So Sir Victor–"

"Perhaps Mrs Entwistle was going around to Sir Victor's to clean," Diane insisted. "So, she'll know something."

"She won't have murdered anyone."

"But she's seen something."

"You've already been round to her house," Pat said.

"It's not her house, we should search," Diane said, "but her son's house."

"Well, we do need to report these bloody – sorry, Belle – clothes to that nice detective," Pat said.

"There's no time," Diane insisted. "She might hide the evidence."

"Well, yes, I suppose so."

"Belle?"

"I have to look after the shop," Annabelle said, quickly. "Sorry."

"That settles it," Diane said. "Come on, Pat."

And Pat had no choice but to obey her chief editor.

332

However, before they could collect their coats, bags and walking stick, the doorbell rang. The curate's wife came in dressed in a little black number from Selfridges with a designer black jacket, black scarf and black millinery with a fishnet veil. She carried a black Dolce bag and a black, ultra-thick waste bag with ties.

"Belle," she wailed. "These. Oh, I can't bear it. Take them."

"Oh dear," Annabelle said.

"Thank you," the curate's wife said. "I'm all over the place, I mean. A widow. At my age. Look at me! Just look. Gucci with Balenciaga."

"Oh dear," Annabelle said.

"You look lovely," Pat said. "Di?"

"You–"

"Yes, Di, doesn't she?"

"Yes. It's a great loss."

"Well, thank you," the curate's wife said. "Terrible. These are… well, some of his things."

She dumped the black bag on the counter.

"You're getting rid of a lot," Diane observed.

"Needs must," the curate's wife said. "I can no longer bear it here. London beckons."

"Are you suffering?" Pat asked.

"Everything's turned into a blur," the curate's wife said.

"Oh dear."

"It's terrible," the curate's wife continued. "I've had to wear waterproof mascara and my contacts just fall out."

"Oh dear."

"Belle, please, could you be a dear in my hour of suffering?"

"Of course," Annabelle said.

"I've more of these disgusting bags. Could you pop round and collect them for me?"

"Oh... sorry, but they are quite heavy."

"Pat and Di can help you, I'm sure."

"Well..." Pat said.

"Er..." Diane said.

"Quite," Pat added.

"That's settled then," the curate's wife said. "Tomorrow, ten sharp."

She turned on her pointed heel and reached for the door handle.

Pat intercepted her. "Who do you think... no, never mind."

"Who do I think killed my poor Gary?" the curate's wife said.

"Well... yes."

"Mrs Jones."

"Mrs Jones!"

"She brought Gary a cup of tea before service," the curate's wife continued. "Perhaps she poisoned it."

"Why would she do that?"

"She hated him."

"Why would Mrs Jones do that?" Pat asked her.

"He simply asked her to make a cappuccino for me."

"Oh my!"

"I mean her tea was like poison already."

"It is an acquired taste, I'll admit."

"Ten sharp."

The bell rang, the door slammed and the curate's wife disappeared along the High Street.

"I can't go tomorrow, sorry, but I'm on shift here," Annabelle said.

"We all have our rods to bear," Diane said.

"I'm not going alone," Annabelle said.

"We'll come with you," Pat assured her.

"What about the tea theory?" Diane asked.

"The poison was in the chalice," Pat said, "and, besides, imagine how weak Mrs Jones's first cup would be and how cold by the time she'd taken it across to the church."

"Good point."

Annabelle picked up the black bag, then shrieked as she dropped it.

"Belle?"

"Belle?"

"What if there's another body in this bag?"

"There wasn't one in the other bag," Pat said. "Just clothes."

"Oh. Yes. Sorry. But she's getting rid of bags, so doesn't that make her the murderer?"

Pat shook her head.

Annabelle nodded.

"Let's get going," Diane said.

"Yes."

Pat drank the remains of her hot chocolate. It was cold, reminding her of Mrs Jones's tea. For a moment, she mentally juggled a teacup from the Parochial Hall to the Vestry and then, somehow, to the chalice.

Could the curate have drunk tea to avoid drinking the wine?

No, clergymen drank it because they had to dispose of the consecrated wine and she'd never met a clergyman who didn't like a drop of wine.

"Pat, you coming?"

"Yes, Di. Bye, Belle."

Pat followed Diane out onto the High Street. It was a short walk to Tinsel Road and they both paused where Sergio had met his end. There was a sad bunch of flowers sellotaped to a railing.

"Mrs Entwistle," Diane said.

"How do you know?" Pat asked.

"Those are out of season."

338

They reached Mrs Entwistle's son's house. Matthew Entwistle had been something of a tearaway, running about the church with his aeroplane when his mother had been sorting the flowers, encouraging Zara Pheasant to steal and he'd sprayed graffiti all over the Village Green noticeboard. The latter had been doubly galling as his spelling had been atrocious.

But then, he'd made good – a new house, recently bought, a flash car and holidays in the Caribbean, which all went to show that bad apples could come good.

Pat and Diane glanced up and down the street to check the lace-curtained windows. None seemed to twitch.

At Matthew Entwistle's place, there was a short drive leading up to a garage beside a paved front garden. A small border had been disturbed and the flowerbed churned up.

"Look!" Pat said, pointing with the end of her walking stick. "Moped tracks."

A blue convertible BMW was parked at the back of the house. It didn't appear to have any damage due to an accident, when they bent down to examine it.

"Ooh."

"Ah."

"Wrong sort of tyres," Pat said. "These are Goodyear."

"How do you know?" Diane asked.

"It's written on the side."

"So, this car didn't run over Sergio."

"No and he's in the Caribbean," Pat said. "But those bike tracks suggest Sergio was here. But why?"

"Delivering pizza?"

"All the addresses were in the opposite direction and Mrs Entwistle's son is in the Caribbean."

"There has to be a reason."

They started to look around.

The house exuded silence, the dark windows ominous with their curtains drawn, and the back garden beyond the decking looked like a desolate wasteland.

"Poor Mrs Entwistle," Pat said. "The state of that garden must drive her to distraction."

Diane tried the back door – locked.

A forlorn plant pot with a dead twig sticking out of it guarded the sealed cat flap.

"She comes here every day without fail to water the plants and yet, there's no real evidence of any green fingers here at all," Pat continued.

"Perhaps inside."

"But how?"

Diane smiled and bent down – "oh, my back!" – and picked up the plant pot. Underneath shone a bright new key.

They nodded to each other and went in.

The kitchen gleamed like a starship command centre, but the cupboards only contained a few tins and the huge fridge boasted plenty of room for three bottles of expensive lager.

"What are we looking for?" Diane asked.

"House plants," Pat said.

They found an office full of computers, joysticks and a widescreen. Littering the desk was a collection of small plastic triangles with prongs.

"What are these?" Diane asked.

"Pizza stands," Pat said.

"You couldn't put a pizza on one of these."

"They keep the cardboard box off the pizza."

"But what keeps the plastic off the pizza?"

There was a large, open plan lounge with an enormous television surrounded by speakers of many sizes. The sofa was leather and luxurious.

"No house plants," Pat said.

"She must have been doing something else."

"Upstairs?"

They climbed the stairs.

There were three bedrooms off the landing and two bathrooms. The master bedroom was dark, with red highlights, a colossal bed and black, silk sheets, and a door to an en-suite.

Pat checked behind the drawn curtains for any plant pots but there was nothing, not even a bonsai tree tucked in the corner.

"It's quite hot and muggy, isn't it?" Diane said. "We should open a window and let some air in."

"Best not," Pat said, "we *are* trespassing."

"You're right, but what does Mrs Entwistle do here?"

Pat shrugged.

"We best go," Diane said as she led the way out.

Except that Pat paused on the landing. It was even warmer than the rest of the house, despite the radiator being icy to the touch.

"There are no plants here at all," Diane called out from halfway down the stairs.

Pat bent down and touched the carpet. Her knees clicked.

Diane appeared, her eye line level with Pat's fingers. "What is it?"

"Dents." Pat pointed out the two rectangular impressions in the grey shagpile. Directly above her, a black pull-cord dangled from a square hatch.

"Should we?" Diane asked, but it was rhetorical.

Diane helped Pat to stand and then they stretched up, but the hanging black ball was out of reach. Diane found a chair that Pat helped her up and onto. Diane was the taller and she was able to grasp the pull.

The hatch opened and Diane shrieked as a ladder dropped down. Luckily, it paused as the hydraulics took over, so Pat was able to help Diane down and move the chair before the aluminium struts hissed into the dents like a flying saucer's landing legs.

Light shone down as if it was an alien's abduction beam tempting them upwards.

Pat handed her stick to Diane and went up.

344

"Well?" Diane asked, non-rhetorically.

Pat stood on the rung. Her top half vanished into the loft above but Diane heard her comment clearly.

"Di," she said, "I've found the house plants."

21. Confessions

"I don't believe you," Annabelle said.

They had all met after the Oxfam shop's closing time at Diane's cottage.

"It's true," Pat said, "and we have the evidence."

She and Diane put their carrier bags of leafy foliage down in the hall and hung up their coats.

"I'll put the kettle on," Diane said.

"Oh please," Annabelle said.

"Me too," Pat said. "Oh, you've moved the pictures."

"Yes," Diane said, "I wanted to get another one up. You know, Sergio put the nails in the wall originally."

"Poor Sergio," Annabelle said.

It made them all feel even sadder to look upon the many framed pictures, each holding one of the parish magazine's most famous front covers. They harked back to a better age when the magazine had had a print run in the upper thirties and the village hadn't been awash with murder.

"Oh, will you look at this one," Annabelle said. "The village fête with the curate's wife winning the Best-in-Show for her filagree fancies."

"Yes, and here, *Plague at Pentecost*," Pat said.

"*Whitsun Wonder*," Annabelle added moving along the hallway

"*Littering at Lent*."

"*Second Sunday Scandal*."

"I was particularly proud of that one," Diane said.

"It was clever, Di."

"Thank you, Pat."

"And this one," Annabelle said, nearing the kitchen. "*Minister Mercilessly Murdered*... oh, sorry, that's the vicar."

They had a cup of tea in silence. There was a lot to take in, what with all the killings.

"Shall we get a takeaway?" Diane suggested.

"Oh, let's," Annabelle said.

"Yes," Pat agreed.

Diane had Chiang's menu tucked behind the telephone charger.

"Chinese or pizza?" she said.

"Two pepperoni, one Margherita, and one buffalo with olives," Annabelle said.

"That's an awful lot for the three of us," Pat said.

"That was Sergio's last delivery," Annabelle said.

"How about one pepperoni, a Margherita and a buffalo with olives," Pat said.

"We'll never finish three pizzas."

"There might be a clue."

Diane nodded, rang the number and ordered the three pizzas. "How long? Hmm... forty minutes. And who is delivering?"

She hung up and looked at the others.

"Zara?" Pat asked.

Diane nodded.

"So, perhaps Zara killed Sergio for his delivery job?" Pat said. "May I use your phone?"

"Please do."

Pat dialled.

"Odd," Pat mused while she waited, "that's it's still 'dialled' when it has buttons and– *oh!* ...Mrs Pilkington, yes, it's Patricia Thomas here... yes, lovely day... my begonias suffered in the storm, I'm afraid... I have a question for you."

Diane signalled to Annabelle and they went into the kitchen. Diane found the plates, knives and forks, and her pizza cutter. She raised her eyebrows to Annabelle when she took out the wine glasses.

"Oh yes," Annabelle said, "but not too much."

"I've a cheeky little number from Aldi," Diane said. "It's... Beaujolais."

"Does that go with pizza?"

"I think it pretty much goes with anything."

Pat joined them.

"Did you learn anything?" Diane asked.

"I did indeed," Pat said, "although it was tricky to keep that woman on topic."

"But specifically?"

"Lord Bishop Barnaby is the vicar's... *was* the vicar's uncle. On death's door in Torquay and listen, there's no money, but there's a title."

"Sir Victor asked about titles," Diane said. "You saw the vicar's will."

"Yes," Pat said. "So, I think the title goes to the eldest son. With the vicar dead, that's Sir Victor."

"It's a motive for killing his elder brother," Diane said. "Sir Victor is just the sort of arrogant prig who would like being a Lord."

"And he'll get to sit in the House of Lords," Annabelle said. "Or he would have done before they changed the rules."

"And that's in the vicar's will?" Pat asked.

"Yes," Diane said, "and Frances our warden inherits money."

"Really?" Pat said. "From the vicar?"

Diane nodded.

"How much?" Pat asked.

"A great deal."

"But why?"

The doorbell rang.

Diane fetched the pizza boxes and brought them back to the kitchen counter.

"It was Zara delivering," she said.

"She works very long hours," Annabelle said. "She makes the breakfasts in her café and now pizza delivery at this hour."

By this time, Diane had opened the boxes and taken out the small, plastic tripods. "Mrs Entwistle's son had loads of these," she said.

Pat took one and held it up, squinting to focus on it.

"Is it a clue, Pat?" Annabelle asked.

"If it is, I don't see how," Pat replied.

"Well, help yourselves," Diane said, placing fine china plates next to the delivery.

"I don't feel like eating pizza," Pat said.

"Oh... sorry, but I've also quite gone off the idea," Annabelle said.

"Me too," Diane said. "We could try the marijuana."

So Pat and Diane fetched the carrier bags from the hall and they plonked the leafy, bushy plants down on the coffee table.

"They are big," Annabelle said. "I honestly wouldn't have believed it."

"There were bigger ones," Pat said, "which is unsurprising given the hydro... wotnot and the lights. It was like the tropics up there."

"And Mrs Entwistle had been watering them every day?"

"It explains Matthew Entwistle's fortune, doesn't it?" Diane said.

"It's cannabis," Pat said. "An illegal drug."

"Could we go to prison?" Annabelle said, appalled.

"Not if it's for personal use," Diane said. "The law is quite specific on that point."

"Or if it's evidence that we're... er, looking after," Pat said.

"You smoke it," Diane added.

"I've never tried marijuana," Annabelle said.

"It's called skunk these days," Diane said.

"Oooh, really?"

"We could try it."

"No, I couldn't," Annabelle said. "I couldn't smoke, smoking makes me cough, and it makes your clothes reek of tobacco."

"We've no tobacco to cut it with anyway," Diane said.

"Cut it with?" Annabelle asked.

"When you mix drugs with something else it's called 'cutting'."

"Well, I never."

"You can use it as a herb in cooking," Pat said.

"We could make scones[7]," Diane suggested. "Herbal scones."

---

[7] Ingredients: 350g of self-raising flour, 2 tsps baking powder, 2 tbsps caster sugar, 75g of proper butter, 1 egg, 175ml milk, sultanas and 'herbs' to taste. That's nothing like enough, so double or treble the amounts.

"Ooh, they sound good for you," Annabelle said.

"It might go down a storm at the bring-and-buy at the next village fête."

"Quite," Pat said.

So, they opened the bottle of Beaujolais, and set about mixing flour, sugar and butter, beating eggs and measuring semi-skimmed.

"The trick is to put a little lemon juice in the milk if you can't get butter milk," Diane explained.

Directions: put everything in a large bowl and mix thoroughly. Lightly dust your worksurface with flour and kneed all this. Cut into round shapes with a fluted scone cutter. Glaze by brushing with a beaten egg. Pre-heat oven to 200C/Gas 6, which you should have turned on *before* mixing, etc. Bake for 15 minutes or until golden brown.

Serve with strawberry jam and then clotted cream if you are in Cornwall, clotted cream and then strawberry jam in Devon, and whatever you like everywhere else.

"On a scone, is it clotted cream then jam, or jam then clotted cream?" Annabelle asked.

"I don't have any cream," Diane said, "and it's pronounced scone, not scone."

Pat selected a few leaves, washed them in a steel colander, snipped them into small pieces with scissors and then ground them up in Diane's marble mortar and pestle.

Diane put the scone mix into the freezer.

"This is the trick, the colder the dough, the better the scone," Diane explained.

Their patience with this idea lasted ten minutes.

So, Diane popped them into the pre-heated oven at Gas Mark 6 for fifteen minutes or until golden brown. After another glass of red, she gazed through the oven door's glass front.

"A little longer, I think," she said.

A couple of minutes later, she declared them done and out they came to cool.

356

"They smell delicious," Annabelle said, "if a little odd."

They all peered down at the gentle steaming green scones as they cooled on the metal rack.

"I like them hot," Annabelle said.

"Yes," Diane said.

"Well, yes," Pat said.

They each took one, sliced it open, spread butter and took a good bite.

"Ooh oh oh."

"Oh."

"Oh oh."

A hit of red wine rescued their scalded mouths.

The scones didn't keep their heat, or the glasses of light-bodied ruby-shade pain killer worked their magic, for they soon had another scone.

And another.

"Quite morish," Pat said.

"Tasty," Annabelle said.

"Mm-mmm," Diane said.

They took another on plates into the front room and sat in the comfy seats, passing the butter round, but forwent any clotted cream or jam.

"It's not doing anything mind-altering," Annabelle said, licking her fingers.

"I'm not sure what all the fuss is about," Diane said.

"Quite disappointing," Pat agreed.

"Maybe Sir Victor pretended to be the vicar and then locked the door after we'd discovered the body," Diane said.

"I don't think that would work."

"Or... or... he dyed his hair grey and was his reflection," Diane said.

"Reflection?"

"To hide in the church in a mirror."

"There's no mirror in the church," Pat said, "and we saw Sir Victor coming out of Frances's house."

"She has a key."

"And... mmm... mm... a motive," Diane added.

"I feel dizzy," Annabelle said.

"I've done some terrible things in my life," Diane said.

"We all have, Di," Pat said.

"Is this room bigger than when we came in?" Annabelle asked.

"No," Diane said. "It's a trick of the light."

Annabelle stared up at the recessed wattage. "Which one?"

"Any one."

"I've got blotches in front of my eyes now," Annabelle said. "Is that the skunk?"

"Doubt it," Diane said. "It must be a dud batch."

"Maybe it needed more watering," Pat said. "It's not affected any of us."

"Oh, well," Annabelle said. "Any more?"

"All gone here," Diane said. "There are more in the kitchen."

"I'm really hungry. Really, really hungry."

"Me too."

"I'm a little peckish now you mention it," Pat said.

"Do you have anything, Di?" Annabelle said.

"I could cook... wait!" Diane exclaimed. "Didn't we order pizza?"

They all heaved themselves out of the comfy chairs.

"Ooh."

"Ah."

"Oh."

And helped one another back to the kitchen, where Diane popped the pizzas in their boxes into the still-warm oven. She turned it to Gas Mark 4 for ten minutes or until the cardboard went golden brown.

"So," she said dramatically when she returned, "who's for pepperoni, who's for Margherita and who's for buffalo with olives?"

"Or a slice of each?" Annabelle suggested.

"Good idea," Diane said. She waved the knife and cut each in half, then one half into three and served them on big white plates.

"Mmm, delicious," Annabelle said.

Pat shifted an olive like a Chinese master playing Go. "Why these pizzas?" she said.

"You think it's a clue?" Diane asked.

"Pepperoni, Margareta and Buffalo... Pee, Em... Bee... does that stand for anything?"

"With olives," Annabelle added.

"Pee, em, bee, oh... bomb! No, pee, not another bee."

"Two pepperonis."

"Bomp-p!"

They started chuckling at this and found they couldn't stop.

"Anyone want another scone?" Annabelle asked.

"What for," Diane said. "They don't work."

"They're still tasty."

"Scones all round then... and more wine?"

"Yes."

"I'll get them," Annabelle said.

Annabelle got up – "ah" – and went to the kitchen, standing at the sink to gaze out into the dark void. She knew Diane had a functional garden, a large lawn with flower borders. Somewhere out there too was a large pear tree that no longer gave a harvest.

It was late.

A red beam shone, tracking back and forth.

"Fascinating," she said to herself.

She fetched the plate of scones, found a bottle of Merlot and went back to the others.

They were suddenly quiet.

"Were you talking about me?" Annabelle asked.

"No."

"No."

"You were."

"No."

"No."

"I didn't kill whoever you think I killed."

"No, Belle."

"No, we don't."

"Well, good, because I didn't."

"No."

"No."

She put the scones down and took one for herself.

"Thanks, Belle."

"Thank you."

They buttered away in silence.

"There's someone in the garden," Annabelle said, suddenly.

"Nonsense," Diane said.

"Honestly."

"What was he doing?" Pat asked.

Annabelle peered out. "He's measuring."

"Measuring?"

"With one of those laser things."

"Why," Diane said, "I mean, why, would anyone be measuring the garden at... at... whatever time this is?"

"Laser things?" Pat asked.

"You know," Annabelle said, "it's a laser on the end of some stick thing."

"Belle!"

"Yes."

"Get down!"

364

Pat leapt up, grabbed Annabelle and pulled her over. The two went down in a flurry of cardigan.

"What's going on?" Diane asked.

"It's a hitman," Pat said.

"Nonsense."

"Di, are you expecting a tradesman to come and measure your garden?"

"No, but... ah... it's the mara... mara de junna, mara... weed."

"He wasn't weeding," Annabelle said.

"I mean... skunk makes you paranormal."

"Paranoid," Pat said, "not paranormal."

"That's it... paranormalanoid."

Pat shuffled in a combat crawl over to the window and then heaved herself up – "Oh, my knees" – to see over the ledge.

"Wait," Diane said, "the lights are on."

"Oh, yes," Pat said.

"I'll get the fuses!" Diane whispered. She went out on her hands and knees, crawling quickly and rucking up the rug and her stockings.

"What do we do?" Annabelle asked.

"We wait," Pat said, ominously.

The room went dark.

Annabelle shrieked.

"Belle, it's just Di at the fuse box."

"Why didn't she just turn off the light switch!"

"Oh, yes. Di, why didn't you just–"

There was a clatter of crockery and a sudden swearing.

"Are you all right, Di?"

"Yes, just... butter," Diane griped from the darkness.

"Why are we hiding from the measuring man?" Annabelle asked.

"He's not measuring," Pat said. "It's the laser sight of a sniper rifle."

366

"Do you think he'll shoot at us?"

"He might already have shot at us."

"I've not heard a bang."

"If he had a silencer, we wouldn't have heard it."

"I've not heard a phut."

"Good."

"Sorry," Annabelle said, "but this is just paranoia, isn't it?"

"Just because you're paranormal doesn't mean they aren't out to get you," Diane said, sniggering.

"Better safe than sorry, Belle," Pat said.

"But why?" Annabelle muttered.

"Why is it better to be safe-"

"No, why would anyone want to kill us?"

"Why would anyone want to kill the vicar, Sergio, Mrs Boseman, the curate, that tall thin man and whoever's clothes are in the black bag!"

"Oh... sorry."

"And, Belle," Diane said, "we've been investigating. The murderer might want to bump us off because we've discovered who they are."

"But we haven't," Annabelle said.

"They don't know that," Diane said.

"But that's just the murderer being paranoid and the murderer hasn't had any scones."

"Not scones, *scones.*"

"I'm going to look," Pat said.

She opened the heavy drape and twitched aside the net curtains.

Outside it was pitch black.

"What can you see?"

"Yes, Pat, what can you see?"

"Quiet!" Pat said through gritted false teeth.

She peered, wishing her eyesight better by sheer force of will.

It was still pitch–

A face!

A man's face right up against the window.

Pat jerked backwards, partially falling over Annabelle and Diane.

"Run!" she shouted.

They crawled.

As they went away from the window, they crashed into the coffee table and the soft furniture. A glass broke, but this was not the time to spread salt on the carpet.

Diane, knowing the layout better, made it to the hall first.

A shape loomed in the stained-glass panes of the front door.

"Side door," Diane said as she collided with the others.

"But our shoes are in the hall!" Annabelle whined.

"No time," Diane said.

There was nothing for it. They piled out into the cold night in their stockings or slippers, and light cardigans.

Diane's wheelie bins formed a good hiding place. Thank goodness Diane was a keen gardener because it meant they had a bin each. However, in the dark, it was impossible to tell which was grey, which was blue and which was brown.

"These aren't going to protect us," Diane said.

"Why did we come outside?" Annabelle asked.

"We should have stayed indoors and rung the police," Pat said.

"I can't hear anything," Annabelle said.

"Shhh," Diane shushed.

They listened.

Did the hitman have one of those night sights to see the garden clear and obvious in fuzzy green? Or a thermal camera that would show Pat, Diane and Annabelle as cowering figures with limbs turning blue in the cold? Or had he gone home for a nice hot chocolate in a lovely centrally-heated secret lair?

"Shall we go inside?" Diane said.

"Yes," Pat said.

"Yes, please," Annabelle said.

They did.

Diane found the fuse box and the lights came back on. In the sudden brightness, the three of them felt quite foolish, doubly so when they saw the mess of split wine, dropped pizzas, scone crumbs and butter. It had all been ground into the carpet by their hands and knees.

"Oh, what a mess, Di," Annabelle said.

"This takes me back to my student days," Diane said.

"Of course," Pat said. "Sergio was going to take something to the students – dope!"

"And someone killed him for it," Diane said.

"And the hitman is part of a crime syndicate!"

"I'm never touching scones again," Annabelle said.

"It's scones!" Diane corrected.

22. Up the Garden Path

The night before had become a blur. The following day seemed like adverts for stairlifts, funeral finance and Saga holidays after a tense and exciting episode of *Midsomer Murders*. And just as surreal.

Pat had rung up her nephew in Australia.

"Why are you ringing in the middle of the day?" he'd asked.

"It's not... never mind. Listen, I need to know the symptoms of marijuana use."

There was a pause.

"Oh... er... well, yes... it's for a pub quiz."

"Auntie, are you–"

"In the parochial hall."

After that, with a few 'uh-huh's, Pat had learned all about hallucinations, paranoia, red eyes, dry mouth and loss of short-term memory. So, she thought, the mysterious assailant could have been a paranoid hallucination and indeed, along with red eyes and dry mouths, the details seemed to slip away like flour through a sieve with only the chaff left to mull over.

They decided that discretion would be the better part of informing the police. After all, there were plants to repot and scone mix to scrap into the compost. No-one had fancied licking the bowl. What would the police say anyway: a lot of dotty old ladies imagining things because they watched too many crime dramas?

One thing they hadn't forgotten was their appointment at the Church House and the garden gate creaked as Pat, Diane and Annabelle arrived at the curate's cottage the next day.

"If the vicar's is the vicarage," Annabelle said, "then surely this is the curatage?"

"Belle, honestly!" Diane said. "It's just Church House."

"But it's not a house, it's a cottage."

"I think 'curatage' is right," Pat said. "I remember it coming up in Scrabble."

They made their way up the garden path, admiring the flowery borders, dandelion sprinkled lawn and trailing ivy. It was all rather going to seed. The previous curate had been one for his garden, whereas the new curate – the late curate – was more interested in good works, but the hollyhocks had suffered terribly and as for the dahlias... well.

Diane reached for the door pull.

"Wait," Pat said, fishing out her half-moon glasses to check her Accurist. "...and at the third stroke..."

They laughed.

"...now!"

Diane pulled the bell at exactly 10 o'clock sharp.

It didn't ring.

"Di?"

"Yes, Pat."

She pulled again and again – nothing.

"Try the knocker," Annabelle said.

"There's a bell," Diane said.

"But it's not working," Pat replied.

"That's hardly my fault."

"Well..." Diane switched to the knocker and then flapped the letterbox.

A shape appeared in the frosted windows and then the door opened.

"You're late," the curate's wife said. "I said ten o'clock *sharp.*"

"We're only..." Pat began, but it was no use arguing despite the minute hand being at the top of the watch face, and anyway, Pat had put her half-moon glasses away.

"Have you three been crying?" the curate's wife asked.

"Well, no..."

"It's just, er..."

"Hay fever."

The curate's wife arched an eyebrow. "You'd better come in."

There were workmen in brown overalls moving boxes and furniture about.

"You're packing," Pat said as she folded up her walking stick to put away in her large bag. "Are you leaving us today?"

"No, no, I'm staying until Sunday for the memorial for my poor Gary," the curate's wife said, "but then, yes, I'm off to London by train. I've packed everything already, my passport, my– You! Yes, you! Careful with that, it's Dior!"

"Sorry, Miss," the mover replied. He glanced at one of his mates, eyebrows raised and eyes turned to heaven.

"Madam!" the curate's wife reminded him.

To the eyebrows raised and eyes up, the man added a shake of the head.

"We could come back another time," Pat suggested.

"Nonsense," the curate's wife said, "I have to leave. Particularly now there's been another death."

"Another?"

"Sir Victor... haven't you heard?"

"Sir Victor!" Pat exclaimed. It was shocking to lose such a renowned figure from the village, but also because he was the only murderer they had identified. "We hadn't."

"That amazes me. I thought you knew everything."

"We don't–"

"Accident," the curate's wife said. "Fell over when naked and impaled himself on a spike. So embarrassing."

Pat, Diane and Annabelle winced as they looked at each other. Sir Victor had been their only sure suspect and now... it changed everything.

"Coffee?" the curate's wife offered.

"Oh, please," Pat said. "Or tea?"

"Tea, lovely," Annabelle said.

"Tea's fine," Diane added.

"After you've dealt with all the rubbish for the charity shop," the curate's wife said, "and assuming these idiots haven't packed the *barista express.*"

"Miss... Madam," the man said, "we wouldn't–"

"Get on, get on, time and tide, etcetera."

So, the three of them set about sorting old clothes in the box room and filling the black bags.

"Take anything that's not a label," the curate's wife explained.

First, Pat, Diane and Annabelle made sure their own belongings, their coats and scarves, stayed separate as they didn't want them ending up in any black bag. The other clothes were mostly the curate's, although there were a few choice women's outfits.

"Sir Victor, dead," Diane whispered.

"Well, yes, quite, shocking," Pat whispered back. She picked up an elegant chiffon number. "This is brand new."

"I bet it's last season," Diane added, "even if it is designer. Everything has a label."

"Yes," Annabelle agreed. "Look, this is M and S, this is George, this is Yves Saint Laurent, this is Gary and this one's hand wash."

They did their best.

"And Sir Victor's dead," Diane repeated. "He must have killed his brother."

"Who inherits now Sir Victor's dead," Annabelle asked. "Does Frances the warden get even more money?"

"That would depend on Sir Victor's will," Diane said.

"And?" Pat prompted.

"It's not held by my firm," Diane admitted, "but it means Frances has a motive – and a strong motive – to kill the vicar and then Sir Victor."

"Well, yes, quite," Pat replied. "I can't really think straight without a cuppa."

"I'm parched," Diane said.

"Oh yes," Annabelle agreed.

"I'll see about a cup of tea," Pat said and she made her way to the kitchen.

The movers seemed to have disappeared.

"I wondered about that cup of tea," Pat said when she reached the kitchen.

"Can't you see, I'm doing this!" the curate's wife exclaimed. She was trying to get a premium auto-mixer six-speed tilt head back in its box.

"Er... can I help?" Pat asked.

The curate's wife – well, Pat supposed the curate's *widow* or perhaps she was merely a civilian now – anyway, she was struggling with her cake-making equipment. She had an awful lot of stainless steel and much of it was unidentifiable. Pat had found that a good, manual mixing bowl that didn't tilt and a few baking trays served well enough. And no-one needed four different types of display turntables in three different sizes.

Did anyone?

All this high-tech apparatus was at odds with the country cottage kitchen with its weather-beaten oak table, its chipped

Victorian tiling and ancient oak rafters. She envied the curate's house, so much better than her own and so well looked after.

"It's very clean," Pat said.

"Mrs Entwistle does," the curate's widow explained. "Maybe this is the wrong box?"

"Does she?"

"Yes. She does the vicarage, here, the warden's."

"Part of the church arrangements?"

"I don't think so, she just *does.*"

"She missed something," Pat said. She bent down, paused mid-bend as her knees complained. The round bit of dirt that resembled a rabbit dropping was just out of reach.

"Ah!" the curate's wife exclaimed.

The floor was suddenly awash with silver balls. The curate's widow stood holding an empty container for the cake silver dragées that still bounced and rolled underfoot.

"Damn," the curate's widow announced. "They're everywhere."

"Lucky they weren't hundreds and thousands," Pat said. "Shall I get the dustpan and brush?"

"No. No. Mrs Entwistle does."

Back at the box room, the other two looked up as Pat returned

"Tea?" Diane asked.

Pat shook her head.

"We're done here," Annabelle said. "Oh."

There were a lot of black bags heaped in the hallway. It was clear that they'd never get them all down to the charity shop. For the three of them, it was at least half a dozen trips.

"What are we going to do?" Pat said.

"Leave it to me," Annabelle said. She went outside and Pat followed.

The moving men were all standing around smoking in the front garden.

"Excuse me," Annabelle said. "Mr... er... sorry."

"Angus, love," said their gaffer. He took a final drag and dropped his butt into the hollyhocks and weeds.

"Sorry, so sorry, these bags are so heavy and would you mind?"

"Of course not, love," Angus replied. "You shouldn't be troubling yourself with those. Here lads."

The other men moved forward, dropping their cigarettes on the garden path or pitching their tea into the foliage, and each collected three or four bags each. They managed to carry the whole lot in one go.

"In the lorry with 'em," said Angus.

"Oh no, sorry," Annabelle said, "but these are for the charity shop."

"Charity shop?" Angus asked.

"Yes."

"Where's your van?"

"We don't have one. Sorry. But my lovely, little shop is just... down there!"

Angus and the other movers followed Annabelle's pointing to the distant shops on the other side of the Village Green.

"So kind of you," Annabelle said.

"But–"

"So sorry."

Pat smiled as she watched the men heaving the bags down the hill. It was an effort, the bags were big and awkward, and they had to suffer Annabelle's constant apologies as well. But she was sure they were enjoying it. Men liked to show off. They'd get a cup of tea and a chance to avoid the curate's widow's demands for a while. And Annabelle was sure to sell them something to carry on the climb back. She always could wrap men around her little finger.

A screech came from indoors. "I will not!"

Pat hurried back inside to find Diane and the curate's widow facing off one another.

"I'll need the curate's key," Diane said.

"What? Oh! Yes."

The curate's widow went to a drawer and pulled out a key, which she handed to Diane.

"And there's your key," Diane added.

"Mine... but I'm still alive."

"And moving to London."

"I haven't time for this foolishness, Di," the curate's widow replied. She fussed with her cake-making trays, unsure whether to pack them or use them as percussion instruments.

"So," Diane said, holding out her hand, "best return the key now."

The curate's widow bristled.

"If you are going to London," Diane repeated.

"I was given it by the vicar, so I should return it to the vicar."

"Who is no longer with us, so..."

The two glared at each other, neither wishing to give ground.

386

The curate's widow blinked first. "Oh, very well."

She opened her clutch bag and fished out a make-up compact, lipstick, mascara, perfume, credit cards, mobile phone, pack of baby wipes, hand lotion, passport, paracetamol and, finally, a big key. She gave the chunky thing to Diane, whose fingers closed like talons to make a fist.

"But it's not yours!" the curate's widow insisted. "You are to hang it up on the hook for the next curate's wife."

The curate's widow smiled, happy to have won the battle between them.

"I shall hang it up on the hook for the next person in charge of church *cleaning*," Diane replied.

The curate's widow glared.

Touché, Pat thought.

23. Softly, Softly

Diane had the key in her pocket. It felt heavy, substantial like a weapon. As they walked back to the charity shop, she became convinced or, perhaps, she was convincing herself that it had been Sir Victor Pendle-Took who had fired three shots that night on his driveway. She closed her eyes: she could see the flash, Pendle-Took's evil beard and moustache as he leered round to stare at her and his unforgettable cackling laughter.

"Careful, Di," Pat said, gripping her friend's arm and directing her off her collision course with the giant horse chestnut tree.

Di had slept on it – not well, because of the skunk – and her nightmares had inflated the terrifying ordeal into something far worse and somewhat comically exaggerated, but nonetheless, he had shot someone.

And they had been attacked when having those moreish scones, so there was real danger. But had they? Paranoia made it hard to tell. She had to hold on to what she'd seen, if she'd seen it.

"I'll put the kettle on," Annabelle said.

"Good idea," Pat said.

According to the curate's wife, Diane remembered, Sir Victor had had some sort of a fatal and embarrassing accident.

Or was it another murder?

And, above all else, he was the vicar's brother, so there must be a motive to establish. There was money to inherit (so could it be Frances Fairfax?), but Sir Victor wasn't short of a bob or two, and then there was the family title. For an arrogant prig like Sir Victor that was more than enough, surely?

"Here you go," Annabelle said.

"Hmm," Diane said taking the cup and saucer.

Why had she suggested investigating Mrs Entwistle when Sir Victor was the key. And he had a key!

Diane put her teacup down. "We have to go and check."

"I have these black bags to go through," Annabelle said. "Sorry."

"The police will have looked everywhere," Pat replied.

"Yes, Pat," Diane said, "but only for evidence of an accident."

"And not for evidence of a shooting, you mean?"

"Yes."

"Like a body."

"Yes."

"Or bullet holes."

"Exactly."

Pat could always see the nub of the problem. That forensic nature of Pat's mind worried Diane.

"Let's go and have a look," Diane said. "No harm in that. It'll be perfectly safe."

"But I'll have to close up the shop," Annabelle said.

"Pop a sign on it," Diane said. "Say you'll be back in five minutes."

"But that won't be right."

"Come on, Belle."

"Oh… all right."

The only sign she could find said *'Back in Ten Minutes'*.

So, the three lady detectives, for that was indeed what they were, set off with a walking stick, misgivings and utter determination.

"Oh, hello, Mrs Pilkington," Annabelle said, stopping to chat to her friend as she whizzed by at a snail's pace on her mobility scooter.

"Lovely day for a stroll, Belle."

"Yes, Mrs Pilkington. Going far?"

"Oh yes, I've a full charge. I'm off down to the shops on the High Street."

"Lovely."

"Belle!" Diane shouted. She and Pat had paused by the kerb ready to cross Tinsel Lane over to Brighter Avenue.

"Coming!" Annabelle shouted. "Sorry, Mrs Pilkington, I must be off."

"I've some things to drop to the charity shop," Mrs Pilkington said.

"Oh, thank you, except I'm not there."

"Don't worry, Belle dear, I'll drop the bag in the porch for you."

"Oh, that's... oh."

Pat and Diane were pointedly looking left and right, left and right, left and right for traffic. There was none: no other mobility scooter, no mopeds and no SUVs.

"I must dash," Annabelle said.

"Cheerio," said Mrs Pilkington as she turned the throttle and, with all due care and attention, scooted off down Tinsel Lane.

Annabelle caught the others up over on the far side of the road.

"We're on a mission, Belle," Diane reminded her.

"Sorry."

They made their way along Brighter Avenue and then around Orthodox Crescent. The houses along the Crescent were bespoke builds, the unoccupied second homes of city couples wanting to get away for a rare, long weekend.

The final house was the *Architectural Masterpiece* that had won the prestigious *R&NAB Sir Clifford Hughes Memorial Award for Innovation and Originality.* It had been lauded as the definitive construction of country brutalism, *'modern and vibrant, a breath of fresh air amongst the staid brick and thatch dark ages',* heralding a new era of architectural progress.

"God, that's ugly," Diane said.

"Well, quite, it's not pretty," Pat said.

"Sorry... it's not to my taste," Annabelle said.

The stone statues, two hideous gargoyles on pedestals, guarded the open gate as if there had once been a ruined castle or manor house beyond.

"And what are those supposed to be?" Diane asked.

"Monkeys," Annabelle said.

"Nonsense, they don't look anything like monkeys."

"They are," Annabelle said. She pointed to one and then the other. "See no evil and hear no evil."

"Oh yes," Pat said. "Where's speak no evil?"

They looked around but they couldn't see a third monkey. It would not have fitted with the tree of stainless steel that shimmered in the centre of the front garden's tarmac lawn. The modern art also boasted a dent.

"Frances said she'd hit something in Pendle-Took's drive," Diane said.

A length of *'Police – Do Not Cross'* tape fluttered around one of the stone monkeys' necks like a festive collar and lead.

They stepped onto the herringbone brickwork of the driveway.

"His SUV, undamaged," Diane pointed out, unnecessarily.

Pat and Annabelle peered inside.

"*Architecture Today* and *Private Eye*," Annabelle said.

"Why did he move his car the other day?" Diane asked.

"So the nice detective constable would see it," Pat said.

"You're thinking of Sergio," Diane said.

"Could he have had the damage repaired and then deliberately parked it so that he'd be crossed off the suspect list?"

"No chance," Diane said, "it's weeks before you can get a mechanic to look at a car round here."

"Show us where the shooting was... no wait, hide where you were and we can pretend to be Sir Victor and his victim."

Diane stepped up to the SUV and bent down. "I was – oh, my back – here."

"Right."

Pat led Annabelle to the side of the house.

"Back a bit, left, left, bit more... a couple of yards between you," Diane directed and Pat and Annabelle shuffled about. "That's it."

"Which of us is Sir Victor?" Pat asked.

"Belle."

"We should swap," Annabelle said. "You've got a walking stick, Pat."

"It wasn't a rifle," Diane shouted.

"You best shoot me," Pat said.

"Oh... er..." Annabelle raised her hand, pointed her finger, winced with closed eyes, and then fired. "Bang... sorry."

"It's all right."

"He fired three times," Diane said.

"Do I have to?" Annabelle asked.

396

"Yes!"

"Oh… bang, bang, bang."

"That's four!"

"Oh… sorry, can I start again?"

"If you've got the ammunition," Diane teased.

"Oh… I'm not sure."

"Ammunition!" Pat shouted suddenly. She turned around. "If I'd been shot, I'd have fallen here by the fence."

She checked the floor and then the fence – nothing.

"Maybe Di didn't see anything," Annabelle whispered.

"What's that?" Diane asked loudly from the other side of the SUV.

"Nothing," Pat said. "Wait. We're short women."

"Yes, Pat," Annabelle agreed, although she was fairly tall.

"And Di said the victim was tall and thin," Pat said. "So the man would have been further away."

She worked her way along the fence moving away from Diane towards the big, triple fronted garage.

"Ah-ha!"

"What is it?" Anabelle asked.

"Di, come and see," Pat shouted.

Diane unbent herself – "ooh" – and came around.

Pat's finger pointed at the wooden fence panel. "There, there and there."

The first two places could have been where the wood had split or been knocked, but the last one had hit the post leaving an angry cavity as if some workman had botched drilling a hole and then charged the old dear £280 for the essential 'your fence will fall down, if you don't have it seen to right away' maintenance.

"So, I was right," Diane said.

"I wonder if the bullets are thirty-eights," Pat said.

"Shall we dig it out?"

"We best leave that for the nice detective constable's forensic team."

"I agree," Diane said, "and we don't have anything to pull the bullet out with."

"I've some eyebrow tweezers," Annabelle said.

"Let's see what else we can find," Pat said.

"Oh, what if we're stopped?" Annabelle asked.

"Then we say we're working for the police."

"Oh, sorry, but that's not official."

"We could say we're collecting for the church roof?" Diane said.

Pat shook her head.

Even so, without any excuse, they moved around the house. The modern concrete and plastic cladding loomed above them, creating a strange set of changing perspectives: the sort of thing you'd want to see in a modern art gallery, gasp at the price and then move on towards the more classical galleries or their lovely cafés.

They pushed open the side gate.

At the back, a new patio dominated the space, thrusting into the quaint apple orchard like a metaphor for the spread of concrete urbanisation as it smashed aside hedge and row. Around it, looking like a blitzed building, bricks lay ready to become walls and arches and barbeques. The discarded timber beyond was the remains of the original decking.

A few footprints spoiled the concrete, as if the concrete could be spoiled.

"I wonder who that was?" Diane asked.

Pat checked the concrete was dry with her stick and then knelt down – "Ah" – to peer at the impressions. "It's the detective constable. I saw his shoes when he came to mine the other day."

"Clumsy of him."

A crack cut across the entire grey slab like the remnant of some terrible cataclysm. The God of Good Taste had struck at this offensive man-made abomination and, leaning over, they could look down towards Hell.

"The pour dried too quickly and shrunk," Diane explained. "He must have done this recently."

"Last night to hide a body," Pat suggested.

"Before he... you know, passed on," Annabelle said.

Diane scanned the garden with its stacks of bricks, piles of old decking, concrete mixer, and bags of sand and cement. It covered and crushed the lawn, perennials and flowers. She didn't fancy delving under all the rubble for clues. Going down to the end of the garden to check the rickety wooden shed seemed foolish too. Maybe she could get Pat to mention the possibility to that Kilroy detective and he could get some strong police officers to sift through the mess. There would then be another report for them to accidentally find in his briefcase.

They all peered into the house though the French windows.

"That must be where he fell," Diane said.

The spikes on either side of the fireplace had been taped off. A yellow number, '6', stood guard.

"Well, yes," Pat said. "I don't think we're going to find anything useful here."

"This must have cost a fortune," Diane said.

"Let's go home," Annabelle said, "and have some cake."

Pat agreed, "Good idea."

They picked their way around to the front.

"I thought his deck was nice," Annabelle said.

"It was better than his house," Diane agreed.

"Why change it?"

"Architects," Diane said, "always designing buildings to win awards and never to live in."

They reached the driveway again.

"Shame we can't look inside," Pat said.

"We can't break and enter," Annabelle said.

"We could," Diane said.

"Best not," Pat said. "We could look in the garage."

"That's breaking and entering," Annabelle said.

"Let's look round it anyway," Pat said. "While we're here."

The architect had a triple garage with a gable roof in fine yellow Cambridge brick. The door spanned the entire width of the construction. The good solid English oak-patterned fibreglass made it look like a coach house stable door that opened in the centre. However, it was the sort that went up into the ceiling like a normal garage door at the flick of a remote.

"It's locked," Diane said.

"It goes up," Pat said.

"It's still locked."

They put their hands over their eyes to see if they could peer inside through the smoked glass windows.

"Maybe there's only his lawnmower inside," Annabelle said.

"He's got no lawn, Belle," Diane said.

His SUV, its green metallic paint looking splendid in the afternoon sun, sparkled in the drive.

"He's not put his car away," Annabelle said.

"There might be windows on the other walls," Pat said.

They went back to the garden again and this time circled the garage. They found a side door.

Diane tried it: it clicked.

They looked at each other, well aware that they shouldn't, that it was a sin and that they'd get into trouble, but also knowing that they were going inside.

Pat found the light switch.

The *buzzzz-ping* revealed a huge space bigger than Diane's cottage. In the middle stood an SUV, a black, sinister vehicle poised to leap out into the night.

"So? He has two," Diane said.

"Red paint," Pat said.

"It's black."

"No. Look!"

On the front radiator grille, along the bumper and the right-hand wing, the black paint was scarred and pitted revealing the silver metal beneath. Here and there, it was etched with scrapes of red paint.

"I don't wish to speak ill of the dead," Diane said, "but we've got him."

"It's method," Pat said.

"Oh yes, and opportunity," Annabelle added.

"Sir Victor killed Sergio," Diane said, "and he killed someone else – I saw him – and he must have killed... Mrs Boseman with the same gun and he was in the church when the curate was poisoned, so he must have killed the vicar!"

"Well, yes, quite, but what's his motive for killing Sergio?" Pat said.

"He killed him, so he must have had a motive."

"Well... hmm, but what?" Pat said. "Let's get back. We'll have a good old think over a cocoa."

"And biscuits," Annabelle added.

"Good idea."

They closed the door behind them and made their way to the gate, the driveway and back towards Orthodox Crescent, but there weren't only stone statues on guard.

Blocking their way, a tall, thin man stood like a panther ready to strike. He wore a dark suit, white shirt and red tie, black driving gloves and a Christmas festive balaclava pulled over his face.

The three old ladies stopped.

"Oh."

"Ah."

"Hmm."

"Äntligen! De gamla damerna!"

24. Wild Goose Chase

Pat stood, frozen, knowing her knees were slowly locking into position as she clenched the handle of her stick tightly. Their gasp over, the others stood on either side of her, waiting soundlessly.

The Mexican stand-off stretched time.

Each side waited for someone to crack and make the first move.

Until the man realised that they were harmless old ladies and he was an armed hitman.

He drew his gun from a hidden shoulder holster in a single, fluid, well-practised action while simultaneously pulling out a black silencer from his pocket. But he was wearing gloves and so fumbled it at the last moment. The suppressor dropped to the brick-paved driveway with a musical note like a tubular bell.

"Skit!" he exclaimed, bending down to retrieve it.

"Run," Diane said.

The three of them kerfuffled back to the rear garden. Diane had the forethought to bolt the wooden gate behind them before she joined Pat and Annabelle clambering over the cast-off decking and skirting the stacks of bricks.

The gate rattled.

"Quick!" Diane said.

The gate bulged with the impact of a shoulder charge, the wood and the bolt competing to be the first to break. On the second attempt, the wood split, the bolt pinged away and the top hinge failed. The remains of the gate formed a low barrier, but that was soon kicked aside.

The man leapt into the garden; the gun now elongated with a silencer as if he was compensating.

"Du kan springa... Nej! You can run, but you can't hide."

Silence.

He was hunting old ladies: they couldn't run, so they had hidden.

The garden had a high fence surrounding it, a few trees, stacks of bricks and construction equipment. There were plenty of solid obstacles to skulk behind. He jumped up onto the partially constructed patio to gain height, all the time keeping a beady eye on his surroundings.

"All right," he shouted, "you can hide, but I'll find you. Best come out. I will count to ten. Ten..."

Diane craned around in the garden shed, shifting a rake and a hoe, to peer through the grease and grime of the Perspex window.

"Isn't it a hundred in hide and seek?" Annabelle said.

"Er... nio... neun... nine!"

"What's he doing?" Pat whispered.

"...åtta..."

"Counting," Diane said, "in Swedish."

410

"How do you know it's Swedish?"

"...sju..."

"I've seen enough Scandi noir to know."

"...sex..."

"Perhaps we could arm ourselves with a fork or a spade," Annabelle whispered.

"He's got a gun," Diane said.

"...fem..."

"Why does he want to kill us?" Annabelle whispered.

"...fyra..."

"We've discovered something that incriminates someone to one of the killings," Pat said.

"...tre... Three! That's it, three..."

"But which one?" Annabelle whispered.

"...two..."

"Perhaps he'd listen to reason," Pat said, "if we explained how little we actually understood."

"...one! Ready or not, here I– *arrgh!*"

"He's fallen down," Diane observed.

"Skit! Helvete! Jävla!"

"Go! Go! Go!" Diane yelled. She smashed open the shed door clattering out hoes and rakes to add to the minefield of obstacles.

The others launched themselves into the daylight, pausing only to hold the door open and say "After you" a couple of times.

The hitman knelt on the patio, one leg trapped in the great crack in the concrete.

The women faced him.

His gun had fallen from his grip. It lay a few feet away from him, but yards from their position.

He reached.

His hand didn't touch the handle.

Annabelle, the nearest, stepped forward.

412

He made another attempt, touching the handle.

Annabelle dithered.

The man yanked his foot up, gaining a few inches, and his face contorted in a spitting rage.

"Run!" Pat shouted.

They ran, skirting the house again and hobbling along the brick driveway to Tinsel Lane.

"Belle, why didn't you get the gun?" Diane demanded.

"We were safe in the shed," Annabelle said.

"With the gun–"

"Quiet!" Pat insisted. "Follow me."

They fled down Tinsel Lane towards the shops.

Pat risked glancing back.

The man was in pursuit, crying out with every other step as he lolloped towards them. Even with his injury, he was gaining.

"Faster," she said, "Fast– oh!"

Her breath wheezed as it struggled in the old leather of her lungs. When she'd run for the Whallop Harriers Under-15s, she had not seen stars circling encroaching darkness quite so soon. Their 500-yard dash became more of a 200-yard lurch interspersed with 5-yard lollops.

Phut!

A bullet whizzed past her.

Somehow, Pat was once again racing against school favourite Tania Rehnquist in the village fête for at least another 50-yards, running so fast that her stick barely touched the ground.

Mrs Pilkington appeared, nearly running them over in her bright red, sporty mobility scooter.

"Careful!" she shouted and then she remembered to honk her hooter.

The three ran around her.

"Ha!"

"Ah!"

"Oh... sorry."

"Watch out!" Mrs Pilkington shouted.

Years of habit, training and carefulness made them pause at the kerb to cross Gladstone Road.

Pat risked another glance.

The man limped up to Mrs Pilkington.

"Get out!" he shouted. "Din dumma gammal kvinna!"

"Now listen, young man," Mrs Pilkington replied, "I–"

The man pointed his pistol at Mrs Pilkington's head. "Get out! Get out! Get out!"

"Good heavens!" Mrs Pilkington said. She struggled with her stick, jamming it between the fold-up armrest and the battery as she always did.

"Get out!"

Mrs Pilkington tried her best.

415

"Mrs Pilkington is being mobility-scooter-jacked," Pat said.

"Should we help?" Annabelle said.

"He has a gun," Diane shouted back.

"Oh... yes. Sorry."

The man finally yanked Mrs Pilkington out of the scooter and she fell on the pavement, and then he struggled to free the walking stick, gave up and instead leapt over it, leaving the armrest up and caution to the wind.

"Come on," Pat said. She hadn't really recovered, but they were now being chased by an armed lunatic in a motorised vehicle.

They attempted a sprint, looking left and right until they reached the far pavement.

The gunman flung the stolen machine forward at the heady maximum speed of 4 miles-per-hour!

Mrs Pilkington's shopping bounced around in the basket, her fizzy pop shaken towards an explosive degree. A clutch of pedestrians had to dodder out of the way.

416

"He's after us!" Di screamed.

The man levelled his gun.

Pat took a sharp left, stumbled down the kerb and nearly came to grief in a pothole. People had already written to the council about it. Thank goodness she had her stick, otherwise, she'd have come a cropper.

"He can't go down the kerb," she explained, without looking round to see if the others were following.

The man realised – Pat had stupidly explained it out loud – so he careened further on to the zebra crossing and the dropped kerb, his wheels bibbling on the raised bumps of the pale paving.

He was close and they'd run out of puff.

"Split up," Pat shouted, but she was already on her own.

Behind her, the mobility scooter *bip-bip-bipped* onto the pavement.

She went another car length along the parked cars and then zigged through a gap back across the road.

"Jävlar!"

Metal scraped paving, wheels crunched... a woman pulled her pram back just in time!

The mother screamed.

The pram slipped from her fingers and rolled away.

The baby bawled.

The pram reached the top of the kerb.

In front of Pat, Mr Henderson faffed with his mobility scooter. He'd just struggled out of it with his stick.

Villagers stood frozen in horror as the pram bumped down onto the road and came to a safe halt.

Oh, thank goodness, Pat thought as she turned her attention to Mr Henderson and his mobility scooter.

"Excuse me," Pat said as she lurched onto it with the last of her oomph, jamming her stick into the metalwork by the seat. She turned the key, but it didn't start!

"Mrs Thomas, I say," Mr Henderson started to say.

No, wait!

Pat realised it was electric.

She turned the knob, gripped the lever and took off, the wheels spinning to gain traction.

The scooter scooted!

Really scooted!

Good grief, Pat thought, Mr Henderson was a speed freak – the thing was doing 5, if not 6, mph. Her scarf almost streamed out behind her in her slipstream.

She had to slow down.

But how?

There were a bewildering number of controls of all shapes and sizes: a knob, a button, a lever... the list just stopped there.

Then the headrest exploded – *Phut-booff!* – as the gunman fired again.

And that persuaded Pat to put the plastic handle hard against the easy-grip rubber.

But it wasn't enough.

Yard by yard, inch by inch, the other mobility scooter closed the distance. The man aimed, a leer of triumph, and he fired at point-blank range.

Click.

"Skit!"

Pat veered wildly from side to side, but there were iron benches, panicking pedestrians, pretty trees and litter bins.

The other scooter got its front wheel beside Pat's rear and then he sidled up.

He drew level.

In desperation, Pat leaned backwards and grabbed at Mrs Pilkington's shopping from the hitman's basket. She hurled it backwards. A yoghurt split, the fizzy pop ricocheted and then exploded – *BOOM-fizzzz* – like a rocket, the milk bounced off and splattered whitely on the paving.

Their wheels locked!

The man turned his handlebars to force Pat off into the buildings. She hit the flowers put outside Celia's, trashing the heads and upturning the display.

Pat steered into him, forcing him outwards.

He punched at her, but missed.

Pat drew her walking stick and struck furiously.

The man got Mrs Pilkington's stick out, struck back.

Pat lunged.

He countered.

Slash.

Cut.

Parry.

Riposte.

Desperate flailing.

Pasado.

Straight thrust.

Bonetti's defence.

Capo Ferro.

Thibault.

Pat tried a heroic remise.

He feinted left.

She fell for it.

He performed a sweeping envelope action and Pat's stick went spinning away.

Pat grabbed the handlebars to regain control of her vehicle.

The High Street came to an end!

Pat turned left, going around the Chinese and Pizza restaurant. Mr Chiang[8] had been putting out cardboard boxes for recycling all

---

[8] Editor's note: There is a rule in crime fiction about not having a 'Chinaman', because of the overuse of stereotypical characters in the 1920s.

afternoon, effectively constructing a barrier. Pat careened through, smashing the brown corrugated, double-wall hither and thither.

And then the pavement ran out!

She turned sharply. The scooter hurtled off the kerb, flying through the air for inches before slamming down onto the hard tarmac. The main A-road was wide. Suddenly, she was no longer a fast vehicle, but a slow and plodding target.

A Porsche zoomed past, blaring its horn, revving its engine and grating its exhaust.

Pat drove over the solid white line into the other lane.

An open-topped lorry screeched to a halt and jack-knifed. Apples and oranges cascaded like a waterfall of 5-a-days, ready to be swerved around, squashed and pulped.

Pat wheeled round and headed for the village again.

The other scooter was still trapped by fallen boxes, but not for much longer.

She turned right, back to the High Street: Chiang's, Celia's, Conkies, Baxters and the Oxfam shop whizzing past at a dizzying rate.

Mr Henderson walked along side with his stick.

"Excuse me, Mrs Thomas, but do you think I could have my scooter back?" he said.

But she left him behind as he was getting on a bit and couldn't keep up.

And then disaster!

She hit the wretched pothole and the wheel jammed.

She pulled herself out of the scooter and staggered towards Pheasant's Café. A safe haven was what she needed and a cup of reviving tea wouldn't go amiss.

But the other scooter appeared in front of her, blocking her escape.

The gunman got out of his chair, menacing – except when the walking stick threatened to trap him again – and dangerous. He ejected the magazine from his gun and reloaded, pulling the slide back in a practised, savage movement to chamber a fresh round.

"What... what..." Pat managed. Pheasants Café was mere feet away with fresh tea and she could see the carrot cake, cream buns and the specials board.

"You killed him?" the man said, his eyes mean, narrowed and focused as he hobbled towards her.

"Me?"

"Yes, you... or one of the others."

"Us?"

"Yes, you and Pendle-Took killed him."

"Killed who?"

"Lars!"

"Who?"

"My brother."

"Who!"

"My brother, Lars."

"I've never heard of him," Pat explained. "We're investigating the murder of... well, lots of people, but primarily today, Sir Victor Pendle-Took."

"Pendle-Took's dead?"

"Yes. Murdered."

"Who by?"

"By whom," Pat said. "No, wait, this Lars must be the man that Diane saw murdered."

"Diane!" The man glanced up and down the High Street.

"Look, Mr Whoever-you-are, if you'd just stop trying to kill me for a moment, I might be able to work this out."

"I don't care!" the man shouted. "I want my revenge. I'm going to kill you and then those other two busybodies."

"But we didn't do it."

"So? There's the small matter of professional pride," he said. "If I can't retire three old ladies, then I'll never be hired again."

426

"But I'm already retired," Pat replied.

"I meant 'retired' youth.... em-istically."

"Euphemistically?"

"Yes."

"What does that mean?"

"Killed."

"I don't think 'euphemistically' means 'killed'."

"No, 'retired' means 'killed'."

"Well, quite, but if you'd been clear from–"

"Håll käften," he said as he grabbed Pat by her cashmere scarf to point his gun in her face. "Tid att dö."

For Pat, everything went grey, dark and moody, her bones chilled as if December had come early and all the things she needed to do flickered before her eyes. The man grinned wide enough to show his sadistic nature and his gold teeth.

And then Annabelle ran him over with Mrs Pilkington's mobility scooter.

He fell.

The gun went off – *Phut!*

It wasn't pleasant.

25. Arrests

Detective Constable Kilroy checked the passport. The Scene-of-Crime Officer had kindly slipped it into the transparent evidence bag so that the name could be made out: 'Anders Lindström'.

This was the 'Jack Ketch' he'd met at Pendle-Took's house – a tall and thin man, blond. Or maybe this was the other tall and thin man he'd seen in the Saab. He checked his notebook to remind himself of the foreign number plate: Swedish.

Miss Richards had witnessed Pendle-Took shooting a tall and thin man.

Finally, he thought, it seemed likely that he'd solve a case: Pendle-Took killed Lindström's colleague with a gun.

A definite result – phew.

Except, without a body, they couldn't bring it to court and the murderer, Pendle-Took, was the victim of an unfortunate accident, so it felt like a pyrrhic victory.

He handed the evidence back to the Scene-of-Crime Officer.

The police were still securing the scene, but the ambulances nearby were packing up. They hadn't been needed despite the panic recent events had caused. The village had rallied round with flasks of sweet tea.

"There's this," the man said. It was a walking stick, the sort that split into three sections.

"I think I know who owns that," Kilroy said, taking it.

The police constable wrapping the 'Police Line – Do Not Cross' tape around the crime scene let out a cry of disbelief.

"What is it?" Kilroy asked, but he saw that the tape only reached halfway between the metal railing and the litter bin.

"It's run out," the constable said.

"There's more in the incident room," Kilroy replied.

"This is the last roll."

"We had plenty."

"For a couple of deaths, this is number... I've lost count."

Kilroy went through the list of deaths in his head: vicar, Sergio, Mrs Boseman, curate, the unknown victim Miss Richards witnessed, Pendle-Took and now this Lindström. At least Pendle-Took had been an accident and with any luck, Sergio was simply a hit-and-run.

"Seven," he said.

"Struth."

"Do the best you can."

Kilroy found the old ladies in Pheasant's Café. He'd known they would be Thomas, Richards and Harrison before he got there, because he knew his luck wasn't going to change.

Mrs Thomas gave him a wan smile as she comforted Mrs Harrison. Miss Richards was bringing across a tray of coffees, hot chocolates and cream buns.

"I didn't mean to," Mrs Harrison sobbed. "I'm so sorry."

"You saved our lives," Mrs Thomas said.

"This is becoming less of a cosy mystery and more like a Scandi Noir all the time," Miss Richards said.

"Ladies?" Kilroy said. "Is this yours?"

"Oh, Detective Constable, thank you," Mrs Thomas said taking back her walking stick. "Please sit."

Kilroy scrapped a chair across and joined them. "Any ideas?" he asked.

"He was a hitman–"

"I killed him," Mrs Harrison wailed.

"No, Belle, it was self-defence."

"That is for the courts to decide," Kilroy said, although he regretted saying it straight away.

Mrs Thomas's stare was like that of a superbeing with laser beam eyes.

432

Kilroy shuffled in his seat and wished he could have a cream bun. Much as he wanted a collar, he couldn't bring himself to arrest these poor, sweet old ladies, even though they had conspired to brutally run someone over. Imagine bringing her into court as a witness, he thought. Twelve good men and true would hate him for certain.

Instead, he dug into his Mackintosh pocket and dumped the contents on the table: notes, chalk for drawing around bodies, his pen torch, the receipt for his new Mackintosh, a shotgun cartridge and eventually a packet of tissues. He gave one to Annabelle.

She blew in it, loudly.

Kilroy gave her another.

"You saved our lives," Mrs Thomas said.

"Yes," Kilroy agreed. "A public service. Please, go on about this hitman."

"He was sent to kill someone," Mrs Thomas explained, "but he thought that Sir Victor had killed his brother, Lars–"

"Who?"

433

"Lars, his brother," Mrs Thomas continued. "They were professional assassins."

"In Conky Whallop?" Kilroy sighed: of course, in Conky Whallop, where else? "Why?"

"Drug money."

A quaint English village with a picturesque green, a medieval church, ramshackle cottages and overrun with dotty old ladies was, of course, the operating centre of a drugs cartel.

"Mrs Entwistle watered the plants in her son's house," Mrs Thomas said.

Kilroy sighed again, fetched a cup of tea and a slice of lemon cheesecake.

"Mrs Thomas–"

"Pat, please."

"Pat, please explain."

"Sergio was a drug mule."

That seemed unlikely to Kilroy as he stabbed with his cake fork. "Go on."

434

"He took marijuana to the students in Upper Whallop and the whole operation was run by Sir Victor Pendle-Took," Pat said. "He gave up his architecture business on account of a building collapsing."

"Shame he didn't give up his business on account of the buildings that stayed up," Diane added.

"So," Pat continued, "when the vicar was killed, Sir Victor saw the police cars gathered around Mrs Entwistle's house with their lights flashing."

"They weren't round her house," Kilroy said.

"But they were. She lives next to the church."

"Ah."

"So, Sir Victor assumed the marijuana farm had been discovered and it was time to cover his tracks. He killed Sergio with his black SUV and hid it in the garage, and then he paraded his green one about the village to establish that he'd not hit anyone."

"Right," Kilroy said, nodding. He had wondered why the architect's car, complete with *Architecture Today* on the passenger seat, had been parked next to his. "So, he was killed by his gangland connections."

"Unfortunately not," Mrs Thomas said. "The hitman thought Sir Victor was still alive. He didn't know that Pendle-Took had been murdered."

Kilroy's portion of cheesecake fell from his fork and splatted on his plate. It summed up the case for a brief moment before he squished it back on his fork and into his mouth.

"But," Kilroy said, "Pendle-Took wasn't murdered."

"Please don't speak with your mouth full, Detective Constable."

"S–" – Kilroy swallowed – "Sorry."

"Of course, he was murdered," Pat said.

Kilroy shook his head.

"He was murdered," Pat repeated.

"No," Kilroy said, "He was found... well, that is to say, he was... and... found and the

436

circumstances were, basically, and to cut a long story short, he was... well, you know... the thing is... best not speak ill of the dead."

Pat raised an eyebrow. "I am a woman of the world."

"If you must know, he was naked, watching a pornographic film with a polythene bag over his head and a segment of orange in his mouth."

"Autoerotic asphyxiation."

Kilroy breathed a sigh of relief. "Yes."

"See, that wasn't difficult, was it?"

"No."

"We are women of the world, you know."

"Of course."

"I've come across plenty of debauchery in my time. I mean, I once had a typing job in Ely."

"Well... yes."

"And?"

"And?"

"And there's more about the death," Pat said, "isn't there?"

"Well, he fell over when he was... and landed on the fireplace. The... er, a sticky up metal bit stabbed him in the back. Accident, so there's no crime to solve."

"A puncture on the left side between the second and third ribs that penetrated the heart," Pat said.

"Yes, and death would have instantaneous and... you've been reading my forensics reports again," Kilroy said.

"I haven't," Pat assured him, "I simply examined his clothing. The bloodstains are quite revealing."

"The wounds would still match if it was an accident."

"Well, yes, quite, but it's tricky to take your clothes off after instantaneous death."

"Yes, but... ah... oh."

"Therefore murder."

438

Kilroy sagged: the weight of all the impending paperwork seemed to rest upon his shoulders. Another murder and he'd yet to close a case. He had forensics reports and police statements and yet these old ladies seemed to know more than... wait a minute!

"Clothes?" Kilroy said.

"They were handed in at the Oxfam shop," Pat said.

"Left in the porch," Annabelle wailed between sniffs.

"By the murderer?" Kilroy said.

"It seems an unlikely way to dispose of the evidence," Pat said, "but it would raise money for a good cause."

"So, we're looking for a brutal killer with a charitable heart."

Kilroy went through it in his mind. Pendle-Took shot this Lars Lindström and then, later that evening, he had been murdered and the circumstances had been faked to look like an embarrassing accident. Finally, the murderer must have dropped the clothes off at the charity shop on the way home. An idea began to form at the edge of his mind, a glimmer of–

"What's this?" Diane asked.

"Shotgun cartridge," Kilroy replied, "and it's evidence."

Kilroy took it off her and Pat took it off him.

"Where did you find this?" she asked.

"Major Naseby's... and he had a cartridge missing."

"Did he now?" Pat said, weighing the ammunition in her hand.

"So Major Naseby shot Mrs Boseman!" Diane said.

"Wrong sort of gun," Kilroy said.

"I went there with the Church Committee," Diane said. "He had his shotgun against the dresser. Anyone could have wandered in and taken it."

"Church Committee?" Kilroy asked.

"We raise money for charity," Diane explained. "Mrs Entwistle, the curate's wife, Betty and myself."

"All key holders," Kilroy said aloud.

Charity begins in the home, Kilroy thought, as the idea began to surface again. That would mean... but the bell above the café door tinkled and a tall, well-dressed man with a square jaw, shaven head and piercing blue eyes marched up to their table.

"Right," the newcomer said in a no-nonsense, getting-on-with-it tone of voice, "I'm Inspector Rex Raymond and I'm taking charge of this débâcle."

"Finally," Diane said under her breath, "a proper inspector."

"You, Mrs Thomas–"

"Miss Richards."

"And Harrison," he continued, pointing to Annabelle and then to Pat, "are under arrest."

"On what charge?" Diane exclaimed.

"I'd have thought that was obvious," Inspector Rex Raymond stated. "Half a dozen murders and you're always on the scene – and that can't be coincidence – and several witnesses have reported a car chase, gunshots and one of you holding some bloke while another of you ran him over."

"Oh... sorry," Annabelle said. "I am sorry."

"Save it for the judge, Mrs Richards."

"Miss," Diane said. "And I'm not her."

"This is ridiculous," Pat said.

"Inspector," Diane said, "you are a complete–"

"You have the right, etcetera," the inspector said. "Killjoy, read them their rights. And properly – I don't want any more screw-ups – and then bring them to the station, pronto."

Kilroy took a deep breath. "You have the right to remain silent–" but after that, he was unable to get a word in edgeways.

26. Little Grey Cells

The walls were grey.

Pat stared at a grey wall.

Diane stared at a grey wall.

Annabelle stared at a grey wall.

The walls were grey.

They were not the same grey walls, although they were identical in every respect, except for the number of lines scratched here and there like white picket fences. The marks spoke of time passing, an age built up like the grey painted walls, brick-by-brick, row-by-row, sentence-by-sentence; just as Pat's Accurist watch marked the aeons as they passed, tick-by-tick.

"This is ridiculous," Pat said aloud.

"What was that?" Diane shouted back from the next-door cell.

"I said THIS IS RIDICULOUS."

"YES."

"What was that?" Annabelle's voice was distant.

"SHE SAID," Diane shouted, "THIS IS RIDICULOUS."

"WHAT?"

"Oh for heaven's sake," Pat said. She stood up and went to the iron door. She banged it until her hand hurt. "POLICE, POLICE!"

The shutter in the cell door scraped open and a grizzled face appeared. "What?"

"Can we be locked in the same cell," Pat asked, "so that at least we can have a conversation without shouting?"

"Can't do that," said the police sergeant, "health and safety."

"I beg your pardon."

"Health and safety... one of you could be a murderer."

"Look, I can assure you that none of us is a murderer. We're more amateur sleuths."

444

"Lord help us."

"WE'RE INVESTIGATIVE REPORTERS!" Diane yelled.

"Quiet you."

"Don't take that tone with me, officer."

"Quiet you, Madam."

"*Miss* Richards!"

"Quiet."

"I am on first name terms with the Chief Constable, Sir Benjamin Clough, you arrogant, jumped up-"

"DI," Pat shouted. "YOU'RE NOT HELPING."

"Oi," said the copper, "that's deafening."

"Then put us in the same cell."

"One of you could be the murderer."

"Then if that murderer murders someone, your list of suspects goes down from three to two."

"Oh yes."

"So?"

"But if I put two in one cell and one in another," the officer said, his brain clearly working, "then I'll know who's the murderer for certain."

"How so?"

"Well, if one of you in the cell with two is killed, then it's the survivor and, if neither is killed, then it has to be the one in the cell on their own."

Pat blinked as she thought through the logic.

"But," she said, "what if the murderer is in the cell with the two prisoners and doesn't kill the other one?"

"Why would they do that?"

"To confuse you."

"Eh?"

"PUT US IN THE SAME CELL."

The shutter scraped shut.

"Honestly!" Pat said, incensed.

446

And then the key rattled and she was let out. They collected Diane on the way and he put them into Annabelle's cell.

"And a cup of tea," Diane said, but the door slammed shut. "Well, really."

"Could you not ask the Chief Constable to let us out?" Annabelle said. "Seeing as you are acquainted."

"I'm not sure that would help," Diane said.

"Why not?"

"He'd probably make sure we stayed the night."

"But you know him," Pat said. "You said you were on first name terms."

"Yes... from protests."

"Oh, Di," Pat said.

"What protests?" Annabelle asked.

"The usual," Diane replied, "fox hunting, nuclear bases, genetically modified crops, the cancellation of *Last of the Summer Wine*... that sort of thing."

"Oh, well, we'll have to stay here then," Annabelle said. "I'm sorry there's not much room."

"We'll make do," Pat said. "Now, let's... oh, they took my handbag."

"I've got a tissue," Diane said.

"No, it's not that, it's my notes. They're in my bag."

"Oh, we could start from scratch."

"They might be a good idea," Pat said. "My notes weren't that helpful."

"So, what are the cases?" Annabelle asked. "I'm losing track."

Pat counted on her fingers: "The vicar, Sergio, Mrs Boseman, the curate, Lars Lindström, Sir Victor and finally Anders Lindström."

"That's an awful lot," Diane said.

"I am sorry about the last one," Annabelle said.

"Seven," Pat said. "The problem is that people are being murdered faster than we can solve them."

"Well," Diane said, "the last one, this Anders Whatshisname was killed by Belle."

"I'm sorry, I'm so sorry, I've said I'm sorry," Annabelle said. "I am sorry."

"Belle," Pat said, "you saved our lives and, besides, you running him over didn't kill him. It was his gun, so it was an accident."

Annabelle sniffed. "Was it?"

"Yes."

"And I witnessed Sir Victor kill Lars Whatshisname," Diane said.

"Lindström," Pat said.

"Which is two murders solved," Diane said. "And I bet Pendle-Took killed his brother."

"I think this Lars Lindström is buried under Sir Victor's new patio," Pat said, "which leaves us with a problem."

"What's that?" Diane asked.

"Sir Victor was an architect."

"I don't see what difference that makes."

"He would never lay his own patio," Pat explained. "He'd draw it, certainly, he'd describe its outstanding features, definitely, he'd prepare a speech for the award ceremony, undoubtedly, but build it? Unthinkable. He wouldn't get his hands dirty, so he must have been helped."

"Ah."

"Perhaps," Annabelle said, "whoever helped him, then killed him."

"But why wouldn't they simply kill Pendle-Took and dump his body in the patio?" Diane said.

"I think," Pat said, "that disposing of Lars Lindström would be fine as he wouldn't be missed."

"Anders Whatshisname missed him."

"I meant officially, such that the police would search, and hiding a body in a patio is rather obvious."

"It was in that soap," Annabelle said.

"Yes, so... whoever killed Sir Victor needed it to look like an accident, so that it wouldn't be investigated."

"Oh, yes," Diane said. "Whoever murdered the others like the vicar and curate."

"Someone he knew."

"One of us," Annabelle said.

"Not one of us," Diane said.

"Sorry, I meant one of us in the village."

At that moment, the key rattled in the lock and the door swung open.

"You're free to go," the sergeant said.

"Yes, thank you, officer," Pat said, "but we haven't finished yet."

"That's as may be, but we need the cell."

"You've got two others spare."

The sergeant sighed and his shoulders drooped. He was trained to cope with the youth of today with all their gangs, knife crime and rap-and-drill music. They were younger every year and knew all their rights. It was all 'don't dis me', never respecting others, but this made sense – he'd been young once, though he felt every month pass as if it was a year. However, old ladies hadn't been covered much at Hendon Police College.

"So," Pat said, "that leaves the vicar, Mrs Boseman, the curate and Sir Victor to solve."

"Yes."

"Yes."

They stared at the grey walls for inspiration. The sergeant followed their gaze, saw nothing and then shook himself out of his reverie.

"Out!" he said.

And the police sergeant marched them towards the front desk, realised they were somewhat slower and backtracked.

"This way, dearies," he said.

452

"Don't 'dearie' me," Diane replied. "There must be a canteen in this place. Police are always drinking tea."

"And detectives drink coffee," Annabelle said. "Funny that."

"So long as there's plenty of sugar," Diane added.

"Sugar!" Pat said, snapping her fingers. "Of course."

By this time, they'd reached the front desk and the police sergeant returned their confiscated items: Pat's handbag and walking stick, Annabelle's belt, Diane's bootlaces. Pat checked was pleased to find the shotgun cartridge was still amongst her things.

"What's that?" the sergeant asked.

"Lipstick," she said, "passion red."

"Right."

She dropped it back in her handbag and fussed out her notebook, ripping out a sheet, so that she could write a note outlining their discoveries.

"Could you give this to the nice detective constable, please?" she asked.

"The nice... detective constable?" the sergeant said.

"Yes"

"Madam, which one would that be?"

"Detective Constable Kilroy."

"Killj– yes, madam. Right away."

The sergeant took the slip of paper, but his glance towards the wastepaper bin was too obvious.

"Now, please."

"Yes, Madam."

"We'll wait."

"Oh for... yes, Madam."

He sloped off down a corridor mentioning to the walls, floor and ceiling that life was too short.

Pat glanced around taking in the posters: 'Possession of Cannabis carries a maximum sentence of 5 years', 'carrying a gun, a realistic imitation of a gun or ammunition in public is illegal', and 'Have you seen Fluffy?' At least she had never seen Fluffy.

The police sergeant reappeared.

"And?" Pat asked.

"He wasn't there," the police sergeant said, "so I left it on his computer keyboard."

"Well, I suppose that was the best you could do."

"Yes, madam."

"So, if you'd take us to the police canteen, sergeant," Diane said.

"Well, yes, I could do with a cuppa," Pat said.

"Will they have muffins or crumpet?" Annabelle said.

The police sergeant coughed pointedly. "Ladies! Café! Outside!"

27. A False Trail

Kilroy had to pass on his case notes to Inspector Rex Raymond. Like a guilty schoolboy, he moved some stupid note off his computer keyboard and started hammering out an attempt at a report. He'd had no time to do it properly due to the ever-increasing number of murders.

He needed coffee.

He got a coffee.

A piece of paper was in the way of his coaster.

He moved it.

The problem with the report was deciding which fact went with which murder. The vicar's was straightforward with the nine keyholder suspects, but then it became confused. Sergio knocked over could still be a hit-and-run accident. Mrs Boseman appeared to have been over-murdered and everyone in the village had given Mr

Boseman an alibi and he'd given everyone in the village an alibi.

And then there was the curate, a murder that he himself had almost witnessed. He knocked together a witness statement from himself by copy-and-pasting from the other statements, while being careful to change the wording here and there.

Sir Victor Pendle-Took, who might have had the best motive to kill the vicar, had killed a Swedish hitman only to have been killed in turn by someone unknown.

Could the vicar's death be pinned on Pendle-Took?

No, that was an uncharitable thought.

Mrs Annabelle Harrison had killed the Swedish hitman's brother, also an assassin, and she'd been sent to the cells for something that clearly wouldn't get a conviction in court. Miss Richards had been a lawyer and had pointed that out as soon as they'd reached the police station. Her arguments had been legal, compelling and forthright, and then full of rather blue language.

It was all about results for Inspector Rex Raymond. No doubt, with three old ladies in the cells, the murders could be divvied up between them.

That was an uncharitable thought too.

Idly, he fiddled with a piece of paper on his desk.

The three old dears had gone now, without a word.

Hansel and Gretel had followed a trail of breadcrumbs.

Theseus had had a thread for the labyrinth.

The 'hare' littered their path in a paper chase.

What was needed was a clue – he put the scrap of paper down – some small and telling detail that would unravel the mess.

A clue?

He found he was fiddling with some scrap of paper on his desk again.

Irritated, he put it aside and deleted the section about needing a clue. Let the inspector figure it out. He was paid enough.

Kilroy chucked the paper into the bin. He missed. Typical, he thought.

He got back to the report, typed away furiously, and finally, clicked send: done.

Oh, hell, he'd spelt Miss Fairfax as Miss 'Farfax'.

Too late to do anything about it now.

A shadow loomed over him. "You off the case?"

"Wragg?"

"Bad luck." DC Wragg looked almost sympathetic.

"Thanks," Kilroy said.

Kilroy remembered that DC Wragg had had long hair, but since the arrival of Inspector Raymond, many officers had adopted number one cuts. It was a uniform spreading through the plain clothes division and another reason why Kilroy didn't fit in.

"You'll be on Operation Borrow," Wragg said.

"What's that?"

"The dog fouling epidemic."

Almost sympathetic.

He'd have a Scotch, Kilroy decided. After all, he'd been working at the weekend and deserved it.

"Bye, Wragg."

"Ciao, Killjoy."

So, Kilroy collected his Mackintosh and–

"This yours?"

DC Wragg held up a note he'd picked up off the floor. Kilroy didn't recognize the handwriting, but it was going to be paperwork, he knew it.

Except it was a note from Mrs Thomas.

"Well, well, well," he said, unaware of the cliché.

28. Elementary

"Mrs Thomas," Detective Constable Kilroy said, "this is well after my shift and... something smells good."

"Never mind that," Pat said. "Come in, shoes, coat."

Kilroy handed over his crumpled and filthy Mackintosh.

"Oh my, you have been in the wars."

Kilroy removed his scuffed shoes and noticed that his socks were as mismatched as they had been during his last visit, although they were the other way around.

"I've a pair like these at home," he said. "I got your note."

"Excellent."

Pat showed him into her kitchen. The other two old ladies sat around the table. They appeared to Kilroy to be like a coven of witches, but smiling and – *shudder* – so helpful. Something boiled and bubbled on the cooker, and smelled sweet, wonderful and bad for you.

"Detective Constable," Diane said.

"Yes, sorry, Detective Constable," Annabelle said.

"Ladies. Evening. What's this about?" Kilroy asked.

"We don't know," Diane said. "Pat won't tell us."

"But it involves baking and wine," Annabelle added.

"I can't drink," Kilroy said. "I'm on duty."

"Nonsense," Pat said, "you told me when you arrived that it was well after your shift."

"And I'm driving."

"You'll have to get a taxi."

"I'm–"

"You'll *have* to get a taxi."

"Hmmm."

462

He stood at the head of the table.

"Please," Pat repeated, indicating one of two empty chairs.

So, Kilroy sat, scraping the chair across the linoleum.

The table had been laid with a chequerboard tablecloth and a single, silver cup. Kilroy considered it like a chess grandmaster trying to fathom how to achieve checkmate with only one piece. It had an engraving: 'Cambridge and Norfolk District' and 'Mr E. B. Thomas'.

"All I could find," Pat said taking it off him. She went to the work counter and poured from an already open bottle of Pinot Noir.

Pat placed it back on the table and took her seat.

"Now," she said and took a sip.

"Don't we get a glass?" Annabelle said, glancing over her shoulder at the wine glasses arranged neatly near the bottle.

"Now, Di, you take a sip," Pat said, handing the golf award to Diane. "Blood of Christ."

"Is this a religious thing?" Kilroy asked.

"Quiet," Pat said. "Take a sip, Di."

Diane smiled and took a gulp.

"Not too much," Pat interjected. "How's the taste?"

"Palatable," Diane said.

"Now you, Belle."

Diane passed the cup to her left as if it was port and Annabelle took a sip.

"Well, Belle," Pat said, "how's the taste?"

"Er... well," Annabelle said, taking a sniff, "I'm getting sort of raspberry, maybe walnut, a hint of cinnamon and warm evenings by the fire."

"In other words, red wine," Pat said.

"Oh. Yes. Sorry. Wine... red. Yes. Definitely."

"We saw you pour it from the bottle," Kilroy said.

"Ever the detective, eh?" Diane said.

464

Pat took the cup from Annabelle and placed it in the centre of the table. She swirled it by sliding the base in a circle while she looked at Diane, then Annabelle and finally DC Kilroy.

"You're recreating the murder of the curate," Kilroy said.

"Exactly," Pat said. "The question is how does one put arsenic into the wine in front of everyone?"

Kilroy realised this wasn't chess, but a magic trick. "Go on."

"This is red wine in a goblet and it's been drunk by all three of us."

"Yes."

"Leaving one person left."

Kilroy didn't like where this was going. "Yes?"

"So, Detective, please," Pat said sliding the cup towards him. "Drink."

DC Kilroy looked at her suspiciously.

"You want to know how the curate was killed."

"Oh yes," Annabelle said, excitedly. "Sorry."

"So, Detective Constable, drink."

Kilroy leaned back in his seat and folded his arms across his chest.

"It's safe," Pat said. "You saw me drink, Di and then Belle. No one's touched it."

"Hmmm."

"Is it poison?" Annabelle asked.

"No!" Pat insisted. "Detective, please?"

Kilroy reached out, touched the rim of the cup with his forefinger and thumb.

"It's safe?" he checked.

Pat smiled, a twinkle in her eye. "Perfectly."

"It's not been you three bumping everyone off as Inspector Raymond suspects?"

"Officer! Really. Drink."

The surface of the wine was blood red, dark and mysterious.

"Or we'll be offended," Pat added.

Common sense and good manners fought across Kilroy's features with a frown, a twitch and a slow blink of defeat. He picked up the cup. "You say it's safe?"

Pat nodded.

He drank.

And leapt to his feet, knocking the chair backwards and he spat the wine out: good manners be damned, his common-sense thought.

"What the hell!"

Diane laughed aloud.

"Detective, please," Pat said. "Ladies present."

"Sorry, sorry, I beg your pardon, but you've poisoned me?"

"It's chilli powder," Pat explained.

"But it can't be," Annabelle said, "I'd have tasted it."

"And me," Di added.

"I like chilli," Kilroy complained, trying to wipe his tongue with his finger.

"Well, quite, but not in wine when it's a surprise," Pat explained. "Please, sit."

The detective reclaimed the fallen chair.

While he settled, Pat went over to the cooker and turned off the gas. She brought the frying pan over to the table, a cast iron trivet, a mortar and pestle and a plate. Then, very like a magician, she poured a little of the hot substance from the pan onto the plate to form a small pool of congealing, gelatinous goo about the size of a 50p piece.

"Belle, could you get the white wine from the fridge and two glasses please," she said.

"The... why?"

"Belle."

Annabelle fetched the wine – "Sauvignon blanc do?" – from the fridge and Diane collected the glasses.

"Do I pour?" Annabelle asked.

"Please," Pat said.

"I'm on duty," Kilroy said.

"You said–"

"I'm interviewing witnesses so I'm on duty."

"Do you want to know or not?" Pat asked.

"Glass of wine then."

Annabelle poured two glasses of white wine.

Meanwhile, Pat took a teaspoon and doled out a measure of chilli powder onto the goo. Then, having skipped pulling up her sleeves to show that there were no cards concealed, she folded the concoction so that the red powder was sealed inside. She rolled it into a ball and dropped this 'marble' into one of the wine glasses.

"It floats," Pat said rather obviously.

"It does," Kilroy agreed.

Pat put it to one side and took hold of the silver cup.

"Di," she said, "pass me the sieve... on the draining board, and the jug."

Diane got up and brought over the sieve and a measuring jug. Pat poured the red wine from the golf cup into the jug through the sieve. Three tiny objects appeared in the sieve like pips.

"Ah," said Di.

"Penny dropped?" Pat asked.

"Not quite."

"See," Pat said, taking something from the sieve and holding it up for the detective to see. "Lead shot."

"Three," Kilroy counted.

"Well, I'm not as good as the murderer," Pat said. She repeated the process with the hot substance as before, pouring the goo and spooning the red chilli powder on top, but this time she included the lead shot. The resulting 'gob-stopper' went into the second glass of white wine.

It sank to the bottom like an olive in a martini.

Pat took the glass ceremoniously and took a sip.

"Blood of Christ," she said handing it to Diane again.

Diane took a sip and passed it to Annabelle. "Blood of Christ," she said.

Annabelle giggled and so nearly choked on her sip.

Pat intercepted it before it reached the detective. She placed it on the table and swirled it as she had with the goblet of red wine.

"It takes a while," she explained, "but then there's the final hymn, everyone has to leave, Betty has to tidy up her music and then the warden checks everyone is out, leaving the curate to finish the sacramental wine – it can't be simply poured down the sink – and then..."

Kilroy waited, and waited and then said, "And then?"

Pat nodded to the glass of Sauvignon Blanc. The capsule had dissolved enough for a thin trail of red chilli to seep out into the wine.

"What works for chilli works for arsenic," Pat said.

"Then who?" Diane asked.

"There was me," Pat said, "then Diane, Annabelle, *the curate's wife*, and, when we left, Betty and Frances the warden."

"No!" Annabelle said.

"She dropped silver balls all over her kitchen–"

"Silver balls?" Kilroy asked.

"Like hundreds and thousands," Pat explained. "She dropped them deliberately to hide the lead shot that she must have spilt getting it out of the shotgun cartridge."

"It still doesn't work," Kilroy said.

"Why not?" Diane asked.

"Because the curate would have seen her put it in," the detective insisted. "Anyone would have seen. There were people kneeling either side of her, for goodness' sake."

"Another glass of white, please, Belle," Pat said.

"Oh, right, sorry," Annabelle said, getting to her feet.

"Thank you," Pat said. She coughed and put her hand over her mouth. "Excuse me."

They watched as Annabelle poured another glass. and she poured another glass.

"Here," Annabelle said handing it to Pat.

"Thank you... Blood of Christ," Pat mumbled as she put it to her lips, tilted it back and then placed it on the table. Inside the glass, another marble with a red centre lay sunk to the bottom of the white wine like a mine.

"One I prepared earlier," Pat explained.

Diane let out a whistle.

"You can make the sugar thick enough to last for ten minutes, plenty of time," Pat added. "She carried the arsenic up the aisle to the altar in her mouth."

"Whoa ho!" Kilroy exclaimed.

"One slap on her back," Pat said, "and she'd have swallowed it and died herself."

"But maybe not the curate's wife," Kilroy said.

Pat shook her head: "The curate's wife makes the toffee apples for the church fête. She's an expert in confectionery. It took me all day to get this to work and my rather thick sugar needs three pellets to sink."

 "And hers dissolved to leave nothing but a single pellet and a sugary taste."

"Elementary."

"I thought I was the detective."

"Did you?"

"Where will I find this curate's wide?"

"She's staying for the memorial tomorrow," Pat explained. "That's when all the suspects will be gathered together."

"Then that's when we nab her."

Kilroy picked up the third glass as if he was admiring the colour at a wine tasting. On cue, the sweet bled into the wine, transubstantiating the pure and innocent white into rosé.

29. Suspect List

The idea of a memorial service had seemed so sound, particularly as it would be efficient to remember everyone in a single event. And then it had all seemed so tactless. Not as tactless as Diane's suggestion to print a special murder edition of the parish magazine.

"You can't," Pat said.

"It's news!"

"Honestly. Di."

"We have to... freedom of the press."

There had been so many murders and everyone gathered in the church car park like so many suspects in a line-up: this corner for the vicar, that spot by the lychgate for the curate, Mrs Boseman's friends here, Sergio's there and Sir Victor's on one side.

No-one arrived to mourn the Swedish hitmen.

Pat had dressed in black with numb fingers and a distracted mind. It was hard to take in, so thank goodness that social conventions dictated what to wear, how to nod and mumble, and the need to carry on.

She had gone through her notes again. The pencil lines in her notebook were now a spider's web of confusion. Maybe she should pin photographs to the wall in the spare room with differently coloured threads to show the numerous links. She had plenty of wool.

She shivered, fearful that every time they visited the church there would be another death.

Who would be next? Belle? Di? Herself?

Perhaps the murderer or murderers feared that their investigations were closing in, when, in truth, Pat's thinking seemed further away all the time. Her thoughts never knitted together. She was wool-gathering.

With a sigh, she reached for her pashmina shawl.

And then there had been the hurried phone calls to decide who would perform the memorial.

Frances had rung round.

With the vicar gone, it fell to the curate, but with the curate murdered, the buck passed to the lay preacher, but with Sir Victor dead, the decision had been bumped upstairs to the diocese. However, the bishop was away and so they had been told to a) muddle through and b) find a deacon.

Deaconess Patterson had a happy smiling face at odds with her duty as a layperson performing a memorial. She saw, Pat suspected, a chance to shine in the heartland of protestant England. Clearly, no-one had informed her of the seething morass of murderers, drug dealers and hitmen that slithered and scuttled from their dark hiding places, now that the rock had been overturned.

Everyone feared Major Naseby's reaction to a female deacon.

Diane had produced a lovely memorial service booklet with pictures: the vicar, the curate, Mrs Belinda Boseman, Sir Victor

478

Pendle-Took, Mr Sergio McNally. Although it did look like a Parish Newsletter supplement. The order disturbed Pat: importance to the church, rather than alphabetical or chronologically murdered. She was grateful that Diane hadn't included Lars and Anders Lindström.

But then the two Swedish hitmen were the only cases solved officially: killed by Sir Victor and Annabelle, respectively.

The other five stared out from their black-and-white portraits crying out for justice, even if a couple of them did so with inane smiles.

Given that two of them had died in the church, the memorial was moved to the Parochial Hall. The deaconess and Mrs Jones had put out the plastic chairs in a wide circle.

"Perhaps some sherry for afterwards," Deaconess Patterson suggested.

"We've organised a few refreshments," Frances told her.

"It's not coming out of the tea money," Mrs Jones said.

"Everyone please."

They all sat in a circle: Deaconess Patterson, the curate's wife, Major Naseby, Mr Boseman, Mrs Jones, Mrs Entwistle, Mrs Pilkington, Frances the warden, Betty the organist, Diane, Annabelle and Pat herself. Twelve suspects jiffling on their seats like the cast of *Murder on the Orient Express* or a jury ready to reach a verdict.

Or perhaps they were all murderers.

Twelve divided by six victims meant that some had to innocent of any murder. Unless they all did it.

Pat could probably cross the deaconess off the list.

She knew one murderer – and couldn't meet her eye – but had the curate's widow killed more than once?

Detective Constable Kilroy had not liked the curate's widow attending, but he had been overruled. After the memorial, not before.

"But," he'd said, "the inspector might steal my arrest... oh, fair enough."

So, he stood by the door in his crumpled Mackintosh ready to pounce.

The deaconess started proceedings, speaking softly and with reverence. "We are here to remember our dearly departed George... Gary... Belinda... Victor... and Sergio."

Everyone's heads were bowed in silent prayer, any guilty expressions hidden by hats and fringes.

"Oh Lord, we commend their souls to your care."

They all mumbled to their clasped hands, "Amen."

"Does anyone wish to say a few words?" Deaconess Patterson said.

"Poor Mrs Boseman," Betty said. "Zephron, you are so brave."

Mr Boseman nodded an acknowledgement, his pencil moustache turned up slightly as he attempted a smile. He belonged to an earlier age when minstrels, ethics and films were black and white.

481

"We all need to be brave and care for one another," the deaconess agreed.

The company glanced at each other, their thoughts mirroring Pat's own suspicions: one of them, but which one, who, who, who? The question burned in everyone's mind with glances like stabbing accusations

"Will there be cake?" Annabelle asked. "Oh... sorry."

"Anyone else?" the deaconess said.

Detective Constable Kilroy coughed and walked to the edge of the circle to stand at Pat's right shoulder.

The circle of suspects turned their eyes towards him and a hush descended.

"I know that this is supposed to be a solemn occasion," Kilroy said, "but this gathering gives us a chance to uncover the... one of the culprits."

He looked at the assembled company, each guilty of something: scrumping, shooting at scrumpers, publishing scandal, damaging cars, withholding evidence and brewing weak tea.

482

"This is a memorial service," Deaconess Patterson said. "I hardly think it is appropriate. People are grieving."

"Be that as it may," Kilroy replied, "but this is a murder enquiry."

"Well..." but the deaconess sat back in her hard, plastic seat, disapproving.

"I cannot take all the credit for solving this," Kilroy continued. "Mrs Thomas."

"Oh. Well. Yes. Of course."

Pat stood, flexed her knees – "Ah" – and then, having tapped her walking stick on the ground three times to gain everyone's attention, she began.

"Ladies and gentlemen," she said, "murder is the most terrible of crimes. Our lovely village has been struck by this unspeakable offence many times over the last week or so, and I am ashamed to say that one of us here *in this very room* is a murderer."

Everyone leaned forward.

"This has been something of a three-pot problem," Pat said with her finger raised.

"Ooh, this is so exciting," Annabelle said. "Just like the telly... sorry."

"We need to examine each in turn. The vicar stabbed in the church, Sergio run over, Mrs–"

"Is this necessary?" Deaconess Patterson said.

"Yes," Detective Constable Kilroy said.

"Thank you," said Pat. "Where was I?"

"You were killing the vicar in the church," Annabelle said.

"Yes... well, not me," Pat clarified. "Now, let me see. In the church and one of the keyholders must be the culprit."

The curate's wife, Mrs Jones, Mrs Entwistle, Mr Boseman, Betty the organist, Frances the warden and Diane shuffled uneasily.

"Then there's Sergio McNally," Pat continued. "We know that he was murdered by Sir Victor."

Gasps!

"He hid his car in his garage, but it was the murder weapon," Kilroy added.

484

"We found that," Annabelle said.

"Mrs Boseman and Sir Victor are a little trickier to explain," Pat said, "and then there's the curate."

"You know who killed them?" Frances the warden said.

"The curate, yes," Pat replied. "Let me explain, you see, someone in this very room–"

But then, explosively, the door banged open and a madman burst in, his hair wild and unkempt.

"She killed me," he shouted. "Betty, she killed me."

With that, Vlad the Inventor collapsed to the floor, blood oozing from multiple wounds to his chest.

Betty screamed, "Vlad!"

Pat was the first to reach him, throwing her stick aside.

"Who killed you?" Pat asked, kneeling – "Ooh, my knees" – down by his side.

"Betty."

"She's coming," Pat assured him. "Who killed you?"

"Betty, she killed me."

"I'm not Betty," Pat said. "Who did this?"

Vlad swallowed hard and made a Herculean effort to speak each word clearly so that there was no mistaking his meaning.

"Betty. Was the. Person. Who. Killed. Me."

"Betty? Surely not?"

But Vlad was dead, his eyes staring upwards towards the great workshop in the sky and Pat had blood on her hands.

30. Watertight Alibi

"Mrs Kovalyov," Detective Constable Kilroy said, "I am arresting you on the suspicion of the murder of your husband, Doctor Vladimir Kovalyov."

"Suspicion!" the curate's wife said. "We all heard him point the finger."

"It wasn't me," Betty cried out. "Oh, Zephron."

"Betty, I..." Mr Boseman started to say, but there wasn't anything to say. Everyone had heard Doctor Kovalyov's accusation.

"Please, quiet," Kilroy said. "You have the right to remain silent–"

"We all heard him," Mrs Pilkington said.

"Oh yes," Mrs Entwistle said.

"Clear as a bell," Mrs Jones added.

"I heard it too," Annabelle said.

"I didn't have my hearing aid in," Major Naseby said. "What did he say?"

"BE QUIET," Kilroy yelled.

"Sorry," Annabelle said.

"There's no need to shout," Major Naseby said.

Kilroy glared at them all, daring them to interrupt.

"But," the detective continued, "it may harm your defence if you do not mention when questioned – not another word, Major Naseby – something which you later rely on in court. Anything you do say may be given in evidence."

The light applause was silenced by another angry glare from the detective.

"Sorry," Annabelle said.

"What did he say after 'remain silent'?" Diane asked. "It's for the Parish Newsletter."

"Come with me," Kilroy said.

488

Everyone got up – "ooh", "ah", "oh" and "I'm quite capable, I'll have you know" – and made to follow.

"Just Mrs Kovalyov," Kilroy said.

"Detective–" Pat said.

"Just Mrs Kovalyov."

"But–"

"Thank you."

And they were all left in the main hall with the dead body lying between them and the door. There hadn't been such silence in the hall since the night the amateur cabaret had gone the way it had gone and that had been years ago.[9]

Deaconess Patterson let out a cry of anguish.

Everyone looked down at the lino and someone tutted.

----

[9] Editor's note: See *Hall's Horrendous Hiatus* in the parish magazine of that year.

"How can you just sit there?" the deaconess demanded. "It's like... there's been a murder!"

The villagers glanced at the body and then back at the deaconess.

Frances coughed. "There have been six–"

"Seven," Diane said.

"Seven murders," Frances continued, "and so... well, no need to make a scene."

"But..." The deaconess held her hands aloft to appeal to heaven.

"Well, quite," Pat said.

"Can I go now?" Deaconess Patterson asked.

"I guess the memorial is over, so why not," Frances replied. "Sherry and cake? Everyone?"

The deaconess smiled an apology, so sincere and understanding, grabbed her bag and rushed away.

"Not out of the tea money," Mrs Jones said.

490

"It's not out of the tea money," Frances said.

"Pardon," Major Naseby said.

"It's not out of the tea money!" Frances snapped.

"I don't have my hearing aid in," Major Naseby said.

"Then put it in," Frances mumbled.

"What?" Major Naseby replied.

"Let's go to the kitchen and see if we can help," Pat suggested.

This was met with much nodding.

"Pat?" Diane said handing Pat's walking stick back.

"Thank you, Di."

So, they all edged around the corpse to the kitchen and crammed into Mrs Jones's domain.

The sherry went into a charity shop collection of mismatched glasses and the Victoria sponge went on the green side plates. No-one touched the kettle or cups primed with milk.

"The meeting room, I think," Frances said.

In the little room, they sat at the round tables: Major Naseby, Mr Boseman, Mrs Jones, Mrs Entwistle, Mrs Pilkington, Frances the warden, Diane, Annabelle and Pat herself. Nine suspects like the ever-diminishing cast of *And Then There Were None*.

The curate's widow had high-heeled it.

Pat checked the window, but could see no sign of her. Instead, she saw DC Kilroy arguing with Inspector Rex Raymond, the latter leaning over the nice detective constable using his six foot and more height to its maximum advantage. The inspector was a bully, more like a well-dressed skinhead than a keeper of the peace. He took Betty the organist off Kilroy, added handcuffs to her distress and marched her away.

Pat knew she should run after the inspector and explain that there was no way that Betty could have killed her husband – they'd all been in the Memorial Service about to

492

accuse others at the time – but somehow, she knew the exercise wouldn't be good for her.

Kilroy, now abandoned, looked lost and alone in the wide expanse of the car park like a small boy who had mislaid his mother at the church fête.

"Oh dear," she said to herself.

"Will Betty be all right?" Mr Boseman said. "She can't have done it... could she?"

"Of course not, Zephron," Pat said. "It's all been a misunderstanding."

"But Vladimir said she'd killed him."

"Well, quite, but he was wrong. We were all witnesses to her innocence. We all have watertight alibis."

"Yes," Diane agreed. "We're all innocent."

"Of that, yes," Pat replied. "It means someone else killed him."

"But who?" Mr Boseman asked.

"Cake," Annabelle said, coming in with slices of Victorian sponge and Genoise.

"I couldn't eat a thing," Mr Boseman said.

Everyone else had no problem.

Pat wrapped a piece of sponge cake in a serviette.

"I feel like we're getting used to it," Mrs Entwistle said.

"There are less and less of us," Mr Boseman added.

"More cake for the rest of us," Annabelle said. "It's like *Death in Paradise*, isn't it?"

"How do you mean, Belle?" Diane asked.

"Well, in the early series with Inspector Poole, there were eight or nine suspects and it was difficult, but later on, with those other inspectors, there were only three or four suspects, so it was a lot easier to solve."

"You're right," Pat said.

"Although I never solved them," Annabelle admitted, "but in theory, it was easier."

"So, what you are saying," Diane said, "is that we should wait until the killer... or killers

494

have reduced the village population down to a more manageable suspect list."

"Yes… oh… no, not at all. Sorry."

"Or why not wait until there's only one of us left."

"Di, that's in poor taste," Mrs Entwistle said.

"It's true though," Frances said.

"Is there fruit cake?" Major Naseby asked.

"This isn't coming out of the tea money, is it?" Mrs Jones said.

"What do we do now?" Major Naseby asked.

"We could solve the murder," Annabelle said brightly.

"How?"

"Well… we're all falling down, so it's that nursery rhyme, isn't it?"

"Surely not, Belle," Diane said.

"No, it is, it's ring-a-ring o' roses, a pocket full of posies, a tissue, a tissue, we all fall down – don't you see?"

Frances raised an eyebrow. "Not really."

"We're all falling down, one after another, and a tissue might... I don't know. It might be a clue."

"I believe it's 'atishoo' like sneezing," Frances said.

"You need a tissue after atishoo," Annabelle said.

"Mrs Harrison," Major Naseby said, "this isn't helping."

"But it's... oh, the king has sent his daughter to fetch a pail of water... no, that doesn't really work... er... the robin in his steeple!" Annabelle looked at them excitedly. "Don't you see? The church has a steeple and the vicar–"

"Was not called Robin and the curate was called Gary," Frances pointed out.

"He wore red at Christmas!"

"Only as Santa Claus for the grotto."

"And it's nothing to do with posies," Mrs Entwistle insisted suddenly.

"Well," Annabelle said, "I am trying."

"Are we singing ring-a-ring o' roses," Major Naseby said, "because I don't think this has any charge? No, wait, it's turned off... there."

"We were discussing the murders," Diane said. "MURDERS."

"No need to shout," Major Naseby said. "Look, we simply need to establish our alibis."

"Yes," said Annabelle.

"As I was saying," Major Naseby continued, "there's the vicar, that delivery chap, Mrs Boseman – sorry, Zephron – the curate, Sir Victor, those foreign chaps and now the Russian inventor."

"We were all here for the Russian," Diane said.

"Including Betty," Pat added.

"We know who killed the curate," Diane added, "but Pat was interrupted."

"Oh yes," Annabelle said.

"And Sergio and the Swedish brothers," Diane said.

"So it's just the vicar, Mrs Boseman and Sir Victor left," Pat said.

"Right," Major Naseby said. "Where was everyone when the vicar was killed."

"I was watering plants at my son's house," Mrs Entwistle said.

"I was checking the tea money," Mrs Jones said.

"I was at bingo in Upper Whallop," Mrs Pilkington said.

"Annabelle and I were together at mine," Pat said.

"Oh. Yes," Annabelle said.

"I found the body," Diane admitted.

"I was with Sir Victor," Frances said.

"Hardly an alibi now," Diane said.

"And I was at home," Major Naseby said. "Zephron?"

498

"Oh, er... I was with my wife at home," Mr Boseman said.

"Well, no, you're weren't, were you?" Pat said.

"So, it was Zephron who killed the vicar!" Diane said.

"He was with Betty at Chiang's."

"What!" Major Naseby exploded. "Are you suggesting that–"

"Well, yes, quite."

"Zephron?" Major Naseby said.

Mr Boseman shrugged.

"But your wife was bed-ridden and..." Major Naseby was lost for words, but only for a moment. "You cad, Boseman, and... that's a motive to kill that Russian."

"Major Naseby," Pat said. "Mr Boseman was here when Vlad was killed."

"Then it's a motive to kill his wife!" Major Naseby insisted.

"Major Naseby!" Mr Boseman protested.

"Where were you when your poor wife was murdered?" Major Naseby demanded.

"We saw Mr Boseman at Annabelle's shop with Di and the curate's wife," Pat said.

"I saw Mr Boseman in Celia's," Frances said.

"Yes, you did," Mr Boseman said.

"I saw Mr Boseman on the High Street," Mrs Pilkington said.

"Did you?" Mr Boseman said.

"And you?" Major Naseby asked the only person who hadn't seen Mr Boseman.

"I was checking the tea money," Mrs Jones said.

"And I was at home," Major Naseby said. "And, finally, where was everyone when Sir Victor died."

"In bed," said Mrs Pilkington.

"Me too," Mr Boseman said.

"Yes," Mrs Entwistle said.

"Same," Frances said.

500

"We were at Pat's," Diane said.

"She was," Pat said.

"I was in bed too," Annabelle said.

"I was checking the tea money," Mrs Jones said.

"And I was at home," Major Naseby finished. "Does that get us anywhere?"

The general consensus was that it didn't.

"I'll just see to the detective constable," Pat said.

She popped her shawl on, took her slice of sponge cake and quietly made an exit. The others carried on discussing matters further. Much further.

31. The Butler Did It

Pat found the nice detective constable still in the car park, simply standing there. He could have walked to the crime scene of the vicar and curate's murders, or the crime scene of Vladimir's death, or taken his car to any number of other crime scenes, but he didn't seem able.

"It's not going very well, is it?" Pat said.

Kilroy slumped, his shoulders no longer able to support the disillusionment without bending under the weight.

"No," he said.

"Shall we solve one together?"

He turned to face her, mouth open.

The old lady stood in her matching skirt and jacket of old-fashioned taste, her half-moon spectacles dangling on a chain around her neck. She was meek and wrinkled, but then so was his Mackintosh, although her eyes twinkled in a way that his buttons didn't.

"Mrs Thomas," he said, "police work isn't for... oh, what's the use?"

"Good attitude."

"Thank you."

"Here's cake."

"Thank you."

"Things always look better after cake."

"Thank you," Kilroy said as he took a bite and then mumbled through the soft gooey mess, "but the inspector has stolen my collar."

"Don't worry, he's arrested the wrong person," Pat said. "Betty didn't do it."

"The .38 is missing," Kilroy said. "Kovalyov texted me when he got his safe open, so it's pretty much open and shut."

"He wasn't killed with a .38. With that calibre, the bullets would have gone straight through," Pat explained, "but they didn't."

"Ah."

"So Vladimir was murdered with a different weapon," Pat said. "Although the missing .38 rather suggests a different murder."

"Eh?"

"Poisoned, stabbed *and shot.*"

"Or poisoned, shot and stabbed."

"Oh no, the shot was definitely third," Pat said. "The bedside clock proves that."

"Well, it's not my case anymore. The great Inspector Rex Raymond is calling the shots – ha, shots! He's interviewing Mrs Kovalyov now."

"He's interviewing the wrong person then. Betty was at the memorial when Vladimir was shot."

"Damn."

"And there were no exit wounds."

"Oh... yes."

"So, a different weapon was used. I did say."

"Forensics are working on it, no doubt, and if that's the case, then they'll confirm it."

"Why don't we?"

So, Detective Constable Kilroy waited for Pat to fold up her walking stick and then he helped her into his SUV, then took over clicking her seat belt in – "These things are so fiddly, aren't they?" – and heard all about Frances the warden having heating seats in her SUV for the entire journey.

"Imagine," she said, finishing.

Kilroy couldn't.

At Betty and Vladimir Kovalyov's, a *drip-drip... drip* trail of blood led away from his double garage conversion. Looking up, the church brooded at the top of the hill. The inventor had made it to the Parochial Hall.

The big metal garage door was up.

Vlad the Inventor's workshop was pristine except for the dark red splatter on the concrete floor. In the corner, by the door control, a wig lay on the floor smeared with blood.

505

"Odd," Kilroy said.

"Well, yes, quite," Pat replied. "What else?"

"Here's a possible murder weapon," Kilroy said. A nail gun had been stowed on a bracket fixed to the wall along with numerous other tools. "I'll have to have it checked for prints."

"It would be easy to take that off the wall, use it and put it back."

"Wiping fingerprints, no doubt."

"Yes, quite."

"Needs a battery... there!"

In the corner, Kilroy found a stand holding several specialist batteries for various drills, lights and so on. They were all charging.

Pat placed her handbag on the workbench and then bent down to check the floor. Her knees clicked loudly.

"Oh."

"Anything?"

"Well, Detective Constable, there a small tyre track across this blood here."

"Mini... you couldn't drive a car in here with all this equipment in the way."

"Or even a bicycle," Pat said. She stood up. "Oh."

While Kilroy looked around, Pat walked across the garage and tried the door to the house. It opened into a kitchen. They both went in.

On the kitchen table, a laptop sat with a dark screen keeping its secrets.

"I could put the kettle on," Pat suggested.

Kilroy wiggled his finger across the touchpad – nothing happened. "Usually, you turn it off and on again."

"That's what my nephew keeps telling me, so why don't you?"

Kilroy picked it up and examined the various edges until he found the power button. He turned it off, counted ten in his head and then turned it on again.

He stared at the screen as it booted up.

"These things take forever," he said.

"I imagine," Pat said. She wandered back to the garage not sure what she was looking for, but hoping that she'd know it when she saw it.

"Windows," Kilroy said to no-one in particular. "Anti-virus and... oh, something he wrote himself."

Something whirred that wasn't the laptop's hard disc.

Kilroy glanced around, certain he'd seen something in his peripheral vision, but there was nothing.

"There are holes here," Pat said, loudly, but distantly. "Nails. Why would he plan to put pictures in a line along here?"

The program finally loaded and immediately declared that it had identified a woman.

The detective constable leapt towards the garage leaving his conscious mind a step or two behind.

508

He grabbed Pat, pulled her to one side.

"Oi!" Pat shouted. "I'm eighty–"

Vicious spikes of stainless steel zipped through the air where Pat had been standing. The evil-looking pegs stuck out of the plaster wall.

A collection of metal and plastic stood in the centre of the workshop holding the nail gun. The thing swivelled round on tyre tracks, raised the tool and aimed again at Pat.

Kilroy threw himself in the way in an impulsive act of bravery.

The Heath Robinson monstrosity lowered the nail gun.

"What is it?" Pat said, looking around the detective constable's broad shoulder.

The thing took a pot shot at her, missed.

After a zing of ricochet, something glugged. Behind them, a mortally wounded paint tin bled profusely staining a workbench and the floor in a gore of jasmine shimmer.

"It's a robot," Kilroy explained, "and it appears to want to kill you."

"Me? What have I ever done to robots?"

"Let's go to the kitchen... carefully."

They shuffled around, Kilroy keeping Pat behind him.

The robot followed, its uncanny camera lens searching.

Pat opened the door to the kitchen and guided Kilroy inside.

The killer machine followed.

"Right," Kilroy said, "I'll just–"

He turned to the kitchen table and so the robot caught sight of Pat. It fired a few nails fixing the condiments to the tiling. Ketchup splattered everywhere, a vivid reminder of what could have happened.

"You'll have to do it, Mrs Thomas."

"Me? I know nothing of these things."

"Just move the mouse to the program."

"What mouse?"

"The mouse!"

"I know what a mouse is, there isn't one."

"You put your finger on the touchpad."

"I beg your pardon."

"The flat square below the keyboard."

"Oh."

Pat bent down and put her finger on the touchpad. Her bum stuck out pushing the detective constable forward.

"Steady... now move the arrow to shut down the robot."

"Shutdown?"

"Shutdown, off, er... something."

"How about 'deactivate'? I think that's what it says."

"That sounds about right."

"It's there, but nothing's happened."

"Did you click it?"

"Click it?"

"Press the..." – Kilroy raised his hand and gestured with his finger – "...left button at the top of the flat square."

"The... oh yes. There."

The robot eyed Kilroy.

"Try double click."

"Double click."

"Press it twice, quickly."

"I'm doing the best I can," Pat said. "Don't rush me."

"I meant click it twice... I mean, click-click."

"Oh... I see... Hmm, why don't they make these things so complicated. It's all click this, double click that." – *click-click* – "Ah, there... nothing's happened... oh, wait, something's appeared."

"What?"

"I don't know."

512

"What does it say?"

"I'll need my glasses."

"Right."

"They're in my bag."

"Get them out then."

"My bag is in the garage."

"Oh, for... fine."

Kilroy shuffled forward and then in a strange dance, they rotated around the robot and back into the workshop. Pat got her bag, and then they shambled back to the kitchen going around the mechanical killer again.

All the time, the robot fixed them with its cyclops stare.

Pat put her bag on the table and took out her reading glasses.

"Now, let's see," she said. "Do I want to deactivate?"

"Yes, yes, yes."

"How do I do that?"

"Move the mouse... arrow with the flat square and click on the 'yes' button."

"Oh yes... I see."

She pressed the button and the robot's mechanical arms flopped down. The nail gun fell to the floor, fired and pegged Kilroy's Mackintosh to the fridge.

"Holy cow!" Kilroy said. He pulled at his Mackintosh to be rewarded with freedom and punished with a rip.

"Is it safe?" Pat asked nervously.

"Yes," Kilroy said, but he kicked the deadly thing over all the same and recovered the nail gun.

Pat looked around his Mackintosh, her fingers clutching the material leaving claw marks.

"It's dead?" she asked.

"It was never alive."

"Why would anyone make something that dangerous?"

514

"He didn't," Kilroy said. "When I interviewed him, he was stuck in this non-creasing suit. He was making a robot butler to operate his, er... de-clothing machine."

"Why did it shoot me and not you?"

"I don't know."

Pat examined it, stepped gingerly over it and went back into the workshop.

She clicked her fingers. "I have it."

"What?"

"Vladimir made the robot to... whatever," Pat said. "And then he repurposed it to... er..."

"Take over the world by killing all the women in it," Kilroy said. "It's a sort of sexist terminator."

"He found out that Betty was having an affair, I think," Pat said. "Someone must have let slip that the choir had been cancelled."

"Ah," Kilroy said, "I think that was me."

"That was foolish of you."

"I... yes."

"He made this to kill her automatically, probably when he was busy somewhere else establishing an alibi."

"Makes sense, but it killed him."

"Oh, I imagine he wanted to test it," Pat said, "hence the wig in the garage. He pretended to be a woman."

"And it worked."

"Yes."

"He killed himself and tried to blame Betty."

"Not suicide or murder," Kilroy said. "An accident, technically."

"Who'd have thought it, mind?" Pat said.

"Thought what?"

"The butler did it."

32. Chasing a Lead

"The curate's wife!"

Kilroy froze.

"I quite forgot," Pat added.

Kilroy glanced towards the church, its tower visible above the houses opposite, and mentally measured the sprint distance. Then he remembered his car.

"Come on!" he shouted.

He ran to the car, leapt in and jabbed the key into the ignition. The SUV roared, over-revved as Kilroy pumped the accelerator, and then Kilroy had to get out to help Pat into the passenger seat.

He covered the distance to the church in record time.

"The curate's wife is..." Pat tried to say but she was jostled into the electrically windable side window and pushed back into the foam headrest. She also deeply regretted that the

Parish Council had insisted on all those speed bumps. "Oh dear."

Kilroy screeched to a halt, jumped out and ran into the Parochial Hall. Pat fumbled as quickly as she could with the fiddly seatbelt, but the wretched thing flummoxed her.

Presently, the detective constable returned looking sheepish. He was followed by Diane and Annabelle.

"They're all arguing about flowers and tea money," Kilroy said. "The curate's wife isn't there."

"I did try and tell you," Pat said.

"She's moving to London," Diane said.

"Yes," Annabelle said, "we collected all her donations to the Oxfam shop."

"Right!" Kilroy said decisively.

He clambered into his car again, and was out of the car park gate without delay as Pat was still strapped in.

"Directions!" he snapped.

"To London?" Pat asked.

518

"No, the curate's house."

"Oh... yes, quite... do a U-turn at your earliest–"

The SUV screeched into a savage turn, burning rubber on the tarmac.

"Can I get out, please?" Pat asked.

The car lurched to a halt outside the pretty hollyhocks of Church House, bucked savagely as it stalled, and Kilroy was out and running again.

Pat had another go with the seatbelt.

Eventually, the detective constable reappeared looking forlorn.

"She's gone."

"I had gathered that," Pat replied. "She's going to London."

"Right." Kilroy jumped into his car again and–

"By train."

"Sorry?"

"She's going by train," Pat explained.

"How do you know?"

"She always goes by train to London and her car is still in the driveway."

"Oh yes."

"And she always carries her passport."

"Then there's no time to lose," Kilroy said. "Which way to the station."

"Well, towards Upper Whallop, but I really think I'd like to get *ooooooout!*"

The journey to Upper Whallop passed in a flash of the speed camera on the A-road.

Again, Kilroy was the man of action, his Mackintosh spread out like a cape as he fairly flew into the station. It was a quaint set of buildings on the mainline for the stopping trains. Express trains rushed through much as city folk did.

Pat struggled with the seatbelt and, finally, *click!*

"Oh, thank goodness," she said.

520

She almost fell out of the car, but was glad of terra firma. Her shawl had caught on the headrest so she'd abandoned it. She didn't fancy clambering up the SUV again, so she waited, hoping her heart would stop trying to hammer out of her chest. She hadn't had this much excitement since that robot killing machine had tried to murder her and that felt like a lifetime ago.

Finally, the detective constable reappeared looking desperate.

"She's not here and no trains are running," he said.

Pat pointed down the road.

It was Sunday, so, of course, a sign announced the replacement bus service. The coaches alighted and departed from a temporary post that had ivy growing up it. The 4:50 to Kings Cross was still on the A-frame chalkboard.

"Right."

Pat unfolded her walking stick and followed the detective constable as best she could.

It was well past 4:50.

"Tickets," said a man in uniform.

"I'm police," Kilroy said.

"Tickets."

"Oh... for..." Kilroy ran back to the station office.

"Lovely weather," Pat said.

The man glanced upwards. "Yes," he said, "although drizzle later, I shouldn't wonder."

"Rain expected at the weekend."

"Good for the garden."

"Oh yes."

"Not so much for our Jordan's barbeque."

"Well, no, quite."

Kilroy came running back and handed the ticket inspector a hand of cardboard.

"Very well."

"Has the 4:50 gone?" Pat asked.

"Oh yes."

522

"Then I didn't need to get tickets," Kilroy complained.

"Well, there's the other half," the ticket inspector said.

"Other half?"

"Too many for a single bus. Here it is now."

A coach appeared and came to a hissing halt by the temporary stop.

"All aboard," the ticket inspector said.

Kilroy and Pat clambered up.

The driver checked their tickets.

"Thank you, conductor."

"Conductor, is it? Ha," the driver said. "Hardly an orchestra here."

Pat and Kilroy found themselves a seat. Pat tucked her walking stick away in her big bag.

The door closed with a hiss and the coach set off at a leisurely country pace. On either side, a lovely patchwork of fields and hedges stretched out in the late afternoon sunshine. A flock of starlings darted overhead.

"We're not going to catch up with the other coach in time," Kilroy said.

"No," Pat agreed.

"We must go faster."

Kilroy got up but Pat gripped his Mackintosh sleeve, denting the waterproof sealant.

"Do we have to?" she asked.

"Yes."

Kilroy eased her fingers away and then staggered down the central aisle.

"Driver," Kilroy said.

"Please, return to your seat."

"Driver."

"You can't distract the driver when the coach is in motion."

"Driver, I'm police."

"Oh aye."

Kilroy showed off his warrant card.

"How can I help?" the bus driver said.

"Er... follow that bus."

About 1,000 metres ahead, indicating left towards the motorway, another coach negotiated a parked car and the oncoming traffic as it approached a roundabout.

"But I am already," the driver replied, "we're both going to Kings Cross."

"We have to catch it," Kilroy explained.

"Eh?"

"Catch that bus, there's a murderer on board."

"Oh, right ho!"

The driver put his foot down and the diesel engine roared. The vehicle lurched forward, took the left at the roundabout and then gathered speed, closing the gap, before it slowed again.

"Why are you slowing down?" Kilroy yelled.

"It's limited to fifty miles per hour," the driver replied. "Health and safety."

"Can you override it?"

"Oh aye, but that wouldn't be legal–"

"I'm police."

"And we'd have to jack up the back to get at the engine."

"Oh... well, do the best you can."

So, the two buses careened down the M11 at the identical breakneck velocity allowed by their speed limiters, while other cars pulled out into the fast lane and seemingly idled past.

Pat had some boiled sweets in her handbag.

The motorway changed from two lanes to three. The speed of the passing cars increased to 80 mph, 90 mph for BMWs. Audis swerved between lanes. A racing Porsche was so fast Kilroy couldn't catch its personalised number plate. Every single vehicle overtook the two buses, except for a caravan that held them up for a few miles.

That was until they hit road works and everything snarled to a halt.

"We're not moving," Kilroy said.

"Well, you know, stuck here," the driver said.

"Open the door."

"What?"

"Open the door!"

The man pulled a lever and the hydraulics opened.

Kilroy jumped out and ran along the hard shoulder passing all the stationary cars. He saw the passengers in the other replacement bus. The curate's widow glanced out, and raised her arched and plucked eyebrows in alarm.

But then, the traffic started moving and the 500-metre dash became 600, then 700.

Kilroy glanced to his right as the second coach drew level.

He banged on the door.

It opened, but he couldn't jump the gap as the coach was still moving.

He was going to be left behind.

But an arm appeared.

"Grab my hand," Pat yelled, hanging on to the yellow handrail and reaching out.

Kilroy gave a final sprint, caught her hand and clambered in.

The door hissed its hydraulic sigh and closed behind him.

"It's not like this on *Morse*," Pat said.

"No," Kilroy agreed.

The other bus was now a mere seven cars ahead, but the lurch-lurch of progress made the gap impossible to cover on foot. The speedometer flickered between stationary and a giddy 15 or 16 mph with the driver occasionally reaching the dizzying heights of third gear!

Soon enough, they crossed the M25 and entered London.

Again, the gap looked possible, whenever any traffic lights went red.

"We're not going to catch her," Kilroy admitted to himself aloud.

"Caledonia!" the driver said.

"What?"

"Caledonia Street," the driver said again. "It's one-way the wrong way."

"So?"

"We have to do a big loop, Caledonia Road, Kings Cross Bridge, Grays Inn Road and York Way, but you could cut through Caledonia Street."

"Right!"

Kilroy pulled out his phone, checked on Google for the map and saw the shortcut.

By the time they paused at the crossing for a hen party to giggle and shriek across, Kilroy had limbered up and he was ready. Before the bus had stopped completely, he leapt off, sprinted over the crossing, became briefly entangled in pink balloons before he ran on, turning right between the Tesco Express and Miller's pub.

For her part, Pat eased herself down and unfolded her walking stick.

"Thank you, driver," she said as she alighted.

The bus lurched off, jumping forward to fill the car length that had just appeared.

Pat set off down the wide pavement weaving in between all the pub clientele standing about with their pints as if there was all the time in the world.

By the time she reached the end of the road, she faced a wall of brick and arched windows. There was no sign of the nice detective constable amongst the congested reasons that Pat hated visiting London.

She had no idea where a replacement bus would stop.

She hailed a black cab.

"Driver," she said, clambering in, "take me to Kings Cross bus terminus, please."

"It's there," he said.

"Yes, driver, and be quick about it... it's an emergency!"

So, the black cab made use of its tight turning circle and wheeled around travelling the short distance to the ranks of buses and coaches.

One of them was the first replacement bus from Peterborough via too many stations, including Upper Whallop. It was just pulling up.

"Thank you, driver," Pat said, handing over a fiver.

"It's–"

But she was off as fast as her knees allowed, her walking stick stabbing the cobbles, tarmac and paving with great rapidity.

She reached the door as it opened.

The curate's widow was the first out.

"Excuse me," Pat said.

"Oh... Mrs Thomas, you have a taxi for me," she replied, neatly sidestepping her pursuer and clambering into the black cab.

But the driver had got out to confront Pat about the underpayment of the fare.

"Yes," Pat told him, "it's police business."

"You're not police," he said.

"Undercover," Pat replied, struggling towards the parked car.

The curate's widow realised she was alone and clambered out of the other door.

Pat pursued her through the cab and struggled out the other side in time to see the curate's widow show a clean pair of high heels.

The chase went into a huge industrial cathedral of coaches and buses, funnelled and directed by queues of people, cones closing off areas for cleaning, rows of seating and finally, out in the parking area by the buses themselves.

It was a race, high heels versus mobility aid, haring around when they should have been more tortoise-like.

The curate's widow ran between buses for King's Lynn, Norwich and Cambridge, backtracked around Plymouth, turned left at Cardiff and was cornered between Edinburgh and Penzance.

"Mrs..." Pat said defiantly, "for... pity's... can... I... just... breath... back?"

The curate's widow fixed Pat with a stiletto gaze.

Pat waved her hand to ask for a few more moments.

"I'd rather be off, Pat, if you don't mind," the curate's widow said.

She barged past and Pat had no puff left to object.

But Detective Constable Kilroy appeared at the other end blocking the way out between the two buses.

The curate's widow spun on her sharp heel.

Pat raised her walking stick.

33. The Sixty-Per-Cent Solution

It was late when they finally reached Pat's cottage: the early hours of Monday. Kilroy had overruled every one of Pat's 'I'll be fine' and 'I don't want to be any trouble'.

He had a collar, finally, and it had been Armani.

"Thank you, driver," Pat said to the police constable who had driven them, sans flashing blue lights and siren, back to Conky Whallop. "Come in for a drink, Detective Constable."

"I will," Kilroy replied and then he bent down to talk to the constable driving the car. "Thanks."

"Do I get a tip?" the driver said.

"You're not a taxi."

"I am, Killjoy."

"I think..." but the car was gone, its siren bursting into banshee-mode as the constable decided to get home early.

Pat had already opened her front door and gone in.

It was dark and it had rained. Moisture hung in the air, a mist that drifted through the street lights. Somewhere, distantly, some animal of the countryside cried out. He crept up the path not wanting to disturb any neighbours.

Were the begonias moving?

He paused and listened.

A splash of tread in puddle?

The street seemed quiet, the dark shape of the church stood silhouetted against a full moon and the horse chestnut tree loomed with shadows.

Was someone there... or there?

His imagination played tricks on him. It had been a difficult day after a trying week. What he needed was a hot... Horlicks, that was it. That was what old ladies drank. Gentle, sweet old ladies, who gossiped and knitted and baked and made jam.

He had caught the curate's wife and had the solution to the death of Sergio, the curate, the Swedish hitmen and Vlad the Inventor. There was the murder of the vicar, Mrs Boseman and Sir Victor Pendle-Took still to solve, but Kilroy felt positive. After all, it was 5 out of 8, about 60%.

And he was going to make Inspector Rex Raymond look like a fool, which had a certain delight despite being a career-limiting move. Even so, finally, he felt that things were going his way.

He smiled, turned back towards the house, took a few steps and then it came at him, fast and deadly.

"I–"

Then the bell tolled and everything went black.

!!!

"And it's muddy and the soil is clay."

"Belle?"

"It's muddy, the soil's clay," Annabelle said. "I'm so sorry, Pat."

536

"What's the mud got to do with the price of eggs?"

"For digging the shallow grave."

"Shallow grave?"

"For the body."

Kilroy chose this moment to moan. "Oh... ah..."

Annabelle readied her saucepan. Diane, who stood by the door, advanced with a broom.

"What are you doing?" Pat asked.

"He's not dead," Annabelle explained. "Should I finish him off?"

"What? No. Belle!"

"No?"

"No!"

"Oh, sorry. I wasn't thinking."

They glanced down at Kilroy, who stared up at them in horror and disbelief.

"Misunderstanding," Pat explained. She reached down to assist him out of the flower bed, although she was an old lady, so Kilroy found the offer more hindrance than help.

"I see," Kilroy said.

"Let's get you inside and have a look at that head of yours," Pat said. "Any dizziness?"

Kilroy glanced at Annabelle cautiously. "No... could you lower that weapon please, Madam?"

"Oh sorry," Annabelle said. She lowered it, but kept her grip fast on the handle.

"Why on Earth did you–"

"I'm sorry."

Kilroy staggered into Pat's kitchen, where the glasses from her demonstration still shone on the draining board. He let Pat fuss over him with items from her extensive box of medicines: ointments, TCP, plasters, poisons...

"Just... *ouch!*"

"Stay still, Detective Constable," Pat said, waving soaked cotton wool in his face, causing him to recoil.

"What is that?"

"My mother's remedy."

"Sorry," Annabelle said.

"Why?" Kilroy replied. "You're not the one rubbing chilli powder, lemon juice and salt into my wound."

"Oh, Detective," Pat said, "it has none of that in it."

"But I'm the one who hit you," Annabelle said. "So sorry, and thank goodness you're alive. I'd hate to be known as a serial killer."

"You'd have to kill two more," Kilroy said holding the ice to the back of his head.

"How do you know she hasn't?" Diane said.

"Oh, Di, really," Pat said.

"I'm sorry... I didn't mean to kill that other assassin or this one," Annabelle said. "Even if this one turned out to be a policeman. One is enough."

"Well, never – *ouch!* – mind," Kilroy said.

"Sorry again," Annabelle said.

"There," Pat said, "as good as new."

"Thank you," Kilroy said.

Suddenly, Annabelle banged the pan down on the kitchen table.

Everyone jumped.

And then she banged it again.

"I'm not sorry," Annabelle said. "Why am I always sorry? Sorry for this, sorry for that, sorry for the bloomin' other – sorry... pardon my French. Not. I'm not sorry. Bloomin', bloomin'... bloomin'."

Annabelle's auburn hair stood out like flames on her black with black twinset.

"Belle?" Pat asked gently.

"Why was he creeping about outside in the middle of the night?"

"Why were you?" Kilroy asked.

"He was an intruder in a village full of murderers," Annabelle wailed. "I've nothing to be sorry about."

"She hasn't," Diane agreed.

All four glared at each other.

"I'm sorry," Kilroy said, deliberately.

"There. See. He's sorry," Annabelle said.

"Good," Pat said. "Now that's settled, let's have something strong and some ice."

"Good idea," Diane said. "Whisky and a drop of water in mine, please Pat, a little less than half."

"I don't take ice in my whisky," Kilroy said.

"The ice is for your head to stop the swelling," Pat explained. "And after that, it's straight to bed with you."

"I beg your pardon."

"You can sleep in the spare room," Pat explained. "I've Eric's pyjamas, laundered, and a spare toothbrush."

"That's very kind, but... I'll drive home."

"Not after a drink and not with your car parked at the station, you won't."

Kilroy groaned. "Whisky it is then."

He was trapped.

34. Red Herring

"It's nice having a man about the house," Pat said to Kilroy the next day. "I have a few jobs, if you don't mind?"

"No problem, Mrs Thomas."

"Pat, please."

So, Detective Constable Kilroy spent the morning changing the box room's light bulb, getting the spare blankets from the loft, putting the Christmas lights up into the loft, fixing a dodgy drawer, hammering a nail 'just there', cleaning the outside grid and finally moving the water butt and giving up on the rotting section of fence.

"It needs replacing, Mrs Thomas."

"Oh... well, that's a shame."

By this time, the afternoon was nearly over. They'd both slept in, Kilroy far more than Pat, and so breakfast had been at lunchtime and the things-to-do list had left him famished.

Kilroy ordered a taxi to Upper Whallop to collect his car. He had to come back because Mrs Thomas had left her shawl in his car.

"There you go," he said.

"Thank you, Detective."

"Least I could do."

His mobile burbled a tune.

"Kilroy," Kilroy said. "Oh, Inspector Raymond, sir–"

Pat gathered up the plates and wasn't listening.

"Yes, sir, but I worked the weekend and caught the curate's–"

She put them down on the work surface, quietly so as not to disturb the detective constable, rather than to eavesdrop.

"Yes, sir, but–"

And tiptoed closer.

"Yes, sir, b–"

Pulled the door ever so slightly more ajar.

"Yes, sir, the Chief Constable does know–"

Leaned a shade closer.

"He said that about Miss Richards? Surely not in those words?"

Raised an eyebrow.

"Oh, he did, but, sir–"

And Pat wondered what the words had been: Diane could be quite exasperating.

"Sir, I– Yes, I– At once."

Pat waited a few moments for the nice detective constable's breathing to slow down.

"Have you finished?" Pat asked, innocently.

"I could murder him," Kilroy said.

Kilroy's hand shook and he botched putting his phone away. It fell to the floor and he had to grope around his feet.

"Are you all right, dear?" Pat asked.

"Yes!" Kilroy snapped.

"Well, if–"

"Sorry."

"That's all right."

He'd been fine facing the killer robot, fine afterwards, but five minutes of Inspector Rex Raymond lecturing him on his responsibilities and a murderous rage had risen in his blood pressure. He'd lost count of how many times he'd said, 'yes, sir, but'.

"Well, perhaps something to eat," Pat suggested. "This has all been very trying."

"Yes."

"Come on then," Pat said. "Let's walk to Chiang's on the corner. My treat."

Pat fetched her stick and they walked along the High Street in silence.

Kilroy felt like a small boy being dragged along by his aunt. He decided to forget all about it for five minutes and enjoy the scenery – it was a lovely, quaint English village, peaceful with only the occasional net curtain-twitching as they passed.

They went by Pheasant's Café (scene of the killing of Anders Lindström), the Oxfam Shop (scene of the discovery of Pendle-Took's clothes and thus his murder), Baxter's, Conkies and Celia's (how many bodies were hidden in their cupboards?) and finally they reached Chiang's (a murder victim's place of work). On top of the hill, the gothic church (scene of the first and fourth murders) loomed.

So much for taking his mind off things.

"Greetings," Mrs Chiang said as they entered. "Menus, and we have specials. Is this your nephew back from Australia?"

"No," Kilroy said, "I'm a detective constable."

"Oh yes, I remember. Calamari, whole fish with noodles, Hong Kong style, jasmine tea," she said. "Table by window?"

"No, we'll have the one at the back."

Mrs Chiang raised an eyebrow, but sauntered them over to the most secluded table.

"So?" he said.

"Yes," Pat replied.

"I had calamari last time, apparently. Do you want Chinese or pizza?"

"Chinese, I'm less keen on pizza after the other night."

Kilroy had the same as last time: calamari for starters and the fish in a sweet and sour sauce with noodles for his main. Pat, distracted, decided upon the same.

"Anything to drink?" Mrs Chiang asked.

"White wine?" Pat suggested.

"I'm on... I'm dri... yes, white."

Pat turned to Mrs Chiang. "And a bottle of... house white," Pat said handing the menu back.

Mrs Chiang sauntered off to the kitchen leaving them in peace. Presently, she returned with glasses and a bottle of Soave.

"Taste?" Mrs Chiang said.

"It's fine, I'm sure," Kilroy replied.

"Very good."

She poured and then left the bottle on the table before leaving.

They picked up their glasses.

"Perhaps a toast?" Kilroy said.

"To being alive," Pat suggested.

"Are you sure I can stay the night again?"

"Absolutely."

"Then to being alive."

They clinked their glasses and sipped.

Kilroy found he was gulping it back and forced himself to stop.

"I've not had Chinese in years," Pat admitted.

"I'd have thought with it being the only restaurant."

"Yes, but you never act the tourist in your local area."

"No, I suppose not."

"Act the tourist... of course."

"What is it?" Kilroy asked.

"You've come here twice," Pat said, "and ordered the same dish."

"Yes."

"Just as Mr Boseman came to the charity shop twice and on both occasions, he brought our attention to the time."

"Midday, yes."

"Well, that's the point, isn't it? Twice, separated by no more than ten minutes, just as the two times for Mrs Boseman's death are separated by ten minutes."

"Her death was accurately recorded by the monitoring equipment."

"And by the fallen carriage clock."

"Yes."

"So, two times and two killers and two perfect alibis."

Mrs Chiang arrived with their first course.

Kilroy dug in, but Pat struggled with the chopsticks. She raised her hand to attract Mrs Chiang's attention.

"Yes?"

"Could I have a knife and fork, please?" Pat said.

"Knife and fork?"

"Please."

"They are no good for this meal. This Chinese. And pizza eaten with the fingers."

"Please. My arthritis."

"Knife and fork?"

"Please."

Mrs Chang looked doubtful, but she went off and came back promptly with a knife, fork, two types of spoon and a device for opening oysters.

"Mrs Boseman not need chopsticks," Mrs Chiang said.

"I'm sure, thank you... why not?"

"She play piano," Mrs Chiang said. "Very good, fingers very agile, good enough for festival, but wrong sort of music."

"Did Mr and Mrs Boseman dine here often?"

"Every Wednesday, eat-in," Mrs Chiang said. "Peking duck, egg fried rice, prawn crackers, sometimes lemon chicken."

"Mrs Boseman always sat here?" Pat asked.

"With Mr Boseman, every Wednesday."

"The day of their choir practice," Kilroy said.

"Thank you," Pat said and Mrs Chiang left them in peace again.

"Mrs Boseman was bed bound and yet every Wednesday Mr Boseman brought his wife here."

"Ah."

"It was Betty," Pat said. "They were having an affair. Quite shocking really."

552

"Yes, I think I let that slip to Mr Kovalyov."

"Mr Boseman used it as his alibi for the murder of the vicar," Pat explained. "And then realised it would reveal all to Mrs Boseman, which, of course, it must have."

Kilroy glugged his dry white. "Go on."

"Well, Betty also realised that the cat was out of the bag, so to speak. These are quite rubbery, you have the rest of mine."

"Thank you," Kilroy said, dunking and polishing off the calamari.

Mrs Chiang came and collected their plates, fussed back and forth and finally, their main course arrived.

"You were saying," Kilroy prompted.

"So, all three of them killed Mrs Boseman one after the other."

"Sorry?"

"Mrs Boseman poisoned herself early in the morning," Pat began. "She'd been hoarding sleeping pills in case it all became too much."

"She was also stabbed and shot... or shot and stabbed."

"Stabbed and shot, I'm coming to that."

"Sorry. Go on."

"Mr Boseman removed her medical monitor earlier, probably to check this plan would work, and put it on his own wrist. That's why it didn't go off when she passed away from the poison."

"Right."

"Then, thinking she was asleep, he stabbed her."

Kilroy had stabbed a block of fish fillet with his chopstick and it oozed bright red sweet and sour sauce.

"He knew he'd be the obvious suspect," Pat continued, "so he visited all the shops on the High Street to establish an alibi for twelve o'clock. He took his watch off when he was in the charity shop, but it wasn't his watch, it was Mrs Boseman's medical monitor thingummy. That was exactly when the computer registered her time of death."

"Ah-ha."

"Then all he had to do was go home and discover the body."

"But she was also shot."

"Mr Boseman visited the charity shop twice, but the second time it wasn't Mr Boseman, it was Betty the organist."

"Betty?"

"Yes, she had borrowed her husband's gun, gone round to Mr Boseman's and, finding he was out, she shot Mrs Boseman."

"Who was already dead having been stabbed."

"And already dead having poisoned herself."

"Ah."

"She reset the carriage clock to five past twelve and smashed it on the floor to establish that as the time of death. She'd done amateur dramatics and so she pretended to be Mr Boseman, acting the part in the shop to give him an alibi. She did a fine performance, but we'd only just seen

Mr Boseman for real. She had a different hat, the sunglasses rather overdid it and I think her false moustache was falling off."

"Why not an alibi for herself?"

"She was more concerned about Mr Boseman, who she knew would be the obvious suspect."

"Ah-ha."

"So really, neither of them is guilty of murder."

"Inspector Rex Raymond will do them for wasting police time."

"I'm sure he will," Pat agreed, "but they are in love and they will wait for each other."

"A happy ending then."

"Well, yes, quite," Pat said. "Although we are still left with the vicar and Sir Victor."

Kilroy nodded.

"This sweet and sour," Kilroy said, "it's very red."

"Added food colouring and monosodium glutamate."

"Hmmm."

"We should gather everyone together, again," Pat said, "but first there's one last question that needs answering. And you know what that is, no doubt."

"Hmmm," Kilroy agreed. "What is this fish?"

"Herring."

35. One Last Question

"The question, of course, is whether someone is married," Pat said over the breakfast table. She'd cooked bacon and eggs, extra sausages, black pudding and fried tomatoes. When Kilroy had complained that he was still full from the Chinese, she had relented and reduced the rations to a mere full English. It was good to have a man about the house, but he needed feeding up.

"Married?"

"Sir Victor had a sister," Pat insisted.

"There are no other Pendle-Tooks in the village unless the Reverend had a sex change."

"Hardly," Pat said. "Other people's strange lifestyles, the vicar used to say. He was understanding, forgiving even, but also very traditional. He came from an important family."

"Inheritance?"

"Not money per se, there was none," Pat said, "but there is a title."

"The current Lord, the eighth, is very ill," Kilroy explained. "When he dies, the title and estate would have passed to the Reverend."

"A motive, perhaps, for Sir Victor to kill his brother."

"Sir Victor already had a title," Kilroy mused.

"His sort always wants more."

"That's true."

"With the vicar and Sir Victor dead, then the title would pass to the next in line."

"Who is..."

"His sister, who would become Lady Bishop-Barnaby."

"But there's no other Pendle-Took in the village."

"There are plenty of married women in the village," Pat said, "who may have been a Pendle-Took."

"Ah-ha."

"There's Mrs Entwistle, Mrs Jones, Mrs Pilkington..."

"Mrs Thomas, Mrs Richards, Mrs Harrison."

"*Miss* Richards," Pat corrected.

"I beg your pardon," Kilroy said.

"Just don't let Di hear you make that mistake."

"I won't."

"The point is," Pat continued, "that none of them fit."

"No."

"Which leads me to think that *Miss* Richards might be the point."

"Is she?"

"Miss... you see, someone may be married and then divorce and return to their original name, while others keep their married name, but revert to 'Miss'."

"To go back on the market."

"Well, I wouldn't put it quite like that, but yes, quite."

"So," Kilroy said, "we're looking for a Miss or a Mrs."

"Exactly."

"Hardly narrows it down."

"Narrows it to half the population, my man."

"Hmm."

"And we can find out soon enough by checking with Somerset House," Pat said.

"That's just an internet search."

"Quite," Pat said, standing, "I'll ring my nephew in Australia."

Pat went over to her landline, fussed with the controls and then put the receiver to her ear.

"It won't be easy to find Pendle-Took's sister."

"Nonsense," Pat said, "we're looking for Sir Victor's father or mother's children."

"Unless–"

Pat waved at the detective constable to be quiet.

"Ah, Edward," she said. "No, it is not the middle of the night… We've been over this before. Now, get a piece of paper and a pencil, I've some things for you to look up… Well, you're awake now…"

As Pat explained, repeating much of it to her unaccountably dozy nephew, Kilroy finished his toast and the dregs of his tea.

"Put the kettle on again," Pat said.

Kilroy went to the kitchen to make a fresh pot. When he came back, Pat was saying "Ah-ha", "Mmm" and "I see" in various combinations as well as including "Just one last question" a few times.

Kilroy was 'mother' toping up both their cups.

"Thank you, Edward," Pat said. "Yes, when you've found out, you can go back to bed, but it is a Tuesday, shouldn't you be at work?"

Kilroy glanced at her and checked his watch. Was Australia twelve hours ahead or behind?

"Honestly, Edward," Pat said, "how can it be Wednesday there already? Yes, yes, as soon as you can."

Pat hung up.

"He's going to ring me back."

Kilroy nodded: "Well, I must be going. Text me if you find anything out."

"I will."

The detective constable gathered up his Mackintosh, shook his head at the state of it, and made his way out.

"Thank you again for the room and board."

"My pleasure," Pat replied.

Once he was gone, Pat tidied away a few things and did the washing up. Always best to do that before the marmalade goes all hard and difficult.

Presently, the phone rang.

"Edward... hmmm.... yes... that narrows it down... thank you... yes, that's all... goodnight."

Pat jotted down a few notes, folded the paper and tucked it into her handbag. There was just one thing left to discover, so she rang Mrs Entwistle.

"Yes, it's Pat, Pat Thomas, whom do you do for? No... I'm not looking for a cleaner, I just... so, you clean for..."

Mrs Entwistle told her.

"Oh, yes, quite," Pat said, "the vicar and Sir Victor are dead, so not them anymore."

Mrs Entwistle added to the list of her clients.

"Thank you," Pat said. "Just one last question... you dropped some clothes off at the charity shop, didn't you?"

Pat nodded as Mrs Entwistle expressed surprise that anyone had seen her at that hour.

"Thank you."

Pat fetched her coat, handbag and walking stick. But even armed with the weapon that had subdued the curate's wife, she knew she was taking a risk, so she decided to call for backup. The nice detective constable had made it clear that she should. She found the mobile phone her nephew had insisted on buying her.

"Oh, bother."

The detective constable was not in her contacts, so instead, she texted – fiddly wretched thing – Diane and Annabelle. She included as much explanation as she could fit on the tiny screen with as much accuracy as predictive text considered appropriate. It wasn't completely clear, but it wasn't a cryptic crossword question. At least, she didn't think so and she'd sent it already.

Pat reached the lovely Grade II listed Regency building and rang the doorbell. As she waited, she eased her aching legs by leaning on her walking stick. She really ought to settle in her armchair, put her feet up and read a good book.

"Pat!"

"Frances... may I have a word?"

Frances looked suspicious, but stood aside to let Pat into the starship-like interior. Frances followed, her footsteps slapping on the marble floor that linked the various zones into one harmonious whole.

"Don't your feet get cold?"

"Underfloor heating."

"My, fancy that."

Frances took Pat's coat and stick.

"Tea? Or something stronger?" she offered.

"Oh... tea, please."

Frances turned on what was a warp drive thingumajig as far as Pat could tell. Pat's kettle had a button that went red, but this goldfish bowl glowed blue. Something like a computer beeped in the corner.

"Your laundry's done," Pat said.

"So it is," Frances replied. "Take a seat."

There were only tall stools available.

Pat tried her best. "Oh, well, er..."

"Let me help you."

She manoeuvred Pat up onto a stool.

"It's turning," Pat said, alarmed.

"It's so you can adjust the height."

Pat gripped the breakfast bar to hold herself still.

"What do you want?" Frances asked, padding over to the gin and tonic.

"Well, you're thirty-four, aren't you?" Pat said, turning the stool so she could see the churchwarden. She sank by a millimetre.

"How did you know that?"

Pat overshot, turning to see the lounge and garden beyond, then a clock – how long did backup take to arrive? Finally, going all the way around, Pat saw Frances again.

"It's a shame about Sir Victor," Pat said.

"Yes... and George... I mean the vicar."

"Sir Victor visited you the night the vicar died."

"I didn't know him."

"And you visited Sir Victor the night he died"

"I didn't."

"Did you get cement dust on your clothes?"

"Yes, I..."

"I saw your trousers and that waistcoat of yours in the machine," Pat said. "And the sudden completion of Sir Victor's patio was suspicious. Not many people could have done that on such short notice. He must have rung you for help. Offered you a share, perhaps?"

"No."

"It must have been quite a shock," Pat said, "when the black bags disappeared."

"It was..." and Frances realised what she'd said. "The bins were collected."

"Not on a Thursday," Pat said. "You see, Mrs Entwistle keeps such odd hours and so, as she was passing, saw them and dropped them off on her way back."

568

"The interfering old biddy. Oh! You tricked me!"

"Not at all."

"Wait! The Oxfam Shop isn't between my house and Mrs Entwistle's."

"She went to her son's to water her cannabis plants," Pat explained. "The Oxfam Shop is on the way."

"So she worked for that black-hearted bastard as well."

"Sir Victor was your brother."

Frances went slack-jawed for a moment.

Pat could see the family resemblance in her dark hair and widow's peak. She looked so like Sir Victor; it was a wonder no-one had noticed before. She was nothing like the vicar.

"How did you know?" Frances managed eventually.

Pat, letting go of the breakfast bar, held up her hands in a theatrical shrug and said,

"The DNA test results were in his shirt pocket."

"You're an interfering old biddy too."

"Well, quite," Pat said, gradually turning away from Frances. She came to face the clock on the far wall and then the floor-to-ceiling French windows that afforded such a lovely view of the garden and its patio furniture. "Let's see, once you'd buried the Swedish gentleman in the concrete, you stabbed Sir Victor in the back, perhaps trying to emulate the vicar's death, but that didn't work."

"I thought it might draw attention rather than deflect any investigation."

"And so you removed his clothes... why?"

Frances reappeared in Pat's vision.

"I knew there were enough busybodies in the village," Frances replied, "so if I made it embarrassing either people wouldn't talk about it or they'd focus on the more salacious elements."

The churchwarden went over to her kitchen work surface. Just by her elbow, a range of handles jutted from the knife block. The stainless steel glinted in the downlighting.

The clock told Pat that she'd been stalling for five minutes at least, but there was still no-one at the back of the house. Frances was already talking when the roundabout Pat was trapped on turned to face her.

"I'm sorry, Pat," Frances said, "but I'm afraid the vicar's killer has to claim one more victim."

"But why?"

Even this clock, watched briefly on each revolution, didn't seem to tick enough seconds by.

"It's such a lot of money," Frances said behind her, "and it belongs to me. I was cut off from my inheritance just because my mother ran off with Terry Fairfax."

"But isn't Lord Bishop Barnaby broke?"

"Yes, but there's the title and now Victor's millions."

"From his drug money?"

571

"It was such a shock to Victor when I told him we were related," Frances said. "That's why we had the DNA test."

"How come you were brother and sister and didn't know?"

"Ah," Frances said. "You see, Mater and Pater, packed the two brothers off to boarding school early. They went abroad, diplomatic services for the Foreign Office, you know, all rather hush-hush. I was born abroad and, I think, they simply didn't get around to mentioning that they'd had a daughter."

"Didn't mention it!"

"I suspect with them being Lord and Lady Muck, when they realised that it had slipped their minds, they were too embarrassed to bring it up in conversation. I was sent to a different boarding school and our paths never really crossed."

"That's extraordinary."

"And then mother ran off with the gardener taking me with her."

572

"What did your brothers say when they found out?"

"George was nice about it, but Victor thought it was ancestry dot co dot uk gone mad."

"That'll be an internet thing."

"We were happy, Mum and... but then it all went wrong."

"What happened?"

"My step-father ran off with a waitress."

"Waitress?"

"An actress who played a waitress."

"Sorry?"

"She method-acted a waitress, she was a waitress when he met her, she certainly gave him a service... and it's not right that I lose out. I was only a child."

"It's..." Pat felt dizzy going round and round, but she was certain she was slowly descending towards the marble floor. How many more times around would she need to go to get her feet onto the floor?

573

"Mother gave up the money for him," Frances continued, "but she lost him. It broke her heart. She died penniless."

"So you killed your brothers."

"Killed my... no, George was such a nice man. He kept in touch after mother eloped. No, I didn't kill him."

Everything had become a blur of confusion with times, locations and killers spinning in front of Pat's mind's eye as fast as the clock, the patio and Frances zipped by.

"Then who?" Pat demanded.

"I don't know."

"So, Sir Victor killed the vicar?"

"He was an unscrupulous bastard, but no," Frances said. "At the time, he and I were having words about the DNA test. He didn't believe I was his little sister."

All this to-do, Pat thought, and she'd come many full circles to face Frances again and she still had no idea who killed the vicar.

574

"So, you and Sir Victor have alibis for the vicar's murder?"

"Yes."

"What about Sir Victor's death?"

"Oh, I killed him."

In a sudden moment of clarity, the world stopped spinning. Pat's toes had touched the floor. Unfortunately, the seemed like her head was still going round and round.

"Now, Pat," Frances said, selecting a nasty-looking carving knife from the block and drawing it like a stubby samurai sword, "be a good dear and hold still, so I can get the right gap between your ribs."

Frances levelled the blade, closed an eye and aimed at the taper of the left pleat of the back of Pat's coat.

But Pat threw herself forward, her body pitching across the kitchen faster than her knees could get her feet to patter beneath her. Just as she was about to fall, she crashed a counter, banging her elbows. In front of her was a collection of utensils in exciting storage contraptions: knives in a block, spatulas in holders, dangling ladles.

She grabbed a handle, whirled around to face Frances. Although Frances had a stainless-steel knife, Pat was now armed with a large, stainless steel balloon whisk.

Frances jerked back, frightened, and then she realised.

"Really, Pat?"

"Frances, look, I'm sure we can come to some sort of... er... arrangement."

"It's not flowers," Frances said.

"I could give you twenty-four hours' head start."

"Twenty-four hours!"

"Forty-eight?"

"As opposed to killing you and staying in my lovely house with my new fortune, title and everything."

"The vicar had no money and didn't inherit any from Lord Bishop–"

"But Victor was loaded and I get that."

"But how?"

"I'm his sweet little, long-lost sister."

"You can't accept drugs money!"

Frances tilted her head to one side as if she was considering this and then she said, "Yes, I can."

"But you're a churchwarden."

"So? I only moved here to find out about my brothers. What do I care about this village?"

"Oh, Frances, that's so ungrateful, and we welcomed you with open arms."

The door burst open: Diane and Annabelle.

"We got your coded message," Diane said.

"Coded?" Pat said.

"Oh, the full set," Frances said, "more victims for the vicar killer."

Frances lunged at Pat taking her completely by surprise.

Pat flinched, her eyes tight shut for protection and somehow, she deflected the knife with her whisk. They struggled for a moment, the knife twisted towards Pat and bent the wires of her weapon out of shape. It would never beat eggs again.

Then Frances yanked back and whipped Pat's whisk away.

"STAY WHERE YOU ARE!" Annabelle shouted. "I'VE GOT A GUN!"

Annabelle stood facing them both, quite obviously holding her pointed finger inside her cardigan pocket.

Frances started laughing. "Unbelievable! You mad old witches."

"Sorry?" Annabelle said.

"Please, can we be civilised?" Pat said.

"Yes, Frances, it's three against one," Diane added.

But Frances just carried on laughing, her head bent back, her mouth open and then... she coughed. "Glass of water."

None of the others moved, so she had to do it herself. And, to do so, Frances had to put down her knife.

Diane looked for a weapon, but Frances's house was minimalist.

Pat grabbed another kitchen utensil: a wooden spoon.

Annabelle aimed her finger.

Frances finished the Évian straight out of the bottle. She gasped and wiped her mouth.

"That's better," she said and picked up her knife again.

"Wait!" Pat shouted.

"What?" Frances said.

"I have one last question."

"This isn't Mastermind," Frances said. "It's not 'I've started so I'll finish'."

"Yes," Pat admitted, "but why did you decide to kill Sir Victor?"

"If you tell me how you knew it was me."

"It was the crack in the patio."

"That gave me away?"

"Yes, you see," Pat explained, "Sir Victor was an architect."

"And so," Diane added, "he'd never have laid a patio that developed a crack."

"Not at all, Di," Pat countered. "He's an architect, so he'd never have dirtied his hands laying actual concrete, whereas someone who knows bricklaying... like yourself."

Frances laughed, a deep throaty sound.

"So," Pat said, "why did you kill Sir Victor?"

"Once the vicar had been murdered, the idea just popped into my head. And Victor was such an arrogant prig. He had money–"

"Illegal money."

"I didn't know that... and the title would come to him and I had nothing, just because my mother ran off with Lord Bishop Barnaby's gardener. So, with George dead, and as I'd helped him dispose of a body, I confronted Victor and demanded my share... and Victor just laughed, he wouldn't stop and I was talking to him and he wasn't listening. He turned his back."

"I know the feeling," Diane said.

"So, I stabbed him."

"And you thought about faking it to look like the vicar's murder."

"Yes... then I realised that I might be blamed for all the murders, so I made it look like an accident."

"You bundled up his clothes, but you had to go back to your own house for a pornographic film."

"I didn't know where Victor hid his."

"If he had any."

"I'd have thought he'd have the kinky stuff."

"So, it must have come as a shock to find the bin bags with the clothes had vanished."

"Yes."

"So, how did they end up at the charity shop?" Diane asked.

"I'm not answering you as well," Frances said.

"My one last question," Diane prompted.

"Oh... Mrs Entwistle who does, came past, Pat told me, and saw them by the back door and took them."

"She was watering the plants at her son's house," Pat added.

"Pat here has all the answers," Frances said.

"Oh, right," Diane said. "That clears that up."

Annabelle coughed.

They all looked at her.

"I have one last question," Annabelle said.

"I've answered two last questions already."

"Yes, but it's only fair that I get my turn."

"Oh... very well," Frances said. "What is it?"

"Oh... well..."

582

"Come on."

"Sorry... don't rush me. Er... er..."

Just then, a tall man prowled into the open plan space like a lithe panther. His tall, muscular frame powered forward, dominating all with his strong, square jaw, his dark hair shorn to number one hair and his steely eyes. This no-nonsense action hero took everything in with a cold, calculating gaze.

"I'm Inspector Rex Raymond," he asserted, "and I see, Miss Fairfax, that you are not only lovely but also resourceful. You have already apprehended these three busybodies for me."

"I think not," Frances said and she stabbed him in the heart.

Inspector Rex Raymond jerked away, and then stared at this new evidence sticking out from between his ribs. He pointed to the hilt, either for finger prints to be taken or for help.

"Oops," Francis said, but she clearly didn't mean it.

Pat hit Frances with the spoon.

Frances parried that easily.

Annabelle fired with her finger.

That did nothing at all.

So Diane hit Frances with the metal stool.

Frances went down like a sack of potatoes.

Annabelle apologised – "Oh, sorry." – but Frances didn't reply as she was out cold.

Inspector Rex Raymond let out a gasp.

Everyone looked at him.

"One last question," the inspector managed as a thin trickle of blood escaped his mouth. With his dying breath, he said, "What–"

And then the inspector toppled backwards to land on the marble with a thud of finality.

Even so, Pat jumped to the rescue as nimbly as her years allowed, knelt down as speedily as the click in her knee permitted – "ah" – and grabbed hold of the knife as quickly as her arthritis let her.

If she could staunch the bleeding, she thought, but then, the door burst open and several large police officers charged in, shouting and waving taser guns.

Annabelle screamed.

Diane swore.

Pat looked up from where she knelt over the body holding the knife.

"I can explain," she said.

And then Kilroy appeared at the door, took in the scene at a glance and then had to look again.

"I have one question," he said.

"Is it your last," Annabelle said, "because I've not had my last question yet?"

36. Dénouement

Kilroy looked up from the body, stepped out onto the patio for a moment to appreciate the fresh, cool air. He gazed up towards the celestial bowl for inspiration and a light shone on him, ethereal and heavenly. Perhaps the inspector was alive and it was Kilroy being drawn upwards to face that courtroom in the sky for his good deeds to be weighed against his crimes.

But no, it was a torch, its beam dazzling.

"Hello, hello, hello," a gruff voice exclaimed, "what's all this then?"

"Sergeant Drax," Kilroy said, "I've a task for you."

"I answer to Inspector Raymond, Killjoy."

"The inspector is dead," Kilroy explained. "So I'm the senior detective present."

"Interesting method of promotion."

"Sergeant!"

They both stepped inside.

"Sergeant," Kilroy commanded, "take Miss Fairfax into custody."

"You best come with me, Miss," Drax said.

"It's not Miss," said Frances.

"Madam then."

"It's *Lady*," she insisted. "Lady Bishop Barnaby of Bishop Barnaby Manor."

"Right you are, Lady."

"Excuse me," Diane said, "Frances?"

"What?" Frances replied.

"You won't be churchwarden any longer."

Frances laughed at this.

"So," Diane continued, "I'll take your church key."

"That's for the church committee to decide."

But Frances had glanced towards her jacket and Diane soon fished out the big, solid church key.

"Thank you."

"Diane, you utter–"

But the police sergeant took the lady and her stream of unladylike expletives into custody.

They were alone.

"Is there any whisky?" Kilroy asked.

"She's got Bombay Sapphire gin," Diane informed him.

Kilroy helped himself to a generous measure with a wince and a top-up.

The four of them withdrew from the kitchen area to the lounge to leave the crime scene undisturbed.

Kilroy looked around for somewhere to hang his coat and then, seeing the modern décor, simply dropped it on the floor. He took out his phone...

"Listen–" Pat started to say.

"One moment," Kilroy replied.

...and speed dialled.

588

"Ah, DC Kilroy here... Kil*roy*. I need a pathologist and a SOCO team at Miss Fairfax's residence, Conky Whallop."

Kilroy glanced at the kitchen area with its corpse.

"Yes, Inspector Raymond is here," Kilroy admitted. "Quick as you can."

He put his phone away.

"Listen–" Pat began.

"Look, Mrs Thomas," Detective Constable Kilroy replied, "this is work for the police and... oh, what's the point?"

Kilroy sat on the leather sofa and closed his eyes to wait for the pathologist and the SOCO team.

Meanwhile, Pat explained and explained. This went on for quite a while, until, finally, Sergeant Drax bought Doctor Lake into the kitchen.

"Doctor Lake's here," Drax said.

"Doctor Lake," Kilroy said, trying but failing to avoid looking at her admirable chest.

"Detective," she replied.

With effort, Kilroy met her gaze with his attention.

"If you'd be so kind as to examine the victim," he said.

"Well," she said, "death will most probably be due to that knife sticking out of his chest and... oh! That's Inspector Raymond."

"Yes."

"And I suppose you'll be wanting an estimate of the time as I said–"

"I saw the murder through the window," Kilroy said, holding his left hand up to show off his watch.

"I see," Doctor Lake said, snapping on a pair of blue latex gloves.

"Keep me abreast of developments," Kilroy said.

The sergeant guffawed.

"Sergeant, as I have pointed out, I am the senior detective present," Kilroy said, "who's still alive, so you will show some respect."

590

"Killjoy."

Sergeant Drax went out, sniggering.

Kilroy went back to the trio of old ladies.

"Listen," Pat said, "we need to get everyone together."

"You're joking," Kilroy said.

But she wasn't.

!!!

In answer to the 'we'll never get everyone together', Pat, Diane and Annabelle activated the village grapevine via text, phone call and a few whispers over a hedge. Although, in truth, all they'd needed to do was tell Mrs Pilkington. Moments later, the villagers were asking if they needed an umbrella and what they ought to bring.

'No' and 'nothing'.

The Parochial Hall[10] had half the bunting up before Pat got there and pointed out that it was not needed. The trestle tables had been positioned along one wall for all the 'I know you said nothing, but I made this'. There wasn't much; just garlic bread, French loaves, mixed salad, one cheeseboard, two rice dishes, cold meats, hot sausage rolls, chicken wings in barbeque sauce, still frozen oven chips fresh from someone's freezer, crisps, nuts, sandwiches and little sausages on sticks. These were displayed on the first table. The other three tables were desserts. The trifle made by Mrs Pilkington looked particularly rich with the cake layer swilling in sherry.

"Are these apples from my orchard?" Major Naseby demanded.

"Yes," Zara Pheasant said, shaking her head.

"What?"

---

[10] Editor's note: There is a life-drawing class on alternate Tuesday, central heating permitted, so technically the Parochial Hall is a drawing room.

"NO," Zara repeated.

"This isn't coming out of the tea money," Mrs Jones announced as she served some particularly insipid brew from the hatch.

"Oh sorry, I've done it again," Annabelle said.

"It doesn't matter," Pat said, taking a napkin.

"Here, Detective, let me help you," Diane said.

"I'm fine," Kilroy said, "thank you... well, just one... two then, three's enough, seriously, thank you."

They all sat or stood, depending on their legs, and tucked in.

"Well, Detective?" Diane said putting aside her strawberries and cream.

"Hmmm... hmmm... hmmm," Kilroy replied. He licked his lips and then wiped his hands on a Rudolf napkin.

"Allow me," Pat said, getting to her feet.

"Mmmm... mmmm..." Kilroy said, objecting.

Everyone gathered around in a loose semi-circle. There were twelve of them present like a jury that had retired – and most of them had retired – to consider the evidence.

Pat went from person-to-person, examining each in turn, her steely gaze semi-magnified by her half-moon glasses. Her eyes twinkled in the lower half with corrected long-sightedness and knowledge. Finally, she tapped her walking stick on the ground three times to ensure she had everyone's attention.

"Ladies and gentlemen," she began, "thank you all for coming."

Everyone nodded.

"Pat," Mr Henderson said, "can you make do with the whiteboard?"

"I think I can manage without."

"Only the projector is so fiddly to set up for a PowerPoint and I'm not sure where the extension lead is."

"I shall be fine... what's a power point?"

"It's a... I'm not sure. One of those computery things."

"I'll just explain verbally."

"Just that?"

"Yes."

"How disappointing."

Pat coughed pointedly to regain everyone's attention.

"These murders have been like dominoes," she said, "but not all in a neat line. They've been stood up on the table all higgledy-piggledy. When one fell, it knocked others over too, here and there, in something of a shambles. Let me explain."

Everyone leant forward in their seats.

"Now, I'll remind you of those cases already solved."

"Oh good," Annabelle said, "because I was getting a little lost."

"Last, but not least," Pat began. "I have to tell you that Inspector Raymond is no longer with us."

"Well, that's shocking," Mrs Pilkington said, "leaving us in the lurch like that."

"Very disappointing," Mr Henderson agreed.

"He was murdered!" Pat explained.

"Who killed him?" Mrs Pilkington asked.

"I never liked him," Betty said. "He was very rough with me."

"Neither did I," Mr Boseman said.

"Everyone!" Pat said. "It was Frances Fairfax."

"Well, I never," Mrs Pilkington said.

"What did she say?" Major Naseby said.

"How do you know?" Mr Henderson asked.

"Diane, Belle and I saw her," Pat explained, "along with Detective Constable Kilroy here."

"But why?" Mr Henderson asked.

"To cover up her murder," Pat said, "and prevent her arrest."

"The inspector was going to arrest us," Diane said.

"I'm sure that would have been sorted out."

Diane snorted derisively.

"But who?" Mr Henderson insisted.

"Whom did she murder? I shall get to that," Pat said. "Next we must come to Doctor Kovalyov."

"Be brave, Betty," Mr Boseman said.

"Vlad the Inventor was killed by his own invention, which he'd created to murder... I'm sorry, Betty, but his wife, you."

"Oh!" Betty said.

"There, dear," Mr Boseman said, touching her hand. It was utterly flagrant and quite shocking as they had both lost their own spouse so recently.

"So it was suicide?" Annabelle said.

"Accident," Kilroy said.

"But why?" Mr Henderson said.

"The questioning by the police – sorry, Detective Constable – revealed to Vladimir that his wife was having an affair," Pat said.

Kilroy had the decency to look shamefaced.

"You told him that the choir wasn't running anymore so he knew she was up to something," Pat continued. "Every week, Betty went to the Chiang's pretending to be Mrs Boseman. The real Mrs Boseman was, of course, housebound."

"He modified his robot to shoot his wife," Kilroy added.

"And dressed up as her to test it," Pat said, "with tragic results."

"Not for Betty, though," Mr Boseman added.

"Well, yes, quite," Pat agreed. "And before him was Anders Lindström–"

"I'm so sorry," Annabelle said.

"Who was killed when Mrs Harrison here saved all our lives."

Gentle applause greeted Annabelle's blushes.

598

"But why?" Mr Henderson asked.

"I'll get to that," Pat said. "Now, before that, there was Sir Victor Pendle-Took murdered by Frances Fairfax."

"No."

"Really?"

"Well, I never."

"And she was the churchwarden."

"What did she say?"

"She was the churchwarden," Mr Henderson shouted into Major Naseby's ear.

"I'll step up as churchwarden," Major Naseby said, "but I'll need a key."

"That's for the church committee to decide," Diane said.

"Nonsense," Major Naseby said. "I was elected."

"Please, everyone," Pat said. "She killed him in the same way as the vicar was murdered and then she changed her mind. I suspect she thought if it went wrong, she might be blamed for all the murders. So, instead, she made it look like an accident when he was... well, an accident."

"Well, I never."

"Shocking."

"Could you repeat that bit about Sir Victor?"

"Please," Pat said, "we don't want to take all night."

"No."

"Of course not."

"Sorry."

"So," Pat continued, "she made it look like an accident. Of course, this meant she had to dispose of his clothes. She bagged them up ready to dump somewhere, but Mrs Entwistle arrived, saw them and took them to Annabelle's shop."

"Oh, I did," Mrs Entwistle said.

"Now we move on to Lars Lindström," Pat said. "He was killed by Sir Victor Pendle-Took in his driveway. Diane witnessed that."

"I did," Diane said.

"Probably in self-defence," Kilroy added.

"Quite," Pat said. "And it was Frances who helped her brother–"

"Her brother!"

"Really?"

"Well, I never."

"But that makes her the vicar's sister."

"HER BROTHER," Pat said. "And she helped him bury the body in Sir Victor's new patio."

"Really?"

"Sir Victor has a new patio?"

"Well, fancy that."

"It *is* in my ear properly."

"The Reverend Pendle-Took," Pat said, "had been trying to figure out if he'd be Lord Reverend Bishop Barnaby or the Reverend Lord Bishop Barnaby or–"

"You can't be Reverend Bishop," Annabelle said. "It's either 'Your Grace' or 'Right Reverend', although 'Reverend Right Reverend' sounds a little OTT."

"It's a place," Pat said, "Lord of Bishop Barnaby."

"Oh... sorry."

"So, Frances would inherit the title and Sir Victor's considerable fortune–"

"How could he have a fortune?" Mrs Pilkington said, "He was a terrible architect. One only has to look at his–"

"FORTUNE OF DRUG MONEY."

"That's it," Major Naseby said, "speak up."

"Now," Pat continued, "we have the curate poisoned during the communion."

"We all saw that," Mrs Entwistle said.

"I didn't," Mrs Jones said, "I was on teas."

"We've established that it was the curate's wife," Pat said.

"Never?"

"Shame."

"Oh, how dreadful."

"I knew it."

"She's mumbling again."

"Please," Pat said, holding up her hands. "Now, she was arrested in London by the detective constable here."

There was more applause.

"With help," Kilroy conceded.

"Well, yes, quite," Pat said. "Which brings us to Mrs Boseman... oh, Zephron and Betty, sorry."

"It's all right," Mr Boseman said, "we've just been given a caution."

"Yes, both of you attempted to murder her–"

"Never?"

"I didn't catch that either."

"BUT SHE had already committed suicide," Pat managed to say.

"Bad luck Boseman," Major Naseby said, "better luck next time."

"And Mrs Boseman?" Mr Henderson asked.

"She knew that it would come out that her husband and Betty were having an affair," Pat explained. "She couldn't bear that, so she took an overdose. Mr Boseman had told the police, rather stupidly, that Mrs Boseman would confirm his alibi. He and Betty knew she wouldn't, so they both decided, quite separately, to kill her. Mr Boseman had already taken her watch off, the one that monitors her heartbeat, and he came to the shops to gain an alibi. We were all there when he took the watch off to establish the exact time she died, but he'd already stabbed her. Betty also went to murder her and she used her husband's gun. The shooting had to be second as it would have been seen by the one using the knife. She then disguised herself as Mr Boseman to establish an alibi for him."

"Oh," Annabelle said, "how romantic."

"Can you speak up?" Major Naseby asked.

"And Betty," Annabelle said, "your disguise was marvellous. It fooled me completely. It was better than your principal boy in-"

"Belle, please."

"Oh, sorry, Pat."

"Now we get to poor Sergio. Sir Victor saw the police by Mrs Entwistle's cottage. He didn't know they were there for the church and the vicar, so he assumed his criminal enterprise had been discovered. Mrs Entwistle didn't know him, but Sergio did, so Sir Victor must have called Sergio and then run him over."

"I thought Sir Victor was dead," Mrs Pilkington said.

"I'm doing them in reverse order," Pat explained.

"Like a flashback on the telly?"

"Yes, quite," Pat said. "So, Sir Victor, having seen the police cars by the vicarage, ran Sergio over in his car to hide the evidence that he was a drug baron."

"Oh dear."

"Dreadful."

"My hearing aid *is* on."

"In Conky Whallop!"

"I know."

"Each death follows from the murder of the vicar... Sergio because Sir Victor thought his cover was blown, Mrs Boseman because Mr Boseman let slip about seeing Betty, the curate because his wife didn't want to stay in Conky Whallop, Lars and Anders because they were hitmen hired by the students in Upper Whallop–"

"Really?"

"The youth of today."

"Wouldn't have happened in my day?"

"The battery can't be dead. I bought a new one last spring."

"They do need to pay off their student loans."

"OR ANOTHER drug cartel," Pat said. "Sir Victor died because the death of the vicar brought an inherited title into play and Vlad because… er, someone let slip that Betty was having an affair."

Kilroy had at least the decency to cough.

"And finally, Inspector Raymond killed by Frances because he was going to discover that she had killed Sir Victor."

"Well, technically, he was going to arrest us," Diane said.

"Well, yes, quite."

"Which brings us to the unsolved murder," Pat said. "The vicar."

Pat began to move around the assembled parishioners.

"I know that it wasn't Belle," Pat began, "because she was with me at my house when the murder happened."

"Oh yes, and that means you didn't do it either," Annabelle said.

"Quite."

Pat moved on, going clockwise.

"And then we have Mrs Entwistle," Pat continued. "Did the vicar discover your illicit gardening?"

"He loved my flowers," Mrs Entwistle replied.

"All grown in a corner of your son's hydroponic cannabis farm."

"Well, it was so nice to have daffs all year round."

"And that's where you were when the vicar was killed," Pat said. "Going to water the plants."

"Well, that's me in the clear."

"Except for the drugs charges," Kilroy said.

"Oh, oh," Mrs Entwistle said, fussing with her blue rinse.

"And now Mrs Jones," Pat said. "The vicar was spending money on new vestments."

"Not from the tea money," Mrs Jones said.

"But perhaps, yes, from the tea money. You see, he'd discovered just how much is in the tea money. Detective Constable?"

608

"Oh," Kilroy said. "You were charging twenty-five pence for a cup of tea and using barely any tea bags over what, thirty years? No running costs, electricity or staff to pay, so it all added up. Thirty years, fifty-two Sundays in the year, twenty-odd people, two cups each is... a lot."

"That's... over fifteen grand," Mr Henderson said, looking up from his phone. "Fifteen thousand, six hundred."

There was a gasp that went around the circle of people, they glanced at one another, some even licked their lips.

"Well, Mrs Jones?" Pat asked.

"It's twenty-seven thousand, four hundred and sixty-three pounds and eighty-three pence," Mrs Jones said, and then she pinched the bridge of her sharp nose, "but interest rates nowadays aren't what they were."

Kilroy whistled.

"What of it?" Mrs Jones said. "Thrift is a virtue."

"And a motive for murder when the vicar found out," Pat said.

"I didn't kill him," Mrs Jones said. "All I did was tell him the wrong password for the bank account."

"Good God, woman," Major Naseby spluttered. "And all I wanted was an Earl Grey occasionally."

"Not from the tea money!" Mrs Jones screamed.

"She has an alibi for the murder," Kilroy said. "She was skyping her financial advisor when the vicar was killed."

"Well, I have to keep a close eye on investments, they can do down as well as up."

"Mrs Pilkington," Pat said.

"Do your worst, dear," Mrs Pilkington said.

"Had no motive and didn't have a key to the church."

"Oh... I feel left out."

"Now we come to you, Major," Pat said.

610

"What?"

"It's known by everyone that you disagreed with the vicar's ideas about women churchwardens."

"Well, it's madness."

"We have women priests and women–"

"In the cesspools of London, the gutters of Cambridge, the sewers of Ipswich and the bogs of Norwich, perhaps, but in Conky Whallop! Never."

"It's motive enough, but you can't have killed the vicar," Pat said. "You don't have a key either."

"Only because Miss Richards insisted I return it. I was elected, you know, I should have kept it for the year."

"Mr Henderson had no motive or key."

"That's disappointing," Mr Henderson said.

"Zephron here," Pat said, "had a key–"

"The blighter," Major Naseby said.

"And a motive."

"He didn't have a motive," Betty said.

"What if the vicar had discovered your affair, Betty," Pat said. "Thou shalt not commit adultery, after all."

"Patricia, there's no need for this," Mr Boseman said.

"You both had keys," Pat said, "but you both had Peking duck, egg fried rice and prawn crackers at Chiang's."

"That's not right, Pat," Mr Boseman said.

"Oh?"

"We had the lemon chicken."

For a moment Pat was thrown, her deductions clearly a little off, but then she rallied and moved to the next suspect.

"Zara here had neither motive nor key," she said, "which brings us to–"

"Now wait a minute," Major Naseby said, his ruddy face reddening further. "The vicar knew about her thieving. I mentioned this to the Reverend on many occasions. Many occasions. Perhaps, finally, he did his duty and told her off and she murdered him."

"Perhaps, but she didn't have a key."

"That's as maybe," Major Naseby said, "but she is still guilty of stealing. Look! The evidence is over there in that apple flan. You've only got to look under the pastry, dammit."

"Now we come to... oh. Detective Constable Kilroy."

"Me?" Kilroy said.

"Did he start all this off to have a nice juicy murder for his first-ever case?"

"You can't suspect me!"

"Why not you?" Annabelle said. "We all get our turn."

"Detective Constable Kilroy," Pat explained, "didn't have a key."

"So, it has to be Frances who killed the vicar," Diane said. "Both her brothers!"

"No," Pat said. "When the vicar died, she was arguing with Sir Victor about the DNA test. We saw Sir Victor leaving her house, if you remember?"

"Oh yes," Annabelle said.

"I saw that too," Mrs Entwistle said.

"So, who killed the vicar?" Diane asked.

"Why," Pat said, "that was you, Di."

37. Loose Ends

"Nonsense!"

"Di, of all the key holders," Pat said, "you were the only one without an alibi."

"Rubbish," Diane said. "What about the curate?"

"The curate was visiting Major Naseby to stop him murdering Zara Pheasant."

"You what!" Zara said.

"I never!" Major Naseby objected. "I didn't kill her. I never touched her. Look! There she is. Alive."

"The curate's wife?" Diane tried.

"She was on the train from London."

"What about—"

"We've been over this," Pat said. "Frances Fairfax was meeting Sir Victor about the DNA test, so they are both excluded. Mrs Jones was skyping. Mrs Entwistle was watering the cannabis plants. Betty and Zephron were eating at Chaings'. The curate's wife was on the train back from London, so that leaves... well, you."

"You were with me when we found the body," Diane said.

"You killed him and then fetched Belle and me to witness the discovery."

"Why would I want to kill the vicar?"

"He was going to stop the magazine."

"That's not motive enough," Diane replied. "I could have started a village magazine separate from the church."

"Yes, Di, you could," Pat said, "but–"

"All right, all right, but he was going to cancel the magazine. Freedom of the press, Pat, that's something worth fighting for. We have to stand up for our rights!"

"Well, yes, quite, but you'd still have had to hand your church key back."

Diane flinched. "Never!"

"Di, I really think–"

616

"I was someone! Someone, Somerset and Tome."

"Well, yes, quite."

"I was an important solicitor, reduced to... retirement. But I had the magazine – you understand – and the key that went with it."

"We have to accept change," Pat said. "Things come to an end."

Diane was stumped by that one and everyone could see it in her expression. With the dignity of one used to doing the right thing, Diane finished her tea, stood, smoothed down her sensible tweed outfit and jiggled her frivolous pearls into position.

"Well, Detective Constable," she commanded, "get on with it."

Kilroy stood, looked for a napkin and couldn't see one, so he wiped the mayonnaise onto his Mackintosh, getting dirt and cement dust all over his hands.

"Miss Richards," he said, "I am arresting–"

"It brought a little excitement to the village, didn't it?"

"You have the right–"

"It shook things up."

"Remain silent."

"I chose not to."

"No, I'm telling you to remain silent."

"Gagging the press, are we?"

"No, I–"

"I know the Chief Constable."

"And I know why."

"Oh. Well. Long time ago. I'm sure he's forgotten."

"He hasn't. Inspector Raymond told me what he'd said about you."

"Oh... well."

Diane held out her wrists for the handcuffs.

Kilroy shook his head slightly and then gently took her arm to lead her away.

But Pat stepped forward, "Di."

"Yes, Pat."

"Your key."

They stared at each other, amateur sleuth versus retired lawyer, and then Diane handed over the key.

"She can't keep it."

"She'll be parish magazine editor."

"That's for the church committee to decide."

"What did she say?"

"What bit?"

"Any bit?"

"And if I might say so," Diane said to Kilroy as the detective constable took her out, "I consider your behaviour reprehensible and..."

Diane was still giving Kilroy a piece of her mind when he got her to his car. It was a long way to Foal Lane Police Station and Pat felt sympathetic to the nice detective constable's plight.

As he drove off, the other police officers, including Sergeant Drax, watched him go with a mix of admiration and dread. No-one would disagree with Kilroy now. He'd have no more trouble from his insubordinates. They'd all heard Inspector Rex Raymond yelling at the DC when he'd phoned from Foal Lane and all thought it was over for the new DC. But now the inspector was dead and the 'Kill King' had solved more murders in his first week than his colleagues managed to crack in a good year.

"Is it time for dessert?" Annabelle asked.

And it was.

"That was a gripping dénouement," Mr Henderson said. "Most thrilling and informative."

Everyone agreed.

"It is nice apple pie," Major Naseby admitted.

"I didn't hear that," Zara Pheasant replied.

"Dénouement means 'unknotting'," Annabelle said. "Which is strange because after *un*knotting, there are loose ends to *tie up*."

And, indeed, there were.

For a start, there was who owned what Tupperware from the buffet.

As Pat walked home beside the Green, she allowed herself to feel sad. What had happened was bad enough, but what she had done to her friend weighed heavily upon her, heavier even than the portion of trifle that had been foisted upon her as thanks. Conky Whallop would never be the same.

And then she realised she'd left her walking stick in the Parochial Hall and so she was all cross.

!!!

The next meeting of the Conky Whallop parish magazine editorial committee was a sorry affair. Annabelle didn't even apologise for the Christmas napkins. They had tea, left-over trifle and Bakewell tarts to cheer themselves up.

"I've finished page one," Pat said.

621

"It's lovely, Pat," Annabelle said. "But the headline?"

"I know."

"*Chief Correspondent Charged with Clergy Killing.*"

"Well, quite, but I couldn't think of a word beginning with 'C'," Pat admitted.

"Croaking?"

"Oh no," Pat said, "and I only did that one for Diane. I thought I'd go with the new vicar arriving Wednesday for everyone else.[11]"

"I'll miss Diane."

"She's subscribed to the magazine."

"Oh, that brings us up to 31 subscriptions."

---

[11] Editor's note: See the most recent edition of the parish magazine, *New Vicar Arriving Wednesday.*

"Diane already had one," Pat said. "It means we have to mail it to HMP Peterborough. So, it's 26 with 4 mail-outs."

"Oh, and sorry, but we've lost the vicar, curate and Mrs Boseman."

"Well, quite, but I'm sure the new vicar and curate will take a subscription. Although I doubt Frances will keep hers."

"We could mail it?"

Pat shook her head.

"So, only two down," Annabelle said, checking her list and making the necessary adjustments. "That's not too bad considering how many murders we've had. Anything else?"

"Well, yes," Pat said. "We have to decide who's going to be the magazine's chief editor."

"You do it, Pat."

Pat thought about it, nodded and then popped the heavy, iron key into her handbag.

"So what's our next story"? Annabelle asked.

"Well," Pat said, "there is this strange disappearance in Little Shelford..."

The End

David Wake is a writer of science-fiction, steampunk and more. This novel comes in the latter category. He's been a guest of honour at conventions and he co-runs New Street Authors. He also has a police box, a deer-stalking hat, a magnifying glass, a few little grey cells left and an alibi.

Thank you for reading *The Murders of Conky Whallop*. If you liked it, please consider writing a review.

Please don't be inspired to try any of these methods even if you have the opportunity.

For more information, and to join the mailing list for news of forthcoming releases, see www.davidwake.com.

Many thanks to:–

Dawn Abigail, Lee Benson, Helen Blenkinsop, Dawn Bolton, Andy Conway, Jill Griffin, David Muir, Nicky Tate and Lorraine Walker. Gwyneth Hibbert for the poetry font and the cover was by Dave Slaney.

Remember everyone – run, run very fast, save lives…

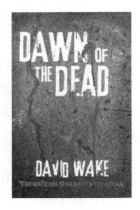

It's the End of the World, but with Pimm's on the patio, video games and working in his pants – Dave's having a great apocalypse.

Until the return-to-work order shatters his peace.

Dawn holds her own – just – as the last woman alive (West Midlands Emergency Area) in a secret bunker.

But then, a surprise visit by the Minister of Resilience, Calmness and Fortitude.

"I genuinely laughed through parts of this book because of how relatable the whole situation was."

★ ★ ★ ★ ★

"David Wake is in possession of a rare gift: combining barbed sideswipes at the socio-political mores of the day with sharp humour."

★ ★ ★ ★ ★

Available as an ebook and a paperback.

A bloke-lit tale of political intrigue and beer

Guy Wilson lives in the past.

Every year, he and his friends re-enact rebellion.

Every year, they celebrate the Jacobite's retreat.

Every year, they have a few drinks and go home...

...except this year, they go too far.

An unstoppable boozing session meets an unbreakable wall of riot police in this satirical thriller. Guy struggles against corrupt politicians, murderous security forces and his own girlfriend in a desperate bid to stop a modern uprising. And it's all his fault.

Will any of his friends survive to last orders?

"Witty, warm and well-written, "Crossing The Bridge" was so enjoyable that I didn't want to finish it."

"My sort of book. Couldn't put it down. Comedy, tension and an uncanny resemblance to the moral fibre of some of our elected representatives."

Available as an ebook and a paperback.

A ripping yarn of cliff-hangers, desperate chases, romance and deadly danger.

Earnestine, Georgina and Charlotte are trapped in the Eden College for Young Ladies suffering deportment, etiquette and Latin. So, when the British Empire is threatened by an army of zombies, the Deering-Dolittle sisters are eager to save the day.
Unfortunately, they are under strict instructions not to have any adventures... but when did that ever stop them?

"Think 'Indiana Jones pace'. It's fast and dangerous and does not involve embroidery!"

★ ★ ★ ★ ★

"A brilliant, fast paced steampunk adventure, trains zombies and zeppelins, what more could you want?"

★ ★ ★ ★ ★

THE DERRING-DO CLUB
Putting their best foot forward, without showing an ankle, since 1896.

The first novel in the adventure series available as an ebook and a paperback.

A ripping yarn of time-travel, rocket-packs, conspiracy and *sword fighting!*

The plucky Deering-Dolittle sisters, Earnestine, Georgina and Charlotte, are put to the test as mysterious Time Travellers appear in Victorian London to avert the destruction of the world...

...but just whose side should they be on?

"Loved it! [...] Fast paced and exciting another great adventure for three Victorian Young Ladies."

"...if I had been wearing a hat, I would have taken it off to David Wake."

THE DERRING-DO CLUB
Putting their best foot forward, without showing an ankle, since 1896.

The first novel in the adventure series available as an ebook and a paperback.

A ripping yarn of strange creatures, aerial dog-fights, espionage and *pirates!*

Strange lights hover over Dartmoor and alien beings abduct the unwary as the plucky Deering-Dolittle sisters, Earnestine, Georgina and Charlotte, race to discover the truth before the conquest begins...

...but betrayal is never far away.

"Well-written, fast-paced, and dangerously addictive – but with some extra thinking in there, too, should you choose to read it that way."

★ ★ ★ ★ ★

"As with previous adventures I really enjoyed the imaginative scene setting, building intrigue into unexpected twists and a spectacular ending."

★ ★ ★ ★ ★

THE DERRING-DO CLUB
Putting their best foot forward, without showing an ankle, since 1896.

The first novel in the adventure series available as an ebook and a paperback.

An Arabian tale of murder, Egyptian gods, mummies, temple raiding and *flying carpets!*

Nine suspects trapped on the SS *Karnak* with a killer! As the Deering-Dolittle sisters, Earnestine, Georgina and Charlotte investigate, mummies rise from the dead, ancient gods send messages and plots turn like cogs.

Their journey is far from straight even on the Suez Canal.

"Well-written and witty, this is a gloriously over the top pastiche of Agatha Christie's 'Death on the Nile' - and much, much more."

★ ★ ★ ★ ★

"You will not put this book down. [...] a quirky funny enjoyable Victorian tale and the last 300 pages fly by."

★ ★ ★ ★ ★

THE DERRING-DO CLUB
Putting their best foot forward, without showing an ankle, since 1896.

The first novel in the adventure series available as an ebook and a paperback.

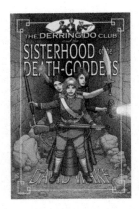

A ripping yarn set in the British Raj with handsome officers, vile thuggees, diabolical plans, a terrifying death-goddess and *a fate worse than death!*

It's soon to be the happiest day of Miss Deering-Dolittle's life, but abandonment, betrayal and an old foe stand to ruin everything – and destroy the British Empire.

All roads lead to the temple of Kali and a desperate last stand against impossible odds. Can our plucky young heroines save the day?

"Charmed meets Indiana Jones. The Derring-Do Club series is wonderful fun. Filled with adventure, atmospheric descriptions and sharp wit, this is an ideal read..." ★★★★★

The first novel in the adventure series available as an ebook and a paperback.

Think *Black Mirror* with a Scandi-crime feel

Twenty years from now, everyone's thoughts are shared on social media: the Thinkersphere. Privacy is dead and buried. Pre-mediated crime is history. So who killed the woman in Chedding car park?

Detective Oliver Braddon is plunged into an investigation to track down the impossible: a murderer who can kill without thinking.

Hashtag is a gritty, dystopian neo-noir that poses uncomfortable questions about our obsession with social media and presents a mind-bending picture of what life might be like when our very thoughts are no longer our own.

"Oh my God what a fantastic concept!"

★ ★ ★ ★ ★

"...and suddenly you need to tell everyone else to go away and let you finish this book!"

★ ★ ★ ★ ★

Book One of the **Thinkersphere** series available as an ebook and a paperback.

The dark sequel to Hashtag

Black Mirror meets Scandi-crime in a mind-bending dystopia where 'likes' matter more than lives.

Detective Oliver Braddon's investigation into an apparent suicide leads him to a powerful media mogul. Is he the killer?

In this alarming vision of the near-future, everyone's thoughts are shared on social media. With privacy consigned to history, a new breed of celebrity influences billions.

But who controls who?

A gritty, neo-noir delving into a conflict between those connected and those with secrets to hide.

"Darker in tone than the previous book, which fits with our now slightly older Braddon's move from new and enthusiastic PC to somewhat more careworn Detective, there's a Scandi-noir feel to this one."

★ ★ ★ ★ ★

Book Two of the **Thinkersphere** series available as an ebook and a paperback.

The mind-bending future continues

Another mass suicide. Or is it murder?

The case drops into Inspector Oliver Braddon's inbox. The world demands answers. With everyone's thoughts shared, liked and monitored, why haven't the police solved the case in the usual 20 seconds?

Braddon's suspicions focus on a disturbing cult, the Church of the Transcendent Cloud, and tech-billionaire, Jacob Lamb, the creator of the Thinkersphere app, *After Life* – except that he's dead.

Plus Sign is a gritty, dystopian neo-noir.

> *"...crackles with humour and tension as the reader is drawn into a world dominated by the all-embracing Thinkersphere and its tantalising app offering the promise of an After Life. Plus Sign is intriguing and alarming in equal measure [...] Thoroughly recommend."*
>
>

Book Three of the **Thinkersphere** series available as an ebook and a paperback.

A tonic for the Xmas Spirit

Being Santa's daughter would be a dream come true for any child, but for Carol Christmas, the fairy tale is about to end. Evil forces threaten the festive season, and only Carol can save the day...

A grim fairy tale told as a children's book, but perhaps not just for children.

"This starts out as a delightfully childlike modern take on the Christmas myth – the kind of Pixar-esque story that can play to the kids and give the adults a knowing wink or two, but it gets dark. Very dark."
★ ★ ★ ★ ★

Available as an ebook, a paperback and an audiobook.

Do you fear technology? We have an App for that.

Your phone is your life. But what if it kept secrets? What if it accidentally framed you for murder? And what if it was the only thing that could save you?

In a world where phones are more intelligent than humans, but are still thrown away like yesterday's fashions, one particular piece of plastic lies helpless as its owner, Alice Wooster, is about to be murdered...

In this darkly comic near-future tale, a very smart phone tells its own story as events build to a climactic battle. Can it save all the virtual and augmented worlds? Can it save the real one? Can it order Alice some proper clothes?

> *"Excellent novel – by turns strikingly original, laugh-out-loud funny and thought provoking."*
> ★ ★ ★ ★ ★

> *"Want to read it again soon..."*
> ★ ★ ★ ★ ★

> *"A thoughtful, tense and funny look at a future that seems to be already upon us."*
> ★ ★ ★ ★ ★

Available as an ebook and a paperback.

An epic tale set in Japan's Samurai era

In the days of the sword, a girl disguised as a boy turns killer to avenge her Samurai master, murdered by a brotherhood of powerful men. Following the trail of blood, a brilliant detective – an Emperor's Watcher – searches for answers only to come face-to-face with an old enemy, a man honour dictates he must protect.

As the death toll rises, and the truth-seeker and ninja assassin find themselves at odds, not only with each other, but also with their fundamental beliefs:

Honour or truth? Instinct or intellect? Justice or revenge?

Roninko is a bloody, action-packed revenge thriller steeped in ancient wisdom. A philosophical and breathtaking story of Bushido.

"This is a beautifully written, atmospheric adventure through ancient Japan. Lovingly researched and with nuanced and interesting characters, I enjoyed this greatly."
★ ★ ★ ★ ★

Available as an ebook and paperback.

Printed in Great Britain
by Amazon

38932956R00364